WHAT
THE FLY SAW

ALSO BY FRANKIE Y. BAILEY

The Red Queen Dies

WHAT THE FLY SAW

Frankie Y. Bailey

MINOTAUR BOOKS
A Thomas Dunne Book
New York

A THOMAS DUNNE BOOK FOR MINOTAUR BOOKS.
An imprint of St. Martin's Publishing Group.

WHAT THE FLY SAW. Copyright © 2015 by Frankie Y. Bailey. All rights reserved. Printed in the United States of America. For information, address St. Martin's Press, 175 Fifth Avenue, New York, N.Y. 10010.

www.thomasdunnebooks.com
www.minotaurbooks.com

Library of Congress Cataloging-in-Publication Data

Bailey, Frankie Y.
    What the fly saw : a mystery / Frankie Y. Bailey. — 1st ed.
        p. cm.
    "A Thomas Dunne Book."
    ISBN 978-1-250-04830-1 (hardcover)
    ISBN 978-1-4668-4910-5 (e-book)
    I.   Title.
    PS3552.A368W48 2015
    813'.54—dc23   2014040206

Minotaur books may be purchased for educational, business, or promotional use. For information on bulk purchases, please contact the Macmillan Corporate and Premium Sales Department at 1-800-221-7945, extension 5442, or write to specialmarkets@macmillan.com.

First Edition: March 2015

10 9 8 7 6 5 4 3 2 1

To the people in my life who remind me to laugh

Acknowledgments

As with any book, this one began in the author's head and evolved with the help of many people. I would like to first offer my thanks to anyone I should forget to mention by name here. Your contribution was much appreciated even if my memory proved faulty when I was writing this.

My thanks to my "first readers," Joanne Barker, Angie Hogancamp, and Joycelyn Pollock. The observant reader will note that Joanne and Angie have minor, recurring characters named in their honor. Joy, I have plans for you in the next book. My thanks to the Sisters in Crime, Upper Hudson Chapter (the "Mavens of Mayhem") and to the Capital Region Romance Writers of America chapter. The members of both chapters have provided me with ongoing support and friendship. The second and third of the month meetings provide me with a place to go where I know I will always find kindred spirits. I want to offer a special thank-you to the Mavens for helping to make my book launch party for *The Red Queen Dies* a success.

Speaking of book launches, I want to thank Susan Novotny and her staff at The Book House of Stuyvesant Plaza for serving as host. Thank you also for showcasing *The Red Queen Dies*.

I want to thank Alice Green, executive director of the Center for Law and Justice and occasional writing partner on nonfiction books, for stepping into her kitchen yet again. I needed a recipe for the muffin that Hannah McCabe eats in *The Red Queen Dies*. Alice came to my rescue.

Thank you to my colleagues in the School of Criminal Justice and my students for continuing to not only put up with, but support a mystery writer in your midst. As usual, a shout-out for fellow mystery lovers, Hans Toch and David Bayley.

Thank you to the readers who have taken the time to drop me a note or to say a kind word about my books when we have met at one conference or another. A special thank-you to the anonymous man who, at a local service station, recognized me from my author's photo and told me he was reading my book and enjoying it. It was great to hear from someone who was reading the first book while I was toiling over the second.

Thank you to the Stanford University Virtual Human Interaction Lab for opening your doors for Friday afternoon tours by the public. It felt a little crazy to hop on a plane to fly to California and put on goggles, but I was glad I did it. My virtual world of avatars is much different—adult sex club, not research on how avatars might be used to help people improve their lives or treat the environment better—but the experience of virtual reality was useful as I thought about immersion and the other issues that I had begun to ponder.

Thank you to the staff person at a local store who explained the use of a bow to me and helped me work on my stance. However, any errors that I have made about bows are completely my own.

Thank you to Dr. Doug Lyle for answering my questions about the damage that might be done by a bow and my follow-up questions about cholera. Again, any errors that I have made were in my translation of what I was told, not the information that I was given. Thank you to my editor, Marcia Markland, and her editorial assistant, Quressa Robinson, for making this book better than it was when you received the manuscript. Thank you to Hector DeJean, Minotaur publicity manager, for helping me get my books and my name out there. Thank you to David Rotstein, executive art director, who designed an incredible cover. Thank you to my copy editor and all of the other production staff at St. Martin's.

Thank you to PJ Nunn of Breakthrough Promotions and to Cheryl and Gina at Partners in Crime Virtual Book Tours.

Thank you to the bloggers who have reviewed my books and will review this one. Thank you for inviting me to do guest posts.

I am proud to be a member of Type M for Murder, a great blog about writing that I share with some of the best writers around.

Thank you to my agent Josh Getzler and the other members of the HSG Agency team. And, finally, thank you to my family, particularly my brother Wayne, sister-in-law, Mae, and fabulous Aunt Kitty.

A Note to the Reader

The "world" of this book is not simply our world six years from now. It is a parallel universe that shares much in common with our world but is not a carbon copy. This world has its own unique past that parallels but also diverges from our own. The technology is inspired by the near-future possibilities being discussed and/or already in development in our world. However, aspects of this technology have developed more quickly than likely in our world. Albany, New York, is a real place, and this book does draw on the real Albany's history, geography, and infrastructure. However, the Albany in this book is the Albany of the world in which it exists. That said, this book is a work of crime fiction, not science fiction. The reader will find a recognizable world with humans who share our strengths and weaknesses.

Who killed Cock Robin?
I, said the Sparrow
With my bow and arrow.
I killed Cock Robin.

Who saw him die?
I, said the Fly
With my little eye
I saw him die.

—from "The Death and Burial
of Cock Robin"
(an English Nursery Rhyme)

WHAT
the FLY SAW

1

Saturday, January 18, 2020
5:47 A.M.

After the storm passed, in the chilly hour before dawn, the last of the "space zombies" found their way back to their nest in the derelict house.

From his command post, the squad leader gave the signal: "Go!"

A black van pulled up in front of the house. Albany PD vice cops wearing protective gear jumped out and stormed up the walk. They used a battering ram to smash open the wooden door.

"Police! Albany PD!"

"Police!"

Their high-powered torches illuminated the grotesque horror movie creatures in the 3-D posters on the walls.

One of the cops ripped down a dangling black plastic replica of the 2012 UFO. He tossed the boomerang-shaped object to the floor.

Hippie freaks, he thought. Ought to make them all go live out in the Mojave Desert and wait for the mother ship to arrive.

He kicked at the nearest mattress on the floor. "Police!" he shouted down at the long-haired occupant. "On your feet!"

Blank eyes in an eerie white-painted face stared up at him.

"Hands up! Hands up!" the cop yelled as the kid stumbled to his feet. He shoved the boy against the wall and patted him down.

Upstairs, in a bathroom, another cop found a girl sprawled out, unconscious, on the dirty tile floor beside the toilet. She had vomited in the toilet bowl. Her jeans were stained with urine and feces.

Reaching down, he shook her, and then rolled her onto her side to see her face beneath the mop of dark hair. A nasty bruise on her cheekbone stood out against the streaked white paint. He moved her red scarf aside to feel for a pulse in her throat. The scarf was damp, like her tee shirt and soiled blue jeans.

"Whaddya have?" another cop asked from the doorway.

"Looks like an OD," the cop inside the bathroom said. "Still breathing, but the wagon had better get here fast."

"Got it," the other cop said, touching the comm button on his helmet.

The cop in the bathroom spotted a smear of blood on the corner of the sink. That explained the bruise. She'd banged her face on the sink when she passed out.

Downstairs in the kitchen, cops surveyed the debris of dirty dishes and rotting garbage—and an impressive array of drugs and paraphernalia.

One lowered her weapon and observed, "With a stash like this, they could have stayed zonked out until the next UFO came to visit."

2

Funeral director Kevin Novak stared at the Cupid and Psyche bronze clock on his host, Olive Cooper's, mantel. He had allowed himself to become marooned on a conversational island with Paige, Olive's great-niece.

As Paige complained about the conversation and laughter filling the long room—the "rabble babble," as she put it—Kevin found a name for what he had been feeling for the past forty-eight-plus hours. Grief.

He was experiencing firsthand what he had often observed when relatives came into the funeral home after the unexpected death of a loved one: that first stage of grieving the experts described as denial, but he often thought of as amazement and disbelief. The stage of bereavement when family members spoke of their dead loved one in the present tense because they couldn't yet believe their lives had been ripped apart.

It seemed, in this state of mind, one went through the usual motions, saying what was expected. But the shell was thin. His was developing cracks. He could tell because he felt no inclination at all to warn Paige Cooper that he had glanced over her shoulder and seen her great-aunt Olive headed their way, and Paige had better shut up. So he must be moving into the next stage: anger.

"Where in the galaxy did Aunt Olive find these people?" Paige said. "Look at them."

"Some of them are from the church's community outreach," Kevin said.

True, Olive's guest list for this celebration of her life reflected her eccentricities. An odd assortment of guests: old friends, relatives, church members and business associates, and other people who tickled Olive's fancy or touched her big heart. But they had all cleaned up and put on their best in Olive's honor.

"It's freezing in here," Paige said. She pulled the belt of her hand-knit cardigan tighter and held her hands out toward the fireplace.

"Feels fine to me," Kevin said.

"It really is annoying we have to come out for this farce when there's a blizzard on the way. The least Aunt Olive could do is heat this mausoleum. Everyone here except her will come down with pneumonia, and we'll still have to do this all over again when she finally does kick off."

"When I finally do 'kick off,' Paige," her great-aunt said, right behind her, "you may feel free not to attend my funeral. In fact, if you die first—maybe of the pneumonia you expect to catch—you'll spare us both that annoyance. And for your information, it was your father who insisted on including you in this shindig."

Paige flushed an unbecoming shade of scarlet. "Aunt Olive, I didn't mean—"

"I know what you meant. Get yourself a glass of champagne, now you're actually old enough to drink, and make the best of the situation."

Olive's sharp gaze fastened on Kevin. "And since you already know you're going to get to bury me when I'm dead, you can relax and enjoy the party."

"I always enjoy your parties, Olive," Kevin said.

"Come with me," she said. "There's someone I want you to meet."

Aware of Paige's suspicious glare, Kevin smiled in her direction. That would teach the little brat to say funeral directors reminded her of vultures without first checking for one of the species within hearing distance.

Vultures sometimes exacted their petty revenge.

"At your service, Olive," he said, offering his arm to the woman, who was eighty-five years old and counting and might well live to be a hundred.

"How have you been?" she asked him.

"Fine," Kevin said. "Never better."

"Don't give me that. Anyone who knows you can tell you're still taking Bob's death hard."

"Having your best friend collapse with a heart attack while you're beating him at tennis, and then die on the operating table, can have that effect."

"It's been over four months since it happened. You should be coping with it by now."

"I am coping with it."

"You're still off-kilter. Not your usual self. That's why I want you to meet Luanne Woodward."

"Luanne? That medium or spiritualist or whatever she calls herself that you found somewhere?"

"I didn't find her 'somewhere.' She was the featured lecturer at a fund-raiser."

"Lecturer? Don't you mean 'performer'?"

"She talked about being a medium and answered questions. She's an interesting woman. I think you could benefit from talking to her."

"I don't believe in that hocus-pocus, Olive."

"I don't believe in most of it, either. I'm almost ancient enough to remember the Fox sisters and their flimflam. But, as I said, Luanne's interesting. I invited her today so you could meet her."

Kevin noticed one of Olive's guests filling his plate high with the urgency of a man who expected the bounty in front of him to disappear.

"And do what?" he said in belated response to Olive. "Sign up for her next séance?"

"That might not be a bad idea. Spiritual therapy, so to speak."

"I get my spiritual therapy at church on Sunday from our minister. You might consider doing the same."

"At my age, I take what I need from wherever I happen to find it. And the fact you're going all righteous on me instead of laughing about my eccentricities, as you like to call them, proves you're off-kilter. We need to get you put to right."

"Olive, I don't think a medium and a séance will do the trick."

"You need an opportunity to confront your feelings."

"I have confronted my feelings. I confronted them after Bob died. I sought counseling from both Reverend Wyatt and Jonathan Burdett."

Olive stopped walking and glared at him. "Now, if you want to talk about hocus-pocus, psychiatrists are right up there. You lie on their couch spilling your guts. And they mumble an occasional Freudian pearl of wisdom while they're thinking about how they intend to spend what they're charging you."

"Burdett offers the option of sitting in a comfortable armchair, and, as you well know, his services are free to church members."

"The church pays his salary, so he's not free. He's full of his diplomas and his jargon, that's what he is."

"And what about your medium? Is she one-hundred-percent jargon free?"

"Not a chance. They all have their language, intended to impress, but she's a hell of a lot more fun than Burdett. So come along and meet her."

"I suppose it would be a waste of time to say no?"

"Yes, it would. You said you were at my service."

"Yes, I did say that."

Not much sleep last night or the night before. His moment of irritation with Paige had given way to weariness. No doubt he would feel the anger later. No chance he'd be able to skip over that stage. Not with the piper to pay.

"Luanne," Olive said to the plump, blond woman sipping from a champagne glass as she observed the people around her. "I'd like you to meet Kevin Novak, the friend of mine I was telling you about."

"I'm so happy to meet you, Mr. Novak," she said in a Southern drawl that suited her pleasant, round face. Her blue gaze met and held his.

If he believed in such things, Kevin would have sworn she'd looked past his tailored suit and crisp white shirt straight into his tarnished soul.

He took a step back, and reached out to steady Olive, whose hand rested on his arm.

"Sorry, Olive," he said. "I just remembered something I need to do."

Luanne Woodward said, "It's all right, Kevin, honey. You don't have to run away from me."

But he did, Kevin thought. He had to run as fast as he could.

3

Saturday evening
6:13 P.M.

Detective Hannah McCabe glanced up from her ORB when Walter Yin walked into the bull pen.

He dropped his hat onto the grinning Chinese dragon standing on his desk. It turned out the dragon, a gag gift from the cops in his old unit, made an excellent hat stand. His new hat, made of high-tech fiber, was a replacement for his battered fedora. His wife, Casey, bought it for him a few months ago. He seemed to have finally gotten it broken in to his satisfaction.

While she was thinking about Yin's hat, she heard Sean Pettigrew, Yin's partner, say, "Was Todd okay?"

Todd was Yin's seven-year-old son.

From her desk across the aisle, McCabe asked, "Did something happen to Todd, Walter?" She had come in a few minutes earlier to send a tag to Research about one of her cases. She hadn't had a chance to talk to Pettigrew.

Yin sat down at his desk. "He's okay. But he gave Casey a scare. He was down the street playing with one of his buddies. They got into a tussle. The kid's parents separated them and called Casey. When she got there, Todd was red in the face and crying, and he was having trouble breathing. She didn't know what was happening, so she got the other kid's father to drive them to the emergency room."

"What was wrong?" McCabe asked.

"The doctor said he was hyperventilating. Probably caused by his temper tantrum, but we need to have him tested for asthma. The doctor gave him a shot, and we brought him home and put him to bed."

"Well," Pettigrew said, "at least, you said he hadn't drawn any more of those pictures since his sessions with the school psychologist."

McCabe remembered what Pettigrew told her about that. Todd had heard a special bulletin about two cops who had been shot and killed during a traffic stop. Two sheriff's deputies in Virginia. But the fact they were cops had been enough to trigger Todd's apprehension about his father's safety. And that apprehension had been expressed in the pictures that he drew.

"Yeah," Yin said, "Casey and I think we're making real progress. Our kid stopped drawing pictures of his daddy the cop being blown away on the job. Now, he's just going ballistic during playtime."

McCabe pushed back her chair and reached for the Elvis 2000 concert mug she'd found on the Web. "Anyone want green pomegranate lemon tea?" she asked.

"Thanks," Pettigrew said, "but I think I'll stick with bad coffee."

"Me, too," Yin said. "Your tea sounds a little too healthy."

McCabe dropped a tea bag into her mug and pressed the hot water button on the beverage unit. "If we're stuck here for a while, both of you will live to regret the caffeine buzz you're going to get from the coffee."

"I'm more likely to get heartburn," Pettigrew said. "I've got my acid reflux pills right here in my drawer."

Yin said, "Sean, if you'd call the nutrition center woman for another date, you could stop taking pills. Having a girlfriend who teaches cooking classes is a lot better than eating cereal for dinner."

"I know. That dinner she cooked for me on our last date was great. But I don't think she'd be up for getting together again."

"Why?" McCabe asked as she sat down with her tea. "Did something go wrong?"

"You could say that," Pettigrew said, glancing at his partner. "After dinner, we were talking, and she asked about my divorce. I was telling her about it when she leaned over and kissed me on the cheek." Pettigrew grimaced. "That was when it happened."

"When what happened?" Yin asked.

"When I dropped my wine glass. Red wine splashed over her and the sofa and onto her white carpet. We both grabbed for napkins to mop up the mess, and that was when I elbowed her in the nose."

"Ouch!" McCabe said.

"She was really nice about it," Pettigrew said. "But I'm pretty sure she'd have other plans if I asked for another date."

Yin said, "How come I'm just hearing about this? When I asked you how your date went, you said you had fun."

"I did. But then I screwed things up at the end."

Yin shook his head. "We've got to work on your dating skills. Maybe we can get Casey to help."

McCabe took a sip from her mug to hide a smile. Yin and his wife were a loving couple, so Yin worried about his partner's lack of a woman in his life.

Or, rather, he worried about the fact that Pettigrew was having a hard time getting over his ex-wife. As Pettigrew's friend, McCabe worried about that, too. He had now been divorced longer than he had been married to Elaine. She had spent most of their seven months of wedlock traveling for her hospitality industry job, and it was Pettigrew who had asked for the divorce. But it was almost two years later, and he still hadn't recovered from his whirlwind courtship and marriage to a woman he'd met on a vacation in Bermuda.

Of course, it hadn't helped that at first Elaine had dropped in whenever she happened to be anywhere near Albany. But Sean said he put a stop to that. And yesterday when he and McCabe were downtown together, attending an awards ceremony, she detected signs that he might be coming out of his doldrums. He even made a couple of jokes.

"All right, Detectives. Listen up," Lt. Jack Dole said as he strode into the bull pen.

McCabe gave her boss her full attention. So did the other detectives in the room. A natural response to a man who was six-foot-four with a shaved head and whose "listen up" was seldom good news.

"We've got confirmation," he told them. "We're expecting at least twenty inches of snow between now and tomorrow night. We're here for the duration. The Comm Center is having trouble with ghost images on the surveillance cameras and echoes from the acoustic devices. We need to have all hands on deck in case patrol needs backup."

"So we're just going to hang around and twiddle our thumbs?" a detective in the back of the room asked.

Dole said, "No, Quincy, the first call we get for backup will be all yours. Of course, your partner may not appreciate that, but you can settle it between the two of you." He glanced around the bull pen. "Meanwhile, let's try to get caught up on some of that outstanding paperwork."

McCabe had already started tackling hers. "Paperwork" meaning the idiosyncratic notes she and everyone else had in their ORBs. Most of them put off transferring their case notes to the Master File.

When the lou was out of sight, Yin said, "It would be nice if our state-of-the-art surveillance system were able to handle the weather."

"The weather's been crazier than usual," McCabe said.

"Just like the world in general," Pettigrew said. "The latest breaking rumor has it Howard Miller is considering heading to Albany for Lisa Nichols's trial. All that media coverage would give his presidential campaign a boost."

"Media coverage while he rants about evil women," McCabe said. "Even Lisa Nichols doesn't deserve Howard Miller and his hatemongers at her trial."

McCabe's ORB buzzed. She checked the ID and touched view. "Hi, Chels. Are you at home because it's your anniversary or because of the blizzard?"

"Blizzard. We closed at four today," Chelsea, her best friend, said. "There was no point in staying open after the travel advisory went into effect. Anyone with good sense had stocked up with food and planned to eat in."

"Well, happy fifth anniversary in spite of the weather. Did you get the card I sent? The gift I ordered isn't going to make it until flights are taking off."

"Hannah, tell me again . . . what's the name of the island your brother and his girlfriend went to on vacation?"

"Roarke's Island. Why? You and Stan thinking of celebrating with a romantic couple's getaway to a jungle oasis?"

"I was afraid you might not have heard, so I thought I'd better tag. Hannah, there was a news bulletin about an earthquake."

"An earthquake?"

"Not a major quake, but the epicenter was near the mainland of San Ramon and the resort island. There was a rock slide on the island." Chelsea paused. "The road leading into the resort is blocked. The people staying there are cut off until help can get to them."

McCabe stood up. "Do the authorities know if the guests at the resort are all right?"

She could feel the gazes from Pettigrew and Yin, who were overhearing the conversation. No point in going out into the hall now.

"According to the bulletin," Chelsea said, "they still have satellite communication. Some minor injuries were reported, but the resort seems to have come through the quake without serious damage."

"Then it's only a matter of sitting tight until a rescue unit can get to them."

"And they should be fine until then. There may be some aftershocks, but they don't anticipate another quake. The bulletin said the resort complex is on high ground and far enough inland to be safe even if there should be a tsunami."

"But I should let my dad know what's going on."

"He might even have spoken to Adam by now. Anyway there's nothing to worry about. You know your brother. Right about now, he's rolling around in his wheelchair, glaring at his fellow guests with his one good eye and ordering them to stop having hysterics. Dr. Adam McCabe, superscientist in action. Of course, he's also probably seriously put out that he's stuck at a resort his girlfriend talked him into going to."

"Poor Mai," McCabe said. "I hope she survives this."

Nodding her head as Yin and Pettigrew offered words of encouragement, McCabe excused herself to step out into the hall and tag her father. He answered, coming on screen with white hair ruffled, cheeks red.

"Pop, don't tell me you've been outside in this weather."

"Had to walk the damn dog," Angus said. "Your juvenile dog walkers went off with their mama and daddy to their grandparents' house."

"We need to give him a name, Pop," McCabe said. "We've been letting this go on way too long. The dog needs a name. And you could have opened the back door and let him go outside on his own."

"I needed to stretch my legs. I've been in the house all day, and I was tired of listening to reporters yapping about the blizzard."

"Well, when you were a reporter, didn't you believe in thorough coverage of major events?"

"I didn't believe in pounding people over the head with bad news. With a real newspaper, you could read the sections you were interested in and leave the rest. With these damn news streams—"

"I know, Pop," McCabe said. "I do have a reason for calling."

"I'm glad to hear it."

"It's about Adam and Mai."

"What about 'em?"

McCabe told him. When she was done, he said, "Well, it sounds like they're both alive and likely well. Not that your brother's going to find it easy going if they have to do any walking."

"I know." McCabe paced in the other direction as two uniforms stopped near her to talk. "Adam took his exoskeleton so he'd be able to get out of his wheelchair, but his exoskeleton isn't designed for navigating post-earthquake terrain."

"So I guess he's in for a spot of humiliation before it's over with."

"Humiliation? Pop, under the circumstances, I don't think—"

"Then you ain't thought, have you? Not being able to walk in that situation is going to go straight to his pride. You know how much he hates having to have people help him."

Yes, McCabe knew that well. She'd spent a large portion of her life feeling guilty because Adam sometimes needed help. Even with his superduper wheelchair and his exoskeleton and all the other gizmos he'd designed to compensate for having only one eye and legs that didn't work, he sometimes needed help.

She said, "Well, it's not like any of the other guests are going to walk to safety. From what Chelsea said, they'll all be waiting to be rescued."

"Let's hope it stays that way," Angus said. "That they can just sit there sipping their drinks and wait for the cavalry to arrive." He shoved his hand through his hair. "I'll get on the horn to my contacts and see what else I can find out."

The uniforms ended their conversation and moved on, and McCabe paced back toward the bull pen. "I tried tagging Adam but I couldn't get through."

"If he could contact us, he would have done it by now."

"But the earlier news stream did say satellite communication was still working."

"They could be restricting use. I'll get back to you when I hear something."

"I'll do the same," McCabe said. "Although you're more likely to hear something before I do. You and the dog be careful during the snow."

"The dog and I know how to take care of ourselves," Angus said.

Pettigrew said, "Your dad hear anything yet?"

McCabe shook her head. "Mind if I check the news stream?"

"Go ahead," Yin said. "We told the rest of the guys."

"Thanks. I just want to see if there's an update, then I'll settle down so we can all try to get some work done."

"Don't worry about it," Pettigrew said. "We're going to be here for a while. We need to stretch the work out so we don't get bored."

McCabe touched the wall, bringing up the news stream.

"I'm Suzanne Price. The lead story this hour is a blizzard named Jezebel, now barreling up the East Coast. After lightning and torrential rains on Friday, the nation's capital is now under a state of emergency with over eleven inches of snow. The National Weather Service is predicting the eastern portion of New York and New England could see double that amount. Wind gusts could exceed seventy-five miles an hour as Jezebel heads north. At the bottom of the hour, we'll be speaking with one of the Weather Service meteorologists about this massive and dangerous winter storm.

"Earlier today supporters of third-party presidential candidate Howard Miller gathered for his arena rally in Roswell, New Mexico. Miller again challenged Janet Cortez, the likely Republican candidate, to a series of Lincoln-Douglas–style debates on what he called the 'overrunning of this country by illegals and criminals from south of the border.' During this same speech, Miller called for the abolition of the Martin Luther King, Jr. holiday, which honors the civil rights leader, anti-war activist, and champion of immigration reform who died a decade ago."

Pettigrew said, "Miller makes ordinary garden-variety bigots look like left-leaning liberals. And the media keeps giving him airtime."

"He'll get more of it if he turns up here for Lisa Nichols's trial," McCabe said.

On the wall, the news anchor continued:

"Mr. Miller repeated his call for embattled President Nora Kirkland to declare her intentions regarding the Democratic nomination. He said the American people have a right to know now if she will seek a second term. Last week, Miller accused President Kirkland of engaging in unlawful surveillance of her political opponents and demanded impeachment procedures be initiated against her. Candidate Miller compared President Kirkland to President Richard Nixon, who was convicted by the Senate of high crimes and misdemeanors and forced from office.

"In other news, the trial of the cyberterrorist accused of hacking into the electrical grid supplying power to the southwestern states has been moved to federal court in Phoenix.

"Here at home in the Capital District, concern continues about water main breaks. The breaks are caused by the freezing and then rapid thawing of the ground in which the pipes, the oldest dating back to the nineteenth century, are buried. These breaks have created problems for homeowners in the affected neighborhoods. Streets have been flooded and houses have been damaged. Albany mayor Beverly Stark has been under fire for what critics have characterized as her lack of attention to needed infrastructure repairs.

"On Tuesday, the trial of Lisa Nichols is scheduled to begin in Albany. Nichols is accused of the murders with phenol injections of two young local women and Broadway actress Vivian Jessup, who was in Albany writing her first play. Nichols, the accused killer, is a well-known photographer and the former fiancée of industrialist-adventurer Ted Thornton, who had established a base in the city before . . ."

McCabe waved her hand, shutting down the stream. "Nothing new."

McCabe rapped on her boss's half-open door. "Lou, could I speak to you?"

Lt. Dole gestured toward one of the chairs opposite his desk. "What's on your mind?"

"Lisa Nichols. Her trial starts on Tuesday morning."

Dole rubbed his hand over his gleaming brown scalp. "You're not trying the case, McCabe. You arrested her; now all you have to do is testify."

"I know, sir. I guess I'm having a hard time accepting the possibility she might walk. If the jury believes that story about her reaction to mixing medications causing her to commit murder—"

"Then they believe it. However it turns out, you've done your job."

"Yes, sir, I know that. But I hope neither side asks for a postponement. I'd like to get my testimony over with, preferably before Howard Miller puts in an appearance and we end up with even more of a media circus."

"Having a nutcase like Miller in town ranting about a 'billionaire's killer blonde girlfriend' and the decadence and corruption of the privileged class isn't likely to do the defense any good."

"No, sir. And since Ted Thornton is the alleged decadent and corrupt billionaire in question, he must be hoping Miller will stay away, too."

"Thornton may decide to keep on sitting this one out down in the City," Dole said.

"There's one other thing, sir. It's about my brother, Adam. I don't think this will affect my duty this weekend, but just in case something comes up . . ."

When she was done, Dole said, "If it looks bad, they'll get a US military unit in there to get them out."

"I hope it won't come to that, sir." McCabe stood up. "Anyway, I just wanted to tell you about it."

"Your brother can handle himself. This is his problem not yours."

"Yes, sir," McCabe said.

The "sir" was both a show of respect and a way of maintaining her professional distance at moments like this. Twenty-five years ago, Patrol Officer Dole had been the first uniform to respond to an emergency call. He'd found McCabe, age nine, trying to stop her older brother from bleeding to death. Adam had survived. The burglar she'd shot had not.

"By the way," Dole said, "your partner's cleared to come back to work."

"He'll be happy about that," McCabe said. "Last time I talked to him, Baxter had about had it with his flu quarantine." She glanced upward at the flickering lights. "It looks like we may need the backup generator before the blizzard's over."

The wind whooshed, rattling the windows in Lt. Dole's office.

9:14 P.M.

After dinner the patients at the psychiatric facility were herded back into the recreation room. Seated in what passed for an armchair, Lisa Nichols read a feature story about the environmental catastrophe threatening China's economy. Well-written story, mediocre photos. She should have been the photographer on that assignment. Her fingers itched for her favorite camera.

She held her hands out, staring at the ragged cuticles. She needed a manicure. She needed nail polish to keep from biting her nails.

One stupid slip of the tongue because she was annoyed, and there went everything she'd worked for and the plan she was supposed to execute. But it would have been fixable. She could have recovered from her stumble if it hadn't been for that black bitch.

She had dealt with the other three. If she had gotten rid of her—Detective Hannah McCabe—everything would have been all right.

Nichols moved her head from side to side. Relax, she told

herself. Think calming thoughts. She could fix this. She had made herself into Lisa Nichols. She had bewitched a man who had his choice of women and had never offered any of them marriage until he met her, Lisa. She could fix this.

The lawyers he hired for her believed there was a good chance they could get her off. Then she would get Ted back. He knew she needed him . . . he would be there to keep her safe, to protect her. She could have that life again. She could carry out her assignment and still have that life.

Shrieks and curses erupted on the other side of the room. Nichols retreated behind her chair. She jumped when a hand grabbed her elbow.

"Sit down and stay seated," the nurse said. Then, in a whisper, "Read this later."

Nichols peered down at the wad of paper that had been pressed into her hand. She slid it into the pocket of her jumpsuit.

Across the room, nurses and orderlies separated the two women wrestling on the floor. Nichols sat down in her armchair. God, please, she thought, let this note be about getting me out of this loony bin and back with Ted.

4

Sunday, January 19, 2020
7:03 A.M.

In the small, but well-equipped station house gym, McCabe stepped into a booth and set the geosimulator for "country run on spring day." Up hills and down, fields and cattle. Soundscape on—chirping birds, the sound of the tractor the farmer was riding, her own feet pounding the asphalt. But she skipped the brainwave function with the subliminal messages, supposed to optimize performance. She never quite trusted those messages even if the federal agency in charge of approving health and fitness products had ruled the input safe.

Three miles and a cooldown later, she headed for the showers. She'd forgotten to pack conditioner. McCabe pulled a comb through curly hair, dark tinged with red courtesy of her African American mother and Scots-Irish father. She twisted it into a top-knot before it could dry. Not stylish, but under control.

Baxter was taking off his thermo jacket when she walked into the bull pen. Face still flushed from the cold, blond hair damp with snowflakes, he looked a lot better than he had a week ago when he had gone home early with a cough and fever.

"Howdy, partner," he said, flashing his grin. "Great morning, isn't it?"

"Wonderful morning," McCabe said. "After four hours' sleep on a cot in the women's locker room, I'm ready to tackle whatever the day brings." She snagged her Elvis mug from her desk. "With this weather, I thought you might try to wrangle another day of sick leave."

Baxter reached for his APD mug. "One of my former colleagues from Vice with an all-terrain offered to swing by and give me a lift. But the city's new snowplows are doing a pretty good job. They've got this extension like an elephant's trunk."

"I've been wanting to see one in action, but I could have skipped the blizzard. And with more snow coming down even as we speak, it's probably going to be a mess for a while."

"Then we'll have to keep on our galoshes," Baxter said, following her to the coffee machine.

"Was your friend involved in the zombie nest raid?" McCabe asked.

"That's why she was heading in early this morning. It turned out to be a major bust. Is this drinkable?"

"Almost. They're trying another brand this week."

"Remember the coffee we had at Ted Thornton's house? Made from real, fresh-from-the-grinder beans."

"And served by Rosalind, your favorite robotic maid."

"My dream woman. So what's happening with that? With Lisa Nichols? I heard the trial starts on Tuesday. Are you due in court?"

"Nope, not until they call me to testify. That could be a while. Got to do jury selection first."

"Twelve impartial jurors. No problem."

"None at all. Only about as easy as establishing a permanent colony on Mars."

"Big-time loss for her dream team when they couldn't get a

change of venue. I guess Teddy didn't have as much influence as they thought."

"Assuming he tried to exercise his influence."

"Right," Baxter said. "He probably opened his checkbook to pay her lawyers and then stepped out of it."

"That might be what happened." McCabe took a sip of coffee. "Aside from being homicidal, she did betray his trust."

"But he still hired her lawyers. So I'm guessing the guy's not quite over his 'killer blonde' yet."

"Then he's out of luck," McCabe said.

Sarah Novak looked down into the backyard from her bedroom window. The door of her workshop had stayed shut during the blizzard. The piece of wood she had wedged against it was still in place. As soon as the snow was gone, she needed to get their contractor over to install the new shelving, and have him take care of the faulty hinge on the door while he was at it.

She heard a movement behind her. She turned and smiled at her husband. "It's Sunday morning. Church is canceled. We're officially snowbound. We might as well go back to bed and cuddle."

Her smiled faded when he didn't respond. "Hello! Earth to Kevin."

Kevin Novak, standing in their bathroom doorway, toothbrush in his hand, shook his head. "Sorry . . . I'm a little groggy."

"The way you tossed and turned last night, I'm not surprised."

"I didn't mean to keep you awake."

"You didn't. I was tired enough to fall asleep," Sarah said. "Before I did, I almost asked what was wrong. But since I had already asked that question earlier in the evening, and you hadn't answered—"

"Everything's okay." Kevin paused and looked at his toothbrush as if he were surprised he had it in his hand. He shoved it into his robe pocket. "Nothing's wrong. I was just wondering how I'm going to get five funeral services done in the next three days with snow piling up on the streets and in the cemeteries. It's one of those moments when being a funeral director is like running an airline."

"Funerals on hold and unhappy customers?"

"But there's nothing to be done about it. And since we don't have church this morning, what say we go down to the kitchen and make a big breakfast?"

"I'd rather cuddle."

"Me, too." He hunched his shoulders in the navy blue robe she had given him for Christmas. "But I think I'm coming down with something. No point in both of us getting sick."

Sarah knotted the belt of her own robe. "If you're coming down with something, a good breakfast with lots of fresh-squeezed orange juice is definitely in order. Aren't you glad I ordered those miniature orange trees when we built the greenhouse? Let's go see what we can find."

"I'll be down in a few minutes. I think I'll have a shower to wake myself up."

"You usually start the process with coffee."

"This morning I feel like starting with a shower. I'm really groggy. Must be a drop in the barometric pressure or something."

"That must be it. The blizzard's probably causing all kinds of weather effects." Sarah pushed her hair back behind her ears. "So I guess I'll go start breakfast."

"Give me ten minutes," Kevin said. "And I'll be down to make my famous bacon and mushroom mini quiches."

"Thank goodness the power didn't stay off," Sarah said. "I was dreading the prospect of shivering while we ate sandwiches."

"Better knock on wood. The blizzard won't be out of here until late this afternoon."

"All the more reason to have a hot meal while we can. See you downstairs."

Kevin watched his wife leave the room. He wanted to call her back. Instead, he went to have his shower.

5

Sunday afternoon
5:14 P.M.

Lt. Dole announced the detectives who had been on blizzard duty could go home if they wanted to tackle the streets. Having had her fill of life at the station house, McCabe opted to make the trip, even if she had to do it at a crawl. She wanted her own bed and to be with her father while they waited for news about Adam and Mai.

McCabe slid her ORB into her field bag. "Need a ride?" she asked Baxter.

He shook his head. "The Vice cop who dropped me off is going to pick me up."

"Is she really? Something going on there?"

Baxter grinned. "Jealous, partner?"

"Not in the least. See you in the morning." She turned to go and stopped. Lt. Dole stood there, his expression grim.

"Come into my office before you leave, McCabe. You better come, too, Baxter."

"Oh-oh," Baxter said under his breath. "What'd you mess up while I was out sick?"

"No idea," McCabe said.

If the lieutenant had been asked to break bad news about Adam . . . but he wouldn't have told Baxter to come in, too. Get a grip, McCabe, she told herself.

In his office, Dole gestured for them to sit down. McCabe sat and waited.

"Just got some news," Dole said. "Lisa Nichols was found dead in her room at the psychiatric facility."

"Lisa Nichols?" McCabe said. "How could she be dead?"

"Suicide. Apparently she was stockpiling her medication or gained access to medication."

"How could she gain access to medication?" Baxter said. "Don't they keep their pills locked up?"

"However she did it," Dole said, "she's dead."

McCabe's gaze met Baxter's. They had worked their butts off on the serial killer case. Finally found what connected two twenty-something young women, Albany born and bred, and a Broadway actress visiting Albany. Finally traced it all back to Lisa Nichols. And now she was dead. She had beaten them after all.

Baxter shook his head. McCabe saw a muscle twitch in his clenched jaw.

"Thank you for letting us know, Lou," McCabe said. "If you don't mind, I'm going to go home now."

She left before Baxter could get up to follow her out. They could talk about it tomorrow.

In his penthouse apartment in the City, Ted Thornton closed his ORB. He turned to Bruce Ashby, his aide and friend, who was waiting for him to answer a question about the bid on the seawall project in Virginia.

Ashby said, "Of course, we could just pull out of this. I know you think it's important, but we could end up losing money on this one."

"Lisa's dead," Thornton said. "Suicide."

Silence. Then Ashby said, "I'm sorry, Ted. I know how you felt about her."

"But you're also pleased that the situation's been resolved."

"It was a difficult situation."

"Damn awkward," Thornton agreed.

"Do you want to make a statement to the press?"

"A statement? You can say I regret the death of my former fiancée. And I intend to return to Albany and continue with the business initiatives under way there."

Ashby said, "We're going back to Albany?"

"We had to sooner or later," Thornton said. He strode over to the bar and reached for a bottle of whiskey. "Make the arrangements. I want to head back upstate as soon as the airship can take off and land."

"That will probably be sometime tomorrow afternoon. But I'll let the pilot know."

"And contact a funeral director in Albany."

"Are you sure you want to do that?"

Thornton took a long sip of his whiskey. "If I don't, who will?"

Ashby looked as if he were about to argue the point. He changed his mind.

"I'll make the arrangements. But you'll probably have to wait until they've done an autopsy."

"Bruce," Thornton said. "Get the hell out of here. Okay?"

"Ted . . . I'm sorry." Ashby left, closing the door behind him.

Thornton stared at the closed door. His mind went back almost thirty years to his first day of college when he'd walked into his dorm room and met Ashby, his new roommate. They looked at each other, grinned, and knew they were going to be friends. Both business majors, they went out for pizza and spent hours talking about their plans to conquer the world of finance. After graduation, when he was starting his own company, he offered his former roommate a job. He never regretted doing that. He had found his perfect second-in-command: hardworking, focused, ultra loyal. But it had been a trade-off. Somewhere along the way, the man he thought of as his best friend had become a workaholic, incapable of an inefficient emotion like compassion.

Not, Thornton thought, that he needed a shoulder to cry on. But having someone to talk to might have helped him sort through what he was feeling right then.

Thornton took another sip of his whiskey and walked over to the window. He stood watching the windblown snow swirl. The lights of Manhattan glowed in the background.

6

"Hi, dog," McCabe said.

The rescue dog she had brought home back in November barked his delight at seeing her. His tail swished so hard, his whole body wiggled.

But he managed to restrain himself from jumping up and knocking her over with his enthusiastic greeting. The obedience training was kicking in. He was eight months old, a mixture of Great Dane on his mother's side and Lab, Dalmatian, and mutt on his father's.

And they really did need to find him a name.

"Pop, I'm home," McCabe called out.

"I know you are," Angus said, coming into the hall from the direction of his home office. "I heard the dog barking his head off." He rubbed his fingers across his forehead, leaving a streak of ink. "I got busy and forgot to make dinner."

"That's okay," McCabe said. "Working on something?"

"Yes, but not that damn memoir. Even with the extension I don't know if I'm going to get that written. But I had another idea. Something I found when I was going through my old files."

McCabe shrugged out of her thermo jacket. "What'd you find?"

"I'll tell you about it after I've done some more digging. I did stop long enough to catch the news stream."

"Me, too. But there was no mention of what's happening on Roarke's Island."

"With the damage to the mainland, sending in a rescue squad for the rich tourists on the resort island ain't the first thing on the prime minister's to-do list. But my contact at the State Department says our government is keeping the pressure on. The president has offered to send support."

"Great. I wish she'd go ahead and do that."

"She's got to wait until the offer's accepted. She can't go sending the US military in just because some of the tourists are Americans."

"Yes, I suppose diplomacy is called for."

"It is when you're dealing with a government that claims the United States is an imperialist dictatorship."

"That would be news to President Kirkland."

Angus didn't bother to respond to that. They'd discussed why Kirkland's presidency was on life support too often for either of them to have anything to add.

"I heard something else on the news stream," Angus said. "What's this about Lisa Nichols being dead? Suicide?"

McCabe stooped down to fish one of her sweat socks from beneath the coffee table. It was soggy from dog saliva.

"My fault for not closing my bedroom door," she said to the dog.

He sat down and slapped his tail against the hardwood floor.

"Lisa Nichols," Angus said. "What happened?"

"I don't know any more than you heard on the news stream," McCabe said. "She apparently took an overdose of whatever pills she was able to get her hands on in the psychiatric facility where she was supposed to be under observation."

"Are you buying that?"

"What else do you think might have happened?" McCabe picked up the plastic-covered magazines from her father's collection that were scattered across the coffee table. She tucked them into the wicker magazine basket.

Angus said, "From what I saw of her when she was being arraigned, she didn't strike me as the type to kill herself."

"I guess you were wrong. Faced with the likelihood of spending the rest of her life in prison if her temporary insanity defense didn't work, it makes sense that she would have been depressed."

"Those high-priced lawyers Thornton hired might have gotten her off."

"But she didn't know that."

"So instead of waiting to see what was going to happen, she swallowed some pills and killed herself?"

"If she didn't kill herself," McCabe said, "then that would mean someone killed her. I think that's rather a leap based solely on your impression of her during her arraignment."

"Don't take it out on me because I'm saying something you're wondering about."

"Pop, how do you know what I'm wondering about?"

"I've known you since you were born. But if you think she did kill herself, then you can let it go and move on."

"Exactly what I intend to do. What would you like for dinner?"

"Anything but chicken. I baked a big hen so I'd have food cooked if the power went out. I ended up giving half of it to Bigfoot."

"Pop, we are not going to name him 'Bigfoot.' So, please, stop calling him that. It's insulting."

"Yeah, your 'Spot' would be a whole lot better for his self-esteem. And what was it your brother wanted to call him?"

"Adam likes 'Muttkenstein.' But we are all going to get a lot more original and come up with a real name. If nothing else, we'll choose a dignified name he can grow into like 'Max.' "

Angus nodded his head toward the dog. "Does he look like a 'Max' to you?"

McCabe looked at the dog and sighed. "Well, we're going to do better than Bigfoot, Spot, or Muttkenstein. Go back to what you were doing and I'll let you know when dinner's ready."

"Don't take too long. I'm hungry now that I'm thinking about food."

"I should have stayed out a little bit longer and you would have remembered to make dinner."

Actually, she was glad to see he was working on something. And that it was important enough to him to write the first draft by hand was a good sign. Even with a signed contract for his memoir about his turbulent years as a newspaper editor, he had spent most of the past six months not writing. But now he had found something he wanted to write about. That was good news.

McCabe headed upstairs to change. The dog followed on her heels.

7

Sunday evening
7:41 P.M.

Sarah Novak glanced up from the old-fashioned jigsaw puzzle, dumped out onto the table a couple of hours ago when the book she was trying to read failed to hold her attention.

"Trying on your new ski outfit?" she asked, taking in her husband's hooded jacket and matching pants.

Kevin reached for his gloves. They were on the dining room table from the last time he came in from looking outside. "I'm going to go in and see what's happening."

"Go in where?"

"The funeral home."

"Kevin, you are not going out in this weather."

"The snow stopped a while ago. Now, it's just blowing around in the wind."

"And that's exactly why you shouldn't be out there driving in it. That's why they're telling people to stay home unless they have an emergency."

"I have an emergency, Sarah. I've got five unattended bodies no one has checked on since Saturday afternoon."

"And what do you think they're going to do? Get up and walk away?"

"Funny. But seriously, Arthur isn't going to be in to start work on them until tomorrow morning. When he left on Saturday, I told him not to try to make it in tonight. Someone needs to make sure everything's all right."

"If everything wasn't all right, the security company would have called."

"They would have called if an alarm had gone off. They aren't monitoring the bodies."

"Monitoring them for what?" Sarah said. "They're dead. What do you expect to happen to them?"

"It's hard to explain. I just don't like to leave them there . . . unattended. Normally, Arthur would be there doing the embalming."

Sarah shook her head. "Arthur's braver than I am to work in a funeral home at night."

Kevin smiled. "And even after all these years, you still haven't gotten over the fact you married a funeral director."

Sarah smiled back. "If you'd told me what you did for a living when we met at that first church social . . . So you're going to go out in the cold and the snow to keep the bodies at the funeral home company. And you're going to be able to explain that to a police officer who wants to know why you were out in the first place after you skid into something."

"I'm not going to take the car. I'll take my snowmobile and go through the park."

"You really are crazy. You know that?"

"And you are a good and understanding wife. I'll be careful."

"Just tag me when you get there."

"I will."

He kissed her cheek.

When the back door closed behind him, Sarah stared down at the pieces of the jigsaw puzzle until the colors blurred.

She looked up when her son, Scott, said, "Mom? You okay?"

"Of course, sweetheart. You need something? How about some milk and cookies?"

Lanky like his father, she thought with a mother's pride, and turning into a handsome young man. "I'll throw in some ice cream," she said.

"I'm not hungry. I heard Dad go out. Everything okay?"

"You know your father. Blizzard or no blizzard, he wanted to go check on the funeral home."

"I got a tag from Meg. She said to tell you everything's okay at Nikki's house."

"And I suppose your sister had some reason for tagging you instead of me."

"She thought it would be faster to tag me," Scott said. "You sure you're okay? When I came in, you looked . . . kind of sad or something."

"A tiny touch of winter blues," Sarah said. "Sure I can't talk you into a snack?"

"I'm in training, Mom."

"I keep forgetting."

"I'm going up to my room and listen to some music."

"Okay. Try not to blow the roof off the house."

She listened to his footsteps as he took the stairs at a run. More training.

A few minutes later, the interstellar rock music he loved and she found unfathomable shook the house.

"Scott!" she yelled. "Turn it down."

The volume dropped to a muted rumble. She picked up a piece of the jigsaw puzzle.

Seeing his wife's worried expression, Kevin Novak pasted on a smile he hoped was reassuring. "Everything's okay here," he said.

"Then why weren't you answering your ORB before?" she asked.

"A pipe down in the basement was leaking. I was down there trying to do a temporary patch job."

"Did you get it fixed?" she asked.

"For now. But I'm going to hang around and keep an eye on it until Arthur gets here in the morning."

"You're going to spend the night there?"

"You and Scott will be okay. If the heat goes off, I brought in some wood. You can make a fire in the fireplace."

"I've already done that," Sarah said. "I wanted a fire. And now I'm sitting here with my stupid jigsaw puzzle while you're there. Kevin, I—"

She paused, her brown eyes wide, the way they were when she was trying not to cry.

"What?" he said, as if he hadn't noticed.

"Nothing. I'll see you in the morning."

"Sleep well," he said.

"You do that, too."

"As well as I can on the cot in the basement."

"Well, that's your choice, isn't it? You want to keep your corpses company."

"Sarah—"

His ORB went blank.

Not quite the understanding wife, Kevin thought. But he couldn't blame her. He was pushing her away, and she knew it. After eighteen years of marriage, she knew when something was wrong between them.

Kevin dropped his ORB onto his desk.

He stood there, considering how he would occupy the time. A glance around his office landed on a photo of Scott posing beside the elk they bagged when they had joined some friends on a hunting trip to Montana a couple of years ago. Kevin had brought the elk down with his compound bow.

Bob had been along on that trip. He had preferred a shotgun.

They'd had a running debate about the virtues of gun versus bow. Cowboys versus Indians, Bob always joked.

Kevin walked over to his office closet where he kept his favorite bow.

8

Monday, January 20, 2020
7:49 A.M.

Monday morning got off to a bad start. McCabe heard the dispatcher's message on her ORB and took a detour on her way to the station house. She pulled up behind one of the police cruisers on a side street and reached for her protective vest.

The uniforms monitoring activity in the park across from City Hall were calling for reinforcements. Knowing how thin they were spread, she felt obliged to respond.

In Albany, political and social action groups commemorated Martin Luther King, Jr. Day by rallying their members to protest in the park. A few of the less committed fringe groups had probably taken the day off, but it had been too much to hope that the stalwarts would decide to stay home because there's been a blizzard over the weekend. This year, with a presidential election looming, tensions ran higher than usual. The right-wing conservatives were waving AMERICA FIRST, SECURE BORDERS signs. Their far-left counterparts had their own signs calling for open borders and an end to international conflict. The animal rights people were out, too. McCabe wasn't sure what new issue had galvanized them.

So far nothing had happened. But only a section of the park had been cleared of snow and that meant the groups were packed in close together. The uniforms were concerned about the barbs being exchanged by members of two opposing immigration groups. One of the groups was displaying HOWARD MILLER FOR PRESIDENT signs.

Halfway across the street, McCabe heard a whizzing sound. Smoke bellowed around the demonstrators. Shrieks, coughs, and choking sounds. And then ripples of anger. One of the protestors rushed the cops. Others followed him into the fray.

McCabe touched the transmitter on her vest. "Dispatch, this is Detective McCabe. Officers need immediate assistance in the park. Smoke bomb tossed into the crowd. We've got a brawl."

"More uniforms en route, McCabe."

Terrific, McCabe thought. I'll get back in my vehicle and wait for them to arrive. She ran toward the chaos.

"Hey, what happened at the protests in the park?" Baxter asked before McCabe could sit down at her desk. "I caught the last bit of it on my ORB as I was pulling into the parking lot. Unless my ears deceived me, I could have sworn I heard something about a raccoon."

"Someone threw a smoke bomb into the crowd. That started a brawl between cops and protestors. And either the smoke bomb or the shouting brought this raccoon out of the bushes." McCabe opened the drawer of her desk and put her field bag inside. "The raccoon was showing his teeth and acting weird. Someone yelled, 'Rabid raccoon!' And we're all—protestors and cops—yielding soggy ground to this raccoon. A cop tries to stun him, but he doesn't go down. He darts right at the cop. A couple of other cops fire and kill him. That got this woman in the crowd yelling about police brutality."

"Toward a rabid raccoon?"

"As she told the reporters who'd showed up just in time to cover the story, there was no way of knowing if the raccoon really was rabid. He might have been angry at being awoken. She said we should have waited for animal control and taken him into 'humane custody.' "

" 'Humane custody,' " Baxter said. "Well, gee whiz."

"Exactly what the uniform who'd almost been bitten said about it."

"So the raccoon incident broke up the brawl?"

"We still had to make some arrests. But when the media arrived, the protestors decided to hold up their signs instead of hitting cops with them. Of course, they still accused us of throwing the smoke bomb."

"Sorry I missed the fun. But now you're here, the lou wants us to have another look at that bar shooting you were working last week. The ADA wants to meet to discuss charging."

The video from the scene was up on the wall, and they were going over McCabe's notes, when Lt. Dole came in to tell them they'd caught a call.

"Funeral director," Dole said. "His embalmer found him dead in the basement of the funeral home when he came in this morning."

"Drive carefully, Detective Baxter," the Voice said as the vehicle they had been assigned rolled out of its slot in the garage and stopped in front of them.

"That would be easier if we'd gotten something better than this piece of junk," Baxter said, eyeing the sedan.

"It'll get us where we need to go," McCabe said. "When the streets are as sloppy as they are today, I'd rather have one of the old cars than be responsible for one of the expensive new ones."

"The department has insurance. And we're less likely to have an accident in a car that has collision avoidance technology."

"That would make sense if you didn't always insist on driving manually."

On Central Avenue, a delivery truck had skidded in the slush and set off a chain reaction of fender benders. Baxter drummed his fingers on the steering wheel while two uniforms tried to cope with angry drivers and clear the lanes; finally, he turned on the siren. The uniforms waved the cars to the left and right. Baxter squeezed through and turned onto a side street.

McCabe didn't remind her partner they were not on an emergency call. She had been tired of waiting, too.

When they pulled into the parking lot behind the funeral home, both the medical examiner's car and the forensics unit van were already there.

"Looks like Jacoby's here, too," Baxter said.

"Good," McCabe replied. "Better the PIO than us trying to deal with witty remarks from the media when they hear a funeral director was murdered in his own funeral home."

Detective Wayne Jacoby, the public information officer, the spokesperson for the department, met McCabe and Baxter at the back entrance of the funeral home.

"Picked up the dispatch on my ORB," he said. "I thought you might need me."

"We do," McCabe said.

They left him talking to the uniform stationed on guard at the door, to deter curious onlookers, and went inside to see what they had.

The funeral director's name was Kevin Novak. His body was in the basement.

McCabe paused in mid-stride. "Hi, Rachel," she said to the assistant medical examiner, who was standing beside the body. "He was like this when he was found?"

"According to the embalmer who found him," Rachel Malone said. "I've been waiting for you before I moved him."

"Sorry for the holdup. Fender benders on Central Ave."

McCabe squatted down for a better look at the entangled limbs of the funeral director, who had an arrow protruding from his chest, and the human skeleton he was clutching. The skeleton grinned up at them.

"Who's his friend?" Baxter asked.

"The skeleton's name is 'Ernie,'" Malone said. "According to the embalmer, Ernie usually stands right here by the table."

She pointed to the stand with the broken hook and chain.

Baxter said, "So the vic pulled our friend Ernie down with him as he was falling?"

"Looks like," Malone said. "But that's up to you guys to figure out."

McCabe turned to the Forensic Investigation Unit tech who was heading up the crime scene search. "Jeff, can you walk us through this?"

"Sure." He pointed toward the other end of the room where a target was set up. "The vic was down there by the target when he was apparently—lab results pending—shot with this bow." He indicated the green-and-brown camouflaged bow on the floor not far from the victim's body.

"Then what?" Baxter asked. "What did he do after he was shot?"

Jeff pointed to the blood spatters. "He walked from the target to the sink over there, and then to where he is now. Then he seems to have collapsed, pulling the skeleton down with him as he fell."

McCabe said, "Any idea what he did at the sink?"

"Don't know yet," the tech said. "We've got residue of something we need to analyze in the sink. He might have poured something out or dropped something down the drain."

"So, he's shot with an arrow and dying and instead of trying to get to his ORB to get help," McCabe said, "he goes to the sink and pours something out?"

"We haven't found his ORB," the tech said. "But we'll do another electronics sweep when we go back upstairs. And we aren't sure how long the residue's been there. It may not be related to the crime. The vic might have gone to the sink to try to find something to stop the bleeding from his wound. There's a cloth on the sink with blood on it."

"Okay, so we need to know about the residue. And, please, check the drain carefully," McCabe said.

"Got it covered," the tech said.

"I know you do. Just saying it for the record. What can you tell us about how the perp got in?"

"No sign of forced entry. We checked with the security company. They say the alarm was turned off using the victim's code."

"What time was the alarm turned off?"

"Sunday evening—last night—at eight thirty-six P.M."

"Thanks. Are you all set with photos and video of the body?"

"We're good. Move him however you like. Let me know if you have anything else you want us to focus on."

McCabe turned back to the assistant ME. "Ready to turn him over?"

"Rigor's already set in. Let's do this carefully."

"I've got Ernie," Baxter said.

McCabe studied the arrow sticking out of the vic's chest. A bubble of blood had congealed in the corner of his mouth and a bit had dribbled down his chin. On his blue-and-white pullover sweater, a spray of blood, as if he had coughed.

Remembering Baxter's gag reflex, she glanced in his direction.

He looked pale, but he said, "I have an uncle who's a bow hunter. When I was a kid, he took me out with him a couple of times. When you're shooting a deer, you always aim for the lungs. Brings 'em down fast."

Malone glanced up from the scan she was doing of the body. "At a guess, I'd say our vic was probably brought down the same way. Looks like the arrow punctured a lung. Internal bleeding before he drowned in his own blood. A nasty way to go."

"Would he have died quickly?" McCabe asked.

"With that kind of injury, a victim can die in minutes or hours. Or not die at all if he gets help," Malone said. "Since we know he moved around, I'd said this vic lived at least five to ten minutes.

I'm going to get him out of here and back to the morgue. His wife is coming in to identify him."

"Who called her?"

"The embalmer who found him," Malone said.

"I wonder if he'll do the embalming on his boss," Baxter said.

"He might have wanted to be cremated," McCabe replied, still studying the body.

"Which are you going to have?" Baxter asked.

"Neither. I don't intend to die. Rachel, we'll check with you later about when the autopsy's scheduled."

Malone closed her bag. She arched her back, stretching. "I expect Dr. Singh will want to get this one done quickly. The quirky ones always get press, and it's better to get out in front of that."

"If we're lucky, we'll wrap this one up before we get crime buffs taking to their threads to speculate about it," McCabe said.

Sitting in a room filled with caskets on display, Arthur Putnam, the embalmer, seemed oblivious to his surroundings. He blew his nose again. "Someone must have thought no one was here and broke in."

McCabe, sitting down with her back to the caskets, said, "The patrol officers who were the first to arrive checked the doors. There was no sign of forced entry."

"Then Kevin must have let whoever it was in. Maybe someone came to the door."

"The question is," Baxter said, "why he would let someone in and then take him or her down to the basement."

"He must have been down there doing target practice," Putnam replied. "And he took whoever it was down there with him."

"So that would suggest the person was someone he knew," McCabe said. "You told us that when you called Mr. Novak's wife to tell her what had happened, she said that her husband had come in because he was concerned about no one being here. Do you think he might have been expecting someone?"

"Who would you expect to come to a funeral home on a Sunday night after a blizzard?"

"If he wasn't expecting anyone, why would Mr. Novak have been concerned that no one was here?"

"Sarah said he was concerned about the bodies. About them being unattended."

"Why did they need to be attended?" Baxter asked.

"Kevin believed in showing respect for the dead. In the old days when someone died, the family would lay the body out in the front room. Someone would sit up with it. Now the bodies come into the funeral home, and we take care of them. And the family comes in to hold visiting hours. But other than that the bodies are alone unless I'm here working—or our backup embalmer, if I'm out for some reason. But neither of us came in during the blizzard. And Kevin had this thing about liking to make sure someone was always here . . . to keep them—the bodies—company."

McCabe caught Baxter's glance in her direction. He managed not to make a wisecrack.

She said, "That must be a comfort to the families that trust this funeral home with their loved ones."

"We've got a good reputation. Kevin—the whole staff—treats the bodies with care. With respect."

"Who will handle Mr. Novak's body?"

Putnam's eyes again filled with tears. "I hope Sarah will let me do it. The last thing I can do for him."

"So it wouldn't be too close to home?" Baxter asked.

"I'd rather do it than trust someone else with the job," Putnam said. "We can bring in someone else to direct the funeral itself." He blew his nose again. "Anything else you need from me?"

"Could you give us a list of the funerals you have scheduled?" McCabe asked. "We need to know who has been in and out the past few days."

"All that information would be in Kevin's office. When Helen, his secretary, gets in, she can pull it all for you."

"Is she on her way in?"

"She hadn't planned to come in today because it's a holiday and with the streets being a mess. But I tagged all the staff and spoke to Helen, and as soon as she got done breaking down, she pulled herself together and said she'd get her husband to drive her in. She said Sarah might need her."

Helen Logan, the funeral director's secretary, sat down on the bench in the foyer to remove her boots. She replaced them with black loafers she took from her tote bag. "Is he—is Kevin—still here?" she asked.

"No," McCabe said. "He's been taken to the morgue."

Logan looked relieved. "I didn't want to see him like that," she said. "Arthur told me it was bad."

"I know this must be difficult for you, Mrs. Logan, but we need your help. We think Mr. Novak might have opened the door to the person who killed him."

"You mean the person might have been someone he recognized . . . someone he knew?"

"We haven't found indication of a break-in, and unless Mr. Novak left one of the doors unlocked when he arrived—"

"Kevin wouldn't have done that. He was careful about locking up at night. About security in general. In fact, we always tease . . . we teased him about who would break into a funeral home. But he said kids playing pranks . . ." Logan picked up her coat from the bench and stood up.

"Shall we go into your office?" McCabe said.

Logan took off her cloche hat and ran her fingers through her short hair. "It's right here off the foyer."

They followed her into a small room that contained a desk, two chairs, and green plants sprouting from pots on every available surface.

"I have allergies," Logan said, seeing their reaction. "The chemicals we use here . . . the plants help detoxify the air." She plucked a dead leaf from the plant on her desk. "About kids playing pranks . . . you don't suppose it could have been a prank that went wrong. Those space zombie kids? I heard something on the news stream about a bunch of them being arrested in a drug raid."

"Over the weekend," Baxter said.

"They're always high and they're into horror movies and *The Twilight Zone* and all that. Maybe this is something . . . maybe they broke in because of the bodies and the coffins. . . ." She stopped, sagging a little. "But you said there wasn't any sign of a break-in."

"Which doesn't rule out the possibility Mr. Novak opened the door to kids or someone else who was here to burglarize or vandalize the funeral home," McCabe said.

Baxter asked, "Who else has the code to the security system?"

"The code? I do . . . and Arthur . . . and the other embalmer who comes in when Arthur is out or needs help. But he's in Florida this week. Why are you asking about the code?"

"The security system had been turned off," McCabe said. "It is possible Mr. Novak forgot to reset it when he came in. But from what you've said about how careful he was about security—"

"Yes, he usually was. But maybe he was so cold when he got here that he just came in and started trying to get warm. He probably wasn't thinking about anyone coming to the door after a blizzard."

"Did anyone other than the people who worked here have the security code?"

"No," Logan said. "No one else."

"What about family members?" Baxter asked.

Logan shook out her black coat and carried it over to the coatrack in the corner. She put her hat on the adjoining hook. Then she turned to face them. "Sarah—Kevin's wife—might have known the code. Kevin might have written it down for her in case there was ever an emergency and he wasn't here and Arthur or I couldn't come in. But people always give their security codes to family members and friends."

"Yes, they do," McCabe said. "We're just trying to get some sense of how many people might have had access to the code."

"Well, I'm sure the people who had it wouldn't have given it to anyone else."

"Yes, I'm sure everyone was careful with the code," McCabe said. "And in all likelihood, Mr. Novak turned the alarm off to get in when he arrived and for some reason didn't turn it back on. Then, later, he himself opened the door to whoever came."

"You mean whoever killed him," Logan said.

McCabe said, "You could really help us right now, if you would."

"What do you need me to do?"

"We need you to go through your records and give us a list of the funeral services you've done recently. And the bodies you have waiting."

"We've got five bodies," Logan said. "But I'm sure none of those family members would have any reason to kill Kevin."

"Probably not," McCabe said. "But, you see, we have a procedure we follow. A process of elimination. Could you also tell us if anyone has recently made an appointment to discuss a service of any kind? I believe some people plan their funerals in advance, don't they?"

"Quite a few," Logan said. "It makes it so much easier on the family. And people also like to do celebrations of life. We have an event planner we work with when someone wants us to help with one of those."

"Do you use an event planner for funerals, too?" McCabe asked.

"When someone wants something really elaborate or unusual. But most people who want something like that would rather do a celebration of life so they can be there to enjoy it."

Baxter said, "So a celebration of life is like inviting everybody to your funeral while you're still alive?"

"That's the general idea. It gives everyone a chance to say the things they want to share with you while you're still alive and can hear them."

"Like a party for yourself," Baxter said.

"Kevin went to a celebration for one of our church members

this past Saturday. We didn't handle it. She planned it for herself. But Olive is a good friend of Kevin's."

"Then would you give us her contact information?" McCabe asked.

"Olive's going to be so hurt when she hears this. She expected Kevin to bury her."

"Is she ill?"

"She's eighty-five," Logan said. "I'll start putting together the information you need."

"Thank you," McCabe said. "But, first, if we could get your help with something else. The forensics team is still at work downstairs, but they've done a preliminary walk-through of the rooms on this floor. Everything seems to be in order up here, but could we get you to step into Mr. Novak's office with us? Just to have a look and see if you notice anything unusual."

"Kevin was a very neat person. It'll be easy to see if anything is out of order." She led the way down the hall.

"Did he usually carry his ORB with him?" McCabe asked. "The forensic techs haven't found it yet."

"I'm sure he would have had it here with him. He would have wanted to be in touch with Sarah, and with the staff, if he needed us."

"Then we may find it in his office," McCabe said.

But she wasn't hopeful about that. Jeff had said his team would have a second look upstairs, but the FIU techs tended to be thorough the first time through. They scanned and recorded as they were making their way to the body. That avoided the problem of having evidence destroyed. The FIU techs were unlikely to have missed the victim's ORB during their first sweep of the house.

Novak's office had a desk, bookshelves, a large sofa, and a seating area with table and chairs.

"Anything look out of place in here?" Baxter asked Novak's secretary. "Anything missing?"

Logan shook her head. "No, nothing I can see."

McCabe said, "Let's have another look for Mr. Novak's ORB."

She took plastic gloves from her field bag and handed a pair to Baxter.

She pulled open the desk drawers, one at a time. Standard desk contents for someone who still used paper—pens, rubber bands, paper clips. No ORB.

"Who's this in the picture?" Baxter asked. He had picked up a photo of a teenage boy with a dead elk. The elk had an arrow in its body.

Logan pressed her fingers to her lips. "That's Scott, Kevin's son. They were on a hunting trip out west."

"A father-and-son trip?" McCabe asked.

"Yes. But they went with some of Kevin's friends. Bob was on that trip."

Baxter put the photo back on the shelf. "Who's Bob?"

"Kevin's best friend. He died back in September. A heart attack."

"That must have been hard for Mr. Novak," McCabe said.

"Yes," Logan replied. "They were playing tennis when Bob had his heart attack. Kevin blamed himself for pushing him too hard. No one else thought it was his fault. Bob's doctor even said it could have happened at any time. But Kevin still beat himself up over it." Logan turned and looked around the room. "This office is all Kevin. The person he was."

"What's with the bird?" Baxter asked, pointing at the black bird perched on a top shelf. "Was he into taxidermy?"

McCabe thought of Tony Perkins in *Psycho* showing Janet Leigh his collection of stuffed birds.

But Logan was saying, "The bird was a gift from Kevin's daughter, Meg. She and her mother were at an estate sale, and she saw it. It's a raven."

"Oh," McCabe said. "Edgar Allan Poe?"

"Kevin used to recite 'The Raven' for the kids and their friends when they were little."

A morbid poem for kids, McCabe thought. But they tended to love it.

"Poe, huh?" Baxter said. "I guess a funeral director would be into all that stuff about ghosts and premature burial."

Logan said, "Aside from his training as a funeral director, Kevin had a degree in folklore. He was fascinated by superstitions about death."

"And, of course," McCabe said, "some people were buried prematurely when they sank into comas."

"No chance of being buried alive these days," Baxter said, as he wandered over to the table by the window. "After you're pumped full of embalming fluid, you're dead when you're buried."

Logan grimaced. McCabe resisted the urge to throw the book on Novak's desk at her partner. "This book about mummies looks fascinating."

"Kevin was always reading. He knew all kinds of things about death rituals and the history of funerals and mummification. He was sometimes invited to give talks to groups."

"So he was somewhat of an authority," McCabe said. "Would it be all right if we look around a bit more on our own? While you're getting together the information we need."

Logan glanced around the office. "Yes, I guess . . . I suppose that would be all right."

"Thank you. We want to see if there is anything that might give us a lead."

"I'll be in my office if you need me."

When she was gone, McCabe turned to Baxter. "Have you ever heard the word 'insensitive'?"

He grinned. "Who, me?"

"I don't think we're going to find much here, but let's go through everything."

"Maybe we ought to open up the bird and make sure nothing's hidden inside."

"I used to love that poem when I was a kid. My dad did a great 'Nevermore.' " McCabe inserted the book about mummies in the open space on the middle shelf. "Our vic seems to have his bookshelves organized by topic."

"Well, his secretary did say he was tidy."

"And it makes it easier to put your hands on a book when you want it."

"I don't have that many books," Baxter said as he pulled some file folders from the desk. "I like to enjoy my ignorance."

"Did you know, Mr. Illiterate, that there's a story about Poe having composed 'The Raven' while he was visiting a tavern in Saratoga?"

"Too bad he didn't do it here in Albany," Baxter said. "The mayor could have starred him in her *It Happened Here* tourist promotion."

"We haven't been hearing too much about that since Ted Thornton left town and presumably took his funding with him," McCabe said. She shook the book she was holding. Nothing fell out. "There's a bit of lore that Poe did come to Albany. One of Poe's enemies claimed that after his wife died, Poe came here in romantic pursuit of Frances Osgood. But that's unlikely given that Poe's wife and Osgood's husband approved of their literary friendship."

"Something you picked up in grammar school?"

"My mother, the protest poet, liked Poe."

"And she told you all about his alleged affair?"

"Not when I was a kid. But I read one of the books she had about him when I was older."

Nothing turned up in their search of Novak's office to suggest who might have killed him. No mysterious notes or files.

Baxter put the raven back on the top shelf. "Doesn't look like it's been opened and sewed back up."

"Glad we've eliminated that possibility," McCabe said. She took a last glance at a photo of Kevin Novak with a lovely dark-haired woman. He sat on the arm of the sofa, smiling down at her. She looked up at him, smiling back.

Murder cases were always easier when there was no grieving widow.

Baxter said, "I guess it's too much to hope the killer tossed Novak's ORB in some handy trash receptacle on the street as he was fleeing."

"If he did," McCabe said, "the trash receptacle's buried under snow the same way our killer's footprints were. Even after the snow stopped, the wind was still whipping it around."

"When the snow melts, the company might be able to pick up the ORB's signal."

"If it's still intact and somewhere the signal can be read."

Logan glanced up as they walked into her office. "Did you find anything?"

"No, I'm afraid not," McCabe said. "And we should go and see Mrs. Novak."

"Poor Sarah and the children." Logan took a sip from the glass of water on her desk. Then she said, "Has anyone contacted our minister, Reverend Wyatt?"

"Not that I'm aware of," McCabe said. "Unless Mr. Putnam or Mrs. Novak contacted him."

"He'll probably be at the house by now if someone thought to call him," Logan said. "You should talk to Reverend Wyatt."

"Why's that?" Baxter asked.

"Because he might be able to tell you something. Kevin is . . . was . . . active in our church. He often worked with Reverend Wyatt on projects."

McCabe said, "What church do you belong to?"

"The New Awakening Church."

"Oh, yes, I've seen your billboards."

"Reverend Wyatt says we don't want to be flashy. But we have to get people's attention before we can get them to listen."

"The advertising campaign seems to be working," Baxter said. "You folks have a pretty big congregation from what I hear."

"Over seven thousand who regularly attend services or programs at the cathedral and several thousand more members in the Capital District and New England who take part via the Web. And people in other places, even abroad, who have found us. Reverend Wyatt says so many people are feeling lost and anxious these days."

"That's very true," McCabe said. "We'll be sure to speak to Reverend Wyatt."

"I'll have that list of anyone who had business at the funeral home in just a minute. I stopped to tag my son and his wife to let them know I'm all right. I didn't want them to hear about what had happened on the news stream."

"Yes, I'm sure it was better coming from you. Did your son and his wife know Mr. Novak well?"

"We're like a family here," Logan said. "Two or three times a year, Kevin and Sarah have a party or a picnic for the staff and their families."

"How many people work here?" Baxter asked.

"About twenty, but some of them, like the woman who does hair and makeup, are only part time. We have four full-time drivers and their assistants. We usually have a full-time assistant funeral director. But David, our last one, moved to California because his new wife has family out there. That came up all of a sudden, and Kevin had planned to start interviewing people for the job next week."

McCabe said, "Could you give us David's contact information? And, please, include the names and contact information for anyone who applied for the position. Including the people Mr. Novak didn't intend to interview."

"There were only three or four people who applied," Logan said. "I'll put them on the list."

9

McCabe said, "Mike, you aren't going to believe this. I'm looking at it, and I don't believe it."

"I'm not going to believe what?"

"The last person who tried to contact Novak about a funeral. The message Novak's secretary found says that this person left a tag on Novak's ORB and also sent one to the funeral home. You're not going to believe who it was."

Baxter stopped at the traffic light. "Okay, I bite. Who was it?"

"Ted Thornton's aide-de-camp, Bruce Ashby."

"Ashby was trying to reach Kevin Novak?"

"He wanted to arrange for a funeral as soon as the body was released. Who do you think Ashby would arrange a funeral for here in Albany?"

"I'm guessing Lisa Nichols."

"My guess, too."

"That's one cosmic coincidence."

"Maybe it isn't a coincidence."

"What else could it be?"

"I don't know what else. But first Lisa Nichols manages to get hold of enough pills to kill herself. And then Ashby tags a funeral director about burying her, and the funeral director turns up dead."

"Come on, partner. You're beginning to sound like one of those conspiracy theory kooks."

"Maybe I am. But there's something about this whole Lisa Nichols case. She kills three women, and then—"

"And then, being more than a little crazy, she decides to kill herself, too. And Ted Thornton, her former fiancé, decides he should bury her. And Ashby, his assistant, probably picks a likely looking funeral director from the Web."

"And it's just a coincidence both things happen at about the time someone kills Kevin Novak?"

"Unless you really believe someone killed a funeral director because Ashby contacted him about handling Lisa Nichols's funeral."

"Okay, that sounds far-fetched. But I'd like to ask Ashby and Ted Thornton about this coincidence."

"And you know I wouldn't mind seeing my favorite robot, Roz, again. But we'd better run a visit by the lieutenant. Anyway, last we heard, Teddy was still down in the City."

"We should find out where he is now."

"After we clear it with the lou, right? Meantime, we have a grieving widow we're supposed to be calling on."

"Yes. We do. And we should focus on that."

"I agree," Baxter said.

"This is a change of pace, isn't it?"

"What is?"

"You being the one who reminds me about proper procedure and not going off half-cocked."

"Well, you did tell me I'd learn something working with a pro like you."

"And it seems you have," McCabe said.

Sarah Novak looked as if she had been hit head-on by a semi truck and emerged with no visible injuries but deep in shock. She was flanked by two men, one of them wearing a clerical collar, the other in a business suit and tie. The cleric introduced himself as Reverend Daniel Wyatt. He said the other man was Dr. Jonathan Burdett, psychiatrist, family counselor, and member of their church congregation.

"We're here to provide Sarah and her children with our support and counsel," Wyatt said.

Burdett nodded in agreement. "Although this is something we all find difficult to comprehend."

Burdett was a large man with a Boston Brahmin accent. Wyatt, on the other hand, had the open-faced look of someone who had grown up in small-town America. The kind of place, McCabe thought, where everyone came out for Labor Day parades and high school football games.

Sarah Novak did not seem comforted by either man's presence. She was sitting in her cozy living room on her color-coordinated sofa. And every few minutes, she would draw another little breath that was just short of a sob and that seemed to be forced from her chest.

Her red lipstick stood out against her colorless face.

The lipstick reminded McCabe of the blood that had been on Kevin Novak's mouth. The blood he must have coughed up from his punctured lung as he was dying.

A teenage boy, the one from the photograph in his father's office, came and stood in the doorway. When Sarah Novak did not look at him, he said, "Mom, do you want me to go pick Meg up?"

She drew a deep breath that shook her body. "Yes, please, go and get your sister. Don't . . . don't tell her what's happened. I'll tell her when she gets here."

"Okay," he said.

"Scott, do you want me to drive you?" Reverend Wyatt asked.

"That's okay," Scott said. "I can take Mom's car." He glanced at his mother. "I won't tell Meg anything. Just that you need her to come home now."

"Thank you," she said. "Be careful. The streets are a mess."

When the front door had closed, McCabe said, "Where is your daughter, Mrs. Novak?"

"She's at a friend's house. Her friend asked if she could sleep over during the blizzard."

McCabe turned to the minister and the psychiatrist. "Gentlemen, we'd like to speak with each of you. But, first, if you wouldn't mind, we would like to interview Mrs. Novak alone."

Wyatt touched Sarah Novak's shoulder. "Sarah, are you up to this?"

"I have to be, don't I?" she said. "Thank you both. I can do this alone."

Wyatt glanced at Burdett. Burdett said, "I think some tea and a light snack would be in order. We'll go out to the kitchen and put something together."

When the two men had gone, McCabe sat down on the sofa beside Kevin Novak's widow. Baxter took the adjacent armchair.

"I know this is a difficult thing to think about, Mrs. Novak," McCabe said. "But can you think of anyone who might have wanted to harm your husband?"

Novak's body jerked as if she had been punched. "Then it wasn't . . ." She paused and then went on. "It wasn't a break-in? Someone there to steal something or to get in out of the cold or to . . . Oh, God."

She covered her eyes with her hands, head bowed.

Baxter said, "There was no sign of a break-in. It looks like your husband either forgot to lock the door or opened the door to whoever killed him."

Head still down, Novak said, "So it might have been someone he knew?"

"Yes, it might have been," McCabe said. "Had your husband quarreled with anyone recently?"

"Anyone except me?" Novak raised her head. Her lips trembled as she tried to smile. "We didn't really quarrel. Kevin hated to quarrel. He lived in an orphanage until he was eight, and he always wanted . . ." She threw her head back. "He always wanted our family to be like his foster parents, Joe and Beth. Never a cross word between them. So we didn't really quarrel." She met McCabe's gaze. "Does that make sense? Sometimes we would almost quarrel, especially when we were first married. But he would never fight back, and so I stopped trying to get him to."

McCabe said, "But there was something you'd wanted to quarrel about yesterday? Last night?"

"I wanted him to tell me what was wrong. He said everything was fine."

"But you thought something was bothering him?" Baxter asked.

"A wife knows, Detective."

"Do you have any idea what might have been bothering him?" McCabe asked.

"It started when Bob died."

She stopped as if she was going to leave it there. Baxter said, "Bob was his best friend, right?"

"Yes. Bob Reeves. He died in September. He had a heart attack while he and Kevin were playing tennis and died during surgery."

"You said 'It started when Bob died,' " McCabe said. "What started?"

"I don't know," Sarah Novak said. "Kevin was . . . I thought at first it was Bob's death. Kevin blaming himself. But I think there was more to it than that. And for the past few days, there seemed to be something else. I don't know what. He didn't want to tell me what was wrong."

McCabe asked, "Do you think your husband's death might be related to what was bothering him?"

"He said he was going to spend the night at the funeral home to keep an eye on a leaking pipe. If it wasn't someone who came there to burglarize the place and found him there . . ." Sarah Novak closed her eyes for a moment. "If it wasn't that . . . then, yes, I think it might have been related to what was bothering him. We tell . . . told . . . each other everything. We never kept secrets. But whatever this was, he couldn't tell me."

"Did he seem frightened? On edge?"

"No, not frightened. More distant and distracted."

"Had that ever happened before?" McCabe asked.

"Sometimes he would be preoccupied. But not like this." Novak's hands clenched in her lap. "He had never deliberately shut me out before."

Baxter asked, "How long had the two of you been married?"

"Eighteen years."

"And in all those eighteen years, he always told you everything?"

"Sometimes he didn't have to," Sarah Novak said. "Sometimes I could almost hear my husband's thoughts. But something happened. Something he couldn't share with me . . . that he couldn't tell me about."

McCabe said, "And if the two of you were so close, he must have realized you knew something was wrong."

"But he wouldn't tell me what it was. And that's why I was so worried. Kevin would never have shut me out unless whatever . . . unless it was too awful to share."

"If he couldn't talk to you about what was bothering him," McCabe said, "is there anyone else he might have confided in?"

"Bob was his closest friend. He had other male friends, but no one he was as close to." Novak frowned. "But he . . . he was so depressed after Bob died that he did speak to Reverend Wyatt. And Reverend Wyatt suggested he see Jonathan."

"See him for therapy?" Baxter asked.

"Yes. For counseling. I don't know what they talked about. Probably about how guilty Kevin felt about Bob's death."

"So we should talk to Reverend Wyatt and Dr. Burdett to see what they can tell us about their conversations with your husband," McCabe said. "Is there anything else you can think of, Mrs. Novak?"

"No. I can't really think right now. I don't want to think right now."

"Then we'll let you get some rest, and we'll talk to you later if we have any more questions."

Baxter said, "Just for the record, were you here at home all last evening?"

Novak's head came up and she fixed him with a hard stare. "No, Detective. I followed my husband to the funeral home and killed him. And I'm a terrific actress."

"Mrs. Novak," McCabe said. "It isn't a good idea to make statements that might be misinterpreted. If you want to make a statement about your husband's death—"

"Yes, I was here at home all last evening. No, I didn't kill my husband."

"What about your son?" Baxter said. "Just for the record."

"My son was here as well. Upstairs in his room. Neither one of us went out."

"Thank you, Mrs. Novak," McCabe said. "I know this is difficult and our questions may seem offensive. But once we're able to eliminate the people close to your husband as suspects in his death, we can focus on finding the person who killed him."

Sarah Novak nodded. "I understand. That doesn't make me like being asked if I killed my husband." She drew a deep breath. "I loved him. I don't know what I'm going to do now . . . I don't know how I'll . . ."

McCabe said, "Maybe you should go upstairs and lie down for a while."

"My daughter's coming home. I have to tell her what's happened. Tell her that her father is dead."

"Maybe your minister or Dr. Burdett could help you do that."

"No, I have to do it on my own."

McCabe stood up. "We're going to go out to the kitchen and talk to Reverend Wyatt and Dr. Burdett. That will give you a little time to get your thoughts together."

"Thank you. You're being kind."

When the kitchen door opened, Wyatt and Burdett broke off their low-voiced conversation.

McCabe said, "Were you able to make the tea? I think Mrs. Novak could probably use a cup."

"Yes, it's ready," Reverend Wyatt said. "I'll take it in to her."

"Thank you. If you wouldn't mind, that would give us a chance to speak to Dr. Burdett privately."

"Of course," Wyatt said. He filled a mug and reached for the tray one of them had found and set out on the counter. Two shortbread cookies were already on a plate.

"Nice touch," Baxter said.

Wyatt blinked at him. "What?"

"The tray and the cookies."

Burdett said, "Rituals are important to a woman like Sarah at a time like this."

Although, McCabe thought, Sarah Novak had presumably never experienced "a time like this." Murder was a bit different from life's other distressing events.

"Let me know when you're ready to talk to me," Wyatt said. "I'll keep Sarah company until you need me."

McCabe left it to Sarah Novak to tell her minister she wanted some time to herself. They needed to get Wyatt out of the kitchen.

As he left, McCabe gestured toward the table in the breakfast nook. "If you'd like to sit down, Dr. Burdett . . ."

"Actually, I think I'd rather stand. I'm feeling a bit restless."

Baxter leaned back against the counter. "We understand from Mrs. Novak that her husband has been seeing you professionally."

McCabe said, "She told us Mr. Novak was having a hard time dealing with his friend Bob's death. That he spoke to Reverend Wyatt and then came to you for therapy."

"I prefer to call it 'counseling,' " Burdett said.

"But you are a psychiatrist," Baxter said. "Right?"

"Yes, but I find the church members that I see are more comfortable with the term 'counseling.' "

"Whatever you prefer," McCabe said. "Are you able to tell us anything about your conversations with Mr. Novak?"

"As you must know, Detective McCabe, such conversations between psychiatrist and patient are confidential."

"Yes, but in this case, since your patient is dead, I think his family would appreciate anything you could tell us."

"No, I'm afraid not."

"Then could you tell us if anything Mr. Novak told you might conceivably have played a role in his murder?"

"To the best of my knowledge, no. There was nothing."

"Aside from your sessions with Mr. Novak as a psychiatrist, could you give us a little background on his activities and his involvement in your church?"

"Reverend Wyatt is the best person to tell you about Kevin's involvement in the church. But I can tell you that he was well respected and well liked by the community at large and by the members of our congregation."

"Even though he was an undertaker?" Baxter asked.

"The responsibility of burying the dead and consoling the living is an important one, Detective," Burdett said. "And Kevin was hardly a somber, brooding type. Nor was he some hovering ghoul waiting for people to die."

"Good to hear that," Baxter said.

McCabe asked, "Dr. Burdett, did you and Mr. Novak ever socialize?"

"We played squash now and then. An occasional game of chess."

"So you knew him well enough to consider him a friend."

"Yes, I would say that."

"But neither of you found the psychiatrist-patient relationship uncomfortable?"

"We both knew it was a transitory relationship. Kevin needed to talk through his feelings about his friend's death. Since I had known them both, I was ideally situated to listen and understand."

"I see. So that was the topic of your discussions? Bob's death?"

"I seem to have admitted as much," Burdett said.

McCabe said, "And is that all you're willing to tell us about that?"

"It is."

"Any other topic you're willing to talk about?" Baxter asked.

"Kevin has a wonderful family. A loving wife. Two beautiful children. He loved his family and was extremely proud of them."

"His wife told us that he had been an orphan," McCabe said.

"And that childhood experience made it important to him to create and maintain a solid family unit."

"Was he concerned about his family?" McCabe asked. "Was there anything that threatened their solid family unit?"

"Kevin was a good husband and father. He felt his own emotional state might be having a negative impact on his family."

"And his emotional state was related to his friend's death?"

"Sometimes the death of a friend or relative—even of a stranger with whom we identify—can send us into a tailspin. Can get us thinking about our own mortality and the ways in which we've failed to be the person we wanted to be. Kevin had very high standards for himself."

"But we're talking murder, not suicide," Baxter said. "Did Kevin mention anyone else he might have disappointed big time? Someone who would want him dead?"

"That is a question that I can answer," Burdett said. "Nothing Kevin told me suggested he felt that he was in danger or believed anyone wished him harm."

"So to the best of your knowledge," McCabe said. "Mr. Novak was his own worst enemy?"

"I think that's an accurate statement," Burdett said.

"Reverend Wyatt introduced you as the family counselor for the church."

"Yes, I work in tandem with Daniel. He ministers to our members' spiritual needs. I help them to work through their psychological issues. As you can imagine, there is often overlap."

"Is that why Reverend Wyatt referred Mr. Novak to you?"

"Yes. He saw Kevin was dealing with guilt about Bob's death and also depression related to that."

"Did that mean he needed a shrink more than a minister?" Baxter asked.

"Or both, Detective. And I prefer to think I help my clients to *expand* their minds to see their lives in more positive ways."

"About your relationship with Mr. Novak," McCabe said. "His secretary mentioned he was active in the church. Did the two of you work together on any church committees?"

"Several. The deacons committee and the committee with oversight of the church budget. The youth committee," Burdett added. "Kevin was the coach of the church's softball team, and he also helped out with family-focused events. Both his son, Scott, and his daughter, Megan, are members of the teen book discussion group I direct. Kevin and Sarah sometimes joined us as group leaders."

"What kind of books do you discuss?" Baxter asked. "Books about religion?"

"Books in a variety of genres. Particularly novels that are engaging enough to hold teenagers' attention, but at the same time pose thought-provoking questions about morality and ethical behavior. Our book selection last month was an adventure novel set in France during the fourteenth century."

"Sounds like a fun read," Baxter said.

"The protagonist was someone with whom even our less-engaged group members could identify. And the plot raised some rather profound questions about how one should behave in a time of war, pestilence, and social turmoil."

" 'A time of war, pestilence, and social turmoil,' " Baxter said. "Sort of like now?"

"Yes, unfortunately. Our reading group members did see the analogies."

McCabe said, "Getting back to Mr. Novak's other activities in the church, Dr. Burdett. Has anything unusual happened on any of the church committees or with the congregation? Anything that Mr. Novak expressed concern about?"

Burdett shook his head. "All large churches have their minor conflicts, but in general—much of the credit going to Daniel's leadership—our church functions well. Problems are usually resolved with compromise."

"So Mr. Novak hasn't mentioned any arguments he might have had with a church member?"

"I don't think you're going to find Kevin's killer among our congregation, Detective McCabe. But in answer to your question, the only incident involving a church member that I can remember Kevin bringing up recently was a humorous tag that he sent me on Saturday afternoon."

"Saturday?" McCabe said. "What was it about?"

"I still have it on my ORB," Burdett said, reaching into his jacket pocket. "One of our members, Olive Cooper, had a celebration of life on Saturday afternoon. She turned eighty-five recently, and she wanted to bring together family and friends to celebrate. I was invited but couldn't attend because of another commitment, a lecture I had promised to give at a local college. After the lecture, I tagged Kevin to ask how the celebration had gone. Here's his response."

He held his ORB out for her to see, and McCabe read the message out loud: "Met Olive's medium. Olive says I should forget about counseling with you and attend a séance."

"So this church member, Olive Cooper, is into woo-woo?" Baxter asked.

"If by that you mean the paranormal," Burdett said, "Olive has a lively intellect. She met this woman at someone else's function. She—the woman—was there as the evening's entertainment, I believe Olive told me."

"And since then Ms. Cooper has been seeing her professionally?" McCabe asked.

"When you meet Olive—and I assume you'll want to talk to her about the party on Saturday—you'll understand. She has a way of bringing people she finds intriguing into her orbit. I don't think—based on my brief conversation with her about this woman—that Olive believes wholeheartedly in contact with the dead. But, as I said, she has a lively intellect. She finds the woman *interesting*. Her word, not mine."

"Have you met this medium?" Baxter asked.

"No, I haven't. I'm sorry I missed the opportunity to do that on Saturday."

"So you took Kevin's tag about her as a joke? You don't think of her as competition?"

"Competition?" Burdett smiled. "No, Detective Baxter. Most of the members of our church would not be drawn to séances. Those who might would be curious in passing, as Olive is. And séances, as I understand what they involve, are unlikely to solve anyone's psychological or emotional problems."

"Is your practice limited to members of your church?" McCabe asked.

"I have other patients and I work as a consultant," Burdett said. "But I do hold a paid part-time appointment as family counselor for our church members."

"Is that usual?" Baxter asked. "For a church to have a psychiatrist on call?"

"It isn't unusual to provide counseling services. These days, with the anxiety level high even among regular churchgoers, it seems prudent if the church can afford to do so."

"Just curious, Doc—how do psychiatrists chill out? You must know all kinds of tricks."

"I prefer to call them strategies. Tricks imply magic or sleight of hand. Strategies can be learned and applied."

"Got it," Baxter said.

McCabe asked, "Is there anything else you can tell us, Dr. Burdett? Anyone else you could suggest we talk to?"

"I think after you've talked to Daniel and to Olive, you'll have a good sense of Kevin's involvement with the church and his friends."

"And I hope you won't mind if we follow up with you if we have other questions as we go on."

"You understand that my responses will be limited by the doctor-patient obligation I still feel to Kevin. The need to keep confidential the more private thoughts and feelings he shared with me."

Baxter said, "Isn't it a little weird sometimes—I mean, knowing all kinds of secrets about the folks in your church and hanging out with them?"

"Sometimes. But no more than Daniel must feel. Or anyone else in whom confidences are confided. One learns to compartmentalize."

"What you're told in your office stays in your office?"

"My relationships with the individuals and the families I counsel require that."

McCabe said, "We shouldn't keep Reverend Wyatt waiting too much longer. Just one more thing, Dr. Burdett. And this is a routine question. Could you tell us where you were on Sunday evening?"

"Snowed in like everyone else, Detective. Unlike Kevin, I didn't venture out even after the snow had stopped. From Saturday evening until Monday morning, I hibernated with my books and music. I used the opportunity to try out several recipes—a stew, a loaf of bread. Hearty winter storm foods." He paused. "And, alas, being a widower and not currently involved with anyone, I spent the time alone."

"But hopefully you enjoyed the solitude," McCabe said.

"Yes, I did. Sometimes a brief respite from the world is exactly what the doctor orders—even for himself."

McCabe nodded. "Cops should keep that in mind. There are days when we could use a little psychological downtime."

10

Sarah Novak left her minister alone in the living room. The tray with the mug of tea and the shortbread cookies sat on the coffee table, untouched.

Wyatt closed his ORB and stood up as they came in. "Sarah went up to her bedroom. She said she needed some time alone."

McCabe said, "Yes, she mentioned she wanted to think about what to say to her daughter."

"Scott should be back with Megan any minute, now," Wyatt said. "Do you want to go into one of the other rooms in case they should return during our conversation?"

"Good idea," Baxter said. "Lead the way."

"Let's use Kevin's study. Sarah said to make ourselves at home."

That was helpful, thought McCabe. An opportunity to have a look in the victim's study without having to ask the widow. Just follow the family minister, who said they had been given permission to wander about.

Kevin Novak's study was his office at the funeral home on steroids. His interest in death and death rituals was reflected in the posters on the wall—from a 3-D museum poster about a King Tut exhibit to an old movie poster about Burke and Hare, the nineteenth-century Scottish murderers who'd trafficked in cadavers for medical dissection. Novak's pop culture collectibles included a hologram on his desk of a New Orleans funeral procession.

Baxter waved his hand and the jazz musicians swung into action with "When the Saints Go Marching In."

"Guy had a sense of humor," Baxter said, waving his hand again to close the hologram.

"Yes, he did," Wyatt said. "Shall we sit down?"

They took seats around a small table in the corner. As his secretary had said, Kevin Novak was tidy. Nothing on the table.

"Reverend Wyatt," McCabe said, "Dr. Burdett was able to give us some sense of what had been troubling Mr. Novak without violating the obligation he felt to preserve doctor-patient confidentiality. We know Mr. Novak felt some guilt abut his friend's death and was depressed. We know you referred Mr. Novak to Dr. Burdett."

"Yes, I thought Jonathan was better equipped than I was to offer the counseling I sensed Kevin needed."

"But apparently—from what his wife said—he was still troubled. So troubled she was concerned about him."

"I think Sarah's perception is probably more accurate than mine, or even Jonathan's. I'm practically a newlywed compared to her and Kevin, but I have learned it's much easier to present a brave face to the world than to your spouse."

"Of course, it seems other people were also concerned about Mr. Novak," McCabe said, taking the opportunity to go in another direction. "Dr. Burdett showed us a tag Mr. Novak had sent him on Saturday. Apparently, when he was at the celebration for Olive Cooper, she was concerned enough to suggest Mr. Novak attend a séance with a medium."

Wyatt grimaced. "If she meant that Woodward woman, I hope she was joking."

Baxter said, "So you don't believe in spiritualists, Reverend?"

"I believe that some, if not all of them, prey on vulnerable people. As to whether or not it's possible to communicate with the dead, I'm of an open mind about that. But if it is, I don't think a medium is required to do it."

"I see," McCabe said. "So you wouldn't have encouraged Mr. Novak to attend a séance."

"I would have encouraged him to continue his sessions with Jonathan. From what I understand, the therapeutic process can stir up disturbing emotions. And it becomes a matter of working through to get to the other side."

"Unfortunately, Mr. Novak never got that opportunity." McCabe opened her ORB and glanced at her Novak file, giving Wyatt a moment to think about that. "Do you know anyone who might have wanted Mr. Novak dead, Reverend Wyatt?"

"No, Detective, I don't. That's what concerns me. If this murder wasn't committed by a stranger, by someone who came in off the street, then that means Kevin was killed by someone he knew."

"Someone you might know as well."

"Yes, and that possibility shakes me to the core."

"I can understand that it would. What can you—"

McCabe broke off at the sound of the front door closing. A young female voice called, "Mom, I'm home. What's going on?"

They listened for a reply. Then Sarah Novak called out, "I'm up here, honey. Come upstairs."

Wyatt took an audible breath. "This is going to be so hard for Meg. She adored her father."

McCabe could empathize with that. She had been a "daddy's girl," too. But that had to do with the fact that her brother had been her mother's favorite child. It wasn't clear what the dynamics were in the Novak family. "As I was about to say, can you tell us about Kevin Novak's involvement with your church?"

Wyatt said, "I have some good memories about that. I was a young assistant minister at another church when I first met the two of them—Kevin and Sarah. Later, when I was thinking of going out on my own, they encouraged me. And they were among the first members of my new congregation."

"How did your boss at your old church take it when you left and took two of his members along?" Baxter asked.

"Actually," Wyatt said, a touch of pride in his voice, "I took about thirty members from the old church along. The senior minister was elderly and contemplating retirement. So he wasn't deeply offended when some of the members followed me."

"If I could ask—just curious," McCabe said, "but if the senior minister was about to retire, why didn't you stay where you were?"

"It wasn't a sure thing that I would become the next senior minister there. By then, it had become clear I had some doctrinal differences with that church. I wanted the freedom of starting a new church from the ground up."

"With some supportive members from your former church?"

"Who believed as I did," Wyatt said. "In case you're wondering what we believe, I can best sum it up by saying we're social progressives who believe strongly in faith-based lives."

McCabe nodded her understanding, thinking she would go to the Web later and see if that meant what she thought it did. Conservative religious practices, but liberal on social issues like the homeless and immigration.

"Dr. Burdett told us Mr. Novak was active in the church," McCabe said. "That he served on a number of committees, and he and his wife were involved with the teen book discussion group. And Mr. Novak himself was a coach."

"Yes, Kevin was incredibly generous with his time in serving the church."

"Did he bury most of the members who died?" Baxter asked.

"Many of them," Wyatt said. "But he didn't have a monopoly if that's what you're implying."

"So, are any of your other members funeral directors?"

"A couple of years ago, we had another member who was," Wyatt said. "But he moved to Portland, Oregon."

Before Baxter could make an observation about that, McCabe said, "Will you be delivering Mr. Novak's funeral sermon?"

"I assume so," Wyatt said. "I never talked about it with Kevin.

But I'm sure he left instructions about his service. No one knew better than he how helpful it is to the family to know what their loved one wanted done."

McCabe felt a twinge of guilt. Somehow she had never gotten around to dealing with her own funeral arrangements. Making a living will had been uncomfortable enough. Dealing with what came after they'd take her off life support and take her organs for donation had been a step further than she'd wanted to go at the time.

Buried or cremated? Neither choice appealed.

She wondered which Kevin Novak had opted for. She glanced again at his mummy poster. Maybe he'd had other plans.

Realizing her mind had drifted, McCabe straightened in her chair and said, "Reverend Wyatt, would you tell us where you were on Saturday evening?"

"Snowed in. At home with my wife, Iris, and our toddler."

"And you were at home until when? Were your church services canceled on Sunday?"

"The live church services were canceled. But I was able to do a Web stream from the small studio I have in my home. My wife is my production manager, so there was no problem about technical assistance."

"Handy to have a wife who can do that kind of thing," Baxter said. "Did she train as a production manager after the two of you were married?"

"No, we met at the studio where I was recording my sermons for streaming. After we were married and the church began to grow, she decided to work for me full time."

Something occurred to McCabe. "Speaking of work, does Mrs. Novak work outside the home?"

"She works at home. She's an herbalist. She has her own line of soaps and other products she sells by mail and at fairs and festivals."

"Was that what she was doing when she and Mr. Novak met?"

"I believe she'd had a number of jobs in sales. After they were married and Scott was born, Kevin encouraged her to do what she really wanted to do and try her hand at her own small business."

"That was supportive of him," McCabe said.

"Yes, it was. Kevin was a good husband. He would have done anything to make Sarah happy."

The problem with that, McCabe thought, was that being happy sometimes came with a price tag.

She heard herself repeating the question she had asked at least three times that day: "Is there anything else you can tell us, Reverend Wyatt?"

"Nothing I can think of. But something else may come to me after I've gotten over the initial shock. After I've really taken in that Kevin is dead and someone killed him. Do you intend to talk to Olive Cooper?"

"Yes, we do."

"Please remember her age. I'm sure she'll be upset when she hears about Kevin."

"Speaking of Ms. Cooper, Reverend Wyatt, I gather you didn't attend her celebration of life on Saturday."

He looked uncomfortable. "I had planned to attend, but something came up last week. As I explained to Olive, with my regrets, I needed to take part in a Web conference with several other participants across the country. It was urgent that we deal with some details and we had difficulty coordinating our schedules. That Saturday afternoon was the only time during the next several weeks when one of the key participants was available."

"I see," McCabe said. "Thank you for explaining."

Wyatt still looked uncomfortable. "I felt dreadful about missing Olive's celebration, but this really was important to the church. I'm involved in several national events that are going to be coming up this fall. This Web meeting included the sponsor who is underwriting these events. Olive is a businesswoman herself. She understood the situation."

There was no sign of Sarah Novak and her children when they went back into the living room.

"Do you need to speak to Sarah again?" Reverend Wyatt asked.

McCabe shook her head. "That won't be necessary."

"I'm sure Sarah will appreciate your consideration," Dr. Burdett said as he came in from the kitchen.

He and Wyatt escorted them to the front door.

Baxter glanced back as the door closed. "What do you think about those two?"

"You first this time," McCabe said. "What did you think?"

"I thought both of them seemed kind of uneasy under all of that 'we're here for Sarah and the children.' "

"Same impression I had," McCabe said. "But maybe—as Reverend Wyatt said—when someone you know is murdered, it just makes you uneasy."

"On the other hand, maybe old Kev told them something neither one of them wanted to share with us."

"There's also that possibility."

"They kept telling us how devoted he was to his family," Baxter said. "But his wife said something was wrong. Could it be he was fooling around on her?"

"That's possible. Except it seems out of character from what we know about him so far. Maybe he had financial problems he didn't want to worry his wife about. We'd better make sure he wasn't in over his head."

"While not ruling out another woman."

"While keeping that in mind," McCabe said. "And it might not hurt to find out some more about this church they all belong to."

11

"I wonder if she knows Teddy," Baxter said.

They were sitting in Olive Cooper's driveway looking at her large, gray stone house. *Mansion* was the word that came to mind.

"I think she must be 'old money,' " McCabe said. "Ted Thornton may be too 'new money' to travel in her circle."

"You ever heard of her?"

"No, but I don't follow Albany society. Maybe my dad will be able to tell us something about her."

Baxter rang the front doorbell. He shot McCabe a grin when the door was opened by a middle-aged human female instead of a replica of the robotic maid who had greeted them the first time they went to Ted Thornton's mansion. Olive Cooper was old school when it came to her servants.

McCabe introduced herself and Baxter and asked if they could speak to Ms. Cooper.

The woman nodded her head. "She's expecting you."

"She is?" McCabe asked.

"Reverend Wyatt called to break the news to her about Kevin."

Helpful of him, McCabe thought. Too helpful?

"I'm Velma, Olive's housekeeper," the woman said. "I'll show you into the parlor. Then I'll go tell her you're here and bring in some coffee."

"Well," Baxter said when they were alone in Olive Cooper's parlor, "this is cozy."

"Yes, it is." McCabe smiled as she glanced around the room. "I don't think I've ever actually seen lace doilies on the backs of chairs. Except in a museum."

"When you're eighty-five, I guess you're into antiques."

"On the other hand . . ." McCabe pointed.

"Hey," Baxter said. "Isn't that—"

When Olive Cooper made her way into her parlor, the two detectives from the Albany Police Department, there to speak to her about the murder of her friend, were caught in the act of trying to stifle their guffaws and giggles.

12

McCabe swallowed hard and got her giggles under control. She did not look at Baxter because she knew that would set her off again.

"Ms. Cooper," she said, stepping forward and trying for some semblance of dignity. "I'm so sorry you walked in on us like this. I'm Detective Hannah McCabe and this is my partner, Detective Mike Baxter. And . . ." McCabe shook her head. "And we are usually so much more professional."

Olive Cooper, tall and straight-backed in spite of the cane in her hand, wearing a lace blouse with a cameo brooch, said, "I gather you saw my painting."

"Your . . . you painted . . . ?" McCabe gestured toward the visual humor that had set her and Baxter off.

"Yes. And I'm so pleased you got it. Some of my older friends don't. But that's probably just as well. They might be scandalized if they did."

"But we do apologize again for our behavior when we're here to discuss a matter you must find distressing."

"In moments of distress, finding something to smile about is a good thing."

She gestured toward her feet.

McCabe glanced downward, past Cooper's ankle-length black skirt. The sneakers the elderly woman was wearing almost sent her into giggles again. Two retro yellow smiley faces looked up at her.

Velma, the housekeeper, returned, pushing a coffee trolley before her.

Cooper gestured toward two of the plush armchairs. "Please sit down, detectives. Velma, would you pour the coffee, please? And then we'll help ourselves to refills."

McCabe sat down. While Velma was serving the coffee, McCabe allowed herself another look at Cooper's painting, which was of a late nineteenth- or early twentieth-century parlor, not unlike the one they were sitting in. In the painting, a woman, lovely but no longer in the first blush of youth, smiled down at the handsome, older man who knelt on one knee before her offering a ruby ring in a heart-shaped box. All very sweet and proper . . . if you didn't notice the woman's striking resemblance to a certain feminist talk show host who was notorious for her polemics against traditional heterosexual marriage as an antiquated and oppressive arrangement that favored men. The woman's suitor in the painting was a double for a notoriously unfaithful actor, one who charmed women both in his films and in real life, and who was now on his seventh or eighth marriage.

Was the lady about to kick the gentleman in his lower anatomy and send him hobbling away? Was that why she was smiling so demurely?

That painting, McCabe thought, told one a lot about Olive Cooper.

"I'll be in the kitchen if you need me," Velma told her employer. She slanted a glance at the two detectives before she left the room.

Cooper said, "Velma has worked for me a long time. Sometimes she's protective."

McCabe said, "We understand Reverend Wyatt called to give you the news about Kevin Novak."

"I suppose he thought it might be too much of a shock for my old heart to hear the news from the two police detectives who turned up at my door."

"Would it have been?" Baxter asked.

"My doctor tells me that my heart is in excellent condition for a woman my age. But Daniel was right. I did appreciate having a little time to collect myself before you arrived."

"Did you consider Kevin Novak a good friend?" McCabe asked.

"A good friend and someone I trusted. I took great comfort from the fact that when I died, Kevin would be there to help me make the transition."

"The transition?" Baxter said. "To the other side?"

Cooper smiled. "Yes, I know that word 'transition' sounds a bit what we used to call 'New Age.' Daniel uses it, but it isn't my favorite. Still, when you're as old as I am, you like to believe that— whatever you call it—there will be an afterlife. That you move from this existence to another form and that it won't be terrifying or even unpleasant."

McCabe said, "Of course, since people are living into their nineties and longer these days, you may have years before you find out."

"True," Cooper said. "So no need to dwell on it. But I will think about it a bit more with Kevin gone. And I'm a selfish, self-obsessed old woman. Poor Kevin is dead, and his wife and children left to mourn him. How did this happen? Do you have any idea who did it?"

"The reverend didn't give you the details?" Baxter asked.

"He was still at Sarah's. Meg had run out of the house. He had to go help bring her back. Tell me what happened."

McCabe said, "Mr. Novak was shot with an arrow from his own bow in the basement of the funeral home."

"Oh, dear God."

"He was spending the night there to make sure everything was all right, and had apparently been practicing with his bow. We don't know who killed him or why. There was no sign of forced entry, so it is possible he opened the door to the person who killed him."

"And took this person down to the basement after letting him in?"

"That seems to be what happened. Unless for some reason, his killer forced Mr. Novak to go down into the basement."

"And then shot him with his own bow?" Cooper frowned. "That's odd, isn't it?"

"Odd that he was killed with a bow?" McCabe asked.

"It was a convenient weapon," Baxter said, as he got up to pour himself another cup of coffee.

"Yes," Cooper agreed. "But if it had been someone who'd come there to rob the place, wouldn't he have brought his own weapon? Except, I suppose, a bow would be much quieter than a gun, wouldn't it?"

"Yes, it would," McCabe said.

"Still, have you ever tried to use a compound bow?" Cooper asked. "If you've never used a bow, you might not even know how to position the arrow or what stance to take. And even with a pulley system, if you're using the bow of someone who is a hunter, who has the bow adjusted for his upper body strength, you might find it hard to make an accurate shot."

"Obviously we need to learn a bit more about compound bows," McCabe said. "I gather you've used one."

"When I was a girl, I won several prizes using a recurve bow. That's the kind Robin Hood used—without the pulley system. Later, when I was married, I did some hunting with my husband, who preferred compound bows," Cooper said. "But I haven't made your lives easier by telling you this. We have archery clubs for both teenagers and adults at the church. A number of the men and several of the women are avid bow hunters. Because of the legal restrictions on using crossbows for hunting and some technical issues that bow users love to debate, they tend to prefer compound bows."

Baxter said, "Isn't hunting defenseless animals kind of a contradiction for members of a socially progressive church?"

"Not really," Cooper said. "One of the environmental problems we're facing is the overpopulation of deer and other wild game. They've been wandering into urban areas for years. Now, they're a serious traffic hazard. The hunters in our congregation only kill what they intend to eat themselves or donate to homeless shelters or food pantries."

"So what you're telling us," McCabe said, "is that there are a number of people in your church with knowledge of and skill with compound bows. Do you know if Mr. Novak was on good terms with the members of the archery clubs? Was there anyone with whom he might have quarreled?"

"Not to my knowledge," Cooper said. "As far as I know, there was no one who had a grudge against Kevin or disliked him enough to want to see him dead."

"Thank you," McCabe said. "We have to assume he may have known the person who killed him, and eliminate his friends and associates as suspects."

"Are the reverend and Dr. Burdett bow hunters?" Baxter asked.

"Not hunters. But they both do target practice with the teen archery club."

Why, McCabe wondered, hadn't Burdett mentioned the church members were into archery when he was telling them about the activities Kevin Novak was involved in? Why hadn't Reverend Wyatt mentioned it, for that matter?

Aloud she said, "We've heard from his wife and Reverend Wyatt and Dr. Burdett that Mr. Novak had been depressed recently. Can you tell us anything about that? Did the two of you talk about what was bothering him?"

"Afraid not. Kevin didn't want to talk. He said he'd been talking to Daniel and Jonathan and seeking their counsel."

"And you recommended he attend a séance with your medium," Baxter said.

Cooper raised a snow-white eyebrow. "How did you hear about that?"

McCabe said, "Mr. Novak mentioned it to Dr. Burdett in a tag when Dr. Burdett asked how your celebration of life had gone."

"And he was happy enough to have an excuse not to attend that," Cooper said.

"Dr. Burdett?" McCabe asked. "Why do you think that?"

"Jonathan tries hard to have the common touch. But it doesn't come naturally to him. I had people from all walks of life at my celebration. Street people I'd met through the church's community outreach. Musicians and artists. And, of course, Luanne, the medium I introduced to Kevin."

"And you think Dr. Burdett would have been uncomfortable in that mix of people?"

"Don't get me wrong," Cooper said. "Nothing against Jonathan. He's a good man. Just comes with a family pedigree that makes him a tad awkward when he tries to engage in social chitchat with a guy who has lived in a cardboard box."

"What about Reverend Wyatt?" McCabe asked. "He explained that he couldn't attend your celebration because of church business, but he also seems to disapprove of Luanne, the medium."

"He hasn't told me that to my face, but I wouldn't be surprised. Daniel is also a good man, and because of that he worries about the wolves that might threaten his flock. Of course, he would suspect a medium who befriends an elderly and wealthy woman might be up to no good."

"Then why hasn't he warned you about that?" Baxter asked.

"Because whatever he might think about Luanne, he knows I'm not doddering. My mind's still sharp, and I'm not about to be flim-flammed. So, rather than have me tell him that, he's biting his tongue and keeping the peace between us." Cooper smiled. "As he knows, when I kick off, the church will receive a significant donation. So I'm sure he'd rather not offend me by suggesting I can't take care of my own business. Come to think of it, I'm surprised Kevin mentioned Luanne to Burdett."

"Why?" McCabe asked.

"Because when I introduced him to Luanne, Kevin got this strange look on his face. She told him there was no reason to be afraid, but that seemed to spook him even more. He said his goodbyes and headed for the door. He said he'd remembered something he needed to do. But it was clear he was trying to get away from Luanne."

Baxter said, "How did Luanne take that? Having Kevin leave the party to get away from her."

Cooper said, "She tried to laugh it off. But I could tell her feelings were hurt. All I could think of to do was take her out to the kitchen for a slice of Velma's special chocolate pecan pie. We didn't have enough to serve all the guests, so Velma hadn't put it out on the buffet."

"Ms. Cooper," McCabe said. "We'd like to speak to Luanne. Could you tell us how to reach her?"

"She was on her way to Boston when she left here on Saturday afternoon."

"With the blizzard coming in?"

"Luanne's from North Carolina, so she's not wild about driving in bad weather. But she was scheduled to do a séance at a gathering on Saturday evening. The host had promised to put her up until after the blizzard was over. So she took off, hoping she'd outrun the storm."

"And she delayed leaving to attend your celebration of life?" McCabe asked.

"I told her I would understand if she didn't come. But she said she wanted to be here. Worse come to worst with the blizzard, she'd just stop in a motel between here and Boston and wait it out."

"And you haven't heard from her since she left?"

"I'm sorry," Cooper said. "I'm being about as clear as fog. Yes, I did hear from her. I got a tag on Saturday evening saying she was in Boston and fine."

"When was she expecting to be back in Albany?"

"Tomorrow, I believe. Do you want me to let her know you'd like to speak with her?"

"If you wouldn't mind," McCabe said. "If she'll send me a tag, we'll be glad to come to her." McCabe gave Cooper her card. "Please contact us if you should think of anything else."

Cooper rose and walked with them to the door of the parlor. "Give me a yell if you want the lowdown on anyone you're talking to that I know."

McCabe laughed. "Thank you. We may do that." She glanced back at the painting of the woman and her suitor. "Did you have training as an artist?"

"One of the subjects I studied at the women's college I attended. Then I got married. Fortunately, my husband was willing to admit I would be much better at managing the money he'd inherited than he would. He played golf, and I kept us solvent."

"You seem to have done a pretty good job," McCabe said.

"Well enough. But I might have made better use of my time. If I were doing it over again, I might have the courage of my convictions."

Velma appeared in the hallway. Cooper must have rung for her. Maybe a buzzer in the skirt pocket in which her hand was tucked.

"Velma, will you see the detectives out?" she said.

"Well?" Baxter asked when they were outside. "What'd you think of Olive Cooper?"

"That she could hold her own with Ted Thornton. And that reminds me. We need to talk to the lou about checking in with Ashby to find out how he came to choose Kevin Novak for Lisa Nichols's funeral service."

13

Albany International Airport

"We're about to touch down, Mr. Thornton," the airship captain announced from the cockpit.

"Thanks, Chuck." Ted Thornton closed his ORB and looked out the window as the ship sank down through the clouds. The winds had died down that morning, allowing them to make the trip up from the City. But they had still encountered a bump or two.

Thornton nodded when he saw that the airport crew had done a decent job of clearing the snow from around the landing site. He was the only user of the site. His money had paid for it, but as he had pointed out to the county board, the site provided an extension of the capacities of the airport. He had even signed the landing site over to the county, and it was now the property of the airport, money well spent to make it easier to commute from the City to Albany via his airship.

That was when he had been making frequent trips back and forth. This was the first time he had been back to Albany since early November. He felt disoriented, a feeling he hated.

He shrugged his shoulders and took a sip of the whiskey on the table in front of him. He looked at his aide, who was poring over files. "Bruce, we may as well hit the ground running. Let's stop at the office on the way home."

Ashby glanced up from his ORB and nodded. "Good idea. There are a few matters we can get taken care of this afternoon."

14

Lt. Dole was gone when they got back to the station. Baxter told McCabe he'd see her tomorrow and headed out. She suspected he had a date. Maybe the cop from Vice who had been giving him lifts.

She sent the lieutenant a tag about Ashby contacting Kevin Novak. Then she sat there staring up at a water spot on the ceiling. Was she seeing connections where there were none? She had been feeling uneasy since they'd found the tracker on her car when they were searching for a serial killer. Arresting Lisa Nichols for those murders hadn't taken that uneasiness away.

She had never asked Clarence Redfield, the crime beat threader, if he had put the tracker on her car. Redfield had certainly had reason to want to know what she was doing. They had assumed he was behind it. But when the case was solved and he was both discredited and beaten down, she hadn't asked him about the tracker.

She could still ask. Not likely he would admit breaking the law by tracking a police officer. He had gotten off lucky that no charges had been filed against him in the Nichols case. But even then he'd refused to cooperate with the DA. If the case had gone to trial, he would have been called as an uncooperative witness.

What was it about Lisa Nichols that had made two such different men stand by her even when she had betrayed them both?

And that still didn't answer the question about the tracker. If Redfield hadn't put it there, who had?

"Hey, Hannah," Yin said as he and Pettigrew came in. "Did you see the news stream this afternoon?"

"Nope, but I heard from my dad that the rescue expedition to Roarke's Island is still pending. I thought I'd wait until the day was over to see what's in the news about my funeral director case."

"You might want to hear what they had to say about Ted Thornton," Yin said.

"What about him?"

"His airship arrived at the airport this afternoon. He's officially back in Albany."

Pettigrew said, "Now that Lisa Nichols is dead—"

"There's no reason for him not to return." McCabe pushed back her chair. "Thanks for the heads-up. See you tomorrow."

"Okay," Pettigrew said. "Have a good evening."

McCabe stopped and turned to look at him. "Know that game we play? Six degrees of separation on our cases? I've got one for you."

"Your funeral director case and our homeless dead guy case?" Pettigrew asked.

"Both mine. One old, one new. And a lot less than six degrees of separation. On the evening Kevin Novak, the funeral director, was killed, Ted Thornton's aide, Bruce Ashby, tagged Novak to discuss arrangements for a funeral. Presumably for Lisa Nichols."

"Wo-o-ow," Pettigrew said, drawing the word out.

"But it has to be a coincidence," Yin said.

"That's what Mike says," McCabe replied. "And it probably is. See you tomorrow."

When she was gone, Pettigrew said, "I can see why Hannah's feeling a little rattled."

"Yeah, but lots of odd things happen that are just coincidence," Yin said. "This Ashby guy probably picked the first undertaker he found on the Web." Yin reached for his hat. "I'm out of here, too. I told Casey I'd be home on time for dinner tonight. She wants me to spend more time with Todd."

Pettigrew wondered in passing what kind of father he would be if he had a son. "Say 'hi' to Casey and Todd for me," he said.

"Okay. And don't forget Casey wants you to come over for dinner in a couple of weeks."

"As long as she promises not to try to fix me up with one of her friends."

"I'll tell her that," Yin said. "Of course, you could get around that situation by bringing a date."

"I'll check my little black book."

"If only you had one," Yin said.

As his partner left, Pettigrew picked up the mug that had been sitting on his desk since that morning and took a sip of cold coffee. He made a face and put it down again.

15

Mayor Beverly Stark was in the middle of dinner at the home of one of her husband's business associates when her ORB buzzed. The caller was her assistant. She assumed it was important because she had told him about her plans. She excused herself and left the table to speak to him.

"Sorry to interrupt your evening, Mayor," Paul Riordan said. "Something's come up."

"A new problem?" Stark asked. "Or a new development in one of the ongoing?"

"New, I'm afraid. The girl with the apparent drug overdose who was found during the raid on the space zombie house. The autopsy revealed something unexpected. She had cholera."

"Repeat that. Did you say cholera?"

"That's what the ME says. They aren't sure yet, but it could be the more drug-resistant strain that they had in India last year. The health department is testing the other kids who were living in the house."

Stark said, "All right. Meanwhile, we need to decide how to handle this. Does the health department have a protocol in place?"

"Beverly," her hostess said, coming into the foyer from the dining room. "Should we hold the next course for a few minutes?"

"I'm so sorry," Stark said. "I'm afraid I'm going to have to leave."

"Oh, dear. Duty calls?"

"Yes," Stark said. "Please forgive me."

16

Tuesday morning, January 21, 2020
9:30 A.M.

"Well, come on in," Luanne Woodward said. "I hope you all don't mind coming out to the kitchen. I'm cooking, and I need to keep my eye on what I got simmering."

McCabe and Baxter followed her down the hall of the house she was renting.

McCabe stopped in the doorway, looking around the kitchen, a homage to the 1950s, right down to the Formica countertops with chrome trim and the linoleum floor.

Woodward said, "Isn't it darling? I knew I had to have this place as soon as I saw the kitchen. I hate all that modern stuff. I should have been born when women still made their own soap and killed their own chickens."

She might have something in common with Kevin Novak's wife, McCabe thought. Sarah Novak did make her own soap.

"I hear being a hardy farm woman was a lot of work," Baxter said.

Woodward smiled, showing her dimples. "But I'm built like a

farm girl, honey. I could have handled it. Trouble was my daddy went and sold off our family farm when tobacco was banned back in 2000. That left us landless." She gestured at the kitchen table. "Sit down and make yourselves comfortable."

McCabe pulled out one of the chairs, which had cherry-red cushions, and sat down. "Where are you from in the South?"

"North Carolina, honey. Raleigh, to be exact." Woodward lifted the lid from a pot and stirred. "Chicken and dumplings: nothing better on a cold day."

"Smells great," Baxter said. "But isn't it kind of early in the day to be cooking dinner?"

"Yes, it is. But I'm going to be busy later today. And I want myself a good dinner to come home to this evening. Making some collard greens and corn bread, too. Though, Lord knows, getting good cornmeal up here is a task."

"How'd you come to be here in Albany?" Baxter asked, helping himself to a few of the chocolate-covered almonds in the bowl on the table.

"Let me pour you all some tea to sip on. That's why I put out the cups." Woodward brought a cherry-red teapot over to the table and set it on a trivet. "Real peppermint. I dried the leaves myself." She pulled out her own chair and sat down. "How'd I get up here? Well, honey, you see, my finger landed on Albany."

"Thank you, the tea smells wonderful," McCabe said as Woodward poured tea into her cup. "Do you mean you picked Albany to move to by chance?"

"I know it sounds odd, but it came to me one day when I was tidying up the house that I needed to get a fresh perspective on the world." She filled Baxter's cup. "I was in my granddaddy's study, and I walked right on over to his map on the wall and closed my eyes and pointed. Had to do it twice. First time, I landed smack in the Atlantic Ocean. But next time, my finger was right on Albany. So I called my sister and told her she'd have to mind the house while I was gone. Then I packed my bags and put them in my little old car and headed up this way. Didn't know a soul and had no idea what I'd find when I got here. But the Lord never sends you where you aren't supposed to be."

"So you're religious?" Baxter asked.

"My people have been Southern Baptist for as long as there've been Woodwards in the state of North Carolina."

"Have you been attending Reverend Wyatt's church since you arrived in Albany?" McCabe asked.

"I went there one Sunday with Olive. But I sort of got the feeling when I met him that the reverend didn't approve of little old me."

"Did you?" Baxter asked, munching on another chocolate-covered almond.

"The rest of the congregation was real friendly. Especially because I was there with Olive. But then when she introduced me to the reverend, he asked me what brought me to Albany. And I told him what I just told you."

"And what did Reverend Wyatt say?" McCabe asked.

"Well, it was just like Olive, sweet old thing, was being devilish and tweaking his nose. She told him I was a spiritualist, and he went all stiff and said, 'A spiritualist?' and I said, 'Yes, sir, I am.' Then he said real fast that it had been nice to meet me, and said to Olive that he hoped he'd see her in church next Sunday." Woodward smiled. "And since he didn't invite me to come on back with her, I took it that he didn't want a spiritualist sitting in his pews."

McCabe said, "But you said that you're a Southern Baptist. So I assume your minister back home in Raleigh doesn't have that problem."

"Not a bit. My minister down home knows that he has his job and I have mine. And the Lord has use for both of us."

"What is your job exactly? As a spiritualist, I mean."

"I knew what you meant, honey. I guess the best way to explain it is that I help people reunite with their loved ones who have passed on to the other side."

"And to do that, you do séances?" Baxter asked.

"Usually that's the way. But every now and then, I meet someone and just feel like I have a message for them."

"Is that the way you felt when you met Kevin Novak at Olive
Cooper's house?" McCabe asked.

Woodward shook her head. "Not a message. I looked into his
eyes and I could feel that man's sorrow. Something was weighing
on him and giving him a lot of pain."

"Ms. Cooper told us that Mr. Novak's reaction to meeting you
was odd. How would you describe it?"

"Well, honey, I think I spooked him. He sure didn't stay to talk."

"And that was the first time the two of you had crossed paths?
You didn't see each other when you attended church with Ms. Cooper?"

"No, we didn't. I asked Olive if we could leave when I saw I was
making her minister uncomfortable. So we didn't stay for the fel-
lowship after the service."

"When was it that Ms. Cooper first mentioned Mr. Novak to
you?"

"That would have been when she invited me to her celebration.
I told her I had already said I'd attend a dinner party in Boston that
evening, but, of course, I'd wait and leave after her celebration. And
she said she was glad that I could be there because she wanted me
to meet her friend Kevin."

"And can you remember when it was that you had this conversation?" McCabe asked. "The date? Or approximately how long
ago?"

"Hold on a minute, honey, and I'll get my ORB. I probably still
have the tag." She got up and retrieved her ORB from the counter
by the bulky white refrigerator. "Okay. Let me see . . . Olive . . . here
we go. It was back in December, right after Christmas. December
29. I went down to North Carolina to spend the holiday with my
sister and her family, and I was just getting back to Albany."

"So on Saturday afternoon, you went to Ms. Cooper's celebration of life where you met Mr. Novak for the first time," McCabe

said. "And then you drove to Boston for the dinner party you'd been invited to attend."

"Just ahead of the blizzard. I was afraid I wasn't going to make it." Woodward sat back down at the kitchen table. "But it turned out to be real nice. I got there, and with the snow coming down, the guests ended up spending the night. So it was real cozy."

"So you did a séance?" Baxter asked.

"That was why I was invited. The power went off. And after the séance, people started telling ghost stories sitting by the fireplace with the candles lit."

"Did anybody show up during your séance?" Baxter asked. "Any of the dear departed?"

"We did contact a couple of folks. One man's wife and another woman's little niece. They wanted their loved ones to know that they were safe and at peace."

McCabe said, "And after spending the night, you came back to Albany?"

"Not until yesterday afternoon. After they'd opened the interstate again and got it nice and clear."

"I'm wondering, Ms. Woodward—"

"Call me, Luanne, honey. And what is it that you're wondering?"

"You said that when you met Mr. Novak, you could sense his sorrow, feel his emotional pain. Now that he's dead, do you sense anything else?"

"You mean, am I in touch with him from the other side?"

"If you were, you would pass that information on, wouldn't you?"

"Absolutely, honey. But I'd probably have to do a séance to get in touch with him."

"I see," McCabe said.

"Would you like me to do one? I did call the police one time about this feeling I had."

"About what?" Baxter asked.

"I had the feeling this man that was missing was dead. Turned out he was. But that was the first and last time that ever happened.

It's the psychics who work with the police." She smiled. "But if you think a séance might help, I'm your woman."

McCabe smiled back and stood up. "Thank you for offering. We'll give it some thought."

Walking to their vehicle, Baxter said, "A séance?"

McCabe said, "I read a mystery once. One of those Golden Age detective novels with an amateur sleuth. As I recall, she brought all her suspects together by staging a séance. Except I don't think we want to explain that one to the lou."

"Probably not."

"But it might be illuminating to have Luanne and Reverend Wyatt in the same room together."

"You think one of them killed Kevin Novak?"

"If Woodward was where she says she was, she has an alibi. Let's hope the reverend hasn't taken to knocking off members of his flock."

Baxter started the car. "He wouldn't be the first minister to go astray."

"No, he wouldn't. But they're usually a fairly law-abiding segment of the demographic. I'm wondering what had Kevin Novak so depressed. He was in therapy with Burdett, but then he was suddenly worse than when he started."

"Maybe he was ill. Went to a doctor and found out he was dying."

"That might make sense if he had committed suicide," McCabe said. "But someone killed him."

"Well, he might have been dying when someone killed him. And if we did ask Luanne to do a séance, maybe old Kev would finger his killer from the grave."

"Right now, he's in the morgue, not his grave. I hope the ME has him at the top of his list."

17

Kevin Novak's autopsy was scheduled for Wednesday afternoon. McCabe and Baxter received that information in the form of a tag sent to McCabe on her ORB. They didn't hear the word "cholera" until they got back to the station house.

The other detectives who happened to be in the bull pen were gathered in front of the wall to watch the mayor's press conference. The mayor, flanked by the ME and some other official types, was making a statement:

> . . . a young woman who died after being brought to the hospital following a police drug raid. The assumption at the time was that her condition was caused by a drug overdose. However—and I want to stress this—this single, fatal case of cholera is no reason for alarm. Sadly, this young woman died because she did not realize she was gravely ill and did not seek medical treatment. We understand that she was not a permanent resident of Albany, and had been coming and going. She may well have contracted cholera elsewhere. Although it is the same strain found in the cases in India last year, we have complete confidence in our ability to respond."

She opened the press conference to questions. One of the reporters wanted to know if this case of cholera might be traced to the water main breaks. Others chimed in.

The mayor held up her hands to silence them.

"Our water supply here in Albany is safe. Let me repeat that—the water main breaks occurring here in the city are not a threat to the safety of our water supply. . . ."

"Then how come they've been telling people to boil their water after a water main breaks?" one of the detectives in the bull pen asked.

"Didn't you hear?" Pettigrew said. "That's just a safety precaution."

After the mayor and the state health department official finished offering their reassurances, the reporters repeated their earlier questions. The mayor repeated what she had said.

The detectives lost interest and drifted back to what they had been doing.

Baxter took out his ORB and wandered out into the hall.

McCabe unwrapped the tuna sandwich she'd bought when they stopped for lunch. When Baxter came back, she said, "Checking in with your friend in Vice?"

"She's a good friend." He reached into the bag for his turkey wrap and baked pickle chips. "I wanted to make sure she wasn't coming down with something."

McCabe said, "Did she tell you anything about the girl who died?"

"One of the cops found her passed out in a bathroom upstairs. It made sense to assume that she'd OD'd."

"So I guess everyone was pretty surprised when it turned out she had cholera."

"The cops on the raid started asking how you catch it," Baxter said. "They wanted to know if there was a vaccine."

"Do they have an ID on the dead girl?" McCabe asked.

"No ID yet. Only lead they have is the scarf she was wearing."

"The scarf?"

"A nurse at the hospital noticed that the scarf looked a lot more expensive than her ratty blue jeans. The scarf turned out to be a designer original. Even had her initials. Or somebody's initials. She might have stolen it."

"What color scarf?"

"No idea. Why?"

"Just wondering if I might have seen her. I passed a group of space zombies when I was on my way home on Friday evening."

"Even if you did see her, it wasn't like you could have known she had cholera."

"No," McCabe said. "I couldn't have known that. So nothing's turned up on her in the databases?"

Baxter shook his head. "No fingerprint or DNA match."

"But she probably has a family somewhere."

"Then I guess someone will notice she's missing and start looking for her."

"Or not," McCabe said. She wrapped up what was left of her sandwich and tossed it into her trash receptacle. "So, shall we check in with the lou about the Ashby situation? I really would like to know how Ashby happened to choose Kevin Novak to bury Lisa Nichols."

"I thought you might have forgotten about that."

"Not when it might be relevant to our case."

Lt. Dole gazed across his desk at the two detectives. "I spoke to the commander. He agreed with me that it was probably a coincidence."

McCabe said, "I know that, sir. But we're interviewing everyone that Kevin Novak had contact with in the hours before he died. Why shouldn't we talk to Bruce Ashby? He left a tag for our victim."

"And that, McCabe," the lieutenant said, "is why the commander also agreed with me that you should interview Ashby."

"And Ted Thornton?"

"If it's necessary. Keeping in mind why you are there. This is not about the Lisa Nichols case. It's about the case that you are working on now. Do you understand me?"

"Yes, sir," McCabe said.

"Loud and clear, Lou," Baxter said. "We ask our questions about Ashby's tag to Novak, and we get out of there."

They were standing by the entrance to the police garage. One of the new high-performance sedans with night-prowl vision came down on the lift and rolled out of its slot.

Baxter said, "My day's been made."

The Voice said, again, "Drive carefully, Detective Baxter."

Baxter turned and looked at the ID device on the wall and then at his partner.

McCabe held up her hands. "I didn't touch it. Honest. It must have seen the car we're getting and thought another reminder was in order."

"Let's get moving," Baxter said, heading toward the driver's side.

McCabe settled into her seat, safety restraints in place. She had learned by now that there was no point in suggesting Baxter slow down when he had one of the new vehicles. Even less chance that he would set the car on automatic pilot and let it drive itself. Fortunately, he was a good driver.

"So, have you gotten your baby back yet?" she asked, referring to the 1967 maroon Mustang that was his pride and joy.

The car had been in the garage of his condo when snow collapsed a portion of the roof. He'd covered the car with a tarp to protect it against the cold, and the damage had been minimal. But Baxter, whose everyday car was a despised hybrid, had been teary-eyed when he got the news.

"Not yet," he said in answer to her question. "They have some more work to do on the finish. But thanks for asking."

"You're welcome." McCabe, who had minimal interest in classic cars or cars in general, had instructed herself to ask periodically. A good partner's duty.

She reached for her field bag and took out her ORB. "I'm glad Ted Thornton's airship was able to make it back to Albany."

"Me, too. I could use a cup of real coffee."

"Olive Cooper's coffee was pretty good."

"She can afford the real stuff, too."

"Yeah." McCabe pulled up the tag that Ashby had left for Kevin Novak.

Baxter drove them across town and up into the hills toward the neighborhood that was home to Thornton and some other members of Albany's well heeled. This was not an old-money neighborhood, but instead an enclave created by businesspeople and other professionals who had made their money on their own.

As they passed the home of Joanne Barker-Channing, McCabe wondered again if her father was seeing the former corporate lawyer–turned–socialite in settings other than Barker-Channing's monthly literary salons. McCabe did not question her father about his social life. They respected each other's privacy. But it was strange to think of him in a relationship with someone other than her mother. Of course, her mother had been dead for almost nine years. She couldn't blame the man for wanting someone in his life again.

Baxter turned into the road leading to Thornton's mansion. There were two guards at the gatehouse today, suggesting Ted Thornton wanted to make sure no members of the press gained access. However, police detectives, when expected, could be admitted.

Today, the circular driveway in front of the house was empty. The futuristic sports car that had been there the first time they came to visit back in October was nowhere in sight. Snow was piled up in the yard, and the two-story solar-paneled mansion with the gleaming windows looked desolate.

Or maybe it felt that way because she was thinking of Lisa

Nichols. Maybe if they got Luanne to do a séance, McCabe thought, Nichols might turn up, too. But right now, as the lou had reminded them, she and Baxter were there investigating the Novak case, not Nichols's death in the psychiatric facility.

Baxter rang the doorbell. "Hope my girl Roz is on the job," he said.

The door swung open. "Please come in, Detectives Baxter and McCabe," said a melodious female voice.

Ted Thornton's maid, a gleaming metallic robot wearing a trim black uniform and white apron, stepped back so that they could enter.

"Hi, Roz," Baxter said. "Great to see you again."

"My name is Rosalind, Detective Baxter. It is good to see you, too. Please follow me."

"Be still my heart," Baxter whispered to McCabe.

"Rosalind," McCabe said, "does Mr. Thornton still have his cat, Horatio?"

Rosalind looked back over her shoulder. "Yes, Detective McCabe, Horatio is still a member of this household."

She sounded, McCabe thought, as if she were quoting someone on the subject of Ted Thornton's Maine coon cat. The cat that had allegedly been Lisa Nichols's undoing because of Lisa's allergy and the medication she had been taking.

At the end of the long hall, Rosalind directed them into the same gallery where they had waited for Ted Thornton the first time they came to his house.

This time he was waiting for them. He turned from his contemplation of one of the miniature airplanes in his transportation collection.

Today he looked his age, McCabe thought. Forty-six, according to the bio she had read. Today he had circles under his large dark eyes but was clad in his usual blue jeans with a black pullover sweater.

He gave them a subdued version of his famous lopsided smile. "Detectives, I wish I could say it's a pleasure to see you again."

"I know you'd probably rather not see us again," McCabe said. She held out her hand. "I'm sorry about Ms. Nichols, Mr. Thornton."

"Thank you, Detective McCabe." He clasped her hand. "I realize you must have complicated feelings about Lisa."

"Yes, I do," McCabe said. "But I'm sure you must have as well. She did kill someone you thought of as a close friend."

Baxter cleared his throat and stepped forward, hand outstretched. "Thanks for fitting us into your schedule, Mr. Thornton."

Thornton shook hands with her partner. "I'm happy to do anything I can to help with your current investigation, Detective Baxter."

He gestured toward the grouping of sofa and chairs. "Shall we sit down? Bruce will be along in a moment. He's trying to work out a problem with one of our subsidiaries in the Russian Federation."

It was closer to ten minutes later when Bruce Ashby joined them. By then, they had served themselves coffee from the trolley that Rosalind had brought in and were making small talk about the weather and climate change and whether President Kirkland's ban on drilling in the Arctic had any chance of surviving the presidential election.

Ashby, McCabe thought, looked as if efficiency was his middle name. His gray tweed jacket, paler gray turtleneck, and creased dark slacks offered a marked contrast to his boss's casual attire.

"Sorry to keep you waiting, detectives," he said. "Ted, I think we may have resolved the main issue, just some minor details to iron out."

"Good," Thornton said. "But getting to why Detectives McCabe and Baxter are here . . ."

"Ted asked me to contact a funeral home to make arrangements for Lisa," Ashby said. "We needed a funeral director who could be trusted to behave in a professional manner, with discretion and respect for Ted's privacy."

"How did you go about finding someone?" Baxter asked. "Check for satisfied customers on the Web?"

"No," Ashby said. "I tagged a friend and business associate of Ted's who lives here in Albany."

"Would you mind giving us the name of the person who recommended Mr. Novak to you?" McCabe said.

"Olive Cooper," Ashby said.

"Olive serves on one of my boards," Ted Thornton added.

"She does?" McCabe said.

Baxter said, "My partner thought it was a real coincidence that you had tagged Novak's funeral home. But now we have our explanation."

"Yes, we do," McCabe said. "We should have thought to ask Ms. Cooper if she knew you, Mr. Thornton."

"Olive's one of my favorite people," Ted Thornton said. "I met her not too long after I opened my office here in Albany. We were competing for the same piece of real estate. We decided to join forces instead."

McCabe turned back to Ashby. "So Ms. Cooper suggested Kevin Novak to handle Ms. Nichols's funeral arrangements, and you followed up with a tag to him."

"As you saw."

"Did you expect to reach him on a Sunday evening?"

"Ms. Cooper told me that I might," Ashby said. "As she put it, funeral directors are always on call because people die at inconvenient hours. But when Mr. Novak didn't answer his ORB, I left a tag. As you know from reading it, I asked him to get back to me as soon as possible."

"You didn't mention Mr. Thornton in your tag," McCabe said. "Or that you had been referred by Ms. Cooper."

"I'm sure Bruce was being discreet," Ted Thornton said. "And that's . . . that's all there was to it, Detective McCabe. Bruce needed a referral from Olive because . . . believe it or not . . . we haven't compiled a list of reliable funeral homes."

"There was the funeral home that Vivian Jessup's daughter used for her mother," McCabe said. "Why not use that one?"

But maybe that would have been in questionable taste, she

thought. Vivian Jessup had been one of Lisa Nichols's victims and Thornton's old friend.

Ashby explained why he hadn't used that funeral home. "That funeral director provided more information than he should have when a reporter asked him about the arrangements for Vivian. We hardly needed a repeat of that with Lisa."

McCabe asked, "Did Ms. Nichols leave a directive about how her services should be handled?"

"No," Ashby said. "What does that have to do with the murder of the funeral director?"

"Nothing," McCabe said. "Unless she had left a directive and specified Mr. Novak's funeral home to handle her services, nothing at all."

"I explained how I came to select Mr. Novak's funeral home," Ashby said.

"Yes, you did," McCabe said.

Baxter said, "We should be moving along."

"Yes," McCabe agreed. She put her cup down on the side table. "Thank you both for your time."

"It is an odd coincidence," Thornton said, rising as she did. "But I assure you that's all it is, Detective McCabe."

"Of course. That was what we assumed. But we did need to check in with you and Mr. Ashby to confirm that."

"I'll ring for Rosalind to show you out."

He touched the bell on the wall. McCabe said, "Will you be doing business in Albany again?"

"I never stopped doing business in Albany," Thornton said. "If you're asking if I will be spending time in Albany again, now that . . . now that there won't be a trial . . . yes, I will."

"I really am sorry it ended as it did," McCabe said.

"That makes two of us."

"If I could ask . . . had you spoken to Ms. Nichols recently?"

She felt Baxter make an anxious move beside her. But Ted Thornton was already responding to her question. "No, I hadn't spoken to her. So I don't know why she killed herself. I assume she felt alone and desperate. And if she did, maybe that was my fault."

McCabe met his dark gaze. No humorous twitch of his eyebrows today. "You can't blame yourself for not standing beside someone who lied and killed."

"I told her that I loved her," Thornton said. "I asked her to marry me."

"And she betrayed your trust."

"She was ill," he said. "She proved that, didn't she, when she killed herself."

McCabe nodded. "I guess she did."

Ashby said, "Is some aspect of Lisa's case still open, Detective?"

"No, not as far as we're concerned. I'm sorry, Mr. Thornton, if I've upset you by bringing it up."

"I'm sure we were all thinking about it. Might as well get it out in the open."

"Then may I ask another question?"

"Hannah . . . Detective McCabe," Baxter said at her shoulder. "We're going to be late for our meeting with the lieutenant."

"Go ahead, please," Ted Thornton said.

"Would you have thought that Ms. Nichols might kill herself?"

His gaze became thoughtful. "No. Given what I'd learned about her skills of self-preservation, no, I wouldn't have expected that. Obviously, I was wrong."

"If there is nothing else, Detective," Ashby said. "Ted has business matters that require his attention."

"And we need to get moving," Baxter said.

Rosalind, the maid, said, "May I show you out now?"

"Yes, thank you, Rosalind," McCabe said. "And thank you for your time, Mr. Thornton."

"I'm glad we could answer your questions," Ted Thornton said, and then with a flash of his old smile, "and remove ourselves from your list of suspects."

McCabe and Baxter walked in silence to their vehicle. When they were in the car, doors shut, Baxter turned to McCabe. "What part of what the lou told us about staying off the subject of Lisa Nichols's death did you miss?"

"None of it," McCabe said. "But I had to ask."

"Let's just hope Thornton didn't object to your questions, or we'll be explaining ourselves to both the lou and the commander."

"I did it," McCabe said. "I'll take the blame."

"I saw it coming. I should have gotten you out of there faster."

"How exactly would you have done that?"

"You mean aside from throwing you over my shoulder?"

"I know I'm sounding like a broken record on this, Mike, but I keep thinking we're missing something about Lisa Nichols's death."

"We aren't missing anything because it isn't our investigation."

"And someone from an appropriate agency will investigate how a death occurred in a psychiatric facility. But I'd really like a look at that report."

"I don't think we're on the distribution list. In fact, what I think is that you should let this go before you get us both in hot water."

"I said I'd take the blame for bringing it up to Ted Thornton."

"Great. So let it go, and we'll be good."

Baxter started the car, mouth tight, hands tense on the steering wheel.

"Sorry," McCabe said. "You're right, I should let it go."

"Good. We have more than enough on our plate with our dead undertaker."

"Very true," McCabe said. She reached for her ORB.

She never liked to rely on her intuition. But there it was again. The twinge of uncertainty she'd had about her partner when they were first assigned to work together.

True, Assistant Chief Danvers was Baxter's godfather, and word had it that Baxter had used that connection to get himself transferred out of Vice and into their squad. But Baxter had more than pulled his weight during the serial killer investigation. And he'd had her back, including suggesting her car might have a tracker.

The argument he was making now about leaving Lisa Nichols's death alone was reasonable. One complaint from Ted Thornton to the mayor about how he was being hounded by APD detectives when he was about to return to Albany . . .

Except, McCabe thought, there were those moments when her partner's easygoing grin and wisecracks seemed to be a cover for whatever was going on beneath the surface. Too bad she couldn't connect him to a brain scanner and ask him a few questions—an unacceptable intrusion as a part of a criminal investigation, according to the courts, but they'd said nothing about doing a mind probe on your partner.

18

On her way home after her shift, McCabe remembered that she needed to pick up the takeout dinner for two that she had ordered from Chelsea and Stan. The restaurant was taking part in another community fund-raiser. This one was to send a local children's choir to a festival in Washington, D.C.

The cross street to Chelsea's Place was blocked off. An ancient water pipe—one of the first installed in the city—had burst, spewing water down the street. The water in the restaurant had been off for two days after it happened. Now the water was back on, but the cross street was blocked. McCabe parked and sloshed her way back to the restaurant through the melting snow.

She greeted the hostess as she passed the reception desk in the foyer and made her way to the dining room.

The back region of the restaurant was in full dinnertime bustle.

"Hi, you two," she called to Chelsea and Stan from the kitchen doorway.

"Come on in, slugger," Stan said, waving her in with the knife in his hand.

McCabe glanced at the two huge glass water bottles in a rack beside the counter. "Is your water out again?"

"No," Chelsea said, taking a container from one of the smaller cooling units. "But we've been getting questions from customers about whether the city water's safe. Since we can't swear that it is, we're using bottled water for the food prep."

"Isn't that kind of expensive?"

"Yes," Stan said.

"We don't have any choice," Chelsea said.

"The mayor says the water's safe if it's boiled," McCabe pointed out.

Stan dumped the garlic cloves he had minced into a sauté pan. "She does, but Chelsea doesn't believe her or the health department."

"Didn't you hear what they said about the girl who died of cholera?" Chelsea asked. "They don't know how she picked up the bacteria, but they're confident it wasn't the water. If they don't know, how can they be confident?"

McCabe said, "The other space zombies in the house said that she had only arrived in town two or three months ago. She was away for a couple of days before she became ill. As the mayor said, she could have picked the cholera bacteria up someplace else."

"But they don't know yet," Chelsea said. She finished wrapping McCabe's entrée, a tofu and walnut casserole with a butternut squash sauce, and put it into a carrier. "This is great with an endive salad."

"I'll tell Pop that. Good luck with the water situation."

"Good luck?" Chelsea glared at her from her five foot four. "Right, that's what we need, Hannah. People are dying of cholera . . . the world's a mess. We could use some luck."

"Chelsea," Stan said. "What—"

"I'm pregnant. I'm going to have a baby. And we can't even drink the water."

"Pregnant?" Stan's smile lit up his face. "You're sure?"

Chelsea nodded. "I had a doctor's appointment this morning."

"When you said you were going shopping for herbs?" Stan sobered. "Is everything okay?"

"Fine. She said last time doesn't count. There isn't any reason this baby shouldn't be healthy."

McCabe laughed. "Chels, this is great." She hugged Chelsea, then Stan. "This is wonderful."

She watched as Stan, laughing, swept Chelsea up and kissed her.

"I'm going now," McCabe said, "and letting the two of you have some time alone to celebrate."

"Wait, slugger, don't go." Stan lowered his wife to her feet. "Stay and have a glass of champagne. Champagne for us. Sparkling cider for Chelsea."

"Love to, but I really have to get home. We'll celebrate with dinner at someone else's restaurant when your anniversary gift finally arrives."

As she passed through the dining room, McCabe wondered if Chelsea was right about the bottled water. On a Tuesday evening, most of the tables were filled. If people were feeling anxious about the water breaks, then accommodating their concerns might be good business, even if it was expensive in the short term.

But if Chelsea, who was pregnant again after a miscarriage, was feeling anxious when she should have been joyful because a girl she had never met had died of cholera, then that—

McCabe's foot slipped on an icy patch on the sidewalk. She managed to stay upright and hold on to the bag in her hand.

"That was close. You okay?"

"Fine, thanks," McCabe said to the man who had seen her near-pratfall. "Fine and dandy."

In her car, McCabe sat remembering last Friday evening. She and Pettigrew had gone downtown to attend an award ceremony for a patrol officer. It had been their turn to go. After the ceremony, she had followed Pettigrew into a pharmacy on North Pearl Street. He needed to pick up his prescription for acid reflux; she wanted to send a holographic anniversary card to Chelsea and Stan. She had been finishing her transmission when the ruckus broke out. . . .

The man, a muscle-bound gladiator in a cheap brown suit, whirled and threw a roundhouse kick. The kick demolished a display of cleaning products before connecting with the security guard's jaw. The guard went down hard, out cold. The man straightened, his ripped pant leg dangling around his calf. "Better not mess with me," he advised the several people who had stopped to stare. They scattered into the aisles.

"I'm sorry, I still don't understand your request," Suzy, the automated shopper's aide, told him. "Why don't I ask a staff person to help? Please wait."

"Shut up!" the man yelled. "I told you I don't need no help!"

McCabe measured her five-eight height and one hundred thirty-eight pounds against his bulk. Her hand moved toward her holstered weapon beneath her thermo jacket. "Sir, I'm an Albany PD detective. I can see you're upset. But you need to calm down."

The man turned to have a look at her. His gaze dropped to the weapon she was pointing at him. He grunted and his nostrils flared.

"That was a really nice kick," McCabe said. "Like something out of one of those old martial arts movies. But you just committed an assault in front of a cop."

"He shouldn't have messed with me," the man said.

"It's in his job description," McCabe said. "He's paid to mess with people. It was your mistake to respond by knocking him out."

"Don't nobody mess with me," the man said. "I'm bad. Bad as Leroy Brown and Stagolee."

"I don't doubt it," McCabe said. "But as you can see, I have a weapon. And even when it's set to stun, getting zapped with it isn't pleasant. I should also tell you that there's another cop here in the pharmacy, and we should have backup in a matter of minutes. I know you're aware of the fact you're on store surveillance cameras. The cam on my weapon is also recording this. So what it comes down to is that if you break mean and bad on me, either I will take you down or another cop will. Am I making myself clear?"

They stared at each other. McCabe wondered who would blink first.

To her relief, Pettigrew spoke from her left, "She's telling you the truth, buddy. I'm the other cop. Better just let it go."

Pettigrew had his weapon trained on the man, too.

The man returned his attention to McCabe. "You're a woman. My mama made me promise to never hurt a woman."

"I'm glad your mother made you promise that," McCabe said, giving him his way out. "So let's do this the easy way. You won't hurt me, and I won't hurt you."

The man licked his lips and nodded.

McCabe reached for her handcuffs. "Detective Pettigrew is going to pat you down for weapons. Then I'm going to put these on you, and you're going to sit down on the floor. Understand?"

"Yeah. I can't hurt no woman."

McCabe sent her silent thanks to his mother.

The man's gaze met hers. "What your mama make you promise?"

The question caught McCabe by surprise. "Nothing," she said.

"Mamas always make you promise something," the man said. "What your mama make you promise?"

"That she'd be the first woman on Mars," Pettigrew said. "Nice suit, but you should have gone with a larger size."

The man edged his feet apart for Pettigrew's pat down. "Got it at the mission," he said, staring down at his ripped pant leg. "They gave me the biggest size they had."

Twenty minutes later, McCabe and Pettigrew walked out of the pharmacy, bringing up the rear, behind the paramedics carrying the stretcher with the sedated guard and the uniforms leading away the gladiator. McCabe took shallow breaths of the stagnant air. "The wind's shifted," she said.

"Essence of stale beer and sweaty gym socks this evening," Pettigrew observed.

Across the street, the readout on the bank building registered seventy-three degrees Fahrenheit, air quality poor. McCabe glanced up at the bulletin board streaming Channel 4 "breaking news"— war news about the casualties in the latest offensive.

Lightning flickered in the silver-tinged clouds looming behind the bulletin board. A rumble of thunder followed. "We'd better get moving or we're going to get rained on," she said. "See you tomor-row."

"Weekend duty," Pettigrew said. "I can't wait."

"Speaking of the weekend, are we still on for next Saturday? The classic crime film festival at the Palace?"

"Front and center for *Dog Day Afternoon*." Pettigrew shot his arm in the air, doing his imitation of Al Pacino. " 'Attica! Attica!' "

McCabe laughed. It was good to see Pettigrew kidding around. "And as my mother would have said, 'Power to the people!' "

She waved and pivoted toward her car, parked halfway down the street.

Another flash of lightning, the first fat drops of rain. Then the sky opened up.

Drenched, McCabe sprinted the last few feet and tumbled into her car.

On the way up the State Street hill, the car in front of her stopped without warning. A second later McCabe saw why. With the white paint on their faces dissolving in the downpour, wet T-shirts and tattered blue jeans clinging to their shuffling bodies, a line of space zombies were following their leader across the street.

A girl in the middle of the line stumbled and fell. The red scarf around her neck stood out like a slash on her throat.

The last two zombies in the line reached down and hoisted the girl to her feet instead of stepping over her. The girl staggered on, held up between them. A burst of wind shook McCabe's car door. She got back in and pulled the door closed. A horn blared behind her.

McCabe cast a parting glance at the girl and her two compan-ions as they shuffled toward the Plaza. "Not your job," she told herself. "You're a cop, not a drug counselor."

And she had gone home.

That was what she was going to do now. Go home.

Pettigrew couldn't decide whether he was angry or relieved when his ex-wife didn't keep their appointment. He was calling it an appointment in his mind, not a date. That was what he had in-tended to make clear to her. In spite of what had happened be-tween them a couple of months ago when she had been in the City and taken the fast trip up to Albany, they were not dating. They were not considering a reconciliation. They'd had sex. That was all. It was still over between them.

But he didn't get to give his speech because she stood him up.

"So sorry, but something came up," her tag said. "I'm stuck in Philadelphia. Let's reschedule."

"Not likely," he mumbled as he closed his ORB.

He got up and started to remove the plates and glasses from the table.

Elaine had always liked playing mind games. She liked to have him dangling on her hook. Liked to think that if she wanted him back she could have him.

Not this time. She was not going to sink her fangs into him again.

He reached for his goggles and settled with his feet up into his favorite armchair. A moment later, he was in his avatar body, Mr. Parker, strolling through the doors of the Key Club.

A hostess dressed as a flapper greeted him. "Welcome back, Mr. Parker. It's good to see you again."

"Thank you, Lola. What's on the program this evening?"

"I'll let you guess. Like my outfit?"

"Very nice. Nineteen twenties?"

"The Roaring Twenties. Tonight we have three fun locations to choose from: Hollywood party, Los Angeles, 1921; Mardi Gras, New Orleans, 1925; Speakeasy, Harlem, New York, 1927."

"I'll go to the speakeasy in Harlem."

"An excellent choice. Twelve of our members are already there. You'll be lucky number thirteen."

"My favorite number," Pettigrew said. "I always play the lottery—uh, the horses—on Friday the thirteenth."

"Please stop by the men's changing room, Mr. Parker, and choose what you'd like to wear. Then go down the hall to the third door on the left. Just knock and say, 'Joe sent me.' "

"Thank you, Lola."

"My pleasure. And don't forget we have some private entertainment planned for later this evening back here in our own club lounge."

"I'll be here. Will you?"

Lola winked. "You bet. See you later."

Settling into his avatar body, Pettigrew strolled down the hall toward that evening's adventure.

Mike Baxter was sitting in a tavern down the street from his condo. Since he usually went to cop hangouts, he was in no danger of having the regulars in the tavern recognize him and want to talk.

He sat on a stool at the end of the bar sipping his beer and pondering his problem. His problem was named Hannah McCabe. If he couldn't get McCabe to leave Lisa Nichols's death alone, she might bring them both down.

What he didn't know was what he was going to do about her.

He drained his mug. "Hey, could I get another beer down here?" he called out to the bartender. "Make that bourbon on the rocks."

"Put some hair on your chest, Mike boy," his godfather would have said if he'd been there.

Right now, Baxter would settle for blurring the edges of his reality.

19

Wednesday, January 22, 2020
1:00 P.M.

Located in the basement of the medical center, the morgue was clean, well-lit, and cold. Or at least it always seemed cold to McCabe. She braced herself against the chill as she and Baxter stepped out of the elevator. She hoped Dr. Singh, the medical examiner, would be able to tell them something that would send them in the right direction. They'd spent the morning going through statements from the people they had interviewed about Kevin Novak. They'd also gone through the crime scene report from FIU and learned Novak had lied to his wife about his reason for staying at the funeral home overnight. FIU had found no sign of a broken or patched pipe in the basement.

The residue in the basement sink had turned out to be unrelated to Novak's murder. The part-time staffer who came in to do the corpses' hair and makeup had poured some leftover dye in the sink after doing a touch-up.

Neither the crime-scene report nor the interviews had given the detectives a solid lead.

"You are on time," Dr. Singh said as McCabe and Baxter walked in. He turned back to his examination of the scans and X-rays of Novak's body. They donned surgical gowns and plastic protective masks and took their positions on the other side of the autopsy table.

Singh pointed at the entry wound in Novak's chest. "If the arrow had struck his heart, he might have died instantly. Instead the arrow pierced his lung." Singh swung back around and pointed at the wall where the images were displayed. "Look at this scan. You can see the bruising to the injured lung. He was bleeding internally, drowning in his own blood."

"But according to our forensic techs, he was able to move around," McCabe said.

"Yes, he would have been able to move," Singh said. "But breathing would have been painful. He would have been coughing a bit."

Singh reached for his scalpel. "Let's open him up."

McCabe couldn't see Baxter's expression behind his mask, but he hadn't moved back from the table. This was his fourth autopsy; maybe he was getting used to the process.

After spreading the chest cavity, Singh said, "You can see how the puncture wound extends through the chest wall, and the damage track in the lung. See the bleeding into the surrounding tissue. . . . Look here. You can see how the blood has clotted in the lung tissues, small airways, trachea, throat, and mouth. . . . He has a little blood in the stomach, too. He must have swallowed some blood when he was trying to breathe."

They watched as Singh completed the autopsy, removing the organs.

"Well, what's your verdict, Doc?" Baxter asked.

"Injuries consistent with the weapon used. Definitely not self-inflicted. A homicide. Sorry I can't be more helpful. This one is rather straightforward."

"Could you give us a time of death?" McCabe asked.

"Based on the conditions Dr. Malone recorded, I'd put the time of death at between ten P.M. and twelve A.M."

"The embalmer arrived at a little after nine thirty the next morning. That would mean he'd been dead for at least nine hours at that point," McCabe said.

"I would agree with that," Dr. Singh said. "As you know, I'll need to get back to you with the results of the analysis of the stomach contents and the toxicology report."

"But you don't anticipate any surprises?" McCabe asked.

"Based on what I've seen, I will be surprised if I should find anything unexpected."

After the autopsy, McCabe and Baxter discussed whether they needed to interview Kevin Novak's children, and they decided they did. Children—especially teenagers—saw things. Sometimes a parent even confided in a child.

McCabe thought Sarah Novak might refuse when she asked if they could come over to speak to her children, but she nodded and said they would be waiting.

When she opened the door for the detectives, Novak seemed to be in much better control of her emotions than she had been on Monday afternoon.

"Thank you for agreeing to let us come by, Mrs. Novak," McCabe said. "We have just a few questions for the children. They might have heard or seen something, or your husband might have mentioned something to one of them."

Novak said, "I agreed to this because my children have been asking me questions about the investigation. I thought it would help them if you would explain what you're doing and how you intend to find the person who killed their father."

"We'll do our best to explain."

Novak turned and led the way into her living room.

The Novak children, Scott and Megan, were sitting on the sofa, one at each end. When McCabe and his mother walked into the room, Scott got to his feet.

It was an old-fashioned gesture of courtesy. Obviously, his parents had raised their son to be well mannered, McCabe thought.

"Please, sit down, Detectives," Sarah Novak said.

She slid past her son and sat down in the middle of the sofa, between her children. Maybe they had been sitting there together like that before the doorbell rang.

Megan was thirteen. Petite, with her mother's dark hair and bone structure.

As McCabe sat down, she saw the thick book open on the girl's lap.

"What are you reading?" she asked.

"A book about the Black Death," Megan replied.

"The Black Death?" Baxter said.

Sarah Novak explained, "Last month, the teen book discussion group read a novel set in France during that era."

"Ahh, so you're doing some background reading," McCabe said.

"I did it before the discussion," Megan said. "I brought in some illustrations I'd found of the plague doctors wearing the masks they wore to protect themselves when they were treating patients. The masks had long bird beaks and were hollow so that they could stuff them with straw and spices. We got into this discussion about medicine in the fourteenth century, and Dr. Burdett offered to loan me one of his books." Megan's clear gaze held McCabe's. "I'm reading it now because I need to finish it so that I can return it."

McCabe said, "Under the circumstances, I'm sure Dr. Burdett won't mind if it takes you a bit longer to get his book back to him."

Megan shook her head. "Daddy said we should always return anything we borrow as soon as possible."

"We saw the raven you gave your father in his office," McCabe said. "Are you interested in birds?"

Megan nodded. "Daddy and I are—we were both interested in birds and the folklore and mythologies about them."

Scott cleared his throat. He had sat back down on the sofa beside his mother. Hands gripped together, he leaned forward.

"Detective, we'd like to know if you have any leads in solving my father's murder."

A teenage boy trying to be the man of the house, McCabe thought.

She responded to him as she would have an adult. "We don't have anything yet that would help us to come up with a list of likely suspects. The forensics unit has collected all of the physical evidence available at the scene. The medical examiner has completed your father's autopsy. And, now, it's up to Detective Baxter and me to go through what we have and try to put it together."

"Like one of Mom's jigsaw puzzles," Megan said.

McCabe nodded. "Exactly. I'm afraid it isn't like in the movies or on crime shows. We have to do this one piece at a time. And that was why we asked your mother if we could speak to the two of you."

Scott Novak sat back and unclenched his hands. "What do you need to know?"

"First of all, if you and Megan would think back over the past few weeks or months—think about the conversations you had with your father. Do you remember anything he said to you that made you think he was worried or concerned about something?"

"I've been thinking about that," Megan said.

"Have you?" McCabe asked.

Megan nodded. "The police always ask questions like that, don't they?"

"Yes, I guess we do."

"About Daddy . . . sometimes it was like he wasn't really listening. Like when he told me this ghost story that was completely off target."

"A ghost story?" Sarah Novak said.

"Oh, Mom, you know how Daddy tells—" Megan paused, then went on, focusing on McCabe and Baxter. "He would tell us stories to make a point about something. I loved scary stories, so sometimes he would tell me ghost stories."

"And he told you a ghost story recently?" McCabe asked.

"Last week. These girls at school were giggling and looking at me and then I realized I'd sat in pasta sauce someone had spilled on a seat in the cafeteria. It was totally humiliating. And I mentioned it to Daddy, and he told me a story. It should have been a story about how silly it was to be self-conscious and let a little pasta sauce mess up my whole day. But instead he told me this story about a woman with an overactive imagination. It wasn't even a real ghost story."

"What happened in the story?" Baxter asked.

Megan made a face. "A woman reports the maintenance man in her office building for not doing his work. He's fired. It turns out he's sick, and he dies. She feels guilty. Then one evening, she's there alone, working late. She comes out and sees a man at the end of the hall. It's dark and she can't see who it is, but she thinks it's the man who she got fired. She runs and pushes the elevator button. The man calls out to her to wait. The elevator door opens and she steps in and screams as she falls to her death. When the police arrive, the man explains he was trying to tell her the elevator was being serviced and he had come upstairs to put the sign up. But for some reason, she was frightened and ran away from him."

McCabe said, "Well it's kind of a scary story."

"Yeah, sort of," Megan said. "But it's not a real ghost story. And it had nothing to do with what I was upset about. Daddy usually did a lot better." She peered around her mother at her older brother. "Didn't he, Scott?"

"Yeah, he did. Dad told great stories. Meg's right. He hadn't been really focusing lately."

Megan said, "Sometimes it was like he was from another planet. Like in that old movie when the pod people from outer space replace the real people and have to try to act like they have human emotions."

Scott said, "Dad had been acting odd since Uncle Bob died. But then for the past three or four days, he was even weirder. . . . I mean, like he was thinking about something else when you were talking to him."

Baxter said, "Did you ask him what was up?"

"Sure," Megan said. "But he would just apologize and say he was thinking about work or something."

"Did he say what the 'something' was?" McCabe asked.

"Like something at church or something. One time, he said he was thinking about a conversation he'd had with Reverend Wyatt about the parking lot."

"What about the parking lot?" Baxter asked.

"Whether or not to expand it," Sarah Novak said, speaking for the first time since her children had begun recounting examples of their father's distraction. "Kevin was on the facilities committee. They were—are—trying to decide whether we should make an offer for the land adjacent to the church so that the parking lot can be expanded."

"More folks joining the church and more cars?" Baxter asked.

"Yes," Novak said. "But Reverend Wyatt thinks it would be a less expensive and greener option to provide more shuttles."

"Is this an issue that's causing conflict in the church?" McCabe asked.

"No. Most people are waiting to see what the committee will recommend."

"What about on the committee?" Baxter asked. "Any animosity there?"

"You can't seriously think someone from the church killed Kevin because of a difference of opinion about expanding a parking lot?"

"No," McCabe said. "Unless more was involved. But sometimes a difference of opinion over a minor issue reflects an ongoing conflict between two people."

Megan said, "Everyone at church liked Daddy." She paused and frowned. "Or, at least, everyone acted as if they liked him. Maybe someone didn't."

Novak glanced at her daughter and said quickly, "The facilities committee was not divided into vicious factions over the parking lot expansion."

McCabe said, "Scott and Megan, anything else you can tell us about your dad?"

Megan shook her head. "Are you coming to his funeral? On cop shows, the detectives always come to the funeral to watch the mourners and see how they're reacting."

"Yes, on cop shows they do," McCabe said. "But it makes people uncomfortable when cops turn up at funerals in real life."

"I think you should come anyway," Megan said. She turned to her mother. "Tell them to come, Mom. They might see something."

Novak met her daughter's gaze. Then she said, "If you think it would be useful to attend my husband's funeral . . . it's all right if you attend."

"Thank you," McCabe said. "We'll discuss it with our lieutenant. If we do attend, we'll be discreet."

"You can sit in one of the anterooms and watch everything on camera," Megan said. "Then you can see if anyone seems weird."

McCabe said, "That's not a bad idea. We'll give it some thought. We should go now and let the three of you do whatever you need to."

She stood up, and Scott came to his feet as well.

"I'll see them out," he told his mother. "Be right back."

He followed McCabe and Baxter outside, pulling the door closed behind him. "I need to tell you something," he said.

"What's up?" Baxter asked.

"You can't tell my mom, okay?"

McCabe said, "We'll try to respect your request, Scott, but it will depend on what it is you tell us."

"I went out on Sunday night," he said in a rush. "That night . . . I went out."

Baxter said, "Your mother said you were up in your room listening to music."

"I went upstairs and turned the music on and put my Do Not Disturb sign on the door, and then I sneaked out down the kitchen stairs."

"Where did you go?" McCabe asked.

"To see if my dad had really gone to the funeral home."

"You thought he might have gone somewhere else?"

Scott glanced away and then back at them. "I could see my mom was upset because he'd gone out. And I knew something weird was going on between the two of them. I wanted to make sure my dad really went to the funeral home."

Baxter said, "Okay. So where else did you think he might be going?"

Scott glanced down at the ground. Then he shrugged. "I didn't know. I just wanted to make sure he was there."

"And was he?" McCabe asked.

"Yeah, like he said he'd be. His snowmobile was out back, and the lights were on upstairs in his office and down in the basement."

"Did you go inside to speak to him?"

Scott shook his head. When he looked up tears had filled his eyes. He dashed at them with his hand. "I didn't want . . . I didn't want him to know I thought he'd been lying to Mom. He was there like he said. There was no reason to go in."

"About what time was it when you were there?" Baxter asked.

"I dunno. It must have been around nine thirty. It took me a while to get there because the power pack on my snowboard kept stalling out."

"Did you see anyone else while you were there?" Baxter asked.

"No. I didn't see anyone at all. It was really weird with the lights out on some streets and the cars buried in snow. Like this blizzard had come and everyone had gone inside and shut the doors."

"They had," Baxter said. "Inside, out of the cold. How long did you hang around outside the funeral home?"

"Maybe ten minutes," Scott said. "I was already cold when I got there, and I couldn't stand around too long. But I didn't want to just turn around and come right back after I'd gone to all the trouble of going over there. Except I needed to get back before Mom tried to bring me up a snack or something and realized I wasn't here."

"So your mother didn't realize you left the house," McCabe said. "Why are you telling us?"

Scott glanced away again. "Because I felt creepy about lying. . . .

I mean about letting Mom lie without knowing it when she said I was here."

"You're a good son, kid," Baxter said.

"Not always. But I have to be now. You know?"

"We know," McCabe said. She touched his arm. "We won't tell your mother unless we have to, okay?"

"Thanks."

He went back inside. Baxter said, "As I said before, partner, I'm betting on another woman."

"Scott didn't say that was what he suspected."

"But he did say things were weird between his parents."

McCabe stopped to gaze at a birdhouse sticking up from the middle of a snowdrift. "So you think Kevin Novak persuaded some woman to come out on a cold, miserable night and meet him for fun and games at the funeral home?"

"That would have been a little kinky," Baxter said. "But it would explain why he had the sudden urge to spend the night there."

"But Scott said he saw his father's snowmobile. No mention of another snowmobile or car or any other means of transportation. If a woman was coming to meet Novak, she apparently still hadn't arrived an hour after he got to the funeral home and turned on the lights."

"Well, we know he lied about the broken pipe. And he didn't put the alarm back on the door, so I say that sounds like he was expecting someone."

"Maybe you're right about the other woman. Maybe she arrived via cross-country skis or snowshoes. Maybe she wasn't coming over, but he just needed to get away from his wife because he felt too guilty to be snowbound with her. But if there is another woman, the question is, who is she?"

"Could be someone at the church. Or maybe a widow he met over her husband's coffin."

"Even if he were having an affair, that doesn't explain why he ended up dead."

"It might. Suppose you're right and he was feeling guilty. He'd cheated on his wife of eighteen years. But he loved his wife and wanted to stay with her. He tells his fling that, and she isn't happy. She's so unhappy she kills him. One of those fatal attractions that ends badly for the cheating husband."

"*If* he was cheating," McCabe said. "It would be nice—and admittedly unexpected—if it turned out he was both in love with the woman he was married to and managed to keep his pants zipped."

"You're sounding a little bitter, partner. Romance gone wrong?"

"What romance?" McCabe said. "Let's get out of here before Sarah Novak starts to wonder why we're hanging around her yard, chatting."

"You were the one who stopped to admire the snowdrifts."

"I was looking at that birdhouse and wondering if Kevin Novak and his children built it."

"Being a good father doesn't mean he wasn't cheating on his wife."

20

"We ought to find out some more about compound bows," McCabe said, as they were driving back to the stationhouse. "I wonder where Kevin Novak bought his."

"There's an archery store out on—"

"I know the one you're talking about. I've seen their ads. He probably would have gone there if he was into hunting as well as target shooting."

"Some of the other members of the church archery clubs might have shopped there, too."

"But," McCabe said, "if Novak was one of their customers, the store might be feeling a little defensive right now. Not the kind of publicity you'd want to have—a customer killed with the bow he bought from your store."

"So, I guess," Baxter said, "we'd do best not to go in flashing our badges." He glanced at her sideways. "Actually, partner, I've got an idea."

"Do I really want to hear this?"

"Well, that depends on how much you want to get some useful information."

McCabe picked up her own car and swung by her house to change.

When she walked into the archery store, she was wearing boots, blue jeans, and a sweater, her hair pulled back in a ponytail. She felt like an actress making her first awkward debut. She had not been particularly good at undercover when she was drafted into the "john patrol" to bust men who were cruising for streetwalkers. In fact, she had soon realized she objected on general principle. Male cops were not expected to strut their stuff in short black leather skirts on street corners.

Well, this time she was sufficiently clothed, and this was a murder investigation not a misdemeanor bust. And all she had to do was smile and be chatty, Baxter had assured her.

The lieutenant had agreed with him that there was nothing wrong with a police detective developing an interest in target shooting and bow hunting as recreational activities and going shopping for a bow. As far as McCabe and Baxter knew, no one at the archery store was a suspect. If the clerks felt like talking about their customers, there was nothing wrong with listening.

When she had suggested Baxter do it since this was his idea—that he go in pretending to be a college kid, like he used to do when he was in Vice—Baxter had given her a wounded look. He didn't, he said, look as young as he did then. Being her partner had aged him.

"And come on, McCabe, if you were a straight male clerk, who would you rather chat with? Me or you?"

The lieutenant had reminded her that if one of the staff at the archery store should be stupid enough to start incriminating himself, she could always pull out her badge and tell him she was a cop.

Easy for them to say this was going to be a breeze, McCabe thought. They didn't have to flirt.

The younger of the two clerks in the store came over to greet her. "Hi, need help with anything?"

"Hello," McCabe said, giving him her best smile. "I could use some advice. I'm not really sure what I'm looking for."

"What would you like to do?"

"I know I want to do some target shooting. And maybe hunting . . . but I haven't decided about that yet."

"Know anything about bows?"

McCabe shook her head, making her ponytail sway. "Not much. But I was talking to someone who said it's a super cool, really arctic sport."

"It is. Let me show you what your choices are, and then you can try our range and get a feel for the different bows."

"That sounds like exactly what I need to do."

The clerk took her over to the display of bows and explained the difference between the recurve bow and the compound bow.

"I really like the way the recurve bow looks," McCabe said. "It reminds me of that movie last year. You know, the one set in post-apocalyptic New France, with everyone wearing those incredible tunics and boots."

"We got a lot of people coming in after that movie," the clerk said. "But you might find the compound bow easier to use. It requires less upper body strength because of the pulley system."

"Oh, I see. And they come in different colors. I love the hot pink one. Hot pink is my favorite color. I always wear hot-pink lip gloss."

"Yeah, I can see you're wearing pink gloss now. Would you like to try it—the bow—on our range?"

"Yes, please. If I'm not keeping you from your other customers. . . ."

"That's why I'm here. To help you find what you're looking for."

McCabe tilted her head and flashed him another smile. Batting her eyelashes would have been a bit too much even if she could have pulled it off.

The range was in the back of the store. It was as high tech as the recurve bow was ancient. The clerk told her, "Our system maps your stance and provides feedback. Watch this."

He turned sideways, bow drawn. On the wall, the system diagramed his shadow image with numbers and arrows.

"What does all that mean?" McCabe asked.

"No need to worry about the details. Just notice your number. Mine is seventy-five percent right now. And it's showing me how to adjust my stance to correct my posture flaws."

"Oh, I see! Now you're at ninety-six percent. Have you ever gotten a perfect one hundred?"

"Once or twice. But the system is based on the form of champion archers. I've only been at this three or four years. Before that, I did my hunting with shotguns."

"But then you got into bows? How did that happen?"

"I have some friends who like hunting with them." He grinned. "And I needed a job. I talked my way into the part-time position they had open here with the understanding that I'd take lessons. Then I was hired on full time."

"You must be a fast learner."

"Your turn. Let's try your stance. Ever fired a shotgun or a rifle?"

"A few times."

"Good. Then you're halfway there."

"I'm so glad you think I'll be good at this. Oh, and it'll be fun to do target practice in the park."

"You shouldn't do that unless the park has a designated archery range. The bow is considered a weapon in the state of New York."

McCabe pressed her hand to her mouth. "Oh, how could I have forgotten. That story on the news stream about the man who was killed with his own bow. The funeral director."

"Yeah, I heard about that. Let's check your stance against the image generated by the system."

"Had he ever been in here?" McCabe asked. She dropped her voice. "I know you aren't allowed to gossip—"

"No, I'm not."

"I'm sorry. I know I shouldn't be so curious. But it's just so weird, isn't it? I knew this girl once who killed someone when he broke into her family's house." McCabe didn't stop to wonder why she was using her own history in her ploy. "Violence is just so weird, isn't it? Not something you expect to happen to people you know."

"No. It's a real kick in the gut when it does."

"Did you hear about it—the murder—on the news stream?"

The clerk shook his head. "My boss heard it when he went out to lunch. He told the staff."

"So everyone here knew him? The funeral director?"

"He used to come in for all his equipment. And he'd bring his son in."

"The family was religious, weren't they? I thought I heard he belonged to that big megachurch."

"He did. The nice part for us is the church has two archery clubs. We get a lot of business from the members. But after what happened, we may not see them in here for a while."

"Oh, you mean after the funeral director being killed with his bow? But maybe they're like people with guns. They don't stop using their guns because someone's killed."

"That's true. So getting back to your lesson—"

"Just one more little question." She leaned closer. "Who do you think did it? Do you think it was someone from the church . . . from the archery clubs?"

The clerk laughed. "I think that bunch is strictly nonviolent. All they want to shoot and kill are deer and other game."

"Really? Not even one suspect among them?"

"No one I've met."

"What about the minister? Have you met him?"

"A couple of times. He seems like an okay guy. Usually religious people make me uncomfortable. But these people—at least the ones from the archery clubs—are just normal people."

"Oh, that's disappointing. I mean not that they're normal . . . but I was hoping you were going to say they were like one of those cults."

"No, they aren't creepy like that. At least, not the ones we see in here."

McCabe smiled. "Then maybe I should start going to their church so I can be in their archery club."

"First, I want you to show me your stance again."

McCabe turned sideways and raised the bow. "Like this?"

"Very good. Now, let's see if you can hit the target."

Fifteen minutes later, she gave the clerk one more big smile as he passed over the box containing her new hot-pink compound bow. "See you on Saturday when I come in for my lesson with your pro."

"I won't be working. But if you stop by during the week to pick up anything else you might need . . ."

"I'll do that. Bye, now."

She waved as she left.

Baxter was sitting in his car in the parking lot. He was pretending to look at something on his ORB, but he glanced up and grinned as she walked past.

21

Angus was at his ease, stretched out on the sofa, reading a book.

"What have the two of you been doing?" McCabe asked, glancing at the dog, sprawled beside the coffee table, fast asleep. "He must be tired. He didn't even notice when the front door opened."

"I couldn't sit here any longer waiting for word about your brother, so I went out to do some research. I took the dog along."

"Does this have something to do with your new writing project?"

"It might."

McCabe strolled past him toward the kitchen. "Okay, Pop, be mysterious. And don't ask me about the case I'm working on."

As she had expected, he was in the kitchen before she could open the refrigerator door.

"I made a turkey casserole," he said. "Pop it in to warm up."

The dog wandered into the kitchen, glanced at the two of them, yawned, and flopped out on the floor.

"He really is tired," McCabe said. She washed her hands and held them under the air jet. "Did you tie him to your car and make him run along behind it?"

"We parked the car and did some walking." Angus sat down at

the kitchen table. "What's been happening with your funeral director case?"

McCabe took plates out of the cabinet. "I bought a compound bow on my way home," she said.

"Find out anything useful while you were at the archery store?"

"No, but I learned the proper stance for shooting a bow. By the way, do you know a woman named Olive Cooper?"

"I've encountered her on occasion. What about her?"

"She belongs to Kevin Novak's church. They were good friends. He attended her celebration of life the day before he was murdered." McCabe saw she had her father's attention. "This is off the record, Pop. Completely confidential."

"Are you playing that tune again? Who do you think I'm going to tell? I'm retired."

"Yes, but you're up to something . . . whatever it is you're working on and don't want to talk about. That's why I'm reminding you."

"You can rest easy, Ms. Detective. I'm not interested in writing about your cases."

McCabe put the salad bowl on the table and sat down. "Then would you tell me about Olive Cooper? What do you know about her?"

"She's tough as old shoe leather. If it hadn't been for her, that husband of hers would have found himself living on the street before he died."

"He was a bad businessman?"

"He was more interested in drinking, gambling, and womanizing. Story was, she put him on an allowance and told him to go to it."

"When we talked to her, she sounded like she might have regretted staying with him."

"Maybe she did. But when he finally killed himself driving drunk, she ended up with his inheritance, which she had grown into a respectable fortune, his family name, and the family homesteads." Angus speared a cherry tomato with his fork. "Not bad for a girl from a little town in the North Country. That was how she met him. His family had a camp up there."

"Umm." McCabe chewed and swallowed. "This casserole is good."

"Woman in the farmer's market gave me the recipe when I bought some mushrooms."

"Did you know Olive Cooper serves on one of Ted Thornton's boards?"

"That doesn't surprise me. If he was looking for an Albany businessperson for a board, Olive's a sensible choice. She's smart and she has connections."

"What do you know about the church she belongs to? The New Awakening Church?"

Angus reached for a whole-wheat roll. "What do you know about the minister?"

"What should I know about him?"

"If you've done your research—"

"As a matter of fact, we had the Research Unit run all of the people involved in this case. According to what they were able to find, Reverend Wyatt was born in West Virginia, into a family of miners. He worked in the mines as a teenager, but then got a scholarship and went off to college. He was majoring in business until he nearly died of meningitis. Then he underwent a religious awakening—hence the name of his church, years later. But before that, he changed his college major to religion, went to seminary, and received an appointment as an assistant minister. Then he started his own church, which has become a faith movement in this area."

"And it could become a national movement within the next year or two."

McCabe chewed and swallowed. "When Baxter and I interviewed him, Reverend Wyatt said he'd missed Olive Cooper's celebration of life because he had to do a Web conference meeting with a sponsor. Something about national events he's going to be participating in this fall."

Angus nodded. "According to a buddy of mine, the reverend

went out and got himself a business agent. He's been negotiating a contract for a series of major arena events across the country. The reverend's planning to take his show on the road with the goal of going big-time."

"This buddy who told you this," McCabe said. "You just happened to be chatting with him about one of the people involved in my murder case?"

"No, Ms. Detective. We happened to be talking a couple of months ago about a book my buddy's working on. We were sitting in a bar in the City having lunch. Did I happen to mention my buddy is a reporter who writes about religion and ethics?"

"Oh."

"Yes, 'oh.' He asked what I knew about Wyatt's megachurch up here."

"Were you able to tell him anything?"

"Not as much as he told me."

"And what he told you was that Wyatt was about to expand his ministry."

"Wyatt's been taking it slow but sure. He started out preaching out of a storefront and worked his way up. Now, he's ready to go big-time. But he's being careful about that, too. Keeping it quiet until everything's in place."

"If your source is reliable," McCabe said.

Her father's blue gaze narrowed. "My source is not only reliable, Ms. Detective, he's one of the best reporters I know."

"Good enough for me. So we have a minister who has enough charisma to expand beyond his base."

"He's pretty good as a performer," Angus said. "He knows how to hold his audience."

McCabe scooped another serving of casserole onto her plate. "This really is good, Pop. You've seen Wyatt on the Web?"

"Seen him in person."

"In person? You've been to his church?"

"I have been known to darken the doors of houses of worship."

"I know. You and Mama used to take me to church. But I didn't realize you had been recently."

"After the damn doctor told me I had to stop drinking and then I had to go in and have my chest cut open, I was considering my mortality."

"Were you?" McCabe nodded. "I can see how that might happen. Did you find Reverend Wyatt helpful?"

"Not particularly. But he preached a good sermon."

"Did you happen to encounter Jonathan Burdett while you were there? He's the psychiatrist who provides counseling to church members."

"That many of their members crazy, huh?"

"That many of them suffering from the anxieties of modern life, according to Burdett."

"Didn't meet him. But I didn't stay for the socializing after the sermon."

McCabe pushed back her chair. "I think we have some frozen yogurt. Do you want dessert?"

"Coffee for me. If I wanted dessert, I'd have real ice cream. What'd your research people find out about Burdett when they looked at him?"

"He grew up in a well-to-do Boston family with connections to Harvard by way of his grandfather and his father, who had both been professors there. Burdett himself was an undergrad at Harvard, did graduate work at Oxford, medical degree from Johns Hopkins, worked in San Francisco and then New York before coming here to Albany."

"Why'd he come to Albany?"

"Not clear. He moved here a year or so after his wife died of cancer."

"He could have wanted a change after that," Angus said.

"And maybe he was attracted to Wyatt's religious movement. Aside from his paid part-time position, he's also involved in church activities and governance."

"So you've got a psychiatrist who's religious."

"And open-minded," McCabe said as she edged the frozen yogurt from behind a bag of broccoli. "He said he was sorry that he'd missed meeting Olive Cooper's spiritualist at her celebration of life."

"Her spiritualist?"

"Luanne Woodward. She's from North Carolina and a favorite with the media there. A number of well-known people have attended her séances. She once helped the police find a missing person, whom she had a feeling was dead. Although she did tell us that's not her usual stock in trade."

"Was she right that time?"

"They found the body where she said it was. But it might have been a lucky guess."

"Oh, thee of little faith."

"Come on, Pop." McCabe came back to the table with his coffee and her frozen yogurt. "Don't tell me you believe in the paranormal."

As she said it, McCabe realized this was one of the few topics they had never discussed. But once, when she had found him stretched out on the sofa, nursing a hangover, he had scowled up at her and observed, "If your mother could come back from wherever she is, she'd be giving me hell for getting drunk."

McCabe said, "You don't believe it's possible for the dead to communicate with the living, do you?"

"Depends on what you mean by communicate," Angus said.

"Meaning you don't want to answer my question."

"Meaning the answer to some questions depend on how they're asked. I try to keep an open mind about what I can't prove one way or the other. But with the Fox sisters as an example, I'd think twice about consulting a spiritualist if I wanted to receive a message from your mother."

"The Fox sisters?"

"Don't tell me you've never heard of them."

"Vaguely."

"Nineteenth century. Three sisters. The younger two, Maggie

and Kate, were at the center of the spiritualism movement in New York State. They claimed they could communicate with the dead and became famous for their 'rappings.' Until Maggie confessed it had all been a hoax. But the spiritualism movement continued among the true believers."

"Did the Fox sisters ever come to Albany?"

"Sure they did. So did Houdini."

"The magician? He believed in spiritualism?"

Angus gave her another one of his looks. "Houdini was a debunker. He gave lectures about how hoaxers like the Fox sisters fooled their clients. In fact, Houdini and Arthur Conan Doyle had a falling out over spiritualism." Angus drained his coffee mug and added, "But Doyle went on believing Houdini's magic was the result of Houdini's supernatural powers."

"Houdini must have found that a little frustrating," McCabe said. "What do you think about Olive Cooper cultivating a medium? Is it out of character? Cooper didn't strike me as particularly gullible. So why would she be hanging out with a medium?"

"Maybe she appreciates the woman's entertainment value. Or, maybe she's an old woman who hopes there might be something on the other side."

"That's more or less what she said about it. And Luanne Woodward is entertaining. But Cooper's minister, Reverend Wyatt, isn't happy about Luanne. Luanne says he wasn't welcoming when Olive brought her along to church. Wyatt told Baxter and me that he objects to the way phony spiritualists prey on vulnerable people."

"So he thinks the woman's a fraud, does he?"

McCabe hunched forward, elbows on the table. "He does. But there is a distinction, isn't there, between being a fraud and sincerely believing in your own powers even if you haven't any?"

"I'd take the fraud. People who suffer from delusions about their own powers can be dangerous. Mind pouring me another cup of coffee?"

22

Thursday, January 23, 2020
9:17 A.M.

"We ought to put your dad on the payroll," Baxter said.

McCabe had given Baxter a run-down of her chat with the clerk in the archery store. Then she'd told him about her conversation with her father.

"He does have useful information sometimes. But I always remind him our discussions are confidential."

"If you can't trust your own father to keep his mouth shut, who can you trust?" Baxter leaned back in his chair. "So where does that leave us? We've got the members of the two archery clubs. But the clerk at the archery store says our church people, even though they like to play around with bows, are real nice people, only dangerous to four-legged animals."

"Unless we want to interview all the club members because they own bows and knew the victim, I think we should accept his assessment for now. We can work our way down the lists if nothing else turns up. Or if something turns up that would suggest we should focus on the club members."

"Okay, that leaves us with our major players. A minister, who has a megachurch and, according to your father's source, plans to go big-time. He seems like a nice guy, too, but he objects to the medium his rich old lady church member brought to church and recommended to our victim. On the other hand, the psychiatrist, aka church counselor, thinks the medium is a passing fad among the church members. Rich old lady says the psychiatrist is a good guy, too, just too full of himself to know how to hang with street people."

"We also have our victim's dead friend, Bob, that everyone keeps bringing up," McCabe said.

"But Bob died of natural causes. And it's understandable our vic might have felt some responsibility for his death if they were playing tennis when his friend keeled over from a heart attack."

"That's understandable. But maybe there's more to the Bob thing. Maybe there's something there that would explain Kevin Novak's odd behavior the past few months."

Baxter said, "I wonder who buried Bob when he died. Would you bury your best friend if you were a funeral director?"

"I guess that would depend on what the friend's family wanted." McCabe reached for her ORB. "We don't know anything about Bob or his family yet."

"I don't even remember the guy's last name."

"Reeves. I thought of George Reeves when I heard it."

Baxter grinned. "Sorry, you lost me. Who?"

"The actor who played Superman on that old TV show. When we were kids, my dad took my brother, Adam, and me down to the City to an event at Rockefeller Center honoring TV actors who were big in the 1950s and '60s. Reeves was one of the people being honored."

"He must have been an old man by then."

"But he was still navigating on his own. I was too young to appreciate it at the time, but they had a really arctic surprise for both him and the audience. Marilyn Monroe gave Superman his award."

"Wow! I've seen some of her movies. Of course, she must have been pretty ancient by then, too."

"She had let her hair go white and she had some wrinkles, but she looked pretty good. My dad jumped to his feet and started clapping as soon as she walked out on the arm of the Marine who was escorting her. Okay, here we go. I've got a September 2019 obituary for a Robert Reeves. I think this is our guy."

McCabe sent the obituary from her ORB to the wall. Baxter walked over to read it. "Robert Reeves, age fifty-four, married . . . an attorney."

"Who practiced family law and estate planning."

"Estate planning," Baxter said. "Could he have been Olive Cooper's lawyer?"

"I think she would have mentioned it if he had been. But we can ask. I wonder if Bob's wife and Sarah Novak are friends."

Baxter sat down on the edge of his desk. "You think they might have shared some girl talk about what was going on with Kevin after Bob died?"

"If they're friends, they might have. We should pay Bob's wife a visit and see if she has any thoughts about how Kevin reacted to her husband's death." McCabe turned back to her ORB. "Let's see if we can find an address for her."

Francesca Reeves owned an upscale women's apparel shop in the mall near UAlbany's uptown campus. When McCabe contacted her, Reeves responded with a tag asking the detectives to meet her there.

A clerk smiled at them as they entered La Femme Naturelle. She was busy with a woman who was peering into a mirror as she held silver bangle earrings up to her face.

McCabe said, "Excuse me, we're here to see—"

"I'm Francesca," said a silky, slightly accented voice.

Reeves was clad in a black sweater and calf-length skirt that might have come from her own shop and wore several silver bracelets. Her shoulder-length silver hair was swept back from her face.

She was chic and beautifully preserved, McCabe thought, but she must be in her late sixties. According to his obituary, Bob Reeves had been closer to Kevin Novak's age than his wife's.

"Please come into my office," Reeves said.

Her office décor was understated French country. Reeves sat down behind her desk. She said, "I can see you're surprised. My husband was fifty-four. I'm seventy-two, almost seventy-three."

Baxter said, "I guess your husband preferred beautiful older women."

Reeves returned his smile. "Our age difference seemed less so when my husband and I first met. He said I was fascinating and 'ageless.' "

And did he eventually stop saying that? McCabe wondered. "How long were you married, Mrs. Reeves?"

"Twelve years. Until he died and became the second husband I was required to bury."

"What happened to your first?" Baxter asked.

"A skiing accident. Bob was his lawyer." She glanced at McCabe. "And since you're here to talk about Kevin Novak, I should tell you that Kevin handled both husbands' funeral services."

"Did both husbands belong to the New Awakening Church?" McCabe asked.

"Only Bob. To my annoyance. Not that I'm opposed to organized religion. But when one is as involved as Bob was, it can be time-consuming." A graceful wave of her hand set her bracelets jangling. "Of course, you must understand that I'm particularly peeved at his church right now. Shortly before he died, my husband sent me off on my own on a jaunt to Paris. One of his many church committees was meeting."

"The parking lot committee?" Baxter asked.

"No, I think it was something about church finances."

"Did he say what it was they were going to discuss?" McCabe asked.

"I don't think it was anything unusual. But he was the chair of the committee, and he felt it would be bad form to take off for a long weekend in Paris—so decadent, you know—when his committee was meeting to discuss church business."

"Did you attend church with your husband?" McCabe asked.

"On appropriate holidays," Reeves said. "But I think Reverend Wyatt suspected me of hypocrisy. And I always felt Bob was uncomfortable about our age difference when he was in the midst of his fellow congregants. I think he was afraid they thought he had really married a wealthy widow for her money."

"Did you," McCabe asked, "know Kevin and Sarah Novak well? Were the four of you close friends?"

"Close friends, no. I liked them both. But—although they tried their best to include me—we didn't have a great deal in common."

"But you and Sarah are both businesswomen," Baxter said. "Do you carry her products?"

"I offered, but Sarah was distressed when she saw my price markup. She wants 'working women' to be able to buy her soaps and lotions." Reeves shrugged. "I, on the other hand, have no objection to helping women feel as if they are treating themselves well when they pay for quality."

That was one way of looking at it, McCabe thought.

"How did your husband's death affect your relationship with the Novaks?"

"Not well. Kevin held himself much more responsible than he should have for Bob's heart attack."

"Did you tell him that?" Baxter asked.

"Yes. But even at the hospital, while we were waiting for my husband to come out of surgery, Kevin had a hard time looking me in the eye."

"And when your husband died," McCabe said, "and Mr. Novak was handling his funeral . . . that must have been awkward for both of you."

"It was," Reeves said. "But I had promised Bob before he went into surgery that if anything happened, I would accept Kevin's help."

"Accept his help?" Baxter said. "With the funeral planning and getting your husband's affairs in order?"

Reeves laughed. "My husband was a lawyer. He would never have died with his affairs in disarray. He wanted my promise that I would allow Kevin to not only see me through his burial but be there to support me through my period of mourning. Unfortunately, he hadn't taken Kevin's feelings into account. We were both relieved when we had gotten through the funeral."

"So you haven't spent a lot of time with the Novaks since your husband died?" Baxter asked.

"No, but Sarah has checked in on me now and then. We had lunch together two weeks ago."

"Was that her suggestion or yours?" McCabe asked.

"Hers. We went to a wonderful little café downtown." Reeves paused. "But she hardly touched her food. And . . . this was unusual for Sarah . . . she not only joined me in a glass of wine, she had several. She was a bit tipsy by the time lunch was over."

McCabe asked, "Did you talk about your husbands?"

"Only in passing. She said, 'Kevin misses Bob.' I said, 'So do I.' And after a moment of silence, she rushed into small talk about her children. I countered with small talk about my shop. She said she had always wanted to go to Paris and told me—a story she'd told me the first time we met—about her college roommate who everyone had thought was ultrasophisticated because she had spent a summer with an aunt in Paris. I told her about my last trip to Paris." Reeves paused, smiling. "And then we had to make an important decision."

"About what?" McCabe asked.

"About dessert. There was a new item on the menu, and we had to decide if we were brave enough to try it."

"What was the new item?" Baxter asked.

"Chocolate fudge walnut brownies made with ground cricket flour."

McCabe said, "I've read about that. The cricket flour is supposed to provide protein and make desserts healthier."

"Did you have the healthy brownies?" Baxter asked, grinning.

Reeves shook her head. "Wine and chocolate work well together.

But we were uncertain about the crickets. I had coffee. Sarah ordered the blood orange sorbet. I'm sure, later that afternoon, she felt rather miserable as she recovered from her lunch of three glasses of wine and a sorbet."

"You said it was unusual for Mrs. Novak to drink," McCabe said. "Did you have the sense she was worried or upset?"

"Both. But if she had intended to talk to me about what was troubling her, she changed her mind. I have been wondering if I should call her. Maybe she would like to tell me now. Or, perhaps, now Kevin is dead, talking would make it worse."

"Do you think it might be some secret involving both Kevin and your husband?" Baxter asked.

Reeves said, "My concern is that there is more to this than I at first thought. Bob's death sent Kevin, his best friend, into a tailspin. And now Kevin has been murdered. Maybe there is something I should know."

McCabe felt a twinge of unease. "But it would be best if you left this investigation to us, Mrs. Reeves. Sometimes asking questions can be a bad idea."

"You can't think Sarah killed her husband."

"We have no reason to think that. But Mrs. Novak does believe whatever was bothering her husband might have somehow led to his murder. So it might be better if you didn't appear too interested."

Reeves tilted her head. "I see. But I assume you would not object to my contacting Sarah to express my condolences. It is only good manners, you see."

"Yes, and I don't think that would be a problem."

"You will let me know if you find anything I should know about my husband?"

Baxter said, "Anything in particular you think we might find?"

"I am a realist, Detective Baxter. My husband was attentive and romantic. We had a marriage we both enjoyed. But he was a man—and a lawyer involved in handling the estates of wealthy clients. I am not the kind of woman who goes through life wearing blinders. I know men—and women—are sometimes tempted by lust or greed." She shrugged. "That is what makes us so fascinating. Even when we try to behave as we think we should, we so often fall from grace."

"That's a generous philosophy," McCabe observed.

"To the extent one can be generous, life becomes much more bearable," Reeves said.

"Yes, I suppose it does. Only two more questions. When was the last time you saw Kevin Novak? And where were you on the night he died?"

"I wondered when you would get to that. Oddly enough, the last time I saw Kevin, it was for only a moment. He saw me and made a hasty departure."

Kevin Novak seemed to have a habit of removing himself from situations he found uncomfortable, McCabe thought. He'd also made "a hasty departure" when he was introduced to Luanne Woodward.

"When and where did you see each other?" she asked.

"About a month ago," Reeves said. "And here I might as well make a disgraceful confession. I love video games. On our first date, I took Bob to a video arcade in the City. On the day when I ran into Kevin and his daughter, Megan, I had borrowed my neighbors' twelve- and thirteen-year-old grandsons for a trip to the video arcade that opened on Wolf Road last summer. It has all of my favorite vintage games, and as one of my young companions said, 'It is awesome arctic.' "

"So Kevin and his daughter came to play videos games," Baxter said, "but saw you and—"

"Kevin stopped in his tracks. Then he nodded to me and said something to Megan. She looked surprised and started to protest. He hustled her out. We never spoke."

"Odd," McCabe said.

"Very," Reeves agreed. "And one of the reasons I was particularly intrigued when Sarah invited me to lunch a couple of weeks later."

"Did you tell her what happened with Kevin at the arcade?" Baxter asked.

Reeves shook her head. "I was about to when she plunged into her small talk about her children."

McCabe said, "That should have been the perfect opportunity to mention you'd seen Mr. Novak and his daughter at the arcade."

"Yes, you would think so. But Sarah was chattering away as if she were afraid to stop talking. It didn't seem the best time to bring up her husband's odd behavior."

"About my other question, Mrs. Reeves—where were you on the night Kevin Novak died?"

"Definitely not struggling through the snow to get to the funeral home and kill him, Detective McCabe. I was indulging myself with a long weekend at a spa in the Catskills. And blissfully snowed in there until Monday afternoon. I didn't hear about Kevin's death until I got back to Albany."

23

Dr. Singh's toxicology report on Kevin Novak was waiting for them when they got back to the station house.

Baxter said, "Nothing illegal. But he was taking a prescription antidepressant."

"I wonder who prescribed it," McCabe said. "His family doctor or the church counselor."

"Singh doesn't say. Maybe we should ask our friend Dr. Burdett."

"Not that the antidepressant is necessarily relevant. But Novak's mental state keeps coming up. Let's see if we can reach Dr. Burdett."

Burdett was sitting at his desk, shelves of books in the background. "Good morning, Detectives. I'm afraid we'll have to keep this short, I'm expecting a patient."

"Just a quick question, Dr. Burdett," McCabe said, sliding her ORB into its dock on her desk so that Baxter could see. "According to the toxicology report on Kevin Novak, he was taking an antidepressant." McCabe read the name out to him. "We wondered if you had prescribed it, or if we should speak to his family doctor."

"I can answer your question. Kevin's GP wrote the prescription after consulting with me. We both agreed Kevin could benefit from an antidepressant that would help him to cope while he was working through his emotional problems." Burdett frowned. "Forgive me, but I don't see why you're concerned about the medication Kevin was taking when he was shot with a bow."

Baxter said, "We're being thorough, Doc. Just making sure nothing turned up in his body that shouldn't have been there."

"Oh, yes, of course."

McCabe said, "Speaking of how Mr. Novak died. Olive Cooper mentioned the church's two archery clubs."

"Yes," Burdett said. "I'm sorry. Did both Daniel and I forget to mention the archery clubs when you asked us about activities Kevin was involved in at church?"

"Yeah, you did," Baxter said. "All those members with bows must have slipped you and the reverend's minds."

"Hardly that many, Detective Baxter. Or, at least, I have no idea who attending church services may own a bow. After all, we are in upstate New York, and hunting is a popular activity. But the clubs are relatively new. There are still only about twenty-five members in the archery club for teenagers, and about that same number in the club for adults. And in those two groups, only about half attends any given meeting or event."

"Good," Baxter said. "That will make it easier if we have to talk to them."

"That's ridiculous," Burdett said. "You certainly don't intend to harass innocent people, including teenagers—"

"We don't intend to harass anyone, Dr. Burdett," McCabe said. "We were simply curious about why neither you nor Reverend Wyatt mentioned the existence of the clubs to us."

"As I said—speaking for myself and, I'm sure, for Daniel—we forgot. We were in shock over Kevin's death. The matter of the clubs slipped our minds."

"Even when we asked you about Kevin's activities at the church?" Baxter said. "Yeah, I guess you were in shock."

McCabe said, "No harm done, Dr. Burdett. Luckily, Ms. Cooper thought to mention the clubs when we spoke to her."

"I'm sure Olive didn't suggest that anyone who belonged to—"

"No, I'm sorry. I didn't mean to imply that," McCabe said. "Ms. Cooper was explaining to Detective Baxter and me about the difference between recurve bows and compound bows and how someone inexperienced with a bow might not even know how to shoot it. And she mentioned in passing that Mr. Novak had belonged to the church archery club."

"We did ask her if you and Reverend Wyatt are hunters," Baxter said. "And she said no, you just liked to do target practice and sometimes worked with the teenage archery club."

Burdett said, "And what did you make of that?"

"Not a thing, Doc," Baxter said. "Should we have made something of it?"

"My patient is waiting," Burdett said. "If there is nothing else . . ."

"No, that's all for now," McCabe replied. "Thank you for taking the time to speak to us, Dr. Burdett. And please forgive us if we've upset you. We were just curious about whether you had any thoughts about the members of the archery clubs."

"I've told you my thoughts. You're wasting your time if you intend to pursue this line of investigation."

"Exactly what we needed to know," McCabe said. "We'll let you go now."

"Good day," Burdett said. The monitor went blank as he ended the transmission.

"Couldn't resist ruffling his tail feathers, could you?" McCabe said to her partner.

Baxter leaned back in his chair and whirled around. "You were the one who implied we were wondering about why he and the reverend didn't mention the archery clubs."

"And his answer was he and Wyatt were just so shocked by what had happened that it slipped their minds."

"Uh-huh," Baxter said. "Guess an eighty-five-year-old woman was better at keeping her composure and remembering what she should tell us than the two of them."

"To be fair," McCabe said, "they had been dealing with Sarah

Novak and trying to help her cope. And they knew Scott had gone to pick up his sister. Their minds might have been on Kevin's wife and children."

"Or their minds might have been on what they were whispering about when we walked into the kitchen."

"There is that possibility," McCabe said. "Whatever was going on, when someone claims he 'forgot' to mention something . . . I would have found it more believable if he had said he and Reverend Wyatt hadn't wanted to have the members of the archery clubs dragged into a murder investigation."

"Right at the end, he did say he was sure none of the club members were involved. But he was still claiming he and Wyatt had just forgotten they should mention the clubs."

"And that's where he lost me," McCabe said. "That, and the fact that toward the end of our conversation, he was getting hostile. Either you were really irritating him, or we were making him nervous about something."

McCabe pulled up the Web on her ORB, searching for the New Awakening Church. She found the site and sent it to the wall.

"What are we looking for?" Baxter asked. "The next archery club meeting?"

"I would think they'd cancel any meeting they have coming up until after Kevin Novak's funeral. But we can see what's on the church schedule, and then check in with Reverend Wyatt."

"About what, pray tell?"

"About whether he would mind if we dropped by. Just a couple more questions we'd like to ask. Of course, one of the questions could be about getting the member lists for the archery clubs."

"Rising majestically from a grove of trees . . ." McCabe said.

They were trudging across the parking lot toward the church.

"Looks even flashier than it did in the hologram," Baxter said.

"With that much glass and that large a cross . . . but it is impressive."

"We should have driven in and looked for that underground parking lot."

"It's probably full, and, besides, we can use the exercise. And now we know firsthand why they need 'traffic coordinators' on Sunday to help people park their cars and board the shuttles to the church. No parking close to church even on a weekday. I guess they really do have people attending all those events we saw on the church calendar."

"That explains why our vic was on a committee to consider the parking problem."

"But we've been assured that had nothing at all to do with his murder," McCabe said.

They reached the church and entered through two massive wooden doors. Baxter stopped and glanced around the empty space of the lobby. "I guess the architect and the interior designer forgot to compare notes."

"Definitely," McCabe said. "This is much better."

Winter sunlight poured from above, washing over white walls. On the walls, carefully spaced Impressionist watercolors of nature scenes. On the floor, interlocking blue and green tiles that gleamed in spite of what must be heavy foot traffic.

They followed the sign directing them down a hall to the administrative offices.

The young woman at the reception desk glanced up and gave them a megawatt smile. "Hello, how are you today?"

"Terrific," Baxter said. "How are you?"

The young woman blinked at the dazzling smile Baxter was giving her.

McCabe said, "We're here to see Reverend Wyatt, please. I'm Detective McCabe, and this is my partner, Detective Baxter."

"But you can call me Mike," Baxter said.

The young woman stood up. "Thank you, Detective Baxter, but I always try to be respectful to my elders. I'll see if Reverend Wyatt is available, Detective McCabe."

She disappeared down a hallway lined with open office doors.

Baxter gave an exaggerated groan. " 'My elders,' the woman said."

"She looks about twenty-two or -three," McCabe said. "That would make you her elder by at least seven years. You did have a birthday back in November."

The young woman came back to the end of the hallway and gestured to them. "Please come this way." She escorted the detectives into a conference room and invited them to make themselves comfortable. "Reverend Wyatt will be with you in a moment," the young woman said.

Baxter sat down at the table and nodded at the wall and its static image. "Sunday morning," he said.

On the wall, a choir in white robes stood on a stage, voices raised in song. Standing by his pulpit in a royal-blue clerical robe, Reverend Wyatt had turned toward the choir. In the background, worshipers filled the stadium-style seating.

McCabe said, "We should ask for a tour of the place."

"I'd be happy to show you around," Wyatt said from the doorway.

"Thank you," McCabe said. "That's not why we dropped by—and we do apologize for not calling first—but if you do have time for a tour . . ."

"Of course. I can certainly spare the time. But why are you here? More questions about Kevin?"

"We're hoping we can get a copy of the membership lists for the church's archery clubs," McCabe said.

"The membership lists?" Wyatt blinked rapidly. "I don't understand."

"We thought Dr. Burdett might have given you a heads-up about that," Baxter said. "We talked to him an hour ago."

Wyatt said, "I've been in meetings all morning. I haven't heard from Jonathan. Are you saying he suggested you ask me for the membership lists?"

"We were talking to Dr. Burdett about something else when the clubs came up," McCabe said. "Olive Cooper had told us the church has archery clubs. We wondered why neither you nor Dr. Burdett had mentioned that."

Wyatt frowned. He glanced at the wall on which his Sunday church service was displayed. "What did Jonathan say?"

"He said the two of you had forgotten to tell us."

Wyatt looked even more uncomfortable. "I'm afraid Jonathan was doing his best to cover for me. When we were out in the kitchen, I expressed my concern that suspicion might fall on the members of the adult archery club because Kevin was killed with a bow."

"So that occurred to you even before you'd talked to us?" Baxter asked.

"I— It was an obvious thought," Wyatt said.

"But you assured us that none of your church members would have a reason to harm Mr. Novak," McCabe said.

"Yes, but police—in crime shows—detectives always look at how someone was killed."

McCabe said, "And so you thought it would be best if you and Dr. Burdett didn't mention the archery clubs?"

"We didn't get that far in our discussion. But later, after you had gone, we realized neither one of us had told you." He shook his head. "I'm sorry. It was an error in judgment."

"Anything else you haven't told us?" Baxter asked.

Wyatt flushed and looked away and then did his best to muster an affronted expression. "I'm not in the habit of lying, Detective Baxter."

That was good, McCabe thought, because he was really rotten at it. She said, "We're sure you aren't in the habit of lying, Reverend Wyatt. But is there anything else . . . any other information . . . that you've withheld because of concern about the welfare of your church members or someone else?"

He stared at her. "I . . ." He rubbed his hand across his mouth. "No, there isn't anything else."

"If there were," McCabe said, "what you ought to keep in mind is that we are good at our job. We usually find out what people are trying to hide."

Wyatt drew himself up. "If you are trying to intimidate me, Detective McCabe—"

"Not at all. I'm simply stating a fact. It makes everybody's life a lot easier when the people we talk to answer our questions truthfully. We don't deliberately harass innocent people. We don't try to arrest people who haven't committed crimes."

"Are you saying, 'Trust us and everything will be fine'?"

"Maybe not fine. But a lot less likely to get complicated."

"I . . . I need to think about something that could affect a number of people."

Baxter said, "If one of those people might have killed Kevin Novak, you'd better think about whether you might be next."

"Detective Baxter is right, Reverend Wyatt. If you have knowledge that could implicate someone, you should tell us."

"I don't know who killed Kevin. If I knew that, I would tell you. I just need to think about this some more." He sighed. "Think and pray."

Baxter said, "Does Dr. Burdett know whatever it is you need to pray about?"

"No, he— No, he doesn't know."

Or at least, McCabe thought, Wyatt hoped he didn't know and was now wondering.

"About the membership lists . . ." she said.

"Is that really necessary? I promise—you have my assurance, that none of the members of the archery clubs were involved in Kevin's death."

"So you don't know who killed Kevin," Baxter said, "but you can assure us none of the—"

"I know my church members," Wyatt said.

"Given the number of church members you have," McCabe said, "it's a little difficult to believe—"

"I meant I know the people in the archery clubs. I've spent considerable time with all of them. They all liked and respected Kevin. None of them had reason to kill him. None of them is capable of murder."

McCabe nodded. "But we'd still like the membership lists, if you wouldn't mind."

"You're going to talk to the teenagers, too?"

"We'd like to see both lists. We'll begin with the adults and then perhaps talk to the teenagers as a group. In that case, we'll ask you and any parents who would like to be present to join us. Is that a reasonable approach?"

"Yes. Yes, thank you. Let's go out to the reception desk and I'll get Jessica to pull up the lists. And then I'll give you that tour I offered."

"Thank you, we'd like to see your church."

"I want to do whatever I can to correct any misconceptions you may have about our church."

"About that Web conference you had on the afternoon of Olive Cooper's party," Baxter said, "rumor has it you're about to take the church big-time."

"If you mean that I'm about to expand beyond the Capital Region and my Web outreach, then, yes, that's true."

"Bad timing having a member of your flock murdered right now," Baxter said.

Wyatt turned and looked at him. "Having a member of my flock murdered at any time would be bad," he said. "If you are implying that I might be concerned about the negative press, yes, I am concerned about that. The sponsor for the arena events we have scheduled is the owner of a chain of family restaurants. We have a contract, but that contract has a morality clause that he will implement if there is any hint of scandal involving this church." Wyatt paused. "So, yes, I would rather this were not happening now. But what I wish even more is that a man I respected and cared about hadn't been murdered." He gestured toward the conference room door. "Shall we go?"

"After you, Reverend," Baxter said.

Baxter's expression was a little sheepish when he glanced in McCabe's direction. Dignity trumps wisecrack, she thought.

They stopped at the reception desk for the club membership lists.

Then Wyatt led them back out into the lobby and in the direction of voices and activity.

"The gymnasium," he said, opening a door.

Inside, two teams of men were playing basketball.

"The exercise facilities are available to our members from six A.M. to midnight every day except Sunday," Wyatt said.

The rest of the tour included a stop at the church library, a recreation room, the kitchen, an adjoining cafeteria. Meeting rooms. Out a side door to visit the greenhouse and admire the gardens. Then Wyatt led them back inside. "I saved the sanctuary for last," he said.

They entered at floor level, near the stage.

McCabe said, "This must seem a long way from the storefront where you started your church, Reverend Wyatt."

Wyatt nodded, gazing up at the rows of seats, the monitors that allowed those in the back rows to have a close-up view of the service. "A very long way."

"Is this where you're going to perform Kevin Novak's funeral service?"

"No, we have a smaller, more intimate space we'll use."

"It is possible that we'll be at the funeral," McCabe said.

Wyatt frowned. "Is that necessary?"

"We might see something useful," Baxter said.

"Mrs. Novak has given her permission for us to attend and view the service from another room on cam," McCabe said.

"You mean spy on the mourners?"

"Spy is rather a harsh word, Reverend Wyatt. If we attend the funeral, we'll be doing our job. Has it been scheduled?"

"Kevin's funeral is tomorrow afternoon. The wake is tonight. Are you—do you intend to come to that, too?"

"No," McCabe said. "But we would like to attend the service tomorrow."

"If Sarah has given her permission . . . did she tell you that it's a private service? You— Unless Kevin was killed by someone who would be invited to his funeral service, you'll be wasting your time."

"Possibly," McCabe said. "But Megan did ask us to attend."

"Are you saying that Megan thinks someone her father knew—"

"Megan watches crime shows, too," Baxter said. "She knows that most people are killed by someone they know."

Wyatt stared at him. "I don't think that is true in this case."

"Why don't you think that, Reverend Wyatt?" McCabe asked.

"I—I just don't think—but, of course, if Sarah has said you may attend the funeral service, I won't object."

But he still looked unhappy that they were going to be there, McCabe thought. And he was still choking on whatever it was he hadn't told them.

24

Back at the station house, they decided to have Research run the names on the membership lists they had gotten from Wyatt. That would tell them if anyone on the lists had priors, particularly any history of violence.

"But I'm not counting on it," McCabe said.

"Who knows," Baxter said. "We may find a few reformed sinners among the faithful."

"We might. But if we do, I don't think Wyatt knows about it. His righteous indignation about our harassing innocent people seemed real enough."

Baxter stood up from his desk and stretched. "Anyway, since we aren't going to have the information back from Research until tomorrow, I say we call it a day."

"No argument from me on that one," McCabe said.

They walked out to the parking lot together. Today, Baxter was driving himself.

"I don't know which is worse," McCabe said, "getting off from work at dusk in the winter or having daylight in the summer but too hot outside to enjoy it."

"You know me," Baxter said. "I always go with summer and heat."

Baxter was in no mood to shop, but his four-year-old nephew had a birthday on Sunday. His sister would not be pleased if he turned up at the party without a gift. He wandered through the toy store, waiting for inspiration to strike.

When he was four, his favorite toy had been a stuffed purple shark he had named Fin. And then his second cousin, Tommy, had made him watch *When Sharks Attack*. After that, playing with Fin had creeped him out. For a while, he had even screamed when his parents tried to get him to go into the water.

His ORB buzzed and Baxter stepped to the side, out of the traffic of parents with children in tow. He checked the ID and clicked view.

His godfather, Assistant Chief Danvers, smiled at him from the monitor. "What's that behind you, Mike boy? Teddy bears?"

"Toy store. My nephew has a birthday."

"Your youngest sister's boy? Buy him some boxing gloves. Little boys love punching."

"I'll see if they have any."

"And when you're done, come join Tommy and me and a couple of the fellows for a drink."

"Sure. I could use one."

"We'll save you a glass of the fine whiskey we're sipping."

And may you all choke on it before I arrive, Baxter thought. "Thanks," he said. "Be there as soon as I finish up here."

"We'll see you soon."

An unexpected invitation meant they'd been thinking. As he was running through the possibilities, Baxter turned back to the toy display and chose a sleek black stuffed seal for his nephew. He added an endangered species interactive book to his basket.

By the time he got out to the parking lot, he had a half-baked plan. He punched his code into his ORB and waited for his contact to answer.

McCabe stopped in the doorway of the living room. Her father glanced up from the book he was reading.

"When I was driving home, I saw a news stream on a bulletin board," she said. "There was something about a US rescue unit being en route to Roarke's Island."

"The island's getting unstable."

"Unstable?"

"Man-made island," Angus said. "They didn't take earthquakes and aftershocks into account."

"What's happening? Is it sinking? Flooding?"

"Moving more than it should. Could do either. The government on the mainland is still busy with the damage there, so Kirkland's sending in the Marines to get the people at the resort off the island. That isn't going down well with some people."

"How could anyone object to a rescue operation?"

"Howard Miller is objecting to spending our tax dollars to mount a rescue operation for people who have nothing better to do than vacation at a resort. Some others are already agreeing with him. They're saying the people on the island should pay for private rescue."

"That's ridiculous. Adam and Mai aren't rich. I'm betting most of the people vacationing at that resort aren't either."

"But they can afford a vacation at a fancy swanky resort."

McCabe let out her breath. "The important thing is that the rescue is happening."

"And Kirkland just put another nail in her political coffin. Even if she were having second thoughts about ceding the nomination to the vice president, this could do her in."

"Rescuing people whose lives are in danger—"

"Goes down better if the people are in the United States, not on a vacation island belonging to another country."

McCabe shrugged off her thermo jacket. "I'm not going to worry about this. If idiots like Howard Miller want to make this a political issue—"

"Everything is a political issue. I thought I taught you that." Angus put down his book and stood up. "Bigfoot's out in the yard stretching his legs. Let him in, will you?"

"Our dog's name is not Bigfoot," McCabe said, heading toward the kitchen. "So when do you think we'll hear from Adam and Mai? Was there any estimate about how long the rescue will take?"

"My contacts are saying they should be off the island by tomorrow afternoon if everything goes according to plan."

"I've got to attend a funeral tomorrow afternoon," McCabe said. Angus followed her into the kitchen. "Whose funeral?"

McCabe opened the back door and the dog rushed in barking his greeting. She remembered in time he was not to be rewarded for barking. She turned away from him.

"He's learning," Angus said.

McCabe glanced over her shoulder. The dog had sat down. When she turned he whacked his tail against the floor, but he stayed seated. "Good boy," she said. "Good boy." She patted his spotted head.

Angus repeated, "Whose funeral?"

"Kevin Novak, the funeral director who was murdered. His daughter wants us to come to the funeral to observe for suspicious behavior. Her mother agreed. The lieutenant gave his permission. So Baxter and I are going to hang out in an anteroom and watch the service on camera."

"You really think the person who killed him is going to turn up at the funeral?"

"It's a private service. If the killer is in Kevin Novak's circle of friends and close acquaintances, then he or she is almost obliged to turn up or have a good excuse not to."

"Like having the flu or not being able to take time off from work?" Angus said. "A person would have to have good nerves to kill someone and then attend the funeral."

"Yes, a person would," McCabe said. "So if the killer's there, maybe he or she won't be able to pull it off."

25

Friday, January 24, 2020
11:45 A.M.

Beyond a few speeding tickets, the members of the church archery club had been law-abiding citizens. Research could find nothing on any of them that would suggest a reason for suspicion. But McCabe and Baxter spent the morning on their ORBs, speaking directly to the club members that they could reach and leaving tags asking the four others to get back to them.

No one they spoke to had anything useful to suggest about who might have murdered Kevin Novak or why. They were uniform in their expressions of shock, dismay, and sorrow. Kevin, they all said, had been a great husband and father, an outstanding member of his church and the community, the last person you'd expect to be murdered. It must be someone who had wandered in off the street, a stranger. No one who knew Kevin would wish him harm.

"Saint Kevin," Baxter said, putting down his ORB.

"Yeah," McCabe said. "Even the people who admitted he wasn't perfect—like being stubborn when he'd made up his mind—still thought he was a great guy."

"So where does that leave us? Do we want to round up the kids in the youth archery club and talk to them, too?"

"Sometimes kids can be a bit more candid than adults. But I don't know how much we'll get out of questioning them as a group in front of their parents."

"You were the one who told Wyatt we'd do that," Baxter reminded her.

"I know. And that could have been a tactical mistake. I was trying to keep him cooperating with us."

Baxter stood up and reached for his mug. "We probably wouldn't have gotten that much from the kids anyway."

"After the funeral, if we still don't have any other leads, we can do a group meeting if the lou signs off on it. Then, if any of the kids seem dodgy, we can follow up with individual interviews."

"Sounds like a plan. With kids, we're going to have parents to deal with whatever we do."

"But I think the church thing may be throwing me a little. Nudge me if I seem to be holding back and not doing something we'd normally do."

"Did you just say that, partner?"

"I'm willing to admit when I might need to reevaluate my approach to a case."

Baxter finished stirring sugar substitute into his coffee and took a sip. "I'll remind you of that the next time you mention Lisa Nichols."

"That case is closed." McCabe reached for her field bag. "I'll let the lou know we're on our way out."

From their vantage point in an anteroom adjacent to the sanctuary, McCabe and Baxter watched the mourners gathering outside and coming into the church. The cameras provided them with close-ups of faces that displayed various degrees of grief, all sharing the seriousness of expression appropriate to the occasion, and mourners greeting each other with handshakes or hugs.

McCabe wondered in passing if Kevin Novak had always planned to have a private service or if his wife had made that decision because of the way he had died. Either way, she was glad that they didn't have to cope with the ghouls—the morbidly curious—who turned up when the funeral of a crime victim was open to the public.

"Looks like the family cars are arriving," Baxter said.

On cam, they could see that two black limousines had pulled up. The man in the front passenger seat, a member of the funeral home staff, got out and opened the back door. He held out his hand to help Sarah Novak from the car. She was followed by Megan. Scott exited from the other side.

Kevin Novak's foster parents were dead. A woman and man who McCabe thought must be Sarah Novak's aunt and uncle from Baltimore got out of the other limousine with a younger woman and man who must be their daughter and her husband. The four followed Sarah Novak and her children into the church.

McCabe and Baxter followed their progress on another camera.

Olive Cooper had come in about ten minutes earlier, leaning on her cane and clutching the arm of the usher. She was seated in the pew behind the front row, which was reserved for the family. As Sarah Novak passed, Cooper reached out to offer her hand. Novak grasped it and seemed to waver. Scott put his arm around his mother. She nodded at him and smiled.

Olive Cooper dug a handkerchief from her purse and dabbed at her eyes.

When the family had settled into their seats, Reverend Wyatt stepped up to the podium. McCabe listened with half an ear to his opening words as she scanned the faces of the mourners.

Dr. Burdett was sitting a couple of rows behind Olive Cooper. He was watching the mourners, too. Was he checking for someone who might be in need of his services, McCabe wondered, or watching for suspicious behavior?

"See Burdett looking around?" she asked Baxter.

"Saw him," he said. "I wonder if he saw who slipped in the side door and sat down in back."

McCabe looked in the direction he was pointing. "Luanne Woodward."

"Dressed all in black, including a big, wide hat."

"If she's trying not to be noticed she should have skipped that hat," McCabe said. "I wonder how she got by the security guards at the doors."

"Southern charm?"

"Or Olive Cooper vouching for her."

"My bet would be Olive Cooper."

"Why would Luanne want to attend the funeral of a man she'd met only once?"

"Maybe she's still curious about why Kev turned tail and ran when Olive introduced them."

"Well, it's not like he's going to sit up in his coffin and tell her," McCabe said. "This funeral isn't quite Poe-ish enough for that."

" 'Poe-ish'? As in Edgar Allan?"

"Didn't you ever read that short story? The one with the corpse that's rigged to accuse the killer, 'Thou Art the Man,' " McCabe said. "Maybe Luanne thinks she can pick up some kind of vibes."

"By connecting with Kev while he's still aboveground?"

"Probably easier than when he's belowground."

McCabe's glance went to the gunmetal-silver coffin. Covered with a huge spray of red and white carnations, it was closed. She wondered if it had been open last night so that the mourners who came to the wake could view the man to whom they were saying good-bye.

"Luanne and Olive came in separately. If Olive did get her through security, maybe Luanne wants to give Olive deniability in case Reverend Wyatt sees her and gets annoyed."

"Except the security guards will probably rat Olive out if Wyatt starts asking questions."

"That would suggest Luanne might have been right about Olive tweaking her minister's nose. I wonder why."

"Especially since Olive said she likes the good reverend."

"Maybe she thinks he's too earnest and conservative. But I wonder if she thought about how Sarah Novak and her children would feel about having a medium at the funeral."

Baxter grinned. "Well, our Megan does like ghost stories. She might be on board with trying to contact her dad so Kevin can tell us whodunit."

McCabe smiled. "Yes, she just might." She glanced at the girl sitting with admirable composure beside her mother. "I like Megan."

"The kind of daughter you'd like to have someday," Baxter said.

"Based on your assumption that I want to have children?" McCabe asked. "It looks like we're about to start."

Clad in white robes trimmed in navy blue, the choir began to sing.

" 'Rock of Ages,' " Baxter said. "A golden oldie."

The song was followed by a prayer from Reverend Wyatt. When he was done, he said, "Sarah and her children will deliver the obituary for their husband and father."

The three Novaks stood up and made their way toward the stage. Baxter said, "That's gutsy."

"Maybe he requested it," McCabe said. "I wonder if that's also why they aren't wearing black."

Sarah Novak was dressed in a royal-blue sheath dress, Megan in a navy-blue skirt and white blouse, and Scott in a dark gray suit.

Novak said, "My son and daughter would like to tell you about their father."

Megan spoke first. "My father was a great dad. He taught me to skateboard and water ski and . . ." She flashed a grin. "And he taught me to play poker, but I wasn't supposed to tell Mom." An impish glance in her mother's direction. "And I probably shouldn't mention it in church."

Scott took over. "Sometimes being a great dad is just listening when you need someone to talk to. Our dad always listened."

"Well, not quite," Baxter said. "Didn't they tell us Kev had been getting an F on listening lately?"

McCabe said, "They're giving him a pass on that now that he's dead."

During the next fifteen minutes, Kevin Novak's children shared stories of their father. Their listeners smiled and even laughed. Some of them wiped away tears. As an obituary intended to celebrate the life of the deceased, McCabe thought, it was a hit.

The children and their mother walked off the stage and returned to their pew.

After a song from the choir, Reverend Wyatt returned to the podium to deliver his funeral sermon. "Some deaths test our faith. The death of a child or a young mother. The death of a man who is in the prime of his life. When a life is snatched away by human hands, we ask where God was in his mercy. How could he allow such evil? We weep and we curse and we wonder how we can go on believing when God allowed a good man to be murdered. . . ."

This was the second funeral McCabe had attended in three months. The other had been for an elderly black woman who had been killed by "droogie boys" who had wanted to make sure she wouldn't testify against them. The three juvenile gang members had been found and arrested. The cops who had worked that one had gotten a break because the victim had fought back and one of the suspects had left a trail of blood. No such luck with Kevin Novak's crime scene. FIU had gone over the funeral home basement. They'd found fingerprints belonging to Novak, his family, and his employees. No fingerprints on the bow except Kevin Novak's own. Smudges, probably from gloves. But no way to match those unless they found the killer with the gloves in his or her possession.

Not a whole lot to go on, McCabe thought. No footprints because of the snow. No signal from Kevin Novak's missing ORB. The only way they were going to connect the killer to the scene was to find the killer and work backward.

"The reverend's got them going," Baxter said. "Not a dry eye in the place."

"Tears at the funeral. Food afterward. And then everyone goes home and the family tries to carry on."

Baxter glanced at her. "Like that when your mother died?"

"I think it's always like that. It would be helpful to be able to fast-forward six months or a year." McCabe reached for the coffee thermos sitting on the table beside her. "All right, so we're sitting here watching the funeral. And everyone is behaving as we would expect mourners to behave."

"The only thing unexpected is our friendly medium from down south among the mourners. Want to try to catch up with her after this is over and hear what she has to say about that?"

"Good idea. I really would like to hear why she's here."

When McCabe and Baxter caught up with her, Luanne Woodward was waiting for the elevator to the underground parking garage. The garage had been reserved for funeral attendees.

"Well, hello, Ms. Woodward," McCabe said. "We didn't expect to see you here."

"Hello. And I told you all to call me Luanne. I came along with Olive. Actually, I drove her out here. I was talking to her last night after she got back from the wake. She told me the funeral service was today, and she asked if I'd like to come."

Baxter said, "Odd she did that when you had only met Kevin Novak that one time at her party."

"Her celebration of life, you mean. And you see that was the point. That I did meet poor Kevin just before he died and he wouldn't stay to talk to me. And Olive and I were talking about whether I might have been able to help him if he had."

"But," McCabe said, "even if you had been able to talk to him . . . he was murdered."

Woodward's round face was somber under the wide-brimmed hat. "But if I had been able to speak with him, to relieve his mind a bit, maybe he would have stayed at home with his family that night instead of going to the funeral home. If he hadn't been there, maybe he'd still be alive."

"That's possible," McCabe said. "But Mr. Novak was conscientious. He would probably have gone to the funeral home to check on the bodies no matter what his state of mind."

"There's no way for us to know. And that's what's bothering me. Maybe that's why I was sent here to Albany . . . to help Kevin. And if that was the reason, I failed him."

McCabe nodded. "So that was what drew you to the funeral."

"And I'm glad I came to pay my respects. But I'd better be leaving before Reverend Wyatt sees me and gets his nose out of joint."

"Aren't you going to wait and give Olive a lift?" Baxter asked.

"No, she told me not to worry myself about that. She said her great-niece Paige would pick her up." Luanne smiled. "She said she's letting her earn her way back into her will. Child must have gotten on Olive's bad side."

"It sounds like it," McCabe said. "Well, we won't keep you if you need to go."

Woodward smiled. "We'll be speaking again real soon."

The elevator came back for the third time, and Woodward waved as she edged her way in with the next group.

"I wonder why she was so sure she'd see us again," Baxter said.

"Psychic," McCabe said.

"But she told us she was a medium, not a psychic."

"I'm not sure what she is. But I have a feeling she might turn out to be useful. Let's have a look at the surveillance cam for the garage before we go."

"I'm sorry the Widow Sarah's opting for a family-only interment," Baxter said. "I always like those movie cemetery scenes where the detectives are standing on the edge of the crowd watching."

26

McCabe checked the readout on the police frequency of her ORB. "Wayne Jacoby," she told Baxter, who was driving. "Must be important, he's on private comm."

"You got something for us, Jacoby?" she asked when the PIO came into view. "Something happening with the media?"

"All hell's breaking loose with the media, McCabe. What I want to know is why you didn't give me a heads-up."

"A heads-up about what? We're on our way back from Kevin Novak's funeral, but nothing happened there."

"I'm talking about your brother."

"My brother?"

"Dr. Adam McCabe. Recently stranded with other tourists on a resort island."

"I told Lt. Dole about that in case I had to leave for some kind of emergency."

"Howard Miller has been objecting to the use of government military resources to carry out the rescue."

"I know that. He said the tourists on the island should pay for their own rescue."

"Apparently, he had a closer look at the list of people rescued from the island. And he saw the name 'McCabe' and remembered that the lead detective in the Lisa Nichols murder case also had been named McCabe."

"Oh hell!"

"And in his own inimical way, Miller managed to tie your brother's presence among the well-heeled tourists President Kirkland was spending money to rescue from their resort island to the murder case in Albany involving the former fiancée of billionaire Ted Thornton."

"Wayne, I'll talk to you about this later. I have to try to reach Adam and warn him that the media—"

"Your brother already knows. The press was there when the rescued tourists got off the ship half an hour ago. They had no trouble recognizing your brother coming off in his wheelchair. They got some really prime footage of his glares and 'no comments' and then an especially nice sound bite when he told a reporter to shove it."

"Oh, no."

"That happened when the reporter asked him about being shot and paralyzed by a burglar, who his sister, even though she was only nine years old, had no hesitation about shooting and killing."

McCabe cursed—a fluent, extended curse.

Jacoby chuckled. "Language seems to run in your family."

"I didn't learn that in my family. I learned it from the cop who was my field training officer. He advised me to save it for occasions that merited such self-expression. And this isn't even slightly humorous, Jacoby. Right now, aside from my brother being harassed because of me, probably everyone from the mayor on down—"

"It isn't that bad, McCabe. But it would have been nice if I had known we might get caught up in this."

"I know. I'm sorry. I should have realized that if Howard Miller was complaining about the rescue, he would seize on anything that he could find to make it look even worse."

"Well, at least, no one in the department—including you—did anything wrong. Now that I know what we're dealing with, I can come up with a statement," Jacoby said. "But you may have to tip-toe through this one with the commander. The mayor called him in after she saw Miller's press conference. He called in Lieutenant Dole. And both of them are likely to be waiting for you when you get back to the station house."

"Thanks for the warning, Jacoby."

"You're welcome. Don't sweat it. It's not like you could control where your brother went on vacation or that he isn't crazy about reporters."

"I think," McCabe said, "that after being stuck for a week on an island that had been hit by an earthquake, my brother might be excused for not being terribly patient when he was bombarded with questions by idiot reporters."

Laughing, Jacoby held up his hands. "Don't get your Irish up again, McCabe. I agree. That's what I'm going to say . . . leaving out the 'idiot.' No one would ever guess that you're related to a former newspaper editor."

"My father was a real journalist, not a bloodsucking parasite."

"Yes, ma'am. Point made. And I'll talk to you later."

"I really am sorry, Jacoby. Next time, I'll remember you need to be kept in the loop. Although I hope there won't be a next time."

"Just remember not to curse like your brother if you find your-self ambushed by a reporter."

"I'll keep that in mind."

"Do that."

McCabe turned to meet Baxter's glance. "If you'd ever like to request a change of partners—"

"Wouldn't think of it. Hanging out with you is fascinating. Never know what's going to happen next."

"It makes me sick to my stomach to think Howard Miller knows my name and he and his people are discussing me and my family."

"Don't let it worry you, partner. Sooner or later, old Howard will get his comeuppance."

"Will he?" McCabe said. "I wish I could believe that. I wish I could believe only a handful of people are even considering voting for him for president."

"Saw your brother on the news stream," Angie Hogancamp, the second-watch desk sergeant, remarked as McCabe and Baxter came in.

"I didn't see him, but heard about it," McCabe said.

"That reporter was up in his face," Hogancamp said.

And Adam, McCabe thought, was not inclined to allow people to get up in his face.

McCabe knocked on Lt. Dole's office door. "Sir, you probably want to see me, right?"

Dole waved her in. "Come in and sit down."

McCabe slid into one of the chairs opposite his desk. "About what happened with my brother, sir—"

"The commander and I had a discussion about that. He said to tell you to avoid conversations with the press and to ask your brother and father to do the same. He'd appreciate it if you would ask your father not to take this opportunity to write an editorial about Howard Miller."

"My father is retired, sir."

"But he still has access if he wants to write an editorial. Having Miller go after you and your brother might make him want to do that."

"I'll ask my father to restrain himself, sir. But I can't control his actions."

"We understand that. Just suggest to him it might be better to let this one go."

"Yes, sir, I'll pass on that suggestion. I'll remind my father that he has never approved of journalists who use their positions to even personal scores. Is there anything else?"

"Do your best to get the Novak murder solved. As in, having this become a cold case is highly undesirable. Do you need more support with this one?"

"Thank you, sir, but I'm not sure having more people working on it would help. It's not like the serial killer case when we were worried about more women being killed and needed as many people working on it as we could get." McCabe paused. "The truth is, sir, this case is just weird. It doesn't seem to be a crime committed by a stranger, but so far we haven't found anyone among Kevin Novak's friends and acquaintances who seem to have a motive."

"I take it nothing happened at the funeral."

"Only Luanne Woodward, the medium, showing up. She came with Olive Cooper."

McCabe told him what Woodward had said about why she was there.

"Her reason for coming to Albany still sounds fishy to me," Dole said.

"Yes, sir, but I guess if you're into the paranormal, listening to your inner voice is what you do. And unless she's able to be in two places at once, she's not a suspect in Novak's murder. We've checked her alibi, and she was in Boston."

"That doesn't mean she isn't planning some kind of con."

"No, sir, it doesn't. Baxter and I will have another look at her to see if we might have missed something. In fact, it's probably time we looked again at everything we have to see if we've missed anything."

"Good idea. You on tomorrow?"

"No, sir. It's my weekend off. If my brother and his girlfriend make it home by then, we'll probably do a family dinner."

27

In the farmer's market, McCabe waved her ORB over the display of speckled yellow eggplant. The nutritional content and a suggested recipe came up. She added two of the eggplants to her shopping basket. Her next stop was the bakery. She was debating whether she should splurge on the pricey organic coconut cake when her ORB buzzed.

McCabe stepped away from the counter, out of the way of a mother with two small children who were demanding gingerbread cookies.

Walter Yin came into view on her monitor. "Hannah, sorry to bother you on what's supposed to be your day off."

"That's okay. What's up?"

"A woman named Olive Cooper's trying to reach you. She says it's urgent she speak to you."

"Thanks, I'll get back to her now."

McCabe walked over to a bench by one of the warehouse

windows and put down her shopping basket. She pulled up Cooper's ORB code.

When Cooper answered, she was holding a sleek black cat with emerald-green eyes. White hair loose and flowing to her shoulders, Olive looked as if she might have cast a few spells in her day.

McCabe couldn't resist asking, "Does your cat know Ted Thornton's cat, Horatio?"

"They've met. They didn't care for each other. Esme found Horatio presumptuous."

"You wanted to speak to me."

"I'm having a séance tonight. I want you and your partner, young Baxter, to attend."

"A séance? With Luanne Woodward?"

"I'm busy now rounding up the people who ought to be here."

"Who ought to be there? Who would those people be, exactly? Is Luanne planning to try to . . . Is this about Kevin Novak?"

"Would I be making a point of inviting you and your partner if it wasn't?" Cooper said, her tone brisk. "Sarah has already agreed to come."

"She has?" McCabe said, feeling as if she were one step behind in this conversation. "She's agreed to come to a séance the day after her husband's funeral?"

"Exactly what she said—she was offended and outraged I could 'even suggest' such a thing."

"But then she changed her mind and agreed to come?"

"She didn't have much choice in the matter. Megan overheard our conversation. When her mother said no, Megan said she wanted to have a séance. She wanted to see if we could reach her father. Sarah tried to argue with her, but Megan was getting upset."

"And so Sarah agreed to come to your séance and bring her daughter."

"I would have thought you'd be pleased to hear I've taken on the task of putting this together. Luanne told me when she offered to do a séance, you thanked her and said you'd give it some thought."

And she had been thinking about it, McCabe admitted to herself. A quirky, back of the mind, last-ditch effort idea. But only to be invoked if they had reason to think Kevin Novak's murderer might be among the people he had known well. And she hadn't gotten as far as figuring out how they would get sensible people to agree to participate in an effort to contact a dead man.

"Has anyone else but Sarah Novak agreed to attend this séance you're planning?"

"I waited until I knew it was going to fly before I bothered to contact you. Jonathan Burdett will be here. Said he was sure it would be interesting as a psychological experiment. I expect Daniel to come, too."

"You do? Reverend Wyatt has agreed to take part?"

"I told him about it, and he expressed his disapproval. First, he'll do his best to talk the others out of coming. When he can't do that, I expect he'll come to try to stop it."

"Why are you sure he won't be able to change their minds?"

"Because they're all curious—even Sarah. They want to know if it can be done."

McCabe suspected there might be more than that behind Olive Cooper's confidence, but she let that go for the moment. "Who else is coming?"

"Bob's fancy French wife, Francesca. She was the only one who seemed pleased to be invited. She said she'd been questioned by you and your partner."

And she had asked Reeves not to get involved, McCabe thought. But apparently an invitation to a séance had been too much to resist.

"Ted Thornton and his assistant, Bruce Ashby, will give us ten," Olive Cooper said. "Eleven if we can get Daniel to join us. But I'm not counting on that."

"Why did you invite . . . why do you want Ted Thornton and his aide to take part in your séance?"

Cooper's gaze narrowed. "I thought you might want them to be here. Ted told me about the visit you and your partner paid him.

He said you were interested in how Ashby came to choose Kevin to contact about burying Ted's 'killer blonde.' "

McCabe said, "I don't suppose you call her that when you're talking to him."

"I'm not that heartless," Cooper said. "I was being sarcastic. The woman was crazy as a loon. Her hair color had nothing to do with it, unless the dye had affected her brain."

"I take it you had met her."

"A couple of times. She didn't impress me either time. But men like Ted have a way of falling hard when they fall. Doesn't make a bit of difference if they're smart, hard-driving businessmen. A woman comes along and gives them the right smile, and they're goners."

"Did Mr. Thornton express any reluctance about coming to a séance so soon after his ex-fiancée's death?"

"He didn't seem bothered by that. He did say he isn't convinced there's an afterlife. I said, in that case, it would do him no harm to come and indulge an old woman—who happens to be a prominent member of one of his boards."

"Anyone else going to be there that we should know about?"

"That should be it. Ten at the table. Eleven if Daniel can overcome his objections and agrees to join us. But, as I said, that's not likely. I'll expect you and your partner at my house no later than eight P.M."

"I'm not sure about this, Ms. Cooper. It's rather an unusual invitation. I need to speak to my supervisor, Lieutenant Dole. I'm also not sure my partner, Detective Baxter, is available. We're both off this weekend, and—"

"I'll see you tonight. Don't bother to eat first. Velma will have a spread laid out."

"Ms. Cooper, I'm really not—"

She was talking to the air. Cooper and her cat were gone.

It was, McCabe thought, unseemly and even offensive to have a séance on the day after a man's funeral. Especially when the man's young daughter had been used to coerce her mother into taking part. But the evening might prove illuminating. Unlikely that Kevin Novak would turn up during the séance. But the situation—with this group of people in the same room—might shake something loose and give them a lead.

As she thought this, McCabe realized that she was much more inclined to believe Kevin Novak had been killed by someone he'd known than to accept the random-stranger-from-off-the-street theory. If no one at the séance had killed Novak, one or more of them might know why someone had wanted him dead.

Like Dr. Burdett, for instance. Or, Reverend Wyatt, who was holding something back, something that he knew about Kevin. And then there was Francesca Reeves, who might know more about what was going on than she claimed. Even Sarah Novak might know more than she was telling them . . . or not be what she seemed.

Gathering the suspects for a séance was not in the manual on homicide investigations. But if someone else proposed doing the gathering, there was no reason she and Baxter shouldn't be there to see what happened.

Unless Lt. Dole disagreed with that analysis of the situation.

McCabe reached for her ORB.

"You want to what?" Dole said.

"I know it's a little strange, sir. But if they're all going to be there, and Olive Cooper has invited Baxter and me—"

"What an eccentric old woman does for her amusement is none of our business. Have you given any thought at all to how this would look if the media got ahold of it? Clarence Redfield might even come out of retirement as a threader to report this one if he heard you and Ted Thornton were both at a séance."

"I think Thornton is coming because Olive Cooper is a friend and on one of his boards. She says he isn't convinced there is an afterlife."

"What Thornton believes has nothing to do with how this would look if—"

"Sir, I really don't think anyone there is likely to call the media and tell them."

"I'll meet you and Baxter in my office at two o'clock. Find him and get him there. Meantime, I'll see if I can reach the commander and run this by him." Dole ran his hand over his scalp and sighed. "If we hadn't just had that dustup with Howard Miller and your brother, I'd actually agree to this. When you get a bunch of nervous people in the same room . . . but under the circumstances, McCabe, we'd better get the commander to sign off."

"Yes, sir. I understand."

"It's annoying as hell to have Howard Miller affecting what we do in a murder investigation."

"Yes, sir."

McCabe thought of her promise to Wayne Jacoby to keep him in the loop. Well, if the commander gave them permission to attend the séance, she would suggest then that they should give Jacoby a heads-up, just in case.

She needed to find Mike. And she needed to let her father, Adam, and Mai know tonight's family dinner might have to be Sunday brunch instead. She had accepted Pettigrew's assurance that he would be able to occupy his Saturday afternoon and evening if she canceled out on the classic crime festival they had planned to attend. Now it looked like instead of film festival or family reunion dinner, she might be attending a séance.

"Okay, the lou's not here," Baxter said. "Tell the truth. You swear you didn't secretly put Olive and her medium up to this?"

It was Saturday evening. They had driven over in their own cars and arrived at the same time. Several other cars were already parked on the street in front of the house.

"Yes, Michael, I swear. I may have joked about a séance. I may even have thought about recruiting Luanne if we needed a last-ditch ploy, but I absolutely did not suggest this. It's a little grotesque the day after the funeral."

"If she really wants to rattle some cages, maybe that's what our girl Olive is counting on. I hope she's still doing her witch imitation with the black cat."

"That might not have been deliberate. She might have been too busy summoning people to the séance to worry about putting her hair up in a bun. And the cat was named Esme."

"But it was black with emerald eyes," Baxter said, grinning. "Sounds like a familiar to me."

"Black animals get a bad rap," McCabe said. "Getting back to the subject at hand, I've been thinking about what Lieutenant Dole said about not being able to control what happens. If something weird does happen—"

"You mean if Kev actually does show up during the séance?"

"Or if Luanne—maybe with Olive's help—tries to make it look like he's attempting to make contact."

"That should get some reaction."

"Yes, and the reactions could range from shrieks and fainting to accusing Luanne of being a con artist."

Baxter shrugged. "Nothing we can do but see how it goes. We should be able to handle whatever happens . . . unless we end up with another body."

"Do not say that. Don't even think it." McCabe tugged at the collar of her jacket. "Okay, we're here. Let's go in and see what happens."

Velma, Olive Cooper's housekeeper, opened the door at their ring. They scraped their shoes on the mat and handed her their coats.

"Go on into the living room," she said, gesturing toward the room off to the left. "Everyone who's here already is in there having refreshments."

The voices coming from the living room were muted. When McCabe and Baxter walked into the room, conversation stopped altogether. They seemed to have that effect on these people, McCabe thought.

The expressions on the faces of Cooper's guests—Sarah Novak and her two children sitting on the sofa, Dr. Burdett standing by the window holding a glass, and Francesca Reeves at the buffet table, helping herself to appetizers—suggested that Cooper had not told them the detectives were expected.

"Hello," McCabe said. "Ms. Cooper invited us to join you for the séance. I hope no one minds."

Luanne Woodward, standing beside Dr. Burdett, smiled. "I'm so glad you could make it. Olive told me she had invited you."

"Olive forgot to mention that to the rest of us," Burdett said. "But I assume she thought you would find this experiment of interest."

"She thought I would as well," Francesca Reeves said. "Find this interesting, I mean."

Megan said, "Do you think if Luanne can contact my father he might tell you who killed him?"

The question was raw and hard to hear.

McCabe said, "We're keeping an open mind about that, Megan. We're not sure that Ms. Woodward will be able to contact your father, so you shouldn't get your hopes up. No offense, Luanne."

"None taken. Sometimes it works and sometimes it doesn't. But Olive and I thought it would be worth a try."

"And really not weird at all," Baxter said.

Scott said, "That's what I tried to tell my Mom and Megan. That this is weird. We shouldn't be doing this."

"Daddy believed in an afterlife," Megan said. "Didn't he, Mommy? And if we can reach him and find out—" She took a deep breath and lifted her chin. "Then that's what we ought to do. We owe it to, Daddy. Don't we, Mommy?"

Novak hugged her daughter and kissed the top of her head. "If this will make you feel better, sweetheart, we'll give it a try."

"It'll make me feel better," Megan said. "Even if it doesn't work."

Scott said, "I still think this is stupid."

"That's you," Megan said. "Me and Mommy want to do it."

McCabe wondered if she had missed that before. Had Megan been calling her mother "Mommy"? Daddy for Kevin, but hadn't Sarah Novak been "Mom"?

And was it really wrong to involve a child of thirteen in a séance even if she wanted to do it? Sarah Novak seemed to think agreeing to what her daughter wanted was better than upsetting her. But if the séance didn't work . . . and it was highly unlikely it would . . .

McCabe gave herself a mental shake. She was here to observe the suspects, not worry about Megan Novak's emotional health. That was her mother's job. Something Sarah Novak was likely to be better at than a homicide cop with no children.

The doorbell rang again. "That should be Ted," Olive Cooper said as she came into the living room leaning on her cane. Cooper's hair was back in its tidy bun, but the black cat was with her. Esme trailed after her mistress but didn't weave around Cooper's feet. Training or instinct, McCabe wondered.

Megan reached down and held out her hand. "Hi, Esme. Come here, Esme."

The cat bounded across the room. Megan rubbed between the cat's ears and nuzzled its chin. When the girl leaned back, the cat sprang up into her lap and settled in to be stroked.

A look of what McCabe interpreted as relief passed over Sarah Novak's face.

"Good evening, everyone," Ted Thornton said from the doorway. As usual, he was flanked by his aide, Bruce Ashby. "Sorry we're a little late."

Olive Cooper said, "You're wearing a suit. I take it you're coming from a meeting you actually thought you should dress for."

Thornton opened his dark eyes wide. "Olive, didn't I understand you to tell me not to come to your house again wearing my worn-out blue jeans?"

Cooper smiled. "So this is in my honor?"

Thornton sobered. "And under the circumstances." He went over to Sarah Novak. "My condolences, Mrs. Novak. I never met your husband, but I understand he was a good man."

She looked up at him from the sofa. "Thank you, Mr. Thornton.

I'm sorry about . . . I heard about your loss, too. Your fiancée . . . former fiancée . . ."

"I hadn't quite figured out what to call her, either," he said. "And it is a bit odd, isn't it? Your husband a victim and my ex-fiancée . . ." He trailed off. "Well, no need to go into that. Lisa isn't why we're here."

"Why are you here, anyway?" Scott said. "If you never met my dad, why are you here?"

"Scott!" Sarah Novak said. "Don't be rude."

"It's a legitimate question," Thornton said. He held the teenager's gaze. "Scott, I'm here because Olive invited me. Simple as that." He turned to look at Olive. "I assume Ms. Cooper needed Bruce and me to round out the number at the table."

Megan's hand had stilled on the cat's back. "How many should be at the table for a séance?" she asked.

Woodward said, "It doesn't really matter, honey. Some mediums are superstitious, and don't like to have thirteen people. I think the only problem with thirteen is that it is hard to find a round table in most people's houses that can accommodate that many folks. But some mediums are still back in the old days when people used to believe the number thirteen was unlucky."

Megan nodded. "Daddy and I had a conversation about that once when he was telling me about the old superstitions."

Woodward said, "Now that we're all here, Olive, do you want to get started? Or do you want us to eat first?"

"If anyone's hungry, please help yourself to more appetizers," Cooper said. "Velma will have supper ready for us after the séance."

McCabe happened to be looking in Sarah Novak's direction and saw her wince.

"If you'll forgive us, Olive, the children and I will go after the . . . after we're done. It'll be getting late for them."

"I'll have Velma pack your supper to take home."

Francesca Reeves said, "Didn't you mention Reverend Wyatt might be joining us, Olive?"

"I was sure he would. But he apparently had business else-where."

Jonathan Burdett said, "I spoke to Daniel before I left to come over. He was somewhat distressed that he hadn't been able to talk Sarah or you, Olive, out of going forward with this. He was think-ing of coming to make one last attempt to change your minds, but apparently he decided not to do that."

"Must have realized it would be a waste of his time," Cooper said. "So we're all here, then. Shall we go into the solarium? Luanne thought that would be the ideal location."

"Why?" Megan asked. She hugged the cat to her as she got up. "Why is that a good location?"

"I like the vibrations in that room," Woodward said. "And we may get a bit of moonlight."

"Go on," Cooper said, leaning on her cane. "I'm slow tonight. I'll bring up the rear."

"May I offer you my arm?" Ted Thornton asked.

Cooper smiled up at him. "Thank you, gallant sir."

They led the way out of the room.

Bruce Ashby, who was walking beside Luanne Woodward, said, "I thought a séance was supposed to be done in a dark room. Or, at least, only by candlelight."

"I believe in allowing natural light to enter in when it will," Woodward told him. "I think that makes it more hospitable for the spirits we want to summon."

Scott said, "What if the wrong spirits come?"

Woodward looked over her shoulder and smiled. "You don't have to worry about that, sweetheart. Nothing bad will get past Luanne. I won't let that happen."

Baxter and McCabe were bringing up the rear of the procession to the solarium. He mouthed, "Woo-woo."

She shook her head at him, but silently agreed. Luanne stand-ing at the portal holding back evil spirits was a step too far.

But Scott seemed satisfied with her explanation. He had put his arm around his sister's shoulders. "You going to take that cat to the séance?"

Megan called out, "Is it all right for Esme to come to the séance, Olive?"

"Fine with me," Cooper said, "if Luanne won't find a cat in the room a distraction."

"Not a'tall," Woodward said. "I like cats. Especially black ones."

And this was getting stranger by the minute, McCabe thought. But they'd come this far.

28

From the front, Olive Cooper's sandstone mansion had appeared to have two levels. When they entered the solarium, McCabe realized the house was designed to fit the downhill slope of the property. They were on the second floor with living quarters above and a lower level, probably the basement, below. Beyond the glass walls of the solarium there was a small balcony and steps leading down to what must be an expanse of lawn.

Although Woodward had mentioned moonlight, when they entered the room, the lights were on: Pale hardwood floor with rugs scattered about. White sofas and chairs. And, taking up the back section of the room opposite the door leading onto the balcony, a large round table more than adequate to seat them all.

On the table, there was a candelabrum holding three white taper candles.

"What's the bell for?" Scott asked, pointing at the silver bell beside the candelabrum.

Woodward said, "It's called a spirit bell. It will allow any spirit who wants to contact us to let us know he's here."

"By ringing the bell?" Francesca Reeves asked, but didn't wait for an answer. "Do you want us to sit in any particular order?"

"Wherever you're comfortable, whoever you're moved to sit beside. I'm going to sit right here. And, yes, ma'am, I will ask any spirit who joins us to make the bell ring. Now please sit down, everyone."

McCabe and Baxter headed for opposite halves of the circle. Maximum coverage.

Sarah Novak had sat down between her two children.

McCabe sat down beside Megan.

When she glanced over, she saw that Baxter was seated next to Francesca Reeves, who had sat down next to Scott.

Bruce Ashby was on Baxter's other side. McCabe smiled to herself as she imagined Ashby holding hands with Baxter. As she thought that, Ashby turned his head and saw Baxter. He had been so busy planting himself next to Luanne that he hadn't noticed Baxter was about to take the seat on his other side. The look he gave McCabe's partner could only be described as sour.

Baxter nodded at Ashby and grinned.

Ted Thornton settled Olive Cooper in the chair next to Jonathan Burdett, who had grabbed the place on Luanne's right.

Between the two men, Ashby and Burdett, Luanne would be hard pressed to get away with any kind of sleight of hand. In fact, neither was likely to let go of her hand.

That worked for McCabe. Luanne was unlikely to let go of their hands either.

"Looks like this seat is mine," Ted Thornton said. He sat down between McCabe and his friend, Olive.

And there they were, McCabe thought. Ten people seated around a round table in a solarium waiting for the eleventh among them to do her stuff.

"The lights are still on," Megan said.

"Got them," Thornton replied.

He was obviously familiar with the house. He strode over to the wall switch. "Ready?" he asked Luanne Woodward.

"Just a moment. Let me get the candles." She stood up, drawing a bulky old cigarette lighter from her pocket. "There we go," she said, when all three candles were lit. She sat back down in her chair and nodded to Ted Thornton. "Anytime you're ready, thank you, sir. Then if you'll come back to the table."

"And we'll all join hands," Baxter said.

"Must we do that?" Ashby asked Woodward.

"Absolutely, hon, that part we have to do. We need to form an unbroken circle."

"It's all right, Ashby," Baxter said. "I washed my hands after I used the john."

Megan giggled. Ashby shot Baxter another sour look.

Sarah said to her daughter, "I don't think it's a good idea for Esme to sit on your lap while we're doing this."

Megan put the cat on the floor. "Stay by my chair, Esme."

"Perhaps I shouldn't repeat the question," Burdett said. "But are you sure a cat in the room is a good idea? If something should happen to startle it . . ."

"Esme is a very calm cat," replied Olive Cooper.

That settled the matter.

"Lights going out," Ted Thornton said from his station by the wall.

Megan gave a small gasp.

Her mother said, "Megan, if you're frightened—"

"I'm all right, Mom. I just need to let my eyes adjust to the dark."

"Mom" again, McCabe thought. Good.

The January night was cloudy, but there was enough moonlight to spill through the solarium ceiling and find its way through the glass walls. The room was in twilight with the lit tapers burning on the table.

"Lovely," Francesca Reeves said.

Ted Thornton sat back down and edged his chair closer to the table.

"Please take hands now," Luanne Woodward said. "And I'll ask you to be silent. No matter what happens, please don't speak unless I—or the person we are trying to reach speaking through me— address you by name."

McCabe took Megan's hand. It was cold and moist. McCabe gave the girl's hand a little squeeze.

On her other side, Thornton's long-fingered hand closed around McCabe's. His palm felt rough to the touch, as if the skin were scraped. She hadn't noticed that the last time they shook hands. He must have been doing something without gloves. What would that have been? McCabe wondered. Thornton was an outdoorsman and adventurer. Maybe he had gone out and climbed a mountain since she and Baxter visited him to ask about why Ashby had contacted Kevin Novak.

His hand was not cold or moist. In fact, he seemed to be quite comfortable with the proceedings. Obviously, he wasn't expecting Luanne to connect with Lisa Nichols, his dead ex-fiancée. Nichols, dead and still crazy, would be sufficient to chill anyone.

She felt Thornton's glance. He leaned toward her as if he were about to whisper something. Before he could speak, Luanne said, "I'm going to blow out the candles one by one. There is nothing to be afraid of. We are all safe here."

Thornton leaned back in his chair.

Luanne said, "We are going to breathe together, in harmony. Take a deep breath and release it slowly. Let your body begin to relax. Another breath . . ."

In spite of her intention to stay alert, McCabe found herself being lulled by the sound of Luanne's voice. She hadn't gotten enough sleep last night, she thought. It had been late when she reached Adam, but she had been relieved when he assured her that he was holding Howard Miller solely responsible for shoving him into the spotlight. Of course—and Mai had pointed this out—he might have done a better job of controlling his temper when he'd gotten that question from the reporter about the burglar and the shooting. Losing his temper was playing right into Miller's propaganda.

McCabe had been grateful that Miller hadn't derailed the progress that she and Adam had been making toward mending their relationship. But she had still tossed and turned before falling asleep.

"I'm going to blow out another candle," Luanne said. "But I

want you to go on breathing gently, breathing in harmony with each other. Go on holding hands. Remember the circle must be unbroken. Keep holding the hand of the person on either side of you."

McCabe felt her eyelids drifting closed. She forced them open and straightened in her chair, glancing around her. Over at Baxter. His eyes were open, too. He was glancing around the table.

McCabe slid a glance to her left, at Thornton. His dark eyes glistened in the dim light. Obviously, Mr. Thornton did not intend to go under.

Ashby, on the other hand, seemed to be drifting. McCabe saw his head jerk.

She couldn't tell if Burdett was feeling the effects of Luanne's relaxation technique. His head seemed to be bowed, but he might have been faking.

Before she could look at Olive Cooper, Luanne blew out the third candle.

At that same moment, the moon disappeared behind a cloud.

Someone—McCabe thought it was Francesca Reeves— whispered something, maybe only a gasped "Oh!"

Luanne said, "It's all right. Continue to breathe, breathing together. Let yourself relax in this warm, safe place. A place where we can welcome Kevin Novak's departed spirit to us."

McCabe had the sense a sigh had passed around the table. A whisper of sound. She found herself wishing the moon would come from behind the clouds again. A little light would be welcome.

You're not afraid of the dark, she told herself.

Thornton's hand tightened ever so slightly around her own. She did not look at him. She wouldn't have been able to see his expression in the dark anyway.

Megan, on her other side, was clutching her hand so tightly that McCabe wanted to flex her fingers. But she stayed still.

Her nostrils twitched. What was that odor? Something barely there, but familiar.

"Kevin," Luanne said. "Kevin, we want to welcome you among

us. We want you to join us here. Your family is here, Kevin. Sarah and Megan and Scott. They want to speak to you."

Megan squeezed even tighter on McCabe's hand. McCabe wondered if she was doing the same to her mother on the other side, or if she was focusing all her anxiety in the hand that was clutching McCabe's. If Sarah Novak knew how frightened her daughter was, she might well stop this now.

Maybe they should stop it before . . . what the devil was that odor? Something she knew.

"Kevin, if you're here," Luanne was saying. "Kevin, ring the spirit bell to let us know you're here."

They all held their breath, waiting. Nothing.

On the other side of the table, Jonathan Burdett cleared his throat. "I think this—"

"Be quiet, please," Luanne said. "We have to wait, we have to give him time. Kevin, we—"

The bell jangled. Once. Twice.

Gasps passed around the table.

"Keep holding hands," Luanne said. "The circle must be unbroken. Kevin, do you want to speak to your family?"

"Daddy?" Megan said. "Daddy, are you really here?"

The bell jangled again. But this time, the sound was above the table, in the air above them. The bell was ringing over their heads.

Afterward, McCabe wasn't sure of the order of events. Whether the scream—from Sarah or Francesca—came before or after the bell crashed to the table. Whether Megan let go of her hand before or after Esme, the cat, ran past their legs from under the table. Whether the outer door to the solarium blew open at the same time something on the other side of the room fell to the floor and shattered.

"Don't move," Luanne said. "Don't move. I'm going to light the candles. Stay where you are. Continue to hold hands."

Megan drew a shuddering breath and fumbled for McCabe's hand. On Megan's other side, McCabe heard Sarah Novak whisper, "It's all right, baby. Everything's all right."

The first candle flared up. The second. And then the third. The people at the table glanced around, seeking information from one another.

"I think . . ." Thornton said, "Olive, I really think this is enough for one evening. I'm going to turn on the lights now."

Cooper had her head turned toward Luanne Woodward. McCabe couldn't make out her expression. But she was staring at the medium, who was looking down at the table.

"Olive," Thornton said. "Did you hear what I said?"

"Yes, yes," she said. "Turn on the lights. We're done."

Thornton let McCabe's hand go, and she realized she had forgotten he was still holding it. He got up. A moment later, the lights in the ceiling fixtures came on.

"What fell?" Burdett asked.

"First, the bell that was supposed to be on the table," Ashby said. "And then something over on the other side of the room."

Reeves stood up. "It sounded like something made of glass."

She headed off to investigate, and the others followed her.

Except for Luanne, who was staring at the bell that was now back on the table. And Olive Cooper, who was staring into space, her expression unreadable.

Baxter had followed the others. McCabe said, "Aren't you interested in what fell, Ms. Cooper?"

"I know what it was. I have a large crystal vase on the side table—had a vase, I should say."

McCabe looked from one woman to the other. "Was this rigged? Was it all smoke and mirrors?"

Luanne Woodward shook her head. She turned and looked at Olive Cooper.

Cooper said, "We had planned something in case Kevin didn't respond."

Woodward said, "But what happened wasn't what we planned."

"So what you're telling me," McCabe said, "what you want me to believe is that the spirit bell rose in the air and rang over our heads and the outer door blew open and the vase fell, all without any help from the two of you."

"That's what we're telling you," Cooper said.

"Someone . . . or something was here," Woodward said. "But I don't think it was Kevin."

McCabe said, "We have had enough of this for one night."

"More than enough," Cooper agreed. She reached for her cane and pushed back her chair with a burst of vigor. "Everyone, don't worry about the vase. Velma will clean it up. Let's go into the dining room."

McCabe waited until Cooper had gotten around the table and began to herd her muttering and shell-shocked guests toward the food. Then she leaned across the table where Woodward was still sitting.

"I want the truth," she said. "Were you responsible for what happened here tonight? I don't care if you are a fake. I'm not interested in what con you might be up to. I have a murder investigation going on."

"I'm not a fake, honey. Sometimes I'm able to reach those who have passed over and sometimes I'm not. But I'm not a fake. And I didn't ring that bell up in the air or slam open that door or make that vase fall. Something else did that."

"Something? But not Kevin?"

"Not unless he's awful angry."

"He was murdered," McCabe said. "That might have pissed him off."

Woodward nodded. "That can do it. A violent death. But I thought with his daughter here wanting to speak to him . . . I hear he loved his daughter and his wife and son. No matter how angry he is, I don't think he would have behaved like that with them here."

"Right," McCabe said. "So you think it was some other malevolent spirit."

"That's what I think, honey."

"Then I guess you'd better watch out."

"We all had," Woodward said as McCabe turned away. McCabe kept walking.

She'd convinced Lt. Dole to allow her and Baxter to waste an evening of their weekend off. What in the name of the Fox sisters had she been thinking?

Out in the hall, she could hear the voices of the others discussing what had happened. The dining room must be in that direction.

"Detective McCabe," a voice said from the shadows of the doorway she was walking past.

Feeling like an idiot, McCabe dropped the hand that had flown to her throat. "What can I do for you, Mr. Thornton?"

"Could we speak in private?"

McCabe peered past him and recognized the shape of a toilet. "In there?"

"Oh . . . sorry, I just stopped in here to wash my . . . we can go back into the living room."

"Never mind. Let's just make this quick."

She motioned him back and ducked into the room, closing the door.

They were standing in the dark. McCabe waved her hand. "Why aren't the lights coming on?"

"Try the wall switch," Thornton said, sounding amused.

"Oh." McCabe fumbled along the wall by the door until she found it.

"Olive prefers to maintain the original design of the house," he said.

"What do you want to discuss, Mr. Thornton?"

His smile faded. "I've been thinking about how Lisa died. I've been told it could be months before the investigation is completed. Her death is going to be examined as a part of an extensive review of procedures at the facility." He paused. "I've thought about what you asked me, Detective McCabe. I don't think Lisa would have committed suicide."

"Then maybe it was a stunt," McCabe said.

"A stunt?"

"An escape attempt. Ms. Nichols knew she going to be transferred to jail when her trial began on Tuesday. Maybe she thought that by staging a suicide attempt she could get herself taken to the hospital. She might have thought it would be easier to escape from a hospital room than from a jail cell."

Thornton shook his head. "She couldn't have thought that taking enough pills to kill herself would be the ideal way to plan an escape."

"She might have miscalculated."

"That doesn't make sense."

"I didn't say it made sense, Mr. Thornton. I understand Ms. Nichols's defense was going to be temporary insanity. Maybe she was still having a problem with rational thought." She held his gaze. "It's an alternative theory. Something that you might find easier to live with than the idea that Ms. Nichols deliberately took her own life."

"Thank you, but what I want is the truth."

"The truth is, everything points to suicide. I haven't seen her autopsy report, but if there was any suspicion it was anything other than suicide, the police would be handling the investigation."

"I understand that," he said.

"I'm sorry that you don't have a sense of closure—"

"Do you?"

"Ms. Nichols's death is not a police matter, Mr. Thornton. Now, if you'll excuse me."

Her hand was on the old-fashioned glass doorknob when Ted Thornton said, "Something's wrong about all this. You feel it, too."

McCabe turned and looked at him. "What I feel is that I am going to stop obsessing over your 'killer blonde.' She's dead. I'm going to let her go. I suggest you do the same."

McCabe stepped into the hall and saw Baxter coming toward her. "Hey, partner," he said. "I thought you'd gotten lost."

"Nope, here I am. And I'm starving." She reached behind her and turned off the light in the powder room, leaving Ted Thornton in the dark.

"Velma's put out quite a spread," Baxter said.

"Then let's go eat. We may as well get a good meal out of this fiasco."

Baxter turned and started back down the hall beside her. "You see Luanne anywhere?"

"I left her in the solarium pondering the malevolent spirit she claims showed up in place of Kevin Novak."

"That's what she's saying, huh?"

"She and Olive admit they were planning something if Kevin didn't show up. But they deny responsibility for the bell in the air, the door slamming open, and the shattered vase."

"Guess we had ourselves a genuine poltergeist."

"What are the others saying?" McCabe asked, dropping her voice as they reached the dining room.

"That they can't believe what happened. Scott was real quiet and Megan had this wide-eyed look," Baxter said. "Their mom hustled them out."

"Good idea," McCabe said.

Baxter glanced back the way they had come. "Hey, have you seen Teddy?"

"He must still be here," McCabe said. "Ashby's sitting there breaking bread with Jonathan Burdett. Let's get some food, and go eavesdrop."

They were at the sideboard, filling their plates, when Ted Thornton came in. Luanne was with him.

"I'm sorry to be so rude, y'all," she said to the room in general. "I needed to think awhile about what happened. I hope none of you were too rattled."

Francesca Reeves laughed. "No more than one would expect when objects begin to fly about."

Woodward looked over at Olive Cooper. "I guess we should be glad Reverend Wyatt didn't come tonight."

Since the two of them had confessed to having some kind of stunt planned, McCabe thought, they obviously hadn't been concerned about whether Wyatt suspected trickery. But what had they planned? And who had they thought it would rattle?

Ted Thornton said, "Bruce, if you've finished eating, we should get going." He turned to his host. "Olive, forgive us for cutting the evening short, but I have some work I need to get done tonight."

"Velma will fix you a plate. And don't tell me you have food at home. We had food left over from my celebration last Saturday even after we'd given away as much as we could. Everyone who goes out of my door tonight is taking food."

Woodward laughed. "Now, Olive, you sound just like my grandma. She used to cook enough to feed an army and she fed everyone who came by."

"I should be running along, too, Olive," Francesca Reeves said. "This has been a fascinating evening, but draining."

"I have to admit I'm rather tired, too," Burdett said.

McCabe glanced at Baxter. "Could we get our plates to go, too, Ms. Cooper?" she asked.

29

Sunday, January 26, 2020
2:52 P.M.

Luanne leaned over her gleaming white kitchen sink and threw up. She had barely managed to snatch the collard greens out of the way and shove them across the counter before it happened.

"Oh, that's disgusting," she mumbled.

But there had been no hope of making it to the bathroom in the hallway. Better in the sink than on her clean floor.

She straightened up and reached into the cabinet for the glass she always drank water out of. She hated being sick. Had hated it since she was a child.

"Please, lord, don't let me be getting the flu."

She sipped lukewarm water from the faucet and then reached for the disinfectant and scrub brush under the sink. She would have to throw the brush away after she'd used it to clean up after her vomit.

It might be something she'd eaten. Maybe the food she'd brought home from Olive's house last night. She had finished the plate before she went to bed. But all she'd had was roast beef and potato salad, and both had seemed fine.

Luanne glanced toward the box on the counter. The box the pie had arrived in. She might as well admit it. Making a lunch of chocolate pecan pie wasn't likely to do anybody's stomach any good. But it had been so nice of Olive to send the pie. She'd even tucked in a note saying Luanne wasn't to worry herself about last night and that Olive would call her as soon as she got back home on Monday.

Olive had mentioned last night she was going down to New York City today to visit with a friend from her college days. When you were Olive's age, Luanne thought, you didn't want to miss an opportunity to visit with an old friend. You probably didn't have that many of them still kicking.

But Olive had a whole lot of energy for her age. And she'd kept her figure. She was straight-backed and skinny as a girl.

"Not that you were skinny even when you were a girl," Luanne said to herself. "And you aren't ever likely to lose those twenty-five pounds when you eat half a pie."

Not that she had intended to eat half a pie. But one slice had led to three. She'd had a lot to think about and she did her best thinking when she was nibbling on something sweet.

She was in the bathroom brushing her teeth when another pain caught her and bent her over. This time, Luanne managed to make it to the toilet. But the mess spattered on the rim and the tile floor.

Her stomach gurgled and she had to slam down the seat of the toilet and scramble to get her panties down before her bowels erupted.

30

Monday, January 27, 2020
7:45 A.M.

"The question," McCabe said to her father as she closed her ORB, "Is how she did it. I spent half the night reading everything I could find about the Fox sisters and other self-proclaimed mediums from the nineteenth century on. But if Luanne Woodward pulled off a trick with the bell when her hands were being held on each side, I don't know how she did it."

Angus reached for the dog's leash. "You could take Bigfoot here for a walk before you go. He might have some useful thoughts on the subject."

McCabe rubbed the dog behind his left ear, one of his favorite spots. "His name is not Bigfoot. And even if I didn't need to get to work, you should get the exercise." McCabe reached for her jacket. "How do you think she did it?"

"You should have asked your brother that question yesterday when he was here for lunch."

"I was trying not to think or talk about work on the one day I had off. But you're right. He might have had some ideas. There must have been some type of control device."

"Or an accomplice."

"Olive Cooper admitted they had been planning something, but her hands were being held, too. Ted Thornton on one side, and Jonathan Burdett on the other." McCabe leaned over and kissed her father on his bald spot. "I've got to go."

"Call your brother and run it by him. With all the gadgets he comes up with, he ought to be able to figure this one out." Angus's blue gaze under his white brows was all innocence when he added, "Unless, of course, the woman did manage to conjure up a malevolent spirit from the other side."

"Who must have been moving quickly to do all he, she, or it did within those few seconds."

"Sit down," Angus told the dog. "We aren't ready to go yet." He looked up at McCabe from his place on the sofa. "How come you're worrying about this when you've got a murder to investigate?"

"Because I need something else to think about other than how little progress we're making on the murder investigation." She waved her hand. "On my way. See you later."

At her desk in the station house, McCabe leaned sideways to pick up her mug. She and Baxter were watching and listening to her brother, Adam. He was talking to them from his office at UAlbany in the School of Biotechnology and Robotics. For the past seventeen minutes—picking up various devices from his work table to illustrate—he had been explaining the science of how one could make a bell rise from a table, ring, and then crash down.

McCabe sent a glance in Baxter's direction. He was leaning back in his chair, hands behind his head. He was probably thinking Adam looked more like a swashbuckler than a scientist. Clad in a black fisherman's sweater, Adam was wearing the black eye patch with the tiny Jolly Roger that Mai had given him. That patch, and the others in his collection, was a substitute for the prosthesis he refused to have for his missing eye.

Even though she had invited Baxter to sit in, she was feeling protective of her brother. And that, McCabe thought, was ridiculous. Adam was more than capable of putting anyone who stepped out of line in his place.

Baxter cleared his throat. "Uhh, so Professor . . . Adam . . . what you're saying is that—?"

Adam smiled. "Sorry for the minilecture. What I'm saying is that I agree with what my sister suggested at the start of this discussion. Even with her hands being held, your medium could have not only levitated the bell but created the other special effects. As I've just explained, causing an object to rise typically involves the use of magnetic forces. There is also some promising research using sound waves. And there are a few other possibilities. For example, your medium might have used a verbal command."

"A verbal command?" Baxter unhooked his hands from behind his head. "She did ask Kevin to ring the bell if he was there."

"Yes," McCabe said. "But she didn't say anything that would be an instruction to the bell to rise."

"Not necessary," Adam said. "Any preestablished phrase would have worked."

"Or you said the bell could have been on a timer," Baxter said.

"A timer that could have been built into the bell itself."

McCabe said, "Thanks, Adam. This has been really helpful. We should let you get ready for your class."

He smiled. "This was an unusual diversion."

"Good meeting you," Baxter said.

"You, too. See you later, sis."

McCabe glanced at Baxter. "And thank you for behaving well."

Baxter grinned. "Would I embarrass you, partner? To tell the truth, I sort of enjoyed that minilecture your brother gave us. He always remembered to explain when he used a four-syllable word."

"He enjoys teaching almost as much as doing research. So, what we've learned is that it would have been possible for Luanne to pull off a hoax with the bell. And if she could do the bell, she could figure out how to rig the door."

"Okay," Baxter said. "But where does knowing this get us?"

"I was thinking about that when I was driving in. I asked Luanne point-blank if she had pulled a hoax. She looked me in the eye and lied. If she would lie about one thing . . ."

"That's what I still don't get. She and Olive admitted to you that they had set up something they planned to use if Luanne couldn't contact Kevin. If they were conspiring, why would Luanne have pulled a hoax on her own?"

"Maybe she was trying to convince Olive, too."

"Okay, so she might be trying to pull off some kind of con involving her wealthy benefactor. But where does that get us with our murder investigation?"

"No idea. But what I keep coming back to is Luanne's interest in Kevin. She came to his funeral."

"A lot of people would have been interested enough to come to a murdered undertaker's funeral if they could have gotten in. That's why the press was hanging around outside."

"I know that, but Luanne—"

"Olive invited her to the funeral. And maybe Luanne saw Kevin's unfortunate demise as her lucky break. But even if she were planning a con, wait for it . . ." Baxter did a drum roll on his desk with his fingertips. "Luanne has eight people who were snowed in with her at a house party in Boston who can provide her with an airtight alibi on the night Kevin was murdered."

"She has an alibi. But what if she also has an accomplice?"

"Who killed Kevin while Luanne was in Boston? Okay, where is this accomplice you just conjured up?"

McCabe held up her hands. "I don't know where he or she is. And if he or she does exist, I don't know what motive this accomplice and Luanne would have for killing Kevin—unless it was to pave the way for a con involving Olive. But since we have no other leads at the moment, would you please humor me?"

"Okay. Since we've spent most of the morning going through all of our bits and pieces of evidence and still have zilch. What do you want to do?"

"I want to pay Luanne another visit. An unannounced visit."

31

Snowflakes fluttered in the air as Baxter pulled to a stop in front of the house Luanne Woodward was renting. "Her car's in the drive-way," he said. "Good sign."

On the front steps, McCabe paused with her hand extended toward the doorbell. "Do you hear that?"

"Smoke detector?"

McCabe rang the bell and then began banging on the door. She turned the doorknob, hoping it might be unlocked.

Baxter said, "I'll go around back and see if I can get in that way."

McCabe pounded on the door again. Then she walked around the side of the house, opposite the way Baxter had gone. There was a window she might be able to break.

She went back to the front door, reaching it just as Baxter opened it from the inside. "The back door was open," he said. "Luanne's lying halfway out the door in her nightgown, unconscious. The smoke alarm is from a roast she had in the oven."

He had his ORB in his hand, "Dispatch, we've got . . ."

McCabe ran into the kitchen. The smell of burnt meat filled the room. Baxter had left the back door open to clear the smoke.

The kitchen was as cold as outside. McCabe dropped to her knees beside Luanne Woodward, feeling for her pulse.

"On their way," Baxter said.

"We need a blanket to cover her," McCabe said. "We shouldn't move her."

"I'll grab one out of her bedroom."

McCabe looked down at the woman, who was clad in a white cotton nightgown with pink lace at the wrists and throat. "Hang on, Luanne. Help's on the way."

Baxter came back with a blue thermal blanket. He passed it down to McCabe. "She threw up on the floor beside her bed."

"She must have been really sick not to clean it up."

"Not to mention not turning off the stove before her pot roast burned."

"We'd better touch base with Lieutenant Dole and let him know what's going on," McCabe said.

"I'll tag him while I'm moving our vehicle out of the paramedics' way," Baxter said.

McCabe glanced out the open back door as the wind picked up, whirling the snowflakes. The temperature had fallen into the twenties last night. How long had Luanne been lying there?

McCabe tried to construct the timeline in her mind. The stove was an old-fashioned burner/oven model in keeping with the retro '50s décor, the kind McCabe's grandmother used to have. If Luanne had been planning to have the roast for Sunday dinner, she would have put it in at around midday. When it was almost done, she might have turned the oven down low to keep it warm until she was ready to eat.

Baxter came back. "The lieutenant said to check in after we get her to the hospital."

"Did you notice the oven setting?" McCabe asked.

Baxter gave her exactly the look she expected. "The what?"

"When you came into the kitchen," McCabe said. "The smoke alarm was on—"

"And I used the broom handle to turn it off." He pointed. "And that mitt thing to grab the pan out of the oven and put it on top of the stove."

"And now the oven's turned off. Did you turn it off when you took the roast out of the oven?"

Baxter frowned. "Yeah, I guess I did. The red light was on."

"Did you notice the temperature setting when you turned it off? It's on the knob."

"Oh . . . that oven setting. No." Baxter paused. "I was thinking about letting you in, and getting help for Luanne."

"No problem," McCabe said, seeing his chagrin. "I was just wondering if maybe Luanne had felt ill after she put the roast in and turned it down really low while she lay down to rest. If that was what happened, the roast might have been baking for quite a while—if it were a large roast—before it burned enough to set the smoke alarm off."

"Maybe that was why she came into the kitchen," Baxter said. "To turn off the oven."

"That's possible," McCabe said. "In fact, that would explain why she was in here in her nightgown. She woke up, vomited beside her bed. Then maybe she thought of the roast in the oven and came in to turn it off. And, maybe, she was also going to get what she needed to clean up the vomit."

"Question is why she opened the back door and started out of it."

McCabe looked down at Luanne. She felt for her pulse again.

She said to Baxter, "This house is spotless. Luanne is probably the kind of woman my mother used to call 'house proud.' If a woman like that felt like she was about to throw up, she'd head for the back door and do it outside rather than on her clean floor."

Baxter pointed. "The sink's right over there."

McCabe wrinkled her nose. "Food and dishes are washed in the kitchen sink, Michael."

"Yeah, but you can always wash—"

The sound of sirens alerted them.

The paramedics rushed in and went through their standard process of evaluation and preparing the patient for transport.

McCabe knew the female member of the team from the days when they'd both been rookies. "Vicky, she threw up in the bedroom. Do you need to see that?"

Vicky Nathan glanced up from her work, her gaze meeting McCabe's. She told her partner, her own counterpart to Baxter, "I'm just going to get a specimen. Back in a moment, then we'll be ready to move."

In the bedroom, Nathan slipped on another pair of gloves and took a small specimen container from her kit. She knelt down and scooped up the watery vomit that seemed to have a trace of blood. "So what did you want to talk about?" she asked McCabe.

"What do you think's wrong with her?"

"You know I'm not supposed to speculate about that. But—off the record—it looks like it could be another case of cholera." She stood up and dropped the specimen container into her bag. "What's up with this one?"

"The murdered undertaker case Baxter and I are working on. We stopped by for another interview with your patient."

"Is she a suspect?"

"We aren't sure what she is at this point."

Nathan nodded. "We'd better get rolling."

"Do you think she'll make it?"

"Right now, she's holding her own. But you know how that goes."

"If she should regain consciousness and say anything on the way—"

"Record it."

"Thanks."

Nathan and her partner carried Luanne Woodward out, and a few minutes later the sound of a siren signaled their departure.

McCabe and Baxter had followed them to the door. McCabe stepped out on the walk, glancing up and down the street. No one had come outside. Maybe Woodward had not lived there long enough for her neighbors to feel that kind of concern. And it was a Monday. Most of them were probably at work or elsewhere.

She glanced again at the house across the street. Had a curtain fluttered back into place at one of the upstairs windows?

"Let's have a quick look around before we head to the hospital," she told Baxter.

"What are we looking for?" he asked as he followed her back inside.

"We don't have a search warrant," McCabe said. "And we need to keep that in mind. But we do have a medical emergency, and we can look for anything that might help in the diagnosis of her illness."

"It would be neglect of duty not to," Baxter said.

"You check her medicine cabinet for any prescription medication. I'm going to have a look in the kitchen. Let's make this fast."

"Meet you at the front door in five minutes."

"Gloves," McCabe said, handing him a pair from her field bag.

"Thanks."

In the kitchen, McCabe closed the back door. Then she moved to the center of the room. She had been accurate in what she had said to Baxter. Luanne's kitchen was spotless: Labeled spice bottles in a rank. Gleaming small appliances in primary colors displayed in an open cabinet.

McCabe slipped on her own gloves and opened the refrigerator. Cooked collard greens in a glass container. She took the container out and set it on the counter and reached for what looked like a foil-covered pie.

Chocolate pecan. Almost half of it gone.

She set it on the counter beside the greens and started opening cabinets.

Nothing else until she got to the trash can in the corner. A gleaming metal can with a foot-operated lid.

The cardboard box was there on top. McCabe pulled it out. Bingo, as her partner was fond of saying. The box Luanne's pie had come in. Plain, white cardboard, but no bakery name or any other identification. Could be from a farmer's market, but they usually used labels or stamps. If your family or guests loved the dessert, they wanted you to be able to tell them where you bought it.

"What's in the box?" Baxter asked from the doorway.

"I think the pie on the counter came in it. Find any medication?

"Vitamins, aspirin, cod liver oil . . . and this." He held up a small plastic bag. "Seems our medium likes to get mellow."

"In keeping with her décor. From what I've read, marijuana was already becoming popular in the 1950s. But I can't quite imagine Luanne sitting in a jazz club. Of course, it might be medicinal."

"No label. But it looks like good, quality stuff."

"You can tell by looking?" McCabe asked, as she slid the foiled-covered pie into one of the brown paper bags that she had found neatly folded in a drawer.

"I spent two and a half years working Vice, remember? I know my drugs."

"Then I'll take your word for the quality. Let's bring it along, in case her doctor wants a look."

"Would I be far off, partner, if I guessed you aren't in the habit of getting mellow?"

"No tolerance. A beer or two or an occasional glass of wine is about my limit."

"And, of course, you do prefer to keep a clear head."

"Never know when you're going to need one, do you?"

32

"I thought that since it was a medical emergency and we don't know what made her ill . . ." McCabe listened while her boss talked. "Yes, sir . . ."

McCabe gestured for Baxter to turn at the next light. "Station house," she mouthed. "Yes, sir, on our way."

"What did the lou say?" Baxter asked.

"He wants us to drop the pie and the other items off at FIU before we go to the hospital."

"Didn't want us to leave the grass locked up in the car, huh?"

"He didn't think being left in the car would do the pie any good, either. And, as he said, the sooner Delgardo's techs get busy, the sooner we'll know what we have."

Baxter shot a glance at the page she had pulled up on her ORB. "What are you looking at?"

"Poisons and symptoms. The lou asked if I thought Luanne had been poisoned."

"Or your pal, the paramedic, could be right. It could be cholera."

"Yeah, but remember, that was off the record."

Midafternoon traffic was heavy, but moving. Baxter pulled into the station house parking lot less than ten minutes later.

McCabe gathered up the bags she needed to deliver to the lab. "Be right back."

She met Ray Delgardo, the head of the forensics unit, on his way out the door of his lab. "Ray, do you have a second?"

"Sorry, Hannah, I've got a meeting."

"Then I won't keep you. I'll ask one of your techs to check the pie."

Delgardo took a step, then turned. "What pie?"

"It's all right," McCabe said. "I know you have to go."

"They can start without me. What pie? What's wrong with it?"

"Maybe nothing. Or it could have accidentally been contaminated with some kind of bacteria. Or it might contain poison."

"Poison." He held the door, gesturing for her to go first. "Where did this pie come from?"

"The refrigerator of a medium who is indirectly involved in the funeral director murder investigation." McCabe followed Delgardo as he headed toward an unoccupied table with assorted lab equipment. She set the bags on the counter. "We found her collapsed on the floor in her kitchen, or, rather halfway out the back door."

Delgardo slipped on gloves and began opening the bags. "What about this box?" he asked. "Does it go with the pie?"

"I think so," McCabe said. "It was in the trash. The pie was in the refrigerator. So were the collard greens. Baxter found the marijuana when he was checking the medicine cabinet for prescription drugs."

"Okay. Fill out the submission forms."

"I hate to ask this," McCabe said. "But could we get a rush on this one? Luanne, the medium, was taken to the hospital. If it turns out to be cholera, we may not need the results of your tests. But if it isn't cholera, if we can help the hospital identify the source of her illness . . ."

"What makes you think it might be cholera?"

"Something one of the paramedics said, off the record."

Delgardo nodded. "We should have something later this afternoon."

"Thanks, Ray."

He was looking at the pie. "It's been a while since we had a case involving food."

McCabe said. "So you're going to check for poisons that she might not have been able to taste?"

Delgardo smiled. "Do you have any suggestions about what we ought to be looking for?"

McCabe shook her head. "Baxter got us back here before I could even work my way through the list. There are a lot of poisons, aren't there?"

"But a few are perennially popular," Delgardo said. "We'll test for those first. I'll tag you when we have some results."

When they got to the hospital, Luanne Woodward had still not regained consciousness. The young doctor who was attending her shook his head. "The stool smear we were able to get was inconclusive. We're waiting for the results of the blood culture. Right now, all we can do is try to keep her stable."

"Do you think it might be cholera?" McCabe asked.

"Sorry, I can't speculate about that. Our instructions are to report any potential new cases to the department of health for confirmation. Any statements will come from a hospital spokesperson. I'm assuming the release of information to police detectives is included in that mandate."

Baxter said, "You sound like you've been in hot water over this kind of thing before."

"And learned the virtue of not speculating."

McCabe said, "We understand. But we do need to be notified if cholera and other naturally occurring illnesses are ruled out." She paused. "I should tell you that we took several items from the victim's home to our forensics lab for testing."

The doctor pushed his retro glasses up on his nose. "Are you saying—sorry if I'm slow on the uptake; I didn't get a lot of sleep last night—are you saying that someone might have tried to kill my patient?"

"We're saying that we're considering all possibilities."

"Okay, got it. And if your forensic guys find anything—"

"You'll be the first to know," McCabe said.

"Or whoever's here," the doctor replied. "I'm due to go off duty in a couple of hours. But I'll put a note in the file that we need to keep you guys in the loop."

"Thanks," Baxter said.

"And please include that we should be notified if the patient begins to regain consciousness," McCabe added.

"That, too. This is something new. Most of the time when we get detectives in here someone's shot or stabbed or beaten someone up."

Baxter said, "Try a chocolate pecan pie."

"A pie?"

"We found it in the refrigerator. Just thought we'd have it tested," McCabe said. "Thanks for your help. We'll be in touch with you or whoever's on duty when we have our lab results."

McCabe glanced out at the slate-gray sky visible from the enclosed pedestrian bridge that linked the medical center to the garage on the other side of the street. "Well, at least it looks like we aren't going to get any more snow right now. I think we should let Olive Cooper know Luanne's in the hospital."

"Tag her or drop by?" Baxter asked.

"Let's drop by," McCabe said. "Luanne is her friend. We should give her the news in person."

In the garage, Baxter stopped walking and pointed. "We've got a flat tire."

"I hate changing flat tires," McCabe said.

"Lucky for us, we happen to be driving one of the police fleet's new vehicles on this fine day."

"Why is that lucky? Unless it's going to change its own tire."

"We're about to find out. I haven't finished reading the manual yet, but we can pull it up and follow the instructions."

"Are you saying this car really can change its own tire?"

"Almost," Baxter said, opening the driver's-side door. "What it does is identify the problem and perform a temporary repair, if possible. If the tire needs to be changed, it has auto assist to help with the process. This baby can jack itself up."

"Helpful, on its part." McCabe leaned back against a column and took out her ORB, leaving him to share this moment with their vehicle.

A few minutes later, he said, "We've picked up a piece of metal. We could eject it and attempt a temporary seal, but changing the tire is the recommended action."

"We should certainly follow the recommended action," McCabe said.

Baxter took the spare tire out of the trunk.

McCabe was in the middle of a tag to Lt. Dole when she saw the rear of the car rising from the ground. "Mike, wait, don't you need to back it out of the space so it'll have more room?"

"We're fine," Baxter said. "It calculated the space available to make the change."

"Okay. If you and the car say so."

"This is great. It's loosening the bolts. All I have to do is catch the flat tire and then put the spare in place."

"Proving even changing a flat tire can be fun," McCabe said.

Five minutes later, Baxter slammed down the trunk. "Ready to roll," he said.

"I told Lieutenant Dole we're going to swing by and let Olive know about Luanne."

"The driver she hired just dropped her off from her trip to the City. She went down there yesterday morning to visit one of her old friends from college," Velma, Olive's housekeeper, told them when they asked to see her employer. "She's tired. She never sleeps well in a hotel room bed. Even in those fancy hotels down in the City."

"We're sorry to disturb her," McCabe said, feeling a little guilty. They were talking about an eighty-five-year-old woman. "We won't keep her long. But we have some news we think she'd want to know."

Velma said, "I hope it's not like the last news you came with. Go into the sitting room. I'll let her know you're here."

The lamps were turned on in the sitting room, the curtains drawn against the gray day. A fire crackled in the hearth. McCabe imagined curling up with a book in one of the plush chairs.

Baxter wandered over to the painting of the woman and her suitor. "This still gives me a kick," he said. He turned back to McCabe. "That reminds me. Whatever happened with you and that guy you were seeing?"

The question caught McCabe off guard. "What guy?"

"The guy I kept trying to get you to fess up to when we were working the serial killer case. I'm assuming it was a 'he' and not a 'she.' "

"Really?" McCabe said. "Why are you assuming that?"

"We've been working together for four months. You get to ask me about my friend from the Vice Unit who was giving me lifts to work."

"Okay. You got me there. It isn't fair that I get to be nosy and you don't."

"So was it 'he' or 'she'?"

"He. And it didn't work out."

"Sorry. Were you left with a broken heart?"

"No. Just left questioning my ability to judge men as romantic partners."

Baxter grinned. "In case you're wondering, I'm still available."

"Thanks for telling me. I'll keep that in mind. Now could we change the subject?"

Baxter glanced around. "I wonder where the lady of the house buys her doilies."

"They look handmade," McCabe said.

"They are," Olive Cooper said as she stepped into the room. "I order them from a lacemaker in Devon."

McCabe wondered how long she had been outside the door. For a woman with a cane, she moved quietly. "Sorry to stop by like this, Ms. Cooper. But we have some news about Luanne."

"Sit down, the two of you, so that I can."

McCabe and Baxter sat down in armchairs. Cooper settled herself on the sofa. "What's this news?" she said. "Something about the séance on Saturday night?"

"Indirectly, perhaps," McCabe said. "We went to Luanne's house this afternoon to speak to her about the séance. We were still curious about what happened at the end with the bell and the door."

"I'm curious about that myself," Cooper said. "What did she say about it?"

"Nothing," Baxter said. "She wasn't in any condition to carry on a conversation."

"Are you telling me she was drunk?"

"No, not drunk," McCabe said. "We found her unconscious in her kitchen. The back door was open and she was lying in the doorway in her nightgown."

"Good lord!"

"She's still alive," McCabe said. "At the hospital and holding her own when we were there."

"What happened? Was she attacked?"

"There was no evidence of that. It seems to have been something that developed during the course of the day. She had put a roast in the oven. In fact, it was the sound of her smoke detector that alerted us that something was wrong. She had been in bed and been sick to her stomach—vomited. She got up, went into the kitchen, and apparently passed out."

"With the back door open? Why did she open the door? Could someone have knocked?"

"Knocked?" McCabe asked.

"Like with Kevin," Cooper said. "Someone came to the door of the funeral home, and he let him or her in."

"That's possible," McCabe said, realizing it was. "It is possible someone came to the door," she said, thinking it through as she spoke. "But it would be odd for her to open the door in only her nightgown."

"If she was feeling sick as a dog, she probably didn't care what she was wearing," Cooper said. "If she was as sick as you say, maybe she was glad someone had come to the door."

"So you're suggesting she opened the door, and this person who had knocked went away again without helping her?"

"Well, why do you think she opened the damn door?" Cooper said.

"She might have been delirious and running a fever," Baxter said. "Maybe she opened the door to cool off."

Cooper nodded. "That makes some sense."

"My own theory was more mundane," McCabe said. "I thought she realized she was going to throw up again and rushed over to the door to keep from doing it on the floor or in the sink."

"That makes sense, too."

"But since there's no surveillance system, we have no way of knowing."

"What about the neighbors? Maybe some of them have cameras."

"We'll check that if it becomes relevant," McCabe said, remembering the neighbor across the street who seemed to be peeking out from behind the curtains as the paramedics left with Luanne. "But right now, we don't know if a crime was committed."

Baxter said, "But there was a suspicious chocolate pecan pie in the fridge."

Cooper turned her sharp gaze on him. "Why would a pie be suspicious? In case you haven't noticed by now, Luanne likes her food. And she has a sweet tooth."

"We couldn't figure out where she had gotten the pie," McCabe said.

"Gotten it? Maybe she made it."

"That's possible," McCabe said. "But it was in a disposable pie plate. And there was a white cardboard box in the trash can that the pie might have come in. Except there was no label or stamp on the box." McCabe paused, then said, "When we were here on Saturday evening, you mentioned all the food you had left over from your celebration of life. And you told us the first time we came about taking Luanne to the kitchen to have a slice of Velma's chocolate pecan pie after Kevin Novak left so abruptly when they were introduced. I don't suppose Velma might have sent Luanne a pie?"

Cooper returned her gaze, then she smiled. "That just occurred to you, did it? Velma clearing out our refrigerator and sending Luanne a pie. A pie your partner described as 'suspicious.' Are you wondering if Velma might have sent Luanne a poisoned pie?"

McCabe said, "I certainly didn't intend to suggest that, Ms. Cooper. When my partner said the pie is 'suspicious,' he meant its source. We don't know if there is anything wrong with the pie."

"But I assume you are having it examined by your lab people."

"Yes, since we don't know why Luanne was taken ill. That was why I asked if Velma might have sent Luanne the pie. If we know it came from a safe source—"

Cooper threw back her head and laughed. "I suspect, Detective McCabe, that you are very good at interrogations."

"Thank you, Ms. Cooper. But I'm not interrogating you. Just asking if your housekeeper might know anything about the pie."

"Let's get her in here and find out."

Cooper touched the locket she was wearing.

"Hey," Baxter said. "That's nice."

"A more elegant version of the old MedicAlert," Cooper said.

Velma came in drying her hand on a dishtowel. Did she wash the dishes by hand? McCabe wondered. Surely not when her employer entertained.

"Did you need something, Olive?"

Cooper nodded at McCabe. "Detective McCabe has something she'd like to ask you."

McCabe said, "Ms.— I'm sorry, I don't know your last name."

"Holloway. But Velma's fine. What do you want to ask me?"

"Velma, did you happen to send Luanne Woodward a chocolate pecan pie?"

"Send her a pie?" Velma said. "I didn't have any pie left to send her. She ate the last slice of the one I had left when she was here on Saturday evening."

"She did?"

Velma tucked the dishtowel into the waistband of her apron. "I'd made a butter cream cake and some cookies for dessert, but she asked me if I had any more of the chocolate pecan pie she'd had at Olive's celebration."

"Did she ask you that in front of the other guests at the séance?" Baxter asked.

Velma shook her head. "She came out to the kitchen. Not that it made any difference. I gave her the pie, and she went out there and ate it in front of everyone else."

"This was after the séance?" McCabe asked.

"No, not after. Before. I had put the appetizers out on the buffet table, but she came looking for pie. And then she went back in the dining room and ate it. I had to tell everyone else when I went back in there that we had cake and cookies for dessert later, but that was the last of the pie."

"So someone asked you if there was any more pie?"

"That woman with the accent. The one who was married to Kevin's friend."

"Francesca Reeves," Baxter said.

"That's her," Velma said, in a tone that suggested she didn't quite approve of Francesca. "She said the pie looked delicious and she hoped we were having it for dessert. I had to say Luanne had gotten the last slice."

"So when this conversation about the pie happened," McCabe said, "the guests who were in the dining room would have been—"

"Everyone except the two of you," Velma said, looking from

McCabe to Baxter. "And Ted Thornton and that man who works for him. They came in after the two of you arrived."

"Thank you, Velma," McCabe said. "This has been really helpful."

Velma looked at her employer. "Do you want me to wait and show them out, Olive? You should have a nap before dinner."

Cooper said, "As I've already told you, I don't need or want to take a nap before dinner. But if the detectives have no more questions, you may show them out."

"Nothing else for now," McCabe said. "Thank you both for being so patient with our questions."

"Thank you for stopping by to bring me the news about Luanne," Cooper said. "Please let me know when you find out where the pie came from."

McCabe nodded. "I know you must be as interested in the answer to that question as we are."

"Yes. I am," Cooper said.

Velma took a step toward the sitting room door, then turned and scowled at her employer. "All right, you may not need a nap. But if Paige comes back here, I'm going to tell her you're resting."

Olive Cooper nodded. "You may tell my great-niece that I'm resting, and add that I look forward to having her join me for breakfast tomorrow morning, seven A.M."

A smile spread across Velma's face. "Breakfast at seven A.M. I'll be sure to tell her that."

McCabe recalled what Luanne had said after Kevin Novak's funeral, that Paige had done something to annoy Olive. Great-niece was trying to work her way back into great-aunt's good graces. That was why Paige had been designated to drive Olive home after Kevin's funeral.

Obviously, Paige was not an early riser. Velma's smile as she said good-bye made McCabe wonder what Velma was planning to serve for breakfast.

McCabe shared that thought with Baxter as they were walking to their vehicle.

Baxter grinned. "Yeah, I got the feeling Velma doesn't intend to serve all Paige's favorite seven A.M. breakfast foods. Want to keep Velma, the devoted housekeeper, on the list for Luanne's chocolate pecan pie?"

"Let's hope Luanne hadn't done anything to upset Olive and make Velma consider her persona non grata." McCabe sighed. "But, yeah, let's keep Velma on our list."

33

By the time they'd gotten their orders and found a table, they were both hungry enough to spend the next five minutes focusing on their very late lunch.

Then McCabe's ORB buzzed. She wiped the mayo from her turkey sandwich off her fingers and reached for it. "Delgardo," she told Baxter.

He nodded and took another bite of his pastrami sandwich.

"Ray," McCabe said when Delgardo appeared on the monitor. "Does the fact you're calling mean you have something?"

"We have the results on the pie," he said. "Someone added arsenic to the recipe."

"Arsenic?" McCabe said. "Is it possible to determine the source?"

"Possible, but it could take a few days. We should be able to get back to you before that on the other items."

"Could you have a look at the cardboard box first?"

"I already have someone working on it."

"Thanks, Ray. I need to call the hospital."

"Tell them to contact FIU if they want us to send over our analysis."

The doctor who had been on duty was still there when McCabe asked for him. When he appeared on the monitor, he looked like he was ready to call it a day. "Doctor, I'm sorry to catch you right at the end of your shift. But we have some information about the pie we found in Ms. Woodward's refrigerator. According to our forensics unit, the pie contains arsenic."

"Then that means someone did try to kill her. Is this person likely to try it again?"

"I'm afraid we don't know the answer to that question. But we'll alert your hospital security. In the meantime, please issue an order restricting access to her room."

The doctor took off his glasses and rubbed his eyes. "Could we get a copy of the lab report?"

McCabe gave him Delgardo's code. "He's ready to send it right over. Do you think Ms. Woodward will be all right now that you know what you're dealing with?"

"I think the best answer I can give to that, Detective, is that she's made it this far. Once we confirm that she did consume arsenic, then we start treatment to get it out of her system."

McCabe's next tag was to Lt. Dole. She told him about the arsenic and asked about alerting hospital security. "I'll take care of that," he said. "You and Baxter focus on coming up with a viable suspect."

"Yes, sir, we're on it."

Dole ended the transmission, and McCabe looked across the table at her partner. "Operating on the assumption that arsenic in the pie means Luanne was poisoned, we have several people who were there in the dining room when Luanne came out of the kitchen with the slice of pie that Velma gave her. Even though we're keeping Velma on our list, we should consider other suspects."

"So you think that seeing Luanne eating a slice of pie might have given one of the others an idea about how to get to her?"

"But the big question is why anyone would want to get to her. Is this related to Kevin Novak's murder?"

"Be a real coincidence if it isn't," Baxter said.

"Yes, it would," McCabe agreed. "But we've already been there with Ashby and his tag to Kevin Novak."

"The timing of that was a coincidence," Baxter said. "But I admit we did find a connection—Olive Cooper—the connection between our victim and Ted Thornton."

"And now Olive is the connection between Kevin Novak, our murder victim, and Luanne Woodward, our attempted murder victim." McCabe picked up a sweet potato fry. "Since we can't talk to Luanne right now, I think we should have a chat with the people who were in Olive's dining room."

"That would be Bob Reeves's French wife, Francesca; Jonathan Burdett, the church counselor; and Sarah Novak, the grieving widow. And the two kids, Scott and Megan."

"Of course, the question is why anyone at the séance would want Luanne dead."

"Maybe she and Olive accomplished what they were trying to do. Maybe the séance rattled someone's cage."

"And someone struck out at Luanne to make sure she wouldn't do another séance?" McCabe squeezed another slice of lemon into her tea. "Did anyone at the séance—except maybe Megan—really believe Luanne had contacted the spirit world?"

"If this person wasn't convinced by the séance, then why bother to try to kill the medium?"

"Maybe it wasn't the séance. Maybe Luanne knew—knows—something else."

"But Luanne hasn't been in Albany that long. She only met our vic once. What could she know?"

McCabe reached for her ORB. "No idea, Michael. But we're not accomplishing anything sitting here theorizing. I say we start spreading the word that Luanne is in the hospital."

"As opposed to dead?"

"Lieutenant Dole is contacting hospital security. Whoever tried to kill her must be waiting to hear that she's dead. We let everyone know that she isn't."

"Let's start with the doc. We haven't chatted with him in a while."

Jonathan Burdett lived in a brownstone on a street on the perimeter of Washington Park. Burdett's office was in his home. When McCabe tagged him, he said he would be free shortly. He was about to begin his session with his last patient of the day. Rather than go back to the station house when it was so close to the end of their shift, McCabe and Baxter decided to go to Burdett's office and wait.

"I've been thinking about our first interview with Burdett," McCabe said as Baxter was parking the car. "Remember the tag he showed us that Kevin sent him?"

"Sure. Kevin told him Olive had suggested he drop Burdett and see her medium."

"And Burdett claimed he had been amused, not threatened," McCabe said. "He was sure that Kevin would stay with him. He also said he was sure that, although some church members might have some interest in consulting a medium, it would be only a passing fad."

"So you think he was lying, and he tried to kill Luanne to eliminate potential competition," Baxter said. "Maybe he was afraid if word got around that something happened at Olive's séance, all those curious church members would be flocking to her."

"I'm not suggesting he was trying to eliminate the competition," McCabe said as they crossed from Washington Park to the sidewalk on Willett Street. "I'm just pondering his attitude toward Luanne."

Burdett's receptionist looked up from her desk in the foyer of the two-story house. "Are you Detectives McCabe and Baxter?" she asked.

"Yes, we are," McCabe replied.

"I'm so sorry, but Dr. Burdett had to leave. He asked me to give you this."

She held out an envelope. "Thank you," McCabe said.

She opened the sealed envelope and found a single sheet of monogrammed stationery. With what seemed to be a fountain pen—something she hadn't seen since she was a child when she used to play with the one her father kept on his desk—Burdett had written: *En route to Novak home. Sarah called. Emergency situation with Scott.*

McCabe said, "I'm sorry that we missed Dr. Burdett."

The receptionist smiled and nodded. "I'll tell him you were here."

Out on the sidewalk, Baxter said, "What was that about?"

McCabe passed him the note. "I suppose there was a good reason why he took the time to write a note instead of sending a tag."

"Leaving a note did slow us down," Baxter said.

"Yes, but he told us where he was going."

"Maybe he wants us to come and lend a hand with the emergency."

"Whether that was what he intended or not, he shouldn't be too surprised when we show up."

"I wonder what's wrong with the kid."

"Maybe he broke down. He was trying to step into the role of man of the house. That kind of pressure's a lot for a seventeen-year-old to handle."

They heard the chaos inside when they reached the front door of the Novak house: voices raised, words indistinguishable, but the distress and anger clear.

McCabe rang the bell. The voices rose higher. A woman's voice. Male voices.

McCabe rang the bell again and pounded on the door.

A moment later, the door was flung open. Megan, tears streaming down her face, said, "Scott! Something's really wrong with Scott!"

The shouting inside the house had stopped. Silence.

McCabe looked at Baxter. He shook his head, indicating he couldn't hear anything either.

"Megan," McCabe said, voice pitched low. "Where is Scott? Where's your mother?"

"They're out in the kitchen. Mommy and Scott and Dr. Burdett."

"What were they doing when you came to open the door?"

Megan blinked, her eyes wide. "Scott shoved Dr. Burdett and ran into the kitchen. And he grabbed a knife and told Mommy and Dr. Burdett to stay back."

"Megan, I want you to do something for us. Our car's right there. Go sit in the backseat."

"But, Mommy and Scott—"

"I know. We'll go see what's happening. But we need you out of the house. Will you do that for us?"

The girl nodded. She reached for her coat on the hook by the door.

"Megan," McCabe said. The girl stopped, staring up at her. "Can we get into the house through the back door? Is it unlocked?"

In the light from the foyer, McCabe saw her frown. "It might be. Mommy always forgets to lock it when she comes in from her workshop. Daddy always locked up at night."

McCabe touched her shoulder. "Stay in the car, okay?"

"Okay."

McCabe turned back to Baxter. He said, "Give me an extra couple of minutes to get over the fence."

McCabe watched him disappear around the corner. Then she went in through the front door, closing it behind her.

She drew her weapon, setting it on stun.

"Mrs. Novak," she called out. "Sarah? It's Hannah McCabe. Everything all right?"

"Yes," Sarah Novak called back, strain evident even in that monosyllable. "Scott's a little upset. But everything . . . everything's all right."

Stopping when she reached the closed kitchen door, McCabe called, "Dr. Burdett, how goes it?"

"We're all unharmed," he said, his voice calm. "However, Scott is holding a butcher knife. He wants us to let him think."

McCabe said, "Scott, I'm going to come in, okay? I know you want to think, but I just need to come in and see how everyone's doing."

Silence. McCabe pushed the door inward an inch. "Scott? I'm going to come in."

"I don't want to talk to you," he said in a croaking voice.

"You don't have to talk," McCabe said, stepping into the kitchen, weapon held in the hand behind her back.

Scott was standing by the kitchen sink, facing his mother and Jonathan Burdett. He was holding the butcher knife out in front of him, keeping them at bay.

And the back door was in his direct line of vision. Damn, McCabe thought.

Scott's blue shirt was plastered to his chest with perspiration. He was breathing heavily. Pupils dilated. She looked at Jonathan Burdett. He said, "Scott took some pills a friend gave him. He is having an adverse reaction."

"Don't talk about me like that," Scott said. "I'm here."

"Scott," Sarah Novak held out her hand. "Sweetheart, we know you're here. Everything's all right. Just put down the knife."

McCabe said, "Scott, your mother's right. Just put the knife down on the floor and kick it toward me."

He looked at the knife in his hand. He was breathing harder now.

Burdett said, "Scott, I know you aren't feeling very well. You would feel better if you could lie down."

Scott gazed at him. "I'm feeling dizzy."

"Then let us help you to bed," Sarah Novak said. "You'll feel much better after a nap."

"I can't do this," Scott said.

"You can't do what?" McCabe asked.

"I can't do this."

Scott raised the hand holding the butcher knife. McCabe's fingers tightened on her weapon.

"Scott," she said. "Just put the knife down. Put it down on the counter beside you."

"I can't do this," he said again. "I'm sorry. I can't do this."

"What can't you do?" McCabe asked.

"I'm sorry, Dad. Sorry . . . I didn't mean to do it."

"Scott—," Sarah Novak said, holding her hand out to him.

McCabe fired her weapon at the same moment Scott slashed toward his throat. His hand jerked. He dropped the knife, staggered, fell to the floor.

Sarah Novak screamed. She rushed over to her son.

Dr. Burdett grabbed the crisply pressed, bright orange napkins from the three place settings on the kitchen table. Kneeling beside Scott, he pressed the napkins to his shoulder.

McCabe glanced over at the back door. Baxter had come in. He was on his ORB.

McCabe took a deep breath and another.

"You all right?" Baxter asked.

She nodded and slid her weapon back into its holster. That had been a little too much like when she'd shot Lisa Nichols.

"Is he okay?" she asked Burdett.

"The wound from the knife isn't deep," Burdett said. "But we need to get him to the hospital."

Sarah Novak stroked her son's hair.

"Megan's outside in our car," McCabe told her.

"Thank you," Novak said. She began to hum a song to her son. It sounded like a nursery song.

"Do you know what drug he took?" McCabe asked Burdett. They moved away from the emergency room cubicle where Scott was being treated, finding a corner near a storage area where they could talk.

"His reaction was extreme," Burdett said. "Almost a psychotic episode. It might have been what young people refer to as 'rocket fuel.' Popular years ago. Now making a comeback."

Baxter said, "Is drug counseling part of your work at the church?"

"Indirectly. I facilitate bringing in the experts who can speak knowledgably on the subject."

"I guess Scott wasn't paying attention to what your experts had to say."

"I don't think Scott has used drugs before," Burdett said. "Kevin was as concerned as I am about drug use among the young people in our church. I'm sure he talked to both Kevin and his sister about the dangers."

"If Scott had never used drugs before," McCabe said, "how would you explain what happened tonight, Dr. Burdett?"

"Grief. Stress. Anger. Kevin has been grieving for his father while trying to be strong for his mother and sister. He took the pills to relieve the pressure he was feeling. He had an adverse reaction."

"If he had succeeded in cutting his own throat, that would definitely have been adverse," Baxter said.

Burdett chose to ignore Baxter's observation. "The emergency room physician has ordered full blood work on Scott. That will tell us what drugs he has in his system. In the meantime, he has exhausted himself and should sleep for a while."

"Then we'll check back with Mrs. Novak tomorrow," McCabe said. "We'll need to speak to Scott when he wakes up."

"Is this a police matter?"

"It's a matter that requires a report," McCabe said. "I was required to stun a seventeen-year-old who was high on drugs and tried to cut his own throat." She paused. "There's also the matter of what Scott said."

"What he said? What did he say?"

" 'I'm sorry, Dad. Sorry . . . I didn't mean to do it,' " McCabe quoted.

"He was talking about taking drugs and getting high," Burdett said. "He knew that his father would have been disappointed."

"That may have been what he meant. Please tell Mrs. Novak we'll check back with her tomorrow."

They were halfway to their car when McCabe's ORB buzzed.

"Sorry, Mike, we've got to go back. Luanne is awake and she wants to talk to us."

34

Luanne Woodward was sitting up in bed, but she looked pale and drained. "I come up here," she said, "and someone tries to kill me. Can you believe that?"

McCabe said, "Do you have any idea who might have wanted you dead?"

"That's some question, honey. It must have been someone who knows about my sweet tooth."

"Where did the pie come from?" Baxter asked. He was standing by the window. McCabe had sat down in the chair by the bed.

Woodward said, "All I know is where I found it. I went to open my front door, and there it was on the stoop."

McCabe said, "Why did you open your front door? Did someone knock or ring the bell?"

"Not that I heard. I was on my way out to take my walk before I started my Sunday dinner. I'm supposed to walk every day. But then I saw the box sitting there. And I forgot about taking a walk because I wanted to see what was inside."

"So when you opened the box and found the pie," Baxter said. "Didn't you wonder if you ought to eat a pie someone had left on your doorstep?"

"When I saw the note, I thought Olive had sent it," Woodward said.

"What note?" McCabe asked.

"The note that was taped to the box."

"Was it handwritten?"

"No, but I didn't think anything of that. It sounded like it came from Olive. The note said I wasn't to worry about what had happened the night before at the séance. And it said she would see me when she got back from New York City. She had said she was going down to the City to meet her old friend from her college days."

McCabe said, "That means the person who left the pie knew Ms. Cooper was going out of town."

"Must have. And saying she'd be in touch when she got back made sure I didn't pick up my ORB to thank her."

"What'd you do with this note?" Baxter asked.

Woodward furrowed her brow. "I think I left it there on the counter in the kitchen."

"We didn't see it," McCabe said.

"Well, I don't remember putting it away, but if you didn't see it . . . I know I didn't put it in the trash. So it must be there somewhere."

"Did anyone come by after you received the pie?" McCabe asked.

"No, it was just me on my lonesome. And I was of two minds about that. It would have been nice to have somebody there when I started feeling so sick. But, on the other hand, sick as I felt and bad as I looked, I didn't need anyone around me, pestering me."

"It would have been nice to have someone there when you opened the back door and passed out," Baxter said.

"You know I don't even remember doing that. I could have froze to death if it had got real cold, lying there halfway out the door like that."

"So someone told you how you were found," McCabe said.

"The doctor, when he was telling me how lucky I was not to be dead."

"Very lucky," McCabe said. "Let's talk about the séance."

"What about it, honey?"

"I have a brother," McCabe said. "He's a scientist. Detective Baxter and I had a chat with him about the various ways a bell might be made to levitate from a table."

Woodward held her gaze. "Honey, are you accusing me again of pulling a hoax?"

"I'm saying we know how you might have done it. But the important thing here, Luanne, is that if you're working some kind of scam, you may have created a problem for yourself. The person who killed Kevin Novak may think you really can communicate with the dead."

"You think whoever killed Kevin tried to kill me?"

"That's a possibility. So I think you'd make all our lives a lot easier if you tried telling us the truth about what you're up to."

Woodward pressed her hands to each side of her face. "I guess you may be right. This isn't working out quite the way I was hoping it would when I left North Carolina."

"So you didn't just choose Albany by pointing your finger at your grandfather's map," Baxter said.

"Well, that was just a little prettying up of the truth. I was in my granddaddy's library when I decided I needed to make the trip. And I did look at the map. But I already knew where Albany was and that I was going to come here."

"Why?" McCabe asked.

Woodward sighed. "I'm going to have to tell you a story to explain this. When I was a little girl, my daddy used to come up here to Albany. He didn't go into the tobacco business with his daddy. Instead, he took this job with a munitions company, and for a while they had him coming up here just about every month for some kind of business deal they had going on with the military."

"And what does your father coming up to Albany have to do with what we're discussing?"

"I'm getting to that. I told you I'd have to tell you a story. Anyway, my daddy got old and sick, and Mama had died. He didn't want to leave his house—wouldn't even come and live with me in Granddaddy's house. And he was so mean to 'em, we had a hard time keeping a nurse's aide to stay with him. Then he got so sick he had to go back in the hospital. And he caught pneumonia in the hospital and died." Luanne paused. "That's when I found it. Or, at least, I found it after we'd buried him, and my sister and I were sorting through his things so we could sell his house."

McCabe said, "What was the 'it' that you and your sister found?"

"It was just me that found it. I didn't tell my sister. I decided I should find out what it was all about before I told her. My sister is sensitive, I guess you'd say. She doesn't handle it well when things don't go along the way she thinks they ought to."

"So what did you find that would have gotten her upset?" Baxter asked.

"A folder I found in Daddy's desk drawer. He'd always kept his desk locked, but when he died, I found the key on his key chain."

"What was in the folder?" McCabe asked.

"A report from an investigator he'd hired back in 1972."

She paused, staring down at the blanket over her knees.

Baxter said, "Are you going to tell us what was in the report?"

Woodward looked up, and there were tears in her eyes. "I'm sorry to be dragging this out. But it's hard to tell about losing the last little bit of respect you had left for your own daddy."

McCabe said, "Yes, I guess it would be. But you did say that it was time you told us this story."

"The report was about the child my father had hired the investigator to find. His mother had died, and my daddy wanted to know what became of the child."

McCabe said, "What happened to the child?"

"He was in an orphanage. They hadn't been able to find any next of kin, so they'd put him in an orphanage."

"Why did your father want to find this little boy?" McCabe asked.

"That wasn't in the report. But there was a picture in the drawer with the report. A photograph of a little boy, about a year or so old. And on the back of the photograph, someone—I'm guessing his mother—had written, '*Your son. His name is Kevin.*'"

They were all silent for a moment. Then Baxter said, "Kevin Novak?"

Woodward nodded. "He was my half brother. I think his mama asked my daddy for help when she knew she had cancer. Maybe he sent her some money, but given what the report said about how she and her child had been living, I doubt it. He sure didn't do anything when he found out his son had been put in an orphanage. Just left him there."

"Was your mother still alive when he found out?" McCabe asked.

"She was alive, but he wouldn't have cared about hurting her feelings."

McCabe decided to leave that alone. "So you came here looking for your brother."

"Not looking for him. I knew where he was. I did what my daddy did and hired a PI. I was worried about how I was going to introduce myself. I didn't want to pop up and say, 'Howdy, I'm your sister.' " Woodward smiled. "And then I found out my brother was a funeral director, and I thought I had myself a good idea."

"What?" Baxter asked. "Coming here and seeing if he needed a medium?"

"That didn't come up until I got here and Olive was telling me about him. Like I said, I didn't rush right up here. When I found out Kevin was a funeral director, I knew we had something in common."

"Dealing with the dead?" McCabe asked.

"And both us being interested in folklore and superstition. I found this interview with him on the Web. He'd given this talk and this group had put it up. And he was talking about this discussion node he belonged to where he'd had this conversation with someone about premature burial. I knew about that discussion node, so I decided to join." Luanne smiled. "That was how I met my own brother. On that node."

"When you say 'met,' " McCabe said. "Did you introduce yourself?"

"No, I just started chatting with him about different topics that came up on the node. Other folks were there, chatting, too. But I would comment whenever Kevin said something. And he started responding to what I said. It turned out we had the same sense of humor. We had a chuckle or two together."

"Did he know you were a medium?"

"I didn't mention it."

"And after meeting him on the Web, you decided to come here and meet him in person."

"Yes, and I should have done it sooner. I knew something was going wrong with him."

"How did you know that?"

"He stopped showing up on the node as much. At first, I assumed he was just busy. But when he did come back, it was like he'd just lost all his spirit. Like he was sunk in gloom and didn't really care much anymore about what was being discussed."

"When did this happen?" McCabe asked.

"He stopped logging in for a while back in September. I guess that would have been when his friend Bob died. But he didn't say anything about it when he came back. He just wasn't the same."

" 'Sunk in gloom,' you said."

"I didn't have to see him to know he was drooping over something."

"So this was an old-style discussion node," Baxter said. "No visual contact."

"Or voice contact. Believe it or not, honey, some people enjoy it more when other folks don't know how they look and sound. Just what they think. Leaves a whole lot more room for the imagination."

"Getting back to Kevin," McCabe said.

"I knew something was wrong. I decided to come up here and meet my brother and apologize for the way Daddy had treated him. But I never got any further than that afternoon at Olive's celebration. She introduced us, and he took off running."

"Ms. Cooper introduced you to Kevin as a medium. Did you tell her anything about your relationship to Kevin?"

Woodward shook her head. "I didn't tell anyone. Didn't even tell my own sister. I thought I had to tell Kevin himself first."

"But someone else may have found out," McCabe said.

"And tried to kill me because Kevin and I were kin? Why would anyone care about that?"

"Right now, we have more questions than we have answers," McCabe said. "We'd like to get back into your house again to look for the note that was attached to the box the pie came in."

"Well, honey, I didn't have my key in my nightgown. Unless you brought it out with you—"

"I did," McCabe said. "We locked your door as we were leaving. We have your key secured at the station house."

"Then I guess you won't have any trouble getting back in."

"We'll also be checking with your neighbors to see if anyone happened to notice who left the pie on your doorstep."

"That's fine with me. I want to know who wanted me dead. I want to know if it's the same person who killed my brother before I'd even had a chance to know him."

Let's hope it wasn't your nephew, McCabe thought, thinking of Scott's words before he tried to slash his own throat.

35

McCabe turned from her monitor. "Research is going to see what they can find on Luanne's father and his supposed connection to Kevin's mother."

Baxter raised an eyebrow. "Did I miss something? I thought last night you were buying her story. We were talking about whether any of our suspects could have found out she was his half sister."

"I know we were. But I had time to sleep on it. And when I woke up this morning, I was thinking about how after lying to us with one elaborate story, she decided to volunteer a new one."

"Well, she did almost die. That might have affected her inclination to come clean. Especially after you pointed out the person who tried to kill her might still be out to get her."

"Yes, but didn't you think there was something a bit off about— and I know people react in all kinds of ways to traumatic events. I've seen them do it. I understand she might have been trying not to fall apart. But there was something off about the way she talked about Kevin and his being her half brother."

"They had only met face-to-face once. She did have tears in her eyes at one point."

"Yes, and the tears looked real. But I still want to hear what Research finds."

"You're a hard woman, McCabe."

"I just prefer not to believe any tale that I'm told without checking it out. Verify, Baxter."

"We could always ask her to take a DNA test."

McCabe stood up and reached for her ORB. "I wonder how she'd react to that request. Ready to go in and bring the lou up to speed, so we can head out to Luanne's and look for that note?"

"Right behind you," Baxter said, pushing his chair away from his desk.

"Okay," McCabe said as they stood in the living room of Luanne Woodward's house. "Nothing in here. No note hidden in plain sight among the mail. So let's divide up the rest of the rooms. I'll do the bedroom and bathroom and you can do the kitchen and dining room."

"Hey, that's sexist. Are you saying a male cop doesn't know how to search a woman's bedroom?"

"No, I'm saying Luanne would probably rather not have you looking through her underwear drawer."

Baxter grinned. "Okay, so I've got kitchen duty. But you've got the john. I hope she wasn't so delirious she used the note as toilet paper."

"And I hope," McCabe said, "that was your last bathroom joke for the day."

"Just keeping it light."

In Luanne's bedroom, McCabe started at the dresser and worked her way to the closet. No note under utilitarian cotton underwear and nightgowns. No note in coat or jacket pockets. Or in the nightstand that held a print Bible that looked old enough to be a family heirloom and, in a plastic protective envelope, an old pulp novel from the 1950s with a garish cover of a scantily dressed woman. *Secret Desires* was the title.

McCabe took out her flashlight and looked under the bed. Then she checked under the pillows and finally felt under the mattress.

It was revealing, McCabe thought, that Luanne had no objection to allowing police detectives to search her house. That would suggest she had nothing to hide. Or if she did have something to hide, it was nothing they would find by looking through her cabinets and drawers.

"Anything, Mike?" McCabe asked as she walked back into the dining room.

"Something kind of weird," Baxter said.

He had what looked like a scrapbook open on the table. "Found this over there in the china cabinet."

McCabe glanced at the cabinet, which contained only a few serving platters and a candelabrum. "It was inside?"

"Yeah," he said. "It looks like one of those family photo albums. My folks have some they inherited from one of my aunts."

"We've got some family albums, too," McCabe said. "What's weird about this one?"

"Flip through it. You'll see."

"Luanne mentioned that photo of Kevin when he was a toddler that his mother sent her father. But I don't suppose she would have put it in the family album where her sister or other relatives might see it."

"Didn't see it," Baxter said.

McCabe gave him a questioning glance and flipped back to the beginning of the album. The photos on the first few pages were in black and white, yellowed with age. From the style of the clothing, the early photos dated back to the 1920s or '30s. Changing clothing styles marked the passing years. But there was one thing that remained consistent.

"Cars," McCabe said. "They're all posing in front of, leaning against, sitting on or in a car. I guess Luanne decided to do a family album with a theme."

"Either that or they owned a car dealership. The last car in the most recent photo was manufactured in 2006."

"I'll take your word for it," McCabe said. "But I don't see anything that could help us." McCabe was about to close the album when she stopped and flipped back to the first page. "Mike, did you check the backs of any of these photos? Remember Luanne said Kevin's mother had written a note on the back of the photo she sent to Luanne's father? People used to do that. I remember looking through the old albums that my mother inherited from her mother."

As she was speaking, McCabe was sliding the photos from their slots. "My grandmother had written captions for some of the photos in the beginning, but then she started just writing a note on the back and putting them in the album. If no one could remember who the people were in a photo, they would check the back."

Baxter pulled the album toward him and flipped to the middle. He took out several of the photos and glanced at the backs. "What do yours say?" he asked.

McCabe read, "Carole Ann Simms, Died April 7, 1923." She turned over another. "Jim Robinson. Died July 17, 1928. Here's one from 1934. Same thing. A name and date of death."

"That's what I've got. Name and date of death."

"The last names are different," McCabe said. "But they could be branches of the family. Cousins."

"Or maybe Luanne has some weird thing about collecting photos of dead people with their cars."

McCabe felt the goose bumps rise on her arms. "Okay," she said. "Luanne seems to have an odd hobby. Or maybe it's not so odd for a medium. Maybe these are people she tried to contact. Maybe she always asks for a photo of the dearly departed with his or her car."

"We should ask her about that."

McCabe reached for the photos. "Meantime, let's get these back in the album and go talk to the neighbors. Maybe someone saw something."

"If we're lucky enough to catch anyone at home on a weekday morning."

McCabe turned toward the kitchen. "The refrigerator. You did look inside again?"

"Sure. It was standing right there in front of me."

"Sorry, just wanted to make sure. My dad once tore his office up looking for the slip of paper that he'd written something on. Then he opened the refrigerator to make himself a sandwich and found it stuck to the carton of milk he'd taken out when he was having a cup of coffee."

Baxter said, "I checked everything in the refrigerator, including the food in the freezer. No note."

"What could she have done with that note? If she was telling the truth about it, where is it?"

"No garbage disposal. So she didn't accidentally grind it up."

"She gets the pie. The note's attached to the box. She takes the note off and reads it. She doesn't throw it away or you would have found it in the trash can. She might have torn it up and flushed it down the toilet, but why would she do that, even if she were delirious? The note, according to her, was a friendly note from Olive. No reason to destroy it."

"But it's not in her bedroom or bathroom."

"Or here in the dining room or the kitchen."

"Not in the photo album."

"The paramedics took her purse along. But the contents of the purse were inventoried at the hospital before they locked it away. No note on the list." McCabe froze. "Wait. The lab. Maybe it was with the food that I dropped off at the lab."

"The lab?" Baxter said. "We would have seen it if it had been attached to the box or the pie plate."

McCabe said, "What if the note had gotten stuck to the bottom of the pie plate? Luanne put the pie in the refrigerator. I took it out and took off the foil to look at it and then I started to look for the box it had come in. You came in, we were talking, and I put the pie into a brown paper bag I'd found in a cabinet."

"But if the note was on the bottom of the pie plate, Delgardo's techs would have noticed when they took it out of the bag."

"Maybe. But if the note fell off the bottom of the pie plate and into the bag, they might have missed it." McCabe took out her ORB. "No harm in asking them to check."

She got through to Delgardo himself. He told her to hold. When he returned, he gave a shake of his head. "We have the bags. No note. And nothing in the collard greens, by the way. One set of fingerprints on the containers, but they probably belong to your victim. We'll let you know if they don't."

"Thanks, Ray. The note in the bag was a long shot."

"Well, I'm out of bright ideas," McCabe told Baxter. "Let's go see if we can find some neighbors to talk to."

"Maybe someone really did come to the back door," Baxter said. "Stepped over Luanne's unconscious body and walked out with the note."

"But that person would presumably have been the person who sent or delivered the poison pie. And, in that case, why not take away the rest of the incriminating evidence? The pie itself. The box."

"Maybe it was only the note that mattered."

"That's possible, but—" McCabe stopped, staring at her partner. "The back door was open. The wind was blowing. Maybe Luanne had the note in her hand when she went to the door. Maybe the note blew out into the yard."

"In that case, even if we find it, it's not going to be much help. It's been out there in the rain and the melting snow."

"But if we can find it, Delgardo might be able to tell us something about the paper. And, at least, we'll have proof she did receive a note."

McCabe was heading toward the kitchen as she spoke. Baxter followed behind her. "This is why I joined the cops," he said. "To dig through the mud and muck in someone's backyard."

"Better than what you were doing when you were in Vice," McCabe said. "At least, you won't get stuck by someone's used needle."

"Don't count on that. All kinds of things wash up in people's yards in the city."

They spent the next fifteen minutes or so in Luanne's fenced backyard. The snow had melted as the temperature climbed and the small yard was dead grass, mud, and slush.

"Got something," Baxter said. He was squatting down to peer under a bush with prickly bare branches. "It looks like the edge of a piece of white paper. I can't tell if it has print on it."

McCabe came over to peer at the paper. "Can you hold back the bush? I'll use the trowel we found to try to scoop up the paper and the muck it's stuck in. Maybe Delgardo's techs can save enough of it to tell us something useful."

McCabe turned the glass container she'd snagged from Luanne's kitchen on its side and nudged the paper into it.

"Have we finished our backyard adventure?" Baxter asked.

McCabe nodded. "Let's go see if we can find some nosy neighbors."

They scraped off their boots and tramped back through Luanne Woodward's house to make sure they had turned off the lights, which were manually controlled, like the ones in Olive Cooper's mansion.

"I wonder," McCabe said, "if Luanne knew Olive wasn't into the modern conveniences when she rented this place."

"According to Luanne, she's just a simple down-home girl," Baxter said. "She wouldn't have been influenced by rich folks."

"But she didn't grow up poor, either. We should check into how much granddaddy and daddy left Luanne and her sister. And what, if anything, a half brother might have been entitled to."

"That might give her a motive," Baxter agreed. "But if she was worried about having to share with her newly discovered half brother, why would she come looking for him?"

"And she does have an alibi for the time of his death. And someone seems to have tried to kill her. But no harm in checking off the unexpected-heir-to-the-fortune box."

They knocked on the doors of the houses to the left and right of Luanne Woodward's. No one came to either door. There were no cars parked in the driveways or on the street in front of the houses, so it was possible the residents were at work, not simply avoiding strangers who knocked on their doors.

"Let's try the house across the street," McCabe said. "When Luanne was being taken away by the paramedics, I thought I saw someone at the window over there."

McCabe was drawing her hand back from the bell when the door opened. A blond woman, in her forties, wearing coveralls streaked with paint, smiled out at them. "Saw you coming from the upstairs window," she said. She gestured at her coveralls. "I'm painting the guest room."

"Sorry to interrupt," McCabe said. "We're Albany PD detectives."

"Good," the woman said. "You can tell me what's been going on across the street. I'm dying of curiosity."

She gestured for them to come in. As she was leading them into the living room, McCabe introduced herself and Baxter.

The woman introduced herself as Deb. "Please sit down." She covered an armchair with an old towel before sitting down herself. "So what's been going on?"

McCabe said, "Do you know your neighbor across the street?"

"Luanne? I met her when she first moved in. She told me she was from North Carolina. And she said she was a medium. I've been hoping I'd get a chance to hear some more about that. But when I'm home, she's usually out."

"But you were at home the other day when the paramedics came, right?" McCabe said. "I thought I saw someone at an upstairs window."

"That was me. I was doing measurements for new drapes. My mother-in-law is coming to visit. That's why I'm painting the guest room."

"When you were upstairs on Sunday, did you happen to see anyone come to the door of Luanne's house?"

"There was someone. I thought it might be her birthday or a special occasion."

"Why?" Baxter asked. "Who came to the door?"

"A deliveryman. He drove up, hopped out of his car, and set a white box on Luanne's doorstep. Then he got back in the car and drove away."

"Did you notice a name or logo on the car?" McCabe asked.

Deb shook her head. "No, actually the car was an old heap. I thought he must be using his own car for deliveries."

"What made you think this person was a deliveryman?"

"He was wearing a baseball cap and a jacket. The jacket was red and it had lettering on the back. And he was a kid. I saw him get out and leave the box, and I thought 'deliveryman.' " Deb smiled. "I would have thought pizza deliveryman, but they always have signs on their cars, and he would have rung the bell and gotten money for pizza instead of leaving it out in the cold on the steps."

"So this kid who delivered the box didn't ring the bell?" Baxter asked.

"No, and I was wondering if I should let Luanne know the box was out there. But then I dropped my paint roller and splattered yellow paint on the floor. By the time I had cleaned that up and looked across the street again, the box was gone. So I assumed Luanne had gotten it."

McCabe asked, "Did you see Luanne at all that day?"

" 'Fraid not. My husband came home from a business trip at around four. And we made dinner together and watched an old movie, then went off to an early bed. I didn't think to look back across the street again until the next day when I heard the sirens." Deb looked from McCabe to Baxter. "I've answered your questions. Now, aren't you going to tell me what happened?"

McCabe glanced at Baxter. "I'm afraid we can't discuss the specifics of what happened. But Luanne was taken ill."

Deb said, "I know that. She was taken away in an ambulance. But why are you asking questions about the delivery she received?"

"We're trying to reconstruct what happened leading up to her illness."

"Is Luanne all right?"

"She's still in the hospital," McCabe said. "But her doctors expect her to make a full recovery. About the deliveryman you saw . . . you said he was young, looked like a kid. Can you tell us anything else about him?"

Deb shook her head. "Not much. He was fairly tall. I didn't get a good look at his face because of the baseball cap, but light-skinned, probably white."

"The lettering on the back of his jacket," Baxter said. "Could it have been a sports team?"

"I don't know. It might have been. I was paying more attention to what he was dropping off."

"What about the car," McCabe said. "You said an 'old heap.' "

"It might have been a hybrid. But I don't know that much about cars. This one was gray and boxy."

McCabe looked at Baxter. He shook his head. "Generic older model hybrid."

"What about the license plate on the car?" he asked Deb.

"I think it was New York State. I would probably have noticed if it was anything else. But I wasn't paying attention to that, either." Deb made a face. "I'm sorry I'm not more help. If I had known it was going to be important I would have been glued to the window with my binoculars."

McCabe said, "You've given us a couple of leads we can follow up on."

"Good. I feel awful about Luanne. She could have died over there, and we wouldn't have known until someone found her body." Deb frowned. "I know you said you can't go into specifics . . . but the delivery she received. Was it some kind of prank?"

"No, it wasn't a prank," McCabe said. "But it's nothing you need to worry about. And we should let you get back to your painting. Thank you again for your help."

In the car, McCabe took out her ORB. When Lt. Dole came on, she said, "Sir, we just spoke to one of Luanne's neighbors. She saw the pie being dropped off."

"Could she give you a description?"

"She saw what she assumed was a deliveryman drive up and leave the box on Luanne's doorstep. He was young, wearing a baseball cap and a jacket, and driving an old heap. The car had no markings she noticed."

"So this 'deliveryman' could have been anyone."

"She described him as 'a kid,' sir. Baxter and I are thinking the deliveryman could have been Scott Novak."

"What motive would Novak's son have? Are you thinking it's something to do with the medium claiming to be his father's half sister?"

"We haven't gotten that far in our thinking, sir. Luanne said she hadn't told anyone about Novak being her half brother. So it isn't clear how Scott could have known."

"Then why do you think he would try to poison her?"

McCabe glanced over at Baxter, who was grinning. He had said the lieutenant was going to ask that question.

"We don't know that he did, sir. But we do need to interview him about what happened yesterday."

"Let his mother know you need to interview him."

"He's seventeen years old, sir. Technically—"

"McCabe, the fact that he's an adult to the state of New York isn't going to mean squat to that kid's mother. Her baby boy is lying there in a hospital bed." Dole rubbed his hand over his head. "She and Burdett, the kid's shrink, may have backed your call to stun the kid rather than let him slash his throat, but if you start going after him—"

"Point made, sir. We'll inform his mother."

"Check back in after you do the interview."

"Yes, sir."

McCabe pulled up Sarah Novak's code.

"Hello," Novak said. "Detective McCabe? Do you have news?"

"It looks like you're still at the hospital, Mrs. Novak."

"Yes, I came down to the cafeteria to have some lunch with Megan before her friend's mother picked her up. Scott woke up, but he fell asleep again. I'm on my way back up to his room."

"And we're on our way to the hospital. Would you meet us outside Scott's room in about twenty minutes?"

"Outside his room? What . . . is there something wrong?"

"We'll explain when we get there, Mrs. Novak. See you shortly."

Baxter said, "That story our boy Scott told us about going to the funeral home and standing outside for a while then going home—"

"If he tried to poison Luanne, then that story becomes questionable."

"And the kid could turn out to be one hell of a liar."

McCabe pulled up the Novak file on her ORB. "I hope we're wrong."

"We get paid to solve cases, partner. If we solve Novak's murder, we get the brass off our backs."

"And Sarah Novak's family is her problem. Right?"

"Right," Baxter said. "We're cops, not social workers."

"Of course, we could be getting ahead of ourselves on this. Scott might have an alibi for when Luanne received the pie. He might have told us the truth about what he did when he went to the funeral home on the night his father was murdered."

"He might have," Baxter said. "But don't count on it."

"If Scott does have an alibi, we might be looking for a real deliveryman. Someone hired to deliver the pie to Luanne."

Baxter maneuvered around a garbage truck. "Remember," he said, "what Burdett told us about how he spent his time when he was snowed in?"

"Making a stew and baking bread."

"Wanna bet he could whip up a pie?"

"That brings us right back to motive. Why would Burdett want Kevin Novak dead? Or, if it wasn't Burdett, why would Reverend Wyatt want Kevin dead?"

"Maybe it has something to do with Wyatt's plans to expand his religious movement. The reverend told us that his sponsor for his arena events would drop him if the church were involved in a scandal. Maybe Kev was killed because he knew something that would cause a scandal."

"But if he knew something, would he have revealed what he knew? He was one of the faithful, deeply involved in his church."

"So maybe he found out something about his church leaders that disillusioned him."

"Maybe it was something that Bob knew and told Kevin before he died. That would explain Kevin's depression. Except the problem with that is that Kevin sought counseling from Reverend Wyatt and Dr. Burdett."

"Maybe he was trying to get the goods on them."

"Francesca Reeves would have us believe that she was oblivious to anything that might have been going on with her husband."

"But Bob's fancy French wife was there at Olive's house when Luanne came out of the kitchen with her slice of pie."

"So," McCabe said, "you're suggesting she might have baked one up and hired a deliveryman? Except we know that Francesca was at a spa in the Catskills when Kevin was killed."

"Maybe she hired a hit man."

"A hit man who decided to use Kevin's compound bow instead of a gun? But we know from Olive and the clerk in the archery store that it isn't that easy to pick up a bow and make an accurate shot if you aren't familiar with the weapon."

"That brings us back to Scott. His father. His father's bow. If he thought his father was cheating on his mother—"

"He never came out and said that."

"Implied," Baxter said.

36

Sarah Novak was wearing a black skirt and white pullover sweater. She looked as if she had lost weight overnight.

McCabe said, "Thank you for waiting for us out here, Mrs. Novak. No one is in the lounge. Why don't we step in there for a moment, and we'll explain what's going on."

Novak opened her mouth as if she were going to speak, then she nodded. She walked ahead of them into the visitors' lounge. "What is this about?" she asked. "Do you know who killed my husband?"

"Not yet," McCabe said. "We're still investigating your husband's death. But something else has come up involving Luanne Woodward. Did you know she's here in the hospital?"

"Yes, Olive stopped by. She told me Luanne had been brought in with some type of stomach problem."

"When did she tell you that?" Baxter asked.

"This morning when she came by."

"Actually, there's a bit more to the story," McCabe said. "Luanne received a chocolate pecan pie. She ate some of it and became seriously ill. Detective Baxter and I found her unconscious. There was arsenic in the pie."

"Arsenic?" Novak's gaze held McCabe's. "Is this related some-how to Kevin being killed?"

"We don't know," McCabe said.

"What do you know? You've been investigating my husband's death for days and you still don't know anything. And now Luanne's been poisoned."

"There's something we need to tell you about Luanne," McCabe said.

"She says she and your husband had the same father," Baxter said. "She says she's his half sister."

"That's impossible. Why is she making up a story like that? Kevin was an orphan."

"Luanne says he was sent to an orphanage when his mother died of cancer. Her father hired a private investigator who located Kevin. But as a married man with other children, her father decided to leave Kevin in the orphanage."

"How could he do that? How could he do that to his own child? If he was that kind of man, then Kevin was better off not knowing him." Her gaze fastened on McCabe again. "If this woman is telling the truth, if she knew she was Kevin's sister, why didn't she tell him?"

"She had only that brief encounter with him at Olive Cooper's celebration of life. She said she was waiting for the right time."

"And then he was dead," Baxter said. "And now someone has tried to poison—presumably kill—your husband's half sister."

McCabe gestured toward the chair Novak had begun to lean against. "Maybe you should sit down."

Novak straightened. "What else do you have to tell me?"

"The pie Luanne ate was left on her front steps," McCabe said. "We spoke to one of her neighbors, who told us she had seen the pie dropped off by a young man whom she thought was making a delivery. But there was no company name or logo on the car he was driving. She described it as 'an old heap.' And the young man—whom she described as 'a kid'—was wearing a baseball cap and a red jacket, not a uniform."

"Why are you telling me this?"

McCabe said, "We'd like to ask Scott if he knows anything about the pie Luanne received."

"If he knows anything about it? What does that mean?"

"Exactly what I said, Mrs. Novak. The description we have of the young man who delivered the pie could fit Scott."

"Scott doesn't have a car."

"He might have borrowed a friend's car," McCabe said. "It's possible that he'll know nothing about this. But we do need to speak to him."

"My son experienced a psychotic episode after taking drugs. He tried to cut his own throat. And you want to question him—to accuse him—of trying to kill someone he barely knows? I can't believe you people!"

"Mrs. Novak, we know how difficult this must be for you and for Scott. We understand that. But we have a job to do. If you are concerned that Scott isn't sufficiently recovered to be able to talk to us, then we can postpone this until his doctor gives permission. But we are going to talk to him."

"No. Absolutely not." Novak brushed past them and into the hall.

"Mrs. Novak. Wait. We need to talk about this."

"I'm calling my lawyer. You aren't getting near my son." Novak opened the door of her son's room. "Stay away from my family."

"Mom?" a groggy voice said. "What's wrong?"

"Nothing, sweetheart, it's all right."

Sarah Novak stepped inside the room and closed the door.

Baxter said, "Too bad if we have to arrest the kid to question him."

McCabe nodded. "That's up to his mother. I hope she'll change her mind. In the meantime, we'd better let the lieutenant know we may have to do this the hard way." Ignoring the NO ORBS sign, McCabe took out her ORB. She hoped Sarah Novak had her ear pressed to the door. "And I think we should pay Reverend Wyatt another visit."

When they were shown into his office at the church, Wyatt turned
from the window and came forward to greet them. "Please come
in and sit down."

A decidedly muted greeting, McCabe thought. "Thank you for
seeing us again, Reverend Wyatt."

"Are you here about Scott?"

"Why do you ask?" Baxter said.

"I just spoke to Sarah. She told me a garbled story about Luanne
Woodward, the medium, being Kevin's half sister, and that you suspected Scott of trying to kill her—Luanne Woodward—with a poisoned pie left on her front step. It sounded like something out of a
fairy tale."

McCabe said, "Not quite. But it is rather a twisted tale, isn't it?
We were hoping you might help us to understand what was going
on with Kevin Novak before he died."

"I've already told you I can't talk about that."

"But several things have happened since our last conversation,
Reverend Wyatt. Both Luanne and Scott are in the hospital. Luanne
was poisoned. Scott popped some pills he got from a friend and tried
to slash his own throat."

"I know what's happened, Detective." Wyatt pushed up
horn-rimmed glasses that McCabe hadn't seen him wear before
and pinched the bridge of his nose. "I've been examining my
own conscience about whether I'm to blame for any or all of
this."

McCabe let the silence hang there for a moment, giving Baxter
a small shake of her head before he could speak.

Wyatt adjusted his glasses. "Excuse me," he said. He got up and
went over to his desk. He picked up a black leather-bound Bible and
opened it to what seemed to be a familiar page.

McCabe and Baxter waited. In the distance, they could hear the
voices of a group crossing the courtyard.

Wyatt closed his Bible and put it down on his desk. "You have to understand. This is an incredibly difficult situation because it involves not only Kevin but also Bob Reeves."

McCabe said, "What are we talking about, Reverend Wyatt?"

"I need to ask your discretion. If it turns out there's no need to make public what I'm about to tell you—"

"Then we will do our best to keep it from going public."

"Your best?" Wyatt smiled. "I suppose that's as much of a guarantee of discretion as I'm going to get."

"I'm afraid so. Sometimes the decision is taken out of our hands."

Wyatt nodded. "I have no choice in this. I was trying to protect Kevin's family and Bob's wife, Francesca. But if you are focusing your investigation in the wrong direction and people are being harmed because I am remaining silent . . ."

McCabe said, "Then it's time for you to tell us what you know."

"Yes." Wyatt sighed. He came back over and sat down across from them. "Before his death, Bob Reeves confided a secret to Kevin, his best friend. He asked Kevin to make sure his wife—Bob's wife, Francesca—didn't find out. He didn't want her to be hurt. After some soul searching, Kevin confided the secret to me. He was concerned that what Bob had told him might become known and that if it did, the reputation of the church . . . he was concerned about the damage that might be done if the media learned what Bob had told him."

"What did Bob tell him?" Baxter asked.

Wyatt took off his glasses and held them dangling between his thumb and index finger. "Bob gave Kevin a key with a coded password. The key and password gave Kevin admittance to a club of which Bob was a member."

"What kind of club?" McCabe asked.

"An adults-only club on the Web."

"Adults only," Baxter said. "As in sex club?"

"Yes, that kind of club. The members of the club have avatar identities who—from what Kevin told me—engage in social activities and have intimate encounters."

McCabe said, "Are these encounters restricted to their avatars? Or do the club members also meet in the real world?"

"They only meet in cyberspace," Wyatt said. "That was how Bob rationalized it to Kevin. That if only the avatars were having these encounters, then it had nothing to do with real-world relationships. The members of the club were only indulging harmless fantasies. Like going to an amusement park."

Baxter said, "So why was Bob concerned about his wife finding out he was visiting this amusement park?"

"As I said, he thought she would be hurt. There is the age difference between them, and she might have thought he was dissatisfied with that aspect of their marriage. At any rate, when he realized he would be going into surgery, Bob told Kevin all this and gave him the key. He asked Kevin to resign his membership in the club and delete his account if he didn't pull through."

"So what was the problem?" Baxter asked. "All Kevin had to do was delete the account and that would have been the end of it."

"Bob was using an alias," Wyatt explained, "but if someone had wanted to find out who the members of the club were . . . Kevin wondered if other members of the church might be involved in the club."

McCabe said, "Why did Kevin wonder about that, Reverend Wyatt?"

"Bob's closest friendships were with Kevin and several other members of the congregation."

"As far as Kevin knew," Baxter said. "But there might have been a few friendships Kevin didn't know about. Bob was a lawyer—"

"A lawyer who specialized in estate planning. His clients were often elderly."

"Which doesn't mean they didn't know how to have fun," Baxter said. "Maybe one of his clients brought Bob into the club."

"Whoever introduced Bob to the club," McCabe said, "Kevin was concerned that other members of the church might be involved. Is that right?"

"Yes," Wyatt said. "When he told me about it, so was I. I know now it was a mistake. But I agreed to Kevin's plan to use Bob's access to the club to see if there was any other connection to the church."

"So for the past few months, Kevin Novak had been a member of a Web sex club using his friend Bob's avatar?"

"No, not for the past few months. Only for a few weeks. Then I became concerned that it wasn't appropriate to expose Kevin to . . . I asked him to delete the account."

"And he agreed to do that?" McCabe asked.

"Yes. He said he hadn't found anything. That it was time to do what Bob had asked him to do."

"But you're concerned that during the time he was involved in this club, something might have happened that led to his death?"

"Yes. What if someone realized he was an impostor? What if he was killed because someone was afraid he would expose the club members?"

"Reverend Wyatt," McCabe said, "as long as they're adults only, Web sex clubs are legal."

"I know they're legal," Wyatt said. "But maybe there was someone in this club who wanted to keep his or her identity a secret?"

"That's possible," McCabe said. "Did Kevin say anything to suggest he was concerned that someone in the club suspected he was an imposter?"

"No. I've just been worried about it since he was killed."

"But the reason you suggested to Kevin that he end his investigation of the club was because you were concerned about his psychological well-being."

Wyatt put his glasses back on. "He seemed distracted and preoccupied. When I asked if something was bothering him, he said he was busy at work."

"When we talked before, you suggested he might be experiencing some depression as he worked through his therapy with Dr. Burdett."

"Yes, and I did think his therapy would be easier if he could focus on himself and his family without the distraction of—"

"Romping, naked avatars in a sex club?" Baxter asked.

"I'm sure Kevin did not take part in romps, Detective Baxter.

He said it wasn't required. That some of the avatars simply drank and danced. Or gambled."

Before Baxter could comment on that, McCabe said, "Reverend Wyatt, are you sure that you're the only one who knew what Kevin was doing? That he didn't tell Dr. Burdett or his wife?"

"I'm positive he wouldn't have told Sarah. And I asked him not to tell Jonathan."

"Why did you ask him not to tell Dr. Burdett?" Baxter asked.

"Because, even though Jonathan would never reveal a confidence from someone he was counseling, this was a private matter between Bob and his wife. It was enough that Kevin and I had become privy to that aspect of their marriage."

"So you were being chivalrous," Baxter said. "Protecting Francesca Reeves from the embarrassment of having anyone else know what you would never tell her."

Wyatt flushed. "I know it sounds silly to you, Detective. But after we became aware of Bob's secret life, Kevin and I had enough difficulty looking Francesca in the eye. There was no reason to place Jonathan in that same awkward position."

They picked up Chinese takeout on the way back to the station house.

"I'm going to run this up to Delgardo," McCabe said, holding up the container with the piece of white paper they'd found in Luanne's backyard. "Tell the lou I'll be right there."

They were going to do a working lunch in Lt. Dole's office while they filled him in on what Reverend Wyatt had told them.

By the time McCabe got back downstairs, Baxter and the lieutenant had their plates full and were talking basketball. She filled her own plate while they were debating players and took the opportunity to make a few notes in her ORB. She looked up when they both fell silent. "Did I miss something?"

"Are you trying to tell us we should be focusing on the matter at hand?" Dole asked.

"No, sir. I assumed you'd both get back to that when you were done."

Dole cleared his throat. "Getting to why we're here."

"Yes, sir, as I mentioned when I tagged you, Reverend Wyatt gave us a new lead."

"Something that doesn't involve the Novak kid?"

"That's not clear. It could. But there's also the possibility Kevin Novak got in over his head while he was playing undercover cop. No pun intended."

"No pun about what?"

"A sex club," McCabe said.

McCabe gave the lieutenant a summary of their conversation with Wyatt.

"So the question," Baxter said, "is whether someone figured out a new player had entered the club, a player who was pretending to be one of the regulars."

"And if someone did figure that out," McCabe said, "was this person—or maybe persons—concerned enough about this intruder's presence to try to find out who he was?"

"And if this person or persons was able to find out who Kevin was," Baxter said, "did they track him back to the real world and kill him?"

"That seems like an over-the-top response to someone crashing the party," Dole said.

"Yes, sir," McCabe replied. "Unless this person or persons needed to keep their involvement in the club a secret and feared that Kevin was some kind of twenty-first-century Comstock agent out to stamp out sin and wickedness. In that case, they might have thought he and/or the church he belonged to planned some kind of exposé about the goings-on of the club."

"Killing your vic wouldn't ensure the exposé—if there was going to be one—wouldn't go forward. For all they knew, he might have been making regular reports to his minister or whoever had put him up to going undercover."

McCabe nodded. "That's the glitch in our theory. Even if someone did realize Kevin had assumed his friend Bob's avatar identity, if they had thought about it, they would have realized killing him might not solve the problem."

"Unless they never connected him back to the church," Baxter said. He speared a chunk of chicken with his plastic fork. "Suppose Kevin told Wyatt that he was going to close down the account, but didn't. Suppose he not only kept visiting the club, but began to enjoy himself. What if he decided to meet up with someone he had met in the club in the real world?"

"And hooked up with a psycho?" Dole said.

"That night in the funeral home?" McCabe asked.

"Kinky enough for a sex club hookup, right? But our vic ends up dead."

"Before we start looking for Novak's hookup," Dole said, "let's consider the obvious. We've got a guy, who for whatever reason, was hanging out in a sex club. The guy had a wife. How do you feel about the wife as a suspect?"

McCabe said, "This would give her a motive, sir. But if we can believe what Scott told us, his mother was at home when he left for the funeral home."

"But he didn't say she was there when he got back," Baxter said. "He said he wanted to get back before she realized he was gone."

Dole said, "Are you suggesting she went out after he did and they both ended up at the funeral home?"

Baxter said, "Assuming Scott went there at all. What if the story he told us was intended to provide his mother with an alibi. That would explain why she didn't want us to talk to him, because she was afraid he would slip up and admit he hadn't gone to the funeral home that night."

McCabe shook her head. "Okay, this is getting really twisted. That would mean that she knew what he had told us about going to the funeral home. He asked us not to tell her."

"Even more clever. He completely distracted us."

"Really clever for a seventeen-year-old kid."

Baxter speared another piece of chicken with his fork. "Just playing 'what if,' partner. I thought you liked that game."

McCabe gazed back at him, caught off balance by the ripple of tension.

"What about the other wife?" Dole asked. "Francesca. Any reason she might have gone after Bob's best friend if she found out about the sex club?"

"I don't see her for that, Lou," McCabe said. "She seems sophisticated enough to take learning her husband was a member of a virtual reality sex club—or even had real-life encounters—in her stride. And I'm not sure what her motive would be for killing Kevin, even if she had found out about Bob."

"Okay," Dole said, reaching for his coffee mug. "What about this psychiatrist or family counselor, Burdett? The minister says he told your vic not to tell him."

"Which doesn't mean Kev didn't confide," Baxter said.

McCabe swallowed her bite of egg roll. "I agree with Mike, sir," she said. "If Kevin was trying to work through his guilt about Bob's death, I would think discovering Bob had been involved in a sex club would have been something Kevin would have found hard not to confide to his therapist."

"The reverend did say the reason he told Kev to get out of the club was because he thought being involved might be interfering with his therapy with Burdett."

"Sounds like you should have a chat with the psychiatrist about what he knew and when. And this time make it clear to him that what he knows about Kevin Novak's involvement in this sex club is not a matter of patient confidentiality. It's an important piece of your murder investigation."

37

McCabe told Burdett that it was urgent they speak to him. He said, grudgingly, that he would fit them in between patients. They drove back to Willett Street, and this time caught someone pulling out of a parking space a few doors down from Burdett's building.

His receptionist asked them to go into the waiting room off the foyer.

Baxter nodded toward the large aquarium fitted into a recess of one wall. "The doc seems to be into fish."

"They probably soothe his patients," McCabe said. "I tried raising tropical fish when I was a kid. Keeping the aquarium clean was a pain."

"But you kept it sparkling clean anyway?"

"No, I didn't. My mother had a friend who kept fish. She got him to take them. And she reminded me and my dad that she had objected to getting me fish in the first place."

"Sounds like my mom about the guinea pig I bought with my birthday money," Baxter said. "But my guinea pig solved the problem by dying. My dad said he must have been lonely not having a guinea pig pal."

"Yeah, I read somewhere they're social and do better in pairs."

The small talk they were making was serving to smooth over the brief ripple of tension in the lou's office and the relative silence of their ride over. McCabe still hadn't figured out what that little moment had been about. Maybe Baxter was getting tired of being the junior partner and following her lead. Or, maybe something else was going on. For now, they were both pretending that moment hadn't happened.

About fifteen minutes later, they heard Burdett's receptionist saying good-bye to a patient. She came to the door of the waiting room and said Dr. Burdett could see them now.

Burdett rose as they entered his office and invited them to sit down, but he was not happy to see them. His courtesy verged on frostiness. He sat back down behind his desk. "What can I do for you?"

McCabe said, "We need your help, Dr. Burdett. We've learned Kevin Novak was involved in investigating a matter related to his friend, Bob Reeves. We need to know what he told you about that."

"I'm afraid I don't know what you're referring—to what you're referring."

And the Ivy-educated among us reveal their stress by grammatical stutters, McCabe thought. "Dr. Burdett, we do respect your ethical duty to preserve patient confidentiality. But your patient is dead. He was murdered. And we now—finally—have a lead. Your obligation now is to tell us anything that can help us find a killer before anyone else is hurt or killed. You do know that Luanne Woodward is in the hospital. That someone tried to kill her."

"I spoke to Sarah after your attempt to speak to Scott."

"Did you?" Baxter asked.

"But what happened to the Woodward woman can't have anything to do with Kevin's death."

"How do you know?" Baxter asked.

"I—how could they be connected?"

McCabe said, "We need to know what Kevin told you, Dr. Burdett. We know Bob Reeves belonged to a cyberspace sex club. We want to know what Kevin told you about that."

"I—" Burdett shook his head. "This is—"

"It is possible Kevin's family could be in danger, Dr. Burdett. If he had learned something he shouldn't have about the club members—"

"That wasn't it." Burdett frowned. He laced his fingers together on his desk. "I'm going to tell you this because I'm not sure what's going on. And I am concerned this might not have ended with Kevin's death."

"What are we talking about, Doc?" Baxter asked.

"There was a woman. A woman Kevin met in this club."

"Did something happen between them?" McCabe asked.

"It began with a conversation between their avatars—or, rather, Bob's avatar and this woman's. Kevin hoped the woman would be a source of information about the club and its members. But he found himself attracted to her."

"To an avatar?" Baxter said.

"Have you ever tried interacting in virtual space through an avatar, Detective Baxter?"

"Sure, I used to play lots of games—sports."

"And did you feel any emotions when you were playing? Perhaps you felt a surge of energy or elation when you scored. Or anger at another player who fouled you."

"Yeah, sure."

"Then think of the people interacting in a sex club also feeling emotions through their avatars. But the emotions are related to flirtation and seduction, to acting out their fantasies in an environment where such fantasies are acceptable."

"And that's what happened with Kevin?" McCabe asked. "He got caught up in a fantasy involving this woman?"

"Yes. Their avatars had a virtual encounter and Kevin wondered whether he had been unfaithful to his wife. He wondered if he had used his investigation as an excuse to engage in behavior he found repugnant."

"So he felt guilty about what had happened?"

"Extremely," Burdett responded.

"Does that mean he had only one encounter with this female avatar?"

"That was the only encounter he told me about between their avatars."

McCabe said, "From the way you phrased that, Dr. Burdett, I think my next question should be whether he met the woman behind the avatar."

Burdett cleared his throat.

McCabe said, "We understand your scruples about this, Doctor."

"He . . . In our last session, a few days before he was killed, Kevin told me he needed to see this woman in the flesh so that he could break the hold of the fantasy he had about her."

"So it's possible they did meet in the real world?"

"Yes, it is possible. And I am concerned that somehow that might have led to Kevin's death. Perhaps she tried to blackmail him, and he threatened to contact the police."

McCabe said, "We need to find this woman. Did Kevin tell you anything about her?"

"About her avatar? Yes, he said her avatar was what he called a 'biker girl' in black leather. Her avatar name was Dakota."

"A biker girl," Baxter said. "That's some match for an upstanding family man."

"But one of the attractions of a virtual world, Detective Baxter, is that the participants can transcend the restrictions of their real-world identities. And, of course, in this case, Kevin had assumed the persona of Bob's avatar."

"Was Bob's avatar a biker boy?" Baxter asked.

"According to Kevin, Bob's avatar was a wealthy playboy."

McCabe said, "About Dakota—did Kevin tell you about their conversations? Since his goal initially was to learn about the club, did he manage to get any information from her? Anything that might help us find her?"

"What would help you find her would be to gain entry to the

club," Burdett said. "Unfortunately, Kevin never told me the name of the club. I'm sure he didn't tell Daniel, either. Daniel preferred not to know."

"Reverend Wyatt was sure Kevin hadn't told you anything about Bob and the club," McCabe said.

Burdett smiled slightly. "But you doubted that."

"We thought a man in Kevin's position would want someone to confide in. Someone he could trust to keep his secrets."

"Until the person he confided in revealed his secrets," Burdett said.

"In a good cause, Doc," Baxter said. "This woman Kevin was playing games with could be a psycho."

"Yes, and the most important thing is to make sure Sarah and the children are safe. Kevin would want me to do whatever was needed to ensure that."

"So we don't know the name of this club. And we can't get to it or get in without the key code," McCabe said.

They were sitting in their vehicle, down the street from Burdett's house and office.

"Kev had the key, but it's a good bet he didn't leave it around the house where his wife could find it."

"It was probably on his ORB," McCabe said. "But since it's unlikely we're going to find his ORB, that isn't much help."

"We could try it from another direction," Baxter said.

"What?"

"Our victim's car, partner. If we can reconstruct his movements for the week before he was murdered, we might stumble over the identity of Dakota, the biker girl."

"Mike, that's brilliant."

"You would have thought of it eventually." Baxter grinned. "In another couple of weeks."

"Luckily, one of us is obsessed with cars."

"I still want to know about all those creepy photos of dead people with their cars in Luanne's photo album."

"We have to remember to ask her about that. Let's get back to the Comm Center and see if we can get Pete Sullivan to start a cam search before his shift ends."

"Surveillance cameras all over the city. Unless Kev was driving someone else's car or walking, we should be able to figure out how he spent his week."

Pete Sullivan, the day shift supervisor of the Communications Center, glanced up from his console. "All right, we've got Novak's car with starting location at his home, one week before his death. We should have the readout for you first thing tomorrow morning."

McCabe said, "If his car was at a motel or someplace else where he might have been meeting someone, could you also give us the IDs on the cars parked nearby?"

"Got it," Pete said.

"Thanks, Pete."

When McCabe got back to the bull pen, Yin and Pettigrew were at their desks adjacent to hers, but Baxter was nowhere in sight. He'd left her in the Comm Center finishing up with Pete. "Have you guys seen Baxter?"

"He said to tell you he wasn't feeling well," Yin said. "Upset stomach. He was heading home."

"Probably the lingering effects of having the flu," McCabe said. "We're done for the day anyway. No reason for him to hang around."

She glanced over at the crime-scene photos Pettigrew and Yin were displaying on the wall. "The two of you putting in overtime?" she asked.

Yin said, "We're just wrapping up."

Pettigrew said, "So what's this Baxter was telling us about an avatar?"

"I don't know," McCabe replied. "What did he tell you?"

And if he was sick, why did Baxter stop to tell them anything?

"I asked how the funeral director case was going," Yin said, "and Baxter said you were looking for a biker girl avatar named Dakota." He started to tidy his desk, his daily ritual before leaving. "What does a biker girl avatar have to do with a murdered funeral director?"

So much for discretion, Mike, McCabe thought. "That's what we're trying to figure out," she said.

"Good luck," Yin said. "And see you tomorrow. I get brownie points if I make it home in time for a family dinner again tonight."

Pettigrew lingered, fiddling around at his desk, after Yin had gone. McCabe glanced over at him. "I thought you weren't pulling overtime."

"Just hanging out," Pettigrew said. "How about getting a decent cup of coffee?"

McCabe smiled. "A decent cup of coffee costs more than hardworking cops should spend. Alcohol is cheaper."

"And I could use a drink. Want to go upscale and hit this wine bar I know?"

"Sure. Let's go."

The wine bar was out on Wolf Road. They took separate cars and parked near each other. Something that would be noted, McCabe thought, if they were suspects being followed on Pete Sullivan's surveillance cameras. Lucky they were cops, not suspects.

Pettigrew looked at the wine list and recommended a sauvignon blanc he thought McCabe would like. When she took her first sip, McCabe nodded. "This is really good."

The goat cheese he had ordered to accompany it was good, too. Pettigrew fascinated her. She never knew what he might know about.

"So, Sean," McCabe said, "what is the subject of our conversation?"

He didn't bother to deny that was the reason they were sitting in a wine bar instead of a bar full of cops. He had something he wanted to talk about. "This avatar thing? You ever had one?"

"Back when I was in college. I liked to play Web games."

"Still playing those games?"

"No, I guess I outgrew them. Or got too busy with real life."

Pettigrew took a long sip of his wine. "I have this avatar named Parker. After Charlie Parker, the jazz saxophonist."

"Wasn't Parker black?"

"Yeah. But my avatar's white. And he doesn't look much like either of us."

"Okay. So where do you and Parker, your avatar, hang out?"

"A club. A private club for time travelers."

"Time travelers? Like on those old sci-fi movies where people used to step into portals and be transported?"

"In the club, a hostess greets us and tells us about the available travel locales."

"Actually, it sounds like fun." McCabe leaned forward. "So why are we talking about this?"

"Last time I was Mr. Parker, I spent the evening in a speak-easy in Harlem in the 1920s. I ended the evening by taking a ride with some gangsters who were moving a shipment of bootleg gin."

"Not something a cop should do in real life. But during Prohibition, quite a few of them did, so I don't suppose—"

"Remember that day when we were talking about the frat boys who stopped traffic on Central Avenue? The ones who dressed up like space zombies and danced to Michael Jackson's video?"

"The 'Thriller on Central Avenue' incident. Sure, I remember. You were caught in the traffic jam."

"And close enough to see it all. I wanted to get out of my car and join in."

"Well, we both know you're a music nut."

"I didn't get out of my car because the uniforms showed up and broke the whole thing up. If they hadn't come when they did . . . See, that's the thing, Hannah. Being able to break the rules and get away with it when I'm Parker in cyberspace . . ." Pettigrew's gaze held hers. "I think it might be fooling with my head in real life."

"Then," McCabe said, "why not just stop?"

"I'm not sure I can," Pettigrew said.

"You mean you're addicted?"

"I don't know. I just keep getting drawn back to it."

"Maybe you need to find something else to do. Take up a hobby."

"Or take out a hit on my ex-wife?"

"I didn't realize you and Elaine . . . You hadn't mentioned her lately."

"I'm trying not to think about her. But she keeps sending me tags and not showing up when I agree to meet her. She says she wants me back, but she's playing head games."

"You look tired, Sean. Maybe you ought to see if you can get the lou to let you use a few days' sick leave and get away. Up to the Adirondacks or down to the City. Leave your ORB and your goggles at home and get some R and R."

"Get away from both Elaine and my latent criminal tendencies, huh?"

McCabe reached across the table and touched his hand. "You've got me a little worried about you now. I thought you were almost over Elaine."

"Knowing you ought to be over someone and being over them—"

"True," McCabe said. She reached for another cracker.

Pettigrew leaned back in his chair and looked at her. "That sounds like you're speaking from experience."

McCabe shrugged and spread goat cheese on her cracker. "There was this guy."

"Tell all to Pettigrew, your father confessor."

McCabe laughed. "I thought you were just my friend."

"That, too." He smiled. "The good part is that we keep each other's secrets."

"This really was a secret. And that, my friend, turned out to be my undoing."

"How and why?"

"This guy, who shall remain nameless, grew up in the area. He went off to college, played football in the NFL until he was injured. And then he came home and started a program for kids—"

"If we're thinking of the same nameless guy," Pettigrew said, "his gang intervention program has been controversial."

"That would be the guy."

Pettigrew nodded. "So this nameless guy and you—"

"Met and liked each other. But I wanted to keep a low profile until we were sure that it was more than a fling. So I persuaded him it would be better to wait until we were sure we really were a couple." McCabe took a sip of her wine. "Turns out that suited him just fine. As long as our relationship was a secret, there was nothing at all to keep him from pursuing other women on the side."

"And you found out."

"I happened to drop by his place one evening intending to surprise him. I was the one who got the surprise. She was blond and about twenty-two and her response to being caught with him in a bathtub full of bubbles was to giggle."

"Ouch."

"He pointed out we had never agreed that we were exclusive. When I told him to go to hell, he told me that his interest in me had been in part that he was hoping I would be a source of information about what was going on in the department. Unfortunately, I hadn't been as talkative as he would have liked."

"Ouch, again."

McCabe raised her glass. "Double ouch. But it happened before I was in so deep that it would have really hurt."

"But it did hurt."

"Yes, it hurt, and I'm still bruised. But I'm not going to let him do that to my head." McCabe held Pettigrew's gaze. "And you need to get over this Elaine thing, Sean. Frankly, and pardon my bluntness, the woman's—"

Pettigrew held up his hands. "I know what she is."

"Then tell her to go away and stay away. And if you think you're getting addicted to breaking the law in cyberspace, then throw away your goggles and go talk to someone. I know a psychiatrist who's had recent experience with—"

McCabe broke off.

Pettigrew said, "Don't stop in the middle of your 'stop whining and pull yourself together' speech."

"Sorry, I forgot where I was in my rant. I had a thought."

"About me?"

"I've already told you what I think about your situation. Actually, it was about the psychiatrist I mentioned."

"The one who's had recent experience?"

"The recent experience was with my victim, the funeral director. My vic had an avatar."

"Who was hanging out in cyberspace with a biker girl avatar named Dakota?"

McCabe nodded. "When the psychiatrist was telling us about that, about our victim's secret life, he reminded us of the emotional experience of being inside an avatar."

"So? Your psychiatrist has probably played a few games in cyberspace in his day. It might even have been a part of his training as a therapist. Cyber addiction has been in the mental health manuals for a while now. And avatars are also used in therapy."

"I know." She shook her head. "Getting back to you. I'm sorry about the lecture."

"I forgive you. Obviously your lecture was directed as much at yourself as at me."

McCabe laughed. "Thank you, Dr. Freud. My guy really was a bastard. But I'm not going to take out a hit on him. And I would rather you didn't joke about doing that with Elaine."

Pettigrew raised his glass in a toast. "Here's to always remembering that we are officers of the law."

McCabe clicked her glass against his. "Sworn to protect and serve and not hire hit men to dispose of our exes."

"So getting back to this psychiatrist," Pettigrew said. "Aside from advising me to seek his services, are you looking at him as a suspect?"

"He's on our list. But at this point, so is everyone else."

"Including the woman behind Dakota, the biker girl?"

"Her, too." McCabe smiled. "Of course, since, as you've pointed out, an avatar doesn't have to look like its owner, Dakota could turn out to be six foot two and male."

38

Wednesday, January 29, 2020
8:15 A.M.

"I come in early, and you're already here," McCabe said.

Baxter grinned. "Making up for skipping out on you yesterday. I even brought you a muffin from your favorite bakery."

"Thank you," McCabe said. She sat down at her desk and reached for the Cambrini's bag. "Are you feeling better?" She took a bite of the muffin; it was still warm and smelled of cinnamon.

"A-1. I went by my mom's, and she made me soup and tea to soothe my tummy. I spent the night there, and felt good as new when I woke up this morning."

"Nothing like a mother's TLC. Anything from Delgardo or Pete Sullivan yet?"

"Tags from both," Baxter said. "Both want us to stop in at our earliest convenience."

"Let's start with Delgardo," McCabe said, reaching for a napkin. "I can eat on the way." She sighed. "And although I really appreciate the muffin, you do realize you're encouraging me in my tendency to eat my way through an investigation."

Baxter grinned. "What would a good murder investigation be without food for thought?"

"And bad puns?"

Delgardo was on his ORB when they walked into FIU. He pointed toward a work table on the other side of the room. They went over to join a tech who was glancing into a microscope.

"Hi," the tech said. "We'd better wait for Ray. I think he wants to tell you about this. He's really pleased with the process we used. First time we'd tried it."

"Hope we can understand it," McCabe said.

Delgardo joined them a few minutes later. "Sorry. I was on with my counterpart at the State Police lab. Just wanted to let him know the process we'd talked about worked. But we won't bore you with how we did it. Suffice it to say we were able to extract your piece of paper from the muck and dry it out while preserving the paper itself. We were also able to recover most of the text."

"Then it really was the note we were looking for?" McCabe said.

"If the note was to someone named Luanne—"

"That's it," McCabe said. "Could we see the text?"

Delgardo waved his hand, bringing an image of the document up on the wall.

"So Luanne was telling the truth," Baxter said.

McCabe nodded. "A note telling her not to worry about what happened last night and that the unnamed author of the note will be in touch when the author gets back from the City. No signature. But easy enough to see why Luanne would think it came from Olive."

"Good, quality paper," Delgardo said. "See the watermark?"

"Personal stationery?" McCabe asked.

"Could be. But the person who wrote the note used an old computer and printer."

"Would you be able to match the note with the computer and printer it was produced on?" McCabe asked.

"Probably. The printer would be more useful than the computer."

"Thanks, Ray," McCabe said. "This was fantastic. We'll get back to you."

As they left the lab, Baxter said, "Are we on our way to request search warrants for computers and printers?"

"It may come to that," McCabe said. "But let's see what Pete has and then we'll check in with the lou about what we ought to do next."

"Dead undertaker or poisoned medium," Baxter said. "Who gets priority?"

"I vote for the dead guy if Pete can give us a decent lead."

Pete Sullivan was as pleased with his surveillance work as Delgardo had been with his forensics. Pete pulled up a spreadsheet and an interactive map.

"Okay," he said. "Follow me on this. I'm going to walk you through a week in the life of your vic—at least as much as we can document from where he went in his car. It's your good fortune that it's winter and the weather has been lousy, so most people have been in their cars rather than sloshing along the sidewalks."

Baxter started to ask, "Did you find a meeting—"

"Getting there," Pete said. "Just follow along with me."

McCabe nodded. When you produced results, you deserved to be able to show off a little. Delgardo had given up on trying to explain the science, but he did like displaying the outcome with as much flair as possible. Now, it was Pete's turn.

"We're listening, Pete," she said. "Walk us through it."

"Sit down and make yourselves comfortable," Sullivan said, giving his handlebar mustache a tug. "We have a few stops along the way."

The walk through the seven days leading up to Kevin Novak's death was a study in irony, McCabe thought. A man who didn't know he would soon be dead doing the things they all did. Going to his dentist, picking up cleaning, going to church.

The third trip to his church prompted Baxter to say, "Committees? Or, was he meeting with the reverend?"

"Something we should ask," McCabe said.

Pete said, "This next stop looked like it was going to be a challenge, given your request we identify nearby cars when he was somewhere he could be meeting someone."

The readout and the flashing light on the map indicated his destination was in Guilderland, west of Albany city limits.

"The mall? He went shopping at the mall on Thursday," McCabe said. "How long was he there?"

"Three hours forty-seven minutes," Pete said.

"That's a long time for most men to spend in a mall," Baxter said. "Most of us prefer to get in and out as fast as possible."

"Do we know if he was alone?" McCabe asked. "Maybe he was with his wife or one of the kids. But this is the middle of the day. The kids should have been in school."

Pete said, "He left from his funeral home. No one else in the car when he left, no stops along the way." Pete waved his hand, bringing up more images on the wall. "We've got the surveillance cam images from the mall."

Kevin Novak got out of his car. He had parked in an area where he was one in a stream of shoppers going in and out of the mall. But he was tall enough to stand out, a man in a tailored gray suit and tie among casually dressed shoppers.

Except he had a knapsack. McCabe said, "He has—"

"Hold that thought," Pete said. He froze Novak in midstride and zoomed back for a closer look at the interior of his car. "Unless they're invisible, no passengers in the car."

"No passengers," Baxter said. "But what's with the knapsack? Was he delivering something?"

"He could have been," McCabe said. "But if he had arranged to meet someone to deliver whatever's in the knapsack, why was he in the mall so long?"

"I have the answers to your questions, my friends," Pete said. "Watch what happens."

He released Novak from his freeze frame. "This is where it gets good."

"The bus stop," McCabe said. "He's not going into the mall. He's waiting for a bus."

Pete fast-forwarded. They watched Novak get on a bus.

"What's the number on the bus?" Baxter asked. "Damn, we've lost him."

Pete said, "If we can follow a car, we can follow a bus."

Baxter grinned. "Yeah, I guess you can. But he must not have thought of that, either."

"That's how people get caught," Pete said. "They think they're safe from surveillance if they blend into a crowd."

McCabe asked, "Are you going to make us wait to see where he gets off the bus?"

"The passengers getting on and off are fun to watch. But in the interest of saving time . . ." He brought up another image. "Your victim-to-be, Mr. Novak, caught on camera as he gets off the bus at this stop a few miles farther west."

McCabe said, "I take it this cam footage is courtesy of either the bus company or the Guilderland PD."

"Both. The Guilderland PD has a cam directly across the street from Mr. Novak's destination."

Pete threw another image up on the wall. Inside the bus stop enclosure, Novak pulled a black thermo jacket with red trim and a baseball cap from his knapsack. He took off his suit jacket and put it in the knapsack, then put on the thermo jacket and cap.

They followed Novak on cam as he crossed the parking lot of a motel and went into the office.

Baxter said, "The guy goes to all this trouble, and he picks a cheap motel the cops are watching."

"I guess he was afraid if he went to a good hotel someone would recognize him," McCabe replied.

"Then he should have gone to his biker chick's apartment," Baxter said.

"Assuming that's who he was meeting."

Novak came out of the motel office. He walked down the row

of first-floor rooms, stopped in front of one of them, and unlocked the door.

Pete said, "And in just a few minutes, Mr. Novak's guest will arrive."

"He probably tagged whoever he was meeting on his ORB," McCabe said.

A motorcycle roared up. The rider climbed off, removed her helmet, and ran her fingers through her spiky red hair. She was wearing a black leather jacket, blue jeans, and boots.

"She really is a biker chick," McCabe said.

She strode up to the room Novak had gone into and knocked. He opened the door. She reached around him and tossed her helmet into the room. Then she grabbed Novak and pulled his head down toward hers.

Kevin Novak jumped back from that kiss as if he had been smooched by a lioness.

His visitor followed him into the room and closed the door.

Baxter laughed. "Did he come running out, screaming?"

Pete laughed, too. "I was expecting that. The blinds were closed, so we can't see what happened. But here's our next image. About two hours later."

"Two hours?" McCabe said.

So much for Kevin having been shocked back into fidelity, she thought, as she watched Dakota, the biker girl, come out and roar away on her motorcycle.

"Here comes our boy, Kev," Baxter said.

Carrying his knapsack, Novak came out of the room and walked back to the motel office. There was nothing to read in his expression.

He walked to the bus stop on the opposite side of the road and changed back into his suit jacket. The bus came and he got on board.

Pete showed the detectives the final image: Novak putting his knapsack into his car and driving out of the mall.

"Where did he go after that?" McCabe asked.

"Back to his funeral home, where he remained for the rest of

the day. Then that evening, he went home to his wife and kids."
He waved away the images on the wall. "I have a printout of his
movements for you. But that was the most interesting afternoon
in your guy's week."

"Probably in his whole life," Baxter said.

"And he might have wished he had gone to a movie instead,"
McCabe said. "Pete, do you have anything for us on Dakota, the
biker girl?"

"Got her name—born Mary Ann Wilson, known as Dakota.
Also have her home and work addresses."

"Dare we ask what kind of work she does?" Baxter asked.

"She works at a beauty spa—as in hair salon—on Madison
Avenue. She does facials and massages."

McCabe said, "Thanks, Pete. You're a marvel."

"Tell that to City Hall when the DePloy budget comes up again.
All the Common Council wants to talk about is problems with the
system." Pete tugged at his mustache. "Try explaining to a bunch
of bureaucrats what solar storms and major weather events can do
to a surveillance system."

39

Dakota, the biker girl, was in her Mary Ann persona when she came out of the back room of the salon. Her red hair was smoothed down and tucked behind her ears. She was wearing a pink smock.

McCabe smiled for the benefit of the salon manager. "Would you mind if Ms. Wilson stepped outside with us for a moment? We just have a few questions about something she may have witnessed."

"An accident?" the manager asked.

"Possibly," McCabe said. "We won't keep her long."

Mary Ann had not spoken. She followed them outside.

"Thanks," she said. "You could have screwed that up for me." She leaned back against the wall of the salon. "What do you want?"

"To talk to Dakota," McCabe said.

Mary Ann waved her hand in front of her face. "She's here. Same question. What do you want?"

"Talk to us about the guy you hooked up with last Thursday at a motel out in Guilderland," Baxter said.

"My day off. I had nothing better to do."

McCabe said, "You met him in a cybersex club, right?"

"No law against that."

"None at all," Baxter said. "But this guy was murdered."

"Murdered?" Dakota said. "I had nothing to do with that. He was alive and well when I said good-bye."

"We know he was," McCabe said. "We saw on surveillance cam. What we want to know is what the two of you talked about."

"We were in a cheap motel, not a chat room."

McCabe said, "So the two of you didn't exchange a word?"

"A few. He got all father on me."

"How so?"

"After we'd done the deed, instead of rolling over and going to sleep like most guys his age, he sat up with this look on his face."

"What kind of look?"

"A look like . . . it's hard to describe."

"Try."

"A weird look. Like he was embarrassed and sad and mad all at once. He asked if I did this a lot. I said, now and then. He said I ought to be careful."

"Good advice," McCabe said.

"I told him I knew how to handle myself. That he should have seen my last boyfriend."

"Is he still around?" Baxter asked. "Your last boyfriend?"

"That's what he asked me—Jack, the guy."

"And what did you tell Jack?" McCabe asked.

"You sure you aren't from Vice?"

"We aren't," Baxter stated. "But I have some friends there. You want to talk to us or them?"

Dakota said, "I'll talk to you, and you'll make sure they don't hang me up."

McCabe started to say, "We can't promise—"

"It depends on what you tell us," Baxter said. "Either way, you're better off if we're on your side."

Dakota shrugged. "I told the guy my last boyfriend was a drug dealer and that he was supplying the space zombies."

"You just volunteered that information to this guy, Jack, huh?" Baxter said.

"I was trying to let him know . . . he was getting on my nerves, okay?"

McCabe said, "Your boyfriend, the drug dealer—"

"He's gone. He skipped town one step ahead of the cops. The little zombie girl he'd brought in to be his distributor was in the house the cops raided. He'd had this big fight with her because she told him she was sick and couldn't work that night. He was scared she was going to rat him out."

"This girl was in the zombie nest that was raided?" McCabe said.

"Yeah, she was the one who had cholera. The girl who died after they took her to the hospital."

The girl in the red scarf, McCabe thought, feeling her heart sink. "Did you tell Jack, the guy you met at the motel, about the girl?"

"Yeah, I mentioned her."

"Mentioned her when you were telling him about your ex being a drug dealer?"

"He wasn't really my ex. Just a guy I grew up with. He was trying to go big time by distributing to the zombies." Dakota smiled. "But saying he was my ex really freaked this guy Jack. He looked like he was going to throw up or something. He said he had kids he told not to take drugs. I guess what was getting to him was that he had just finished bonking a drug dealer's ex."

"When did this guy who wasn't really your ex leave town?" Baxter asked.

"Right after the raid on the zombies' nest. He was getting nervous even before that because he thought Vice might be watching. So he'd already bought his plane ticket. He was planning to take his little zombie girl with him, had bought her a fake ID and everything. But she was throwing up all over the place and he ended up leaving her there in the house."

"Where did he go?" McCabe asked.

"Mexico City. He tagged me from there last Saturday."

"We need a name on this friend of yours," Baxter said.

Dakota shrugged. "No skin off my nose. He's gone. You have to get him back before you can mess with him."

She gave them the name. They asked what she had been doing on the night that Kevin Novak was murdered. She said she had been at home with her cat. And a friend who had kept her company during the blizzard. She gave them that friend's name, too.

McCabe and Baxter watched through the window as she went back inside and smiled at the salon manager. Whatever she said about two detectives turning up wanting to speak to her, the manager seemed satisfied. Mary Ann headed back to the client who was waiting for her facial.

Baxter had his ORB out. "We'd better pass on this info."

McCabe added, "And make it clear Dakota cooperated with our homicide investigation."

"Sure," Baxter said. "She'll get a gold star for that from the guys in Vice."

Back at the station house, McCabe paused outside Lt. Dole's office door. "Be there in a minute," she said to Baxter. "I'm just going to give the lou a quick update about the biker girl and her friend, the drug dealer."

"Okay," Baxter said. "I'll start getting what we have up on the wall."

"Lou, have a minute?" McCabe asked.

Dole waved her in. "Find the biker girl?"

"Yes, sir. Turns out she may have really spooked Kevin Novak. She told him her ex was a drug dealer."

McCabe filled him in.

"But you don't see the drug dealer as the killer?"

"No, sir. Not if he really did leave right after Vice raided the space zombies' nest. Sir, there's something else about that. About the girl who had cholera. I think I saw her that evening. She was with a group of zombies. I saw her fall. I thought she was high."

As Dole listened, she told him about seeing the line of space zombies out in the storm, following their Pied Piper toward the Plaza.

"Why are you telling me this, McCabe?"

"Why am I—" McCabe stared at him. "Sir, I didn't . . . If I had gone after her, she might still be alive."

"Who do you think you are?" Dole asked. "Super cop? Do you have psychic powers? How were you supposed to know the girl was sick?"

"I didn't know, but—"

"You don't need this now, McCabe. You don't need grieving parents wanting to know why you didn't save their pretty little white middle-class daughter. What you need to do is solve the case you're working on, like you solved the serial killer case. You need to focus on your job so that when the commander and I get called into the chief's office and your name comes up we can remind the people around the table that you're one of the best detectives in the unit. We need to be able to say that because Howard Miller keeps bringing up your name, and the powers that be aren't thrilled with the attention that one of our cops is getting. So right now, McCabe, you need to keep a low profile. You understand me?"

"Yes, sir, I understand." McCabe stood up. "Baxter and I are going to go over what we have."

"Do that."

Baxter greeted her with some news. "Got the word back from Vice. They have confirmation a passenger by the name of Dakota's drug-dealing friend left town on Saturday morning. That rules him out as a suspect in Kevin Novak's death."

"So we've got Kevin shot with a compound bow by person unknown," McCabe said, turning to the crime-scene images on the board.

"He either let this person in and took him or her down to the basement," Baxter said, "or this person wandered on in after Kev forgot to lock the outer door."

"Kevin is standing by the target when this person picks up his bow and shoots him with it. But there was an arrow lodged in the target. That would suggest Kevin had been doing target practice."

"He's at the target when he's shot. If someone came in uninvited, came down the stairs quietly, he might have been caught by surprise."

"Or if this was someone he knew, Kevin might have been talking to him as he was going on with his target practice. He shoots the arrow, goes to retrieve it from the target, and the killer picks up another arrow, puts it in the bow, and shoots him."

Baxter said, "If you're having an argument with someone, do you walk away from them and leave a deadly weapon within reach?"

"So if Kevin knew this person was there, he didn't feel he was in danger." McCabe glanced again at the crime-scene images. "He didn't know this person was angry enough or afraid enough to kill him."

"This person shoots him with the arrow. But he's not dead," Baxter said. "So why doesn't the killer finish the job? Why leave him alive?"

"Alive but with no way of getting help unless he could get up the stairs. If the killer took Kevin's ORB—"

"But that's no guarantee," Baxter said. "If you want someone dead, you kill him. You don't leave him alive, hoping he'll bleed out before someone can find him."

"Or if you're pretty sure no help is coming, then walking away with the victim's only means of communication and leaving him to die slowly may satisfy your need to make him suffer."

"Assuming nobody comes before he dies. How did the killer know Kevin's embalmer wasn't coming in for his night shift?"

"If this was someone Kevin knew, he might have mentioned he was there alone for the night."

Baxter leaned back in his chair, arms behind his head. "Okay, round two. Who can we eliminate as a suspect?"

"Francesca Reeves has an alibi. Unless she hired someone to do it, I think we can take her off the table."

"And unless an eighty-five-year-old woman was out running around in the streets after a blizzard, we can eliminate Olive."

"That leaves Wyatt, whose wife claims he was with her. Burdett, who claims he was at home alone enjoying his homemade stew."

"According to witnesses, our girl, Luanne, who claims, pending confirmation, to be Kevin's half sister, was in Boston."

"And Sarah Novak says she was at home with her son. But her son says that, although his mother thought he was upstairs in his room all that time, he did sneak out to make sure his father had gone to the funeral home." McCabe sat down at her desk. "We need to talk to Scott."

"We're going to have to arrest him to get to him."

McCabe stared up at the water stain on the ceiling. "Maybe we could get Reverend Wyatt to intervene."

"I haven't gotten the impression that Wyatt has a lot of influence with Sarah Novak."

"No, but she did tell him about our attempt to interview Scott. Maybe if we can get him to tell her about what Kevin was doing—"

"You mean *who* he was doing. Dakota, the biker girl."

"Wyatt doesn't know about her, and there's no reason to bring her up with Sarah. We could just get him to tell her about Kevin's attempt to investigate the club. And then we can explain we need to talk to Scott to make sure he hasn't been holding anything back because he might have thought his father was involved with another woman."

"And we don't bring up that we haven't ruled out the possibility that Scott might not only have thought that, but done something about it?"

"Let's hope his mother's too tired and too distracted by Reverend Wyatt's revelation about Bob and the sex club to lock onto the fact that we now have a real motive for Scott."

"Sounds a little devious, partner," Baxter said. "I'm shocked."

"If Scott was using drugs before his father was killed . . ." McCabe met Baxter's gaze. "Are you saying you want to tell her he's at the top of our list of suspects and suggest she get him a lawyer?"

"Not me. If the kid did it, I'm all for getting him any way we can."

"Great. That's all I need to hear to convince me that involving a minister and a mother in getting to a suspect isn't the least bit unethical."

"If it'll make you feel better, you can run it by the lou." Baxter had his ORB in his hand. "I'll make sure Scott's still at the hospital. They might have let him out."

So, thought McCabe, I obviously have a habit of passing my moral dilemmas onto Lt. Dole. As long as he signs off on it, then I have no responsibility for how it turns out.

McCabe reached for her own ORB.

"I'm going to check in with Luanne," she told Baxter. "See when she's due to be released."

"While you have her, ask her about her creepy photo album."

40

"Scott was released this morning. His mother took him home," Baxter said. "What did Luanne say about the album?"

"That she saw a photo of Bonnie Parker posing with her foot on the running board of a car. And then she saw a photo of the bullet-riddled car that Bonnie and Clyde were killed in. That got her thinking about people who had died in their cars. She started collecting pre-mortem photographs." McCabe paused. "Luanne said that when she and Kevin were chatting on their folklore discussion node, she mentioned her hobby. He was fascinated and she sent him digital copies of a few of the photos. He suggested she think of doing a book on the topic."

Baxter grinned. "And if the reading public is as fascinated as we were, she'll have herself a bestseller."

"Yeah, but Kevin won't be around to see his name in the acknowledgments." McCabe reached for her Elvis mug. "And now that we've satisfied our curiosity, I'm going to call Reverend Wyatt and see if he'll give us a little help getting Sarah Novak to let us see Scott."

On the monitor of McCabe's ORB, Wyatt looked pale. "I might have prevented this," he said. "If Scott believed that his father was being unfaithful to his mother, that would explain why he was so upset, why he took drugs." He squeezed the bridge of his nose. "I might have prevented this if I had known, if I had explained to Sarah." He sighed. "Yes, of course, we need to speak to both of them and clear this up."

McCabe closed her ORB and looked over at Baxter, who had been listening.

He grinned. "Well done, partner."

"Let's get moving," McCabe said.

Reverend Wyatt got them past Sarah Novak's front door. He explained that there was something he needed to talk to Sarah and Scott about, something that might help. The detectives, he said, were there because they also had information.

What information the detectives had, he didn't specify. Just as well, McCabe thought.

"Is Megan at school?" McCabe asked.

"We agreed it was time she went back," Novak said.

"Is Scott upstairs?"

"Yes, and we are not going to go up there until I hear what it is the three of you have to say."

Reverend Wyatt looked unhappy that Novak was grouping him with the police detectives she was barely tolerating in her home. He held out his hand to her. "There is something important I need to tell you. Something for which I need to take responsibility."

Sarah sat down on the sofa. Reverend Wyatt sat down beside her. McCabe and Baxter took the adjacent armchairs.

Reverend Wyatt said, "This is something that I was reluctant to tell you, Sarah. But it has been on my conscience. And the detectives have convinced me that you and Scott should know. You see, Scott may have gotten the wrong idea about what his father was doing." Wyatt cleared his throat. "He may have believed Kevin was being unfaithful to you."

Novak was silent for a long moment. "Wasn't he?" she said.

Wyatt looked shocked. "Sarah, no . . . Kevin loved you. He loved you and his children more than anything in this world."

"I want to believe that," Novak said.

Wyatt took her hand in both of his. "Listen to me. What Kevin was doing was on my behalf and for his church."

He told her about the key Bob Reeves had left to Kevin and Kevin's efforts to find out if other members of the church were involved in the cybersex club. "I should never have encouraged him, Sarah. I knew he was still depressed about Bob's death and certainly his disillusionment when Bob revealed his double life. I should have told Kevin to destroy the key code and get on with his counseling sessions with Jonathan."

"Does Francesca know?" Novak asked.

"No," McCabe said. "She wondered about Kevin's attitude toward her—why he was avoiding her since her husband's death. But, no, she doesn't know about the cybersex club." McCabe paused. "What we wondered was if Scott might have seen or heard something that led him to believe his father was involved with other women."

"What they're thinking, Sarah," Reverend Wyatt said, "is that might explain how Scott is reacting to his father's death."

"You mean, taking drugs and trying to kill himself?" Novak said. "Yes, I suppose believing his father had betrayed his family before being murdered might have been enough to drive him to that."

"Mrs. Novak," McCabe said. "Scott confided something to Detective Baxter and me about the night that his father died. He was concerned that you would be upset if you knew this."

"Knew what?"

"That he left the house that night. That he followed his father to the funeral home. He wanted to make sure that was where your husband was going."

Novak's hands clenched in her lap. "Scott went to the funeral home?"

"He told us that he went there, saw the lights on, and knew his father was inside. Then he hurried home before you realized he had sneaked out. He didn't tell us that he was worried his father might be meeting another woman. But now that we know about your husband's investigation of the cyber club, it is reasonable to assume that Scott may have seen or heard something that made him—"

"Made him think his father might be cheating on his mother," Novak said.

"May we speak to Scott, Mrs. Novak? We'd like to ask him what he knew about his father's investigation of the club. He might have heard or seen something that could help us in our own investigation. Especially since your husband's ORB is still missing."

Novak glanced from her minister to the two detectives. "You know, Detective McCabe, I really don't think so. You've just told me that my son was at the scene of the crime on the night that his father was killed. You've also suggested Scott may have thought he had good reason to be angry at his father. I really don't think I want you and your partner asking my son questions."

"Sarah," Wyatt said. "You can't believe that Scott has anything to hide. If he might know something that could help the detectives find the person who killed—"

"Innocent people end up on death row, Daniel. Innocent people talk with detectives who just want to ask them a few questions, and they find themselves in prison because the detectives have a theory. That's the way it happens."

"Mrs. Novak, we don't have a theory. We want to find the truth."

Novak stood up. "Thank you for coming by and clearing up any misconceptions I may have had about my husband and what he was doing. But you are not going to see my son without a lawyer present."

McCabe said, "Mrs. Novak, you would make this easier on everyone if you would let us speak to Scott."

"I don't want to make your life easier, Detective McCabe. I want to keep my children safe and help them heal. Right now, that means keeping my son away from you and your partner."

Baxter said, "If we have to bring your son in for questioning—"

"I have a lawyer. I'll let him know he may be needed."

Reverend Wyatt said, "Sarah, I understand your concern, but not cooperating with the police—"

"Good-bye, Daniel. Please show the detectives out as you're leaving."

She walked out of the living room.

By the time they reached the foyer, she was at the top of the stairs.

"I'm afraid that might have gone better," Wyatt said.

"Yes," McCabe agreed.

Sarah Novak was the kind of mother you'd want on your side, McCabe thought. But did her determination to keep them from questioning her son mean she thought he might have killed his father?

"I think we'd better go," Wyatt said.

He opened the front door and a woman gasped. McCabe looked around Wyatt and saw Luanne standing there.

41

"Oh, my goodness," Luanne said. "You're all here."

"What are you doing here, Ms. Woodward?" Wyatt asked. "This is not a time when this family would welcome an intrusive visit from someone they barely know. And after what I understand happened at the séance you staged—"

"Reverend, if you'll stop talking, I'll tell you why I'm here. My nephew sent me a tag asking me to come."

"Your nephew? Why would Scott want to see you? And this nonsense about Kevin being your half brother—"

"I'll show you the DNA test when I get it back. Move yourself out of my way, Reverend, before I forget you're a man of the cloth."

"Reverend Wyatt," McCabe said. "If Scott did reach out to Luanne, I think we should let her in."

"I'm sure Sarah couldn't have known about this."

"Out of my way," Woodward said. She gave him a little shove and sailed past him.

"Wait!" Reverend Wyatt shouted.

"Scott!" Woodward called out. "Scott, honey, it's Luanne."

"They're upstairs," Baxter said.

"Did Scott say his mother told him that you're his aunt?" McCabe asked.

"He didn't say anything about it in his tag. He just said he needed to see me." Woodward moved closer to the stairs. "Scott, it's Luanne. Do you want me to come up there?"

A door opened and Sarah Novak appeared in the upstairs hallway. "I want you all to get out of my house now. Do you understand me?"

"Scott asked me to come," Woodward said. "I want to speak to him before I go."

"Mom." Scott appeared, wearing his robe. "Mom, I do want to talk to her."

"Scott, go back to bed."

"Mom, I need to ask her to help me get in contact with Dad. I need to know if Dad hates me."

"Scott, your father loved you," Sarah Novak assured him.

"I killed him. I killed him," Scott said. "I have to know if he hates me."

It was McCabe who told Sarah Novak to call her lawyer and have him meet them at the station house. Baxter had taken Scott back to his bedroom to get dressed. Novak was simply standing there, hands clenched at her sides, staring into space. McCabe touched her arm and told her to call a lawyer for her son.

As she did, she caught a whiff of the fragrance from the séance. The fragrance that had smelled so familiar.

"Are you wearing lavender?" she heard herself ask.

"What?" Novak said.

"Nothing. You need to contact your lawyer."

Luanne Woodward took Novak's arm. "Come along, honey. Luanne's here. It's going to be okay. Is your room down the hall here?"

"Yes," Novak said, and allowed herself to be led away.

Reverend Wyatt, who was standing at the top of the stairs, shook his head. "I can't believe this. I can't believe Scott would kill his father."

McCabe said, "We won't know exactly what happened until we interview him about that night."

"Megan will be home soon."

"I'm not sure what her mother will want to do," McCabe said.

"I'll take care of it," Wyatt said. "I'll wait for Megan and arrange to drop her off at the home of one of her friends."

"Thank you," McCabe said.

Baxter and Scott were coming down the hall. Scott looked thin and tired and a lot like the man that they had seen in the surveillance footage. Scott was his father's son.

And if he had killed his father, his mother might find that was more than she could bear.

At the station house, the lawyer Sarah Novak called spent almost forty-five minutes talking with his client. Then Novak went in and talked to her son. She came out and sat down in one of the chairs in the hallway. Her face was flushed. She was shaking.

McCabe decided to give her some space.

The lawyer went in again. When he came out, he said that Scott, who was legally of age, had decided that he wanted to make a statement. His mother had not been able to dissuade him, but she was registering her objection.

McCabe and Baxter went into the interview room. The lawyer came back in and sat down at the table beside Scott.

McCabe touched the console, turning on the cameras and audio. She noted the date and time, the subject being interviewed, and those present. Then she read Scott his Miranda warning.

"I understand," he said. "I want to make a statement. I can't live with this anymore."

McCabe nodded. "Tell us what happened."

"Dad—he said he was all right. He told me to go home, and not tell Mom what had happened. He said he would call the paramedics and think up a story. He said not to tell Mom because she would be upset. He said the most important thing was protect Mom and Meg." Scott pressed his hands to his eyes and leaned forward over the table. "He said he was all right. I wouldn't have left him if I had known he was dying."

"You shot your father with his bow?" McCabe asked.

Scott sat back. He dashed at the tears on his cheeks, sniffed, and swiped at his nose.

McCabe asked him again. "Did you shoot your father with his bow, Scott?"

He nodded. "Yes, i shot him."

McCabe turned to Baxter. "Mike, could you get Scott some water. And tissues. There's a box on my desk."

"I'll be right back," Baxter said.

"Just relax for a few minutes," McCabe told Scott. "We'll go on as soon as my partner gets back. Okay?"

Scott nodded. He sat there, staring down at the table.

When Baxter returned with a glass bottle of water, Scott took several gulps. Then he reached for a handful of tissues and blew his nose. "Okay, I'm ready now."

"Why did you kill your father?" McCabe asked.

"I didn't intend to," Scott said. "He was talking about drugs, asking me if I had ever used drugs, and that made me . . . I wanted to talk to him about him and Mom and about the woman I'd heard him talking to on his ORB. And he was grilling me about using drugs. I just . . . I didn't even think. I just picked up his bow and an arrow . . . I don't know what I meant . . . I shouldn't have hit him. I didn't even really aim. But he moved just as I . . . I wasn't trying to hit him . . . I just wanted him to stop talking so I could ask him about that woman."

"So you shot the arrow not intending to hit your father. And then what happened?"

"He made this sound and he was clutching . . . and I saw the arrow and the blood. I ran to help him, but he waved me away. He told me to go . . . to go home and not tell Mom what had happened. He said he'd get help as soon as I was gone."

"So your father had his ORB?" McCabe said. "You saw it?"

Scott frowned. "I didn't see it. But he must have had it. He wouldn't have gone to the funeral home without a way to tag Mom and make sure we were okay."

"Yes. Earlier that evening, he did speak with your mother from the funeral home. But we don't know if he had his ORB with him in the basement."

"I didn't see it," Scott said. "Why would he tell me to go if it was upstairs?"

McCabe said, "The woman you mentioned hearing your father talking to . . . when did this happen?"

"I think it was on that Tuesday before . . . before—"

"Before your father died?"

Scott nodded. "Dad was in his office at home. I needed to ask him something. The door was open a little and I started to knock. I heard him say, 'I'm looking forward to it, too.' And then I heard this woman laugh."

"Did you hear the woman speak?"

Scott shook his head. "Dad said, 'Got to go' and he ended the transmission. I thought he might have heard me outside. But he didn't come to the door."

"So you don't think he knew you were there?"

"I think he heard Mom's car. When I got back out to the hall, she was at the door."

"Did your father know you were at home?"

"Yes, but I had told him I had some homework to do. And when he knocked on my door, I had my headphones on listening to music. He probably didn't expect me to come downstairs."

"And you didn't say anything to your father about what you'd heard?"

"I thought maybe I was wrong. That he had been talking to a friend of his or something. I mean, people can have people of the opposite sex as friends. I know girls who are my friends." Scott swallowed hard. "But Mom was acting weird, too. And when he went out to the funeral home that night, she looked so sad. That's when I thought he must be seeing some other woman and Mom must suspect. And I was going to remind him about what he was always telling us about how family was the most important thing in the world. I was going to ask him to stop seeing the woman." Scott swallowed again, and tears started sliding down his face. "I didn't intend to kill him. I didn't . . . I loved my dad."

The attorney said, "You have your statement, Detective McCabe. I think that's enough for now."

"I'm sorry, Scott," McCabe said. "There's something else we need to ask you about."

He raised his head and scrubbed at his nose with the tissues clutched in his hand. "What?"

"Luanne Woodward. You tagged her and asked her to come to your house."

"I thought she might be able to help me contact Dad. I wanted to tell him again that I didn't mean to hurt him. I tried praying, but I . . . I thought maybe she could get through to Dad."

"Because of what happened at the séance?"

Scott nodded. "It was scary with the bell and the door crashing open. But then I thought if Dad was still here, that he might be angry at me. I thought if Luanne could reach him—"

"Scott, do you remember earlier that evening when Luanne came in from the kitchen eating chocolate pecan pie?"

He nodded. "Uncle Bob's wife wanted some. But Velma came in and she said there wasn't any more left."

"Do you know how to cook?" McCabe asked.

"Sure. Mom says everyone should know how to cook. Why?"

"Ever bake a pie?"

The attorney cleared his throat. "Detective McCabe, my client is here to answer questions about his father's death. What is this about?"

"Someone tried to poison Luanne Woodward. Did you do that,

Scott? Did you take a chocolate pecan pie laced with arsenic to Lu-anne's house and leave it on her front steps?"

Scott's eyes went wide. "No! I wouldn't have . . . Why would I . . . ? I don't even know where she lives."

"Did you know Luanne says she's your father's half sister?" Baxter asked.

Scott's eyes widened even more. "She must be making it up. Dad was an orphan."

McCabe said, "But she may really be your father's sister. I'll let her explain that to you and your mother and Megan."

"I didn't do that. I didn't try to poison her."

Sarah Novak was still sitting in the hall when her son was taken out of the interview room. She came to her feet.

"I'm sorry, Mom. I didn't mean to. I didn't mean to," Scott said as he was taken past her.

Novak watched until her son was out of sight. Then she turned to McCabe and Baxter. "I have to go pick up my daughter."

McCabe said, "I'm sorry, Mrs. Novak."

"Thank you."

Novak walked away, back stiff, as if she were in pain.

McCabe said, "I don't think Scott tried to kill Luanne."

Baxter said, "If the kid didn't make Luanne a poisoned pie, who did?"

"There's another question. If Scott didn't take his father's ORB, who did?"

"He could have been lying," Baxter said.

"He could have been. But I believed him."

"Intuition, partner?"

"How to Detect a Lying Suspect 101."

"Okay, if you're right, that would mean after Scott left, some-one else came in. This person would have seen our vic had an ar-row in his chest. Instead of helping him, he or she picked up Kevin's ORB and walked out."

McCabe said, "His son may not have wanted Kevin Novak to die, but maybe someone else did. Someone who decided to make good use of an accidental shooting."

"You have someone in mind?"

"Luanne's photo collection got me thinking about postmortem photographs. Since the nineteenth century, photographers have been taking photos of newly dead people—of babies and dead relatives, of outlaws who had been shot or hung."

"This is going somewhere?"

"Come on. I'll show you."

Baxter sat on the edge of his desk studying the crime-scene images on the wall. "What am I looking for?"

"Our victim with Ernie the skeleton. Suppose Kevin didn't pull Ernie down accidentally when he fell? Suppose he was trying to stage his own death photo?"

Baxter got up and walked over to the wall. "Victim on his side, hugging skeleton. What do you think he was trying to say?"

"What do you think of when you see a skeleton?"

"Graveyards, closets—"

"And doctors?"

"As in Dr. Burdett? What's his motive? And what do you think the lou's going to say when we tell him we have a suspect who confessed to shooting the arrow, but we think someone else might actually be responsible for Kevin Novak's death?"

"If we can prove someone else was responsible," McCabe said, "Sarah Novak and her children might be able to survive this." McCabe brought a document up on the wall. "I asked Research to see what else they could find on Burdett. One interesting tidbit turned up. He has privileges at the psychiatric facility where Lisa Nichols was being evaluated."

Baxter looked from the document to her. "Tell me you aren't on that again. A psychiatrist has privileges at a mental hospital and you think he's part of some kind of conspiracy."

"I said it was interesting. I didn't say anything about a conspiracy," McCabe said. "The only way Dr. Burdett might have been involved in Nichols's death would be if he somehow got her to take the pills. And I don't know why he would want to do that. But learning more about his practice did start me thinking about a question my dad asked. We were talking about Burdett, and he asked how—or really why—someone with Burdett's background would end up in Albany."

"He's from Boston," Baxter said.

"And so was his wife. Maybe he came to Albany because he wanted to be close, but not too close, to family. Maybe he wanted to get out of the City. Since he arrived, he's been active in his church and busy with his practice, but he doesn't seem to have had any romantic involvements."

"Maybe he's still in mourning for his wife."

"That's possible. But what I'm getting at is Burdett's solitary life-style. He told us he was alone during the blizzard because he isn't currently involved with anyone."

"And that means what? If being unattached makes someone suspicious, we'd both qualify."

"True," McCabe said. "But in Burdett's case, what it means is that he doesn't have an alibi for the night of Kevin Novak's murder. We already knew that, but we haven't thought about it in the context of Kevin's sleuthing. Kevin was investigating a virtual reality sex club because he and Reverend Wyatt wondered if Bob Reeves was the only church member who belonged to it. What if Burdett were a member and Kevin found out?"

Baxter looked at the crime-scene image again. "I may be slow, but I think I just got there. If Kevin had discovered Burdett was a member of the sex club and was about to tell Reverend Wyatt, Burdett would have known his days as church counselor were numbered. Wyatt couldn't have risked keeping him on. Burdett would have been out on his ear just as the New Awakening movement was about to go national."

"So," McCabe said. "Want to go run my crazy theory—complete with skeleton—by the lou?"

"Your theory might not be so crazy," Baxter said.

"Except for Luanne. Even if Burdett had a reason to let Kevin die, why would he go after Luanne? All he had to do was sit tight and let Scott be blamed for his father's death."

42

Thursday, January 30, 2020
7:38 A.M.

McCabe was sitting at the breakfast table staring down into her bowl of cereal when her father came in. The dog began to whack his tail on the floor in greeting.

McCabe looked up in time to see Angus glare at him.

"Get up on the wrong side of the bed?" she asked.

"At least I got to bed," Angus replied. "I woke up and came downstairs to get myself a glass of juice, and there you were asleep on the sofa."

"Thanks for throwing a blanket over me. I fell asleep while I was watching a movie."

"What were you watching?"

"A Hitchcock movie that I happened to come across. *Spellbound*."

Angus poured himself a cup of coffee. "You must have seen that movie before."

"Only a few clips."

"Reminded you of Lisa Nichols, did it?" Angus said, sitting down at the table.

"Lisa Nichols was hardly Gregory Peck with amnesia. She killed three people, no doubt about that. What I was thinking about last night was psychiatry and psychiatrists."

"Why?" Angus asked. "Because of that shrink you've got in your funeral director case?"

McCabe scooped up her last spoonful of cereal and chewed. "If Reverend Wyatt goes nationwide with arena events, the membership of his church should boom."

"It should. Unless he bombs."

"And the church's resident counselor would find himself with new opportunities as well." McCabe pushed back her chair and reached for her empty bowl. "Got to get moving." She put her bowl in the sink.

"Wait a minute, what about this psychiatrist and Hitchcock?"

"Don't know yet. I'll tell you tonight."

Lt. Dole walked out of the station house with McCabe and Baxter. He was on his way downtown. With the captain out on sick leave, Dole had to join the commander for periodic meetings at City Hall. McCabe hoped neither she nor her family would be mentioned. Her father had not written an editorial in response to Howard Miller's propaganda. McCabe hoped that meant she was now off City Hall's radar.

"Remember what I said, McCabe," Lt. Dole said. "We clear?"

"Yes, sir, we'll handle this carefully."

In the car, she checked her ORB for an update from Research. She had asked for more specifics about Dr. Burdett's psychiatric practice. In spite of what Olive Cooper said about his inability to relate to street people, it seemed Burdett had done some volunteer work in a group home for troubled teenagers.

At his house on Willett Street, Burdett opened the door himself. He was wearing a richly patterned robe over white silk pajamas. A flicker of surprise crossed his face. "My receptionist isn't here yet," he said. "Am I expecting you at this hour?"

"No, and we apologize for coming by before nine," McCabe said. "I'm afraid we don't have an appointment. But we were hoping that—under the circumstances—you would forgive us for dropping by like this."

"The circumstances," Burdett said. "You mean Scott's arrest for his father's death. I'm not going to say murder, because from what Daniel told me, it was an accident."

McCabe said, "We were hoping you could help us to understand the family dynamics. To be frank, Dr. Burdett, Detective Baxter and I would like to believe Scott. We don't believe he meant to kill his father."

Burdett stepped back. "Come in. If you'll forgive the informality, why don't we go out to the kitchen and have some coffee while we talk."

"Thanks," Baxter said. "I could use another cup. Early start this morning."

Burdett's kitchen reminded McCabe of Chelsea and Stan's kitchen at home, everything a chef needed to put together a gourmet meal. Not to mention whipping up a chocolate pecan pie.

It was lucky Olive Cooper's housekeeper, Velma, was an early riser. She had taken it in stride when McCabe called her at 7:00 A.M. to ask about the recipe for her chocolate pecan pie. Had anyone ever asked her for the recipe? Lots of people, Velma said. Not that she had given it to all of them. She had given it to Francesca Reeves on the night of the séance. Dr. Burdett? Yes, last year, after he'd bought one of her pies at a church bake sale.

"Thank you," McCabe said as Burdett set a cup of black coffee in front of her.

"Cream?" he asked.

"Please," McCabe said, and considered the wisdom of drinking the coffee.

Baxter had no such hesitation. "Good coffee," he said.

"Thank you," Burdett said. He sat down across from them at the kitchen table. "Tell me what I can do to help Scott. You said you want to understand the family dynamics, Detective McCabe."

"There is another twist to this story that Reverend Wyatt might have told you about. Luanne Woodward claims to be Kevin Novak's half sister."

"Daniel told me about that when we spoke about Scott. It strikes me as a bit too much of a coincidence that this woman should turn up now."

"Not a coincidence," McCabe said. "You see, Luanne had located her half brother on a Web discussion node for folklorists and others interested in death and dying rituals. Of course, Kevin was unaware of their relationship, but Luanne felt she was getting to know him. He disappeared from the node for a while, around the time his friend Bob Reeves died. Luanne didn't know what had happened, but when he came back to the group, she did notice he wasn't his usual self. She was concerned something was wrong, and she had the idea of coming up to Albany to meet him and make sure everything was okay with him."

"She came up here," Burdett said. "But she didn't tell Kevin that she was his half sister. That strikes me as odd."

"She only met him once, briefly, at Olive Cooper's celebration of life. You remember that meeting. Kevin sent you a tag about it."

"As I recall from that tag, he wasn't terribly impressed with her."

Baxter said, "You did let us read that tag, Doc. He made a joke about how Olive Cooper wanted him to drop you and start consulting her medium."

McCabe said, "But, of course, you weren't concerned Kevin would do that."

"No, it wasn't one of the things I was concerned about. I wish we had known about this woman's relationship to Kevin. It might have been a real breakthrough in his therapy. He had long-term issues related to his mother's death and the time he spent in an orphanage."

"Did he?" McCabe said. "Thank you for sharing that with us. Understanding Kevin may help us to understand Scott and how he felt when he learned his father was cheating on his mother."

"How could Scott have known that?" Burdett asked.

"Kev got careless," Baxter said. "He left the door of his office ajar. Scott was out in the hall and heard him setting up a meeting with Fran—" Baxter broke off, looking abashed.

"With who?" Burdett asked.

"Uhh, with the woman behind the biker girl avatar."

"You started to say 'Francesca,' " Burdett said. "Are you telling me Francesca Reeves was a member of the cybersex club that Bob— to which Bob belonged?"

"No, he's not saying that, Dr. Burdett," McCabe said. "To the best of our knowledge, Francesca Reeves has no involvement at all in the club."

"Your partner said—"

"Just a slip of the tongue, Doc. My brain's still half asleep."

"He's telling the truth," McCabe said. "Until he's had his second or third cup of coffee, Detective Baxter's brain doesn't shift into gear."

"Mind if I pour myself another cup?" Baxter asked.

"Certainly. Help yourself."

"And, of course," McCabe said, "if Francesca Reeves were a member of the sex club, you would think Kevin would have recognized her, wouldn't you?"

"How would he recognize her?" Burdett said. "The members of this club have avatars."

McCabe nodded. "But I have a friend who is in another club. Not a sex club, a time travel club. And he named his avatar after someone he really admires. And I'll bet if I joined his club and I knew he might be there, I could pick out his avatar. I mean, even though his avatar looks nothing like him, there would be personality traits I would recognize. Wouldn't there?"

"You misunderstand the reason for having an avatar, Detective McCabe. An avatar not only gives its owner a presence in virtual space, it offers the freedom of trying out behaviors—and personality traits—that are different from those one possesses in the real world."

"Yes, but over time, wouldn't one fall into some of one's habits from real life? I mean, wouldn't bits and pieces of one's personality gradually be transferred to the avatar? But I suppose it could go in the other direction, too, couldn't it? The personality that one assumes in virtual space might start to seep into one's real-world existence. I suppose that would be when it could start to become dangerous."

"Of course," Burdett agreed. "That's always been a concern about immersive, interactive media. The wall of separation between virtual worlds and the real one." Burdett reached for his coffee. "This is a fascinating conversation, but getting back to the subject of Scott . . ."

"Which brings us back to Luanne Woodward," McCabe said. She shook her head. "I'm sorry, Dr. Burdett. We've had so many conversations with different people that I've lost track. You do know that someone tried to poison Luanne?"

"Yes, I know—but you can't believe Scott was responsible for that."

"No, actually, Doc," Baxter said, "we think you were."

Burdett stared at him. "What did you say?"

"Dr. Burdett," McCabe said, "we think you tried to kill Luanne Woodward."

"What possible motive could I have for trying to kill a woman I barely know?"

"It was more a matter of what you were afraid she might know," McCabe said.

Burdett laughed. "Are you suggesting, Detective McCabe, that I had something to hide and that I really believed the woman was psychic?"

"No, I'm not suggesting that. Luanne doesn't claim to be a psychic. She's a medium. But it was what she said to you before the séance that might have worried you."

"What she said to me? How do you know what she said to me?"

McCabe raised her cup, then set it back down again. "No psychic powers on my part. I remembered seeing you and Luanne standing together when Detective Baxter and I arrived. I called her this morning and asked if she could recall what you'd talked about."

"And what was it she claimed to have said that made me decide to do her in?"

"Actually, she didn't realize what she'd said. If she had, she might have been more careful when the pie you made arrived on her door-step."

"If you wouldn't mind, Detective, getting to the point—if there is one."

"Before the séance, Luanne saw you standing alone. She went over to join you. She was feeling 'devilish,' as she put it. She knew you and Reverend Wyatt didn't approve of her, and so she wanted to make you a little uneasy. She gave you her 'see right into your head' look—the kind that psychics use—and then she said, 'Your secret's safe with me, honey.' "

Burdett laughed. "This is ridiculous. You think I tried to kill Lu-anne Woodward because she said—"

"You said, 'What secret?' And she said, 'We all have to have our secret lives, honey. A place where we can go and be who we really are. It's all right. I won't tell.' She said you looked startled."

"I suspect I looked amused by her performance."

"Her performance during the séance was fascinating, too. Of course, she denies that the bell ringing and the door slamming open were hoaxes."

"You know, I really am finding this conversation tedious. If you'll excuse me, I need to get ready for the arrival of my first patient."

"We can't place you at Kevin Novak's funeral home on the night he died because the storm had knocked out our surveil-lance system. But we were able to find an image of your delivery-man."

"Of my what?" Burdett said.

"The kid in the park," Baxter said.

"Remember him?" McCabe said. "You came out of your house carrying a paper bag. You walked across the street into Washington Park. You sat down on a bench beside a trash bin. You put the bag on the ground beside the trash bin. Beside. Not in. You walked away, and a young man came over and picked your bag up. And then he scooted off in his old heap of a car."

Burdett stood up. "This is ridiculous. I won't—"

"What happened with Kev, Doc?" Baxter asked. "Was he on to you? Did he know that you were a member of the cybersex club?"

McCabe said, "That would have been a problem, wouldn't it? If Kevin decided to tell what he knew? If he was so guilt-stricken because he had betrayed his wife and his family that he refused to listen when you tried to get him to keep quiet." McCabe fixed her gaze on Burdett. "I may not be a psychic, but I can imagine what happened. You saw Scott leaving the funeral home. You went in and down to the basement. You found something you would never have expected. Kevin had an arrow in his chest, but he was still alive. And you saw your opportunity. You told him you'd get him help and keep quiet about Scott being there if he agreed to forget about the cybersex club. But he said no. He wouldn't play along. He intended to reveal your involvement in the club. So you picked up his ORB—maybe you grabbed it from his hand—and you walked out of that basement, leaving him to die. And then you had to live with that, didn't you?"

Burdett stared back at her. "Yes, I had to live with it. If he had been willing to listen to reason . . . I did try to reason with him. I tried to explain that he would destroy his marriage and my career. . . ." Burdett shook his head. "I begged him to let it go. We would both leave the club, and forget what we knew."

"How did he figure it out?" Baxter asked. "How did he identify your avatar?"

Burdett smiled. "Ironically, the credit for that goes to young Megan."

"Megan?" McCabe said.

"Unfortunately, she is an intelligent and curious child. Last month, when the teen book discussion group read a novel set in fourteenth-century France, she decided to do background research. During our discussion, she shared some information that she had found about the bubonic plague . . . including illustrations of the bird-beaked masks that physicians wore to protect themselves. Her parents were in attendance during our discussion."

"And you loaned her a book," McCabe said. "She was holding it in her lap when Detective Baxter and I went to the house to interview her and her brother. She said she was trying to finish it because she needed to return it to you."

Baxter said, "But how did that tip Kevin off? Were you a big bird in the sex club?"

"My avatar is—was—Edward, a wealthy art collector. A couple of weeks ago, Edward shared some images of beautiful, jewel-encrusted masks with several young women. And Kevin, posing as his friend Bob's avatar, overheard the conversation. As he told me later, he was reminded of a discussion about a different kind of mask during the teen book group meeting. That was enough. He started to watch and listen."

"But if you knew he was there posing as Bob's avatar," McCabe said, "wasn't it a bit reckless to bring up a topic that might remind him of something linked to you?"

Burdett smiled. "Recklessness tends to feed on itself, Detective McCabe. Knowing that he was there and that I was there—in plain sight, but undetected—added a certain thrill. And, to be frank, I underestimated him."

"So that evening at the funeral home, you decided to let him die."

"Yes, I made that decision. But, of course, I should have known that I was only postponing the inevitable. 'Murder will out.' " Burdett glanced down at his robe and pajamas. "I'd rather not go to the police station dressed like this. May I go upstairs and change?"

"Sure, Doc," Baxter said. "You won't mind if I come along and keep you company?"

"I don't think I'm in a position to object."

McCabe watched them go. She sat there for a moment thinking about Kevin Novak and his family. And then she reached for her ORB. When Lt. Dole came on, she said, "Sir, it worked. We're bringing Dr. Burdett in."

"Good job. Be sure you—"

The gunshot was muffled. But the sound vibrated through the house.

"Shot fired, sir," McCabe said. "Baxter went upstairs with Burdett."

"Backup's on the way," Lt. Dole responded.

McCabe shoved her ORB into her jacket pocket. Drawing her weapon, she stepped into the foyer, clinging to the wall. "Baxter?" she called out.

She started up the stairs. "Baxter?"

As she reached the landing, Baxter staggered out into the hallway holding a bloody hand towel to his head.

McCabe ran to him, catching him and lowering him to the floor. "What happened?"

"Burdett . . . We walked into his bedroom. He picked up a lamp . . . bashed me over the head with it."

"The gunshot?" McCabe said. "What?"

"He took a gun out of the nightstand . . . and put it to his head. He's dead."

McCabe glanced toward the door of the bedroom. "I have to go make sure of that."

"He's dead. Believe me."

Burdett was on the floor inside his bedroom. McCabe stooped down beside him, feeling for a pulse. Baxter was right. He was dead. He'd managed to blow away a piece of his skull.

She holstered her weapon and turned. Baxter had come into the room behind her. He was bending down. He straightened, slightly off balance, as she turned.

"Dropped my towel . . . don't want to bleed all over Delgardo's crime scene."

At the hospital, McCabe waited outside the room where Baxter was being examined. Finally, the doctor came out and said she could go in.

Baxter was lying back against the pillows with a bandage around his head.

"How do you feel?" she asked.

"Got a hell of headache," he said. "But that's not my only problem. The suspect I was supposed to be guarding gets a gun and shoots himself."

"Lt. Dole said to tell you that he'll be here as soon as they're done at the scene. Jacoby's dealing with the media. He's going to do a press conference later. And, of course, we're both going to have to give a statement to the guys from Internal Affairs."

"Can't wait," Baxter said.

"That's good. Because I don't think they're going to wait until you get over your concussion."

McCabe woke up in the dark and sat up in bed. She waved her hand in front of the lamp on her nightstand.

She had been dreaming of that moment when she had turned from Burdett's body and seen Baxter bending down to pick up the hand towel on the floor.

There had been something in the towel when he picked it up. Something small that he had been palming.

McCabe leaned back against her headboard. Then sat forward, sniffing the air.

There it was again. That whiff of scent she had caught during the séance and when she was talking to Sarah Novak. . . .

She and Pop had brought in the pots of lavender from her mother's garden and stored them on the porch for the winter.

Even if the bushes had been in flower, the scent would never have reached her closed bedroom window on the second floor.

The Novak case had obviously been triggering a scent memory of her mother's favorite fragrance. Maybe it was seeing a family torn apart by violence. A mother trying to cope.

McCabe waved her hand to turn off the lamp and stretched out again.

What had Baxter picked up in the towel?

43

Sunday, February 2, 2020
3:11 P.M.

McCabe sat down on the bench and looked out across the lake. The dog nudged at her leg. Then, accepting that they were going to take a break in their jaunt through the park, he sat down beside her. He leaned his head against her hand. McCabe obliged by rubbing his favorite spot behind each ear.

McCabe was thinking about the girl in the red scarf, whose name had turned out to be Elizabeth. Her parents had seen the news stream and contacted the police. Elizabeth had left home after an argument. She was nineteen, not a child. Her parents had thought she would come back home when she was ready.

McCabe shut off the mental image of Elizabeth's mother speaking to reporters about their loss. No tears visible, only a trembling mouth and ravaged face.

There were other things she should be thinking about, McCabe reminded herself. On the lighter side, Luanne, perhaps because of her own near-death experience, had admitted she rigged the bell to ring during the séance. She'd thought if Olive was as surprised as everyone else, the stunt would be more convincing. But she hadn't, Luanne insisted, rigged the door and the falling vase. Olive had also denied responsibility. Maybe it had been the wind. Mystery unsolved, and not that important.

The good news was that the DNA test had supported Luanne's claim that she was Kevin Novak's half sister. And Research had found nothing to suggest Luanne had any ulterior motive for seeking Kevin out. Seeing that she was needed, Luanne had swooped in to provide hot meals and moral support for her sibling's family. Scott was still facing charges related to his father's death, but Dr. Burdett's actions ensured Scott wouldn't be charged with murder. There would be a plea deal. And with Luanne's help, the family might well get through what had happened.

But there was the other matter that had not been resolved, the one that McCabe had told no one about. Baxter, and what he had picked up from the floor in Jonathan Burdett's bedroom.

She could always ask. She could say, "What's going on, Mike?"

"Detective McCabe?"

McCabe swung around. Ted Thornton was strolling toward her.

"I thought that was you," he said. "Sorry. I didn't mean to interrupt your . . . contemplation of the lake."

"It is rather a surprise seeing you here, Mr. Thornton," McCabe said, hoping she didn't look as startled as she felt.

"Didn't you think I went for walks in the park? And would it do any good to ask you again to call me Ted?"

McCabe opened her mouth. Decided not to restate what she had told him the first time they met about her preference as a police officer for observing the formalities. Instead, she pretended not to hear the question. "Well, it makes sense that you might take an occasional walk in the park. This park is across from Willett Street. I did hear you once thought of buying up all the houses along that street."

"I don't know how that rumor got started," Thornton said. "I was only going to buy one house. Maybe two." He gestured toward the free end of the bench. "Mind if I sit down? I've been walking for a while."

"Then, please sit," McCabe said.

Thornton gestured at the dog. "Unusual-looking animal," he said. " 'Behold, Mighty Ajax.' "

McCabe's head came up. "What did you say?"

"I was quoting a line from one of your mother's poems."

"Yes, I recognized . . . but I think that line was intended to be ironic."

"That was my impression, too. But your dog does have the look of a mighty hero, doesn't he?"

McCabe looked at the dog. "Ajax?" She shook her head. "That's not right."

The dog was watching her, tongue lolling. "Jax?" she said. He barked his approval.

"Did I miss something?" Thornton asked.

"Unless my father or brother can come up with something better, we just named my family's dog."

"Jax," Thornton said. "It suits him."

"I'm glad to have that settled," McCabe said. "You don't know how long this dog has been without a name. Other than some really awful options."

"Maybe your mother wanted to get her vote in," Thornton said.

McCabe laughed. "I wouldn't put it past her."

Stretched out on the sofa in his condo, Baxter watched the feed from the surveillance camera that was displayed on his wall. He froze the image and turned back to his ORB. "Guess they both felt like a walk in the park," he said to the man who had sent him the feed. "It's a nice day for a walk. A little chilly, according to the weather report, but lots of sunshine."

The man, whose name was Gage, was not amused. "We warned you about keeping your partner away from Ted Thornton, Detective Baxter."

"You warned me?" Baxter said. "Doing that would have been a hell of a lot easier if you had managed to keep Lisa Nichols alive. First, you let one of Miller's operatives pass Nichols a note telling her to trust Burdett. Then, you let Burdett get to Nichols with the pills and whatever story he told her to get her to take them."

Gage's mouth tightened. "The nurse who passed Nichols the note had worked at the facility for twelve years. She passed the note because of the money she was paid to do it. As for Burdett, we had no reason to be interested in him until you told us about his involvement in the sex club. There was no reason to suspect that a psychiatrist with privileges at the facility would be vulnerable to blackmail."

"But you knew Howard Miller would want to make sure Lisa Nichols never made it into the courtroom," Baxter said.

Gage stared back at him. "If Lisa Nichols had cooperated with us, we would have been able to keep her safe."

"She was one of Miller's true believers," Baxter said. "What'd you expect? That she'd be good and cooperate because a couple of G-men told her that Miller would find a way to eliminate her because she'd gone a little crazy and killed three people and he couldn't trust her to keep her mouth shut about her assignment to become Mrs. Ted Thornton with access to all his corporate—"

"This conversation is not about Lisa Nichols," Gage said, allowing his irritation to show. "We're discussing your partner. She has become a problem. We expect you to—"

"I know what you expect," Baxter said. "Burdett's file. What did you find on it?"

"We're still analyzing the contents. We'll get back to you if there's anything you need to know. Meanwhile, Detective Baxter, deal with your partner."

He ended the transmission before Baxter could respond.

Slouched against the piled pillows on his sofa, head throbbing from his recent concussion, Baxter stared at the freeze frame of McCabe and Ted Thornton sitting together on a bench in Washington Park.

"This is all my fault, right, partner?" Baxter said to McCabe's image. "All I had to do was tell you that I'm working undercover for the feds. Tell you that my godfather, the assistant chief, and my second cousin Tommy, who's hated you since you were at the academy together, are big fans of Howard Miller, and they're members of this exclusive little group of rogue cops. If I'd told you that, undoubtedly you would have said, 'Oh, okay, I'll stay out of it.' And this afternoon you would have gone to see some old movie or to get your nails done. This afternoon, you would not be sharing a park bench with Ted Thornton because you would have known that would be a really stupid thing to do. Right?

"Dammit, Hannah!" Fists raised, head thrown back, Baxter let out a roar of rage and frustration worthy of one of the superheroes he had loved when he was a kid reading his dad's old comic books. A full-throated "Arrgh!"

All that did was send a stab of pain through his head. When he opened his eyes again, McCabe was still sitting on that bench with Ted Thornton, cozy as could be.

Author's Note

In *The Red Queen Dies*, the first book in this series, and in this book, I draw on the fascinating history of the real city of Albany, New York. Many people have visited Albany. These visitors include Harry Houdini, the great magician, who suffered an injury while in Albany that may have indirectly contributed to his death. On October 11, 1926, Houdini was performing at the Capitol Theater. During his "Water Torture Cell" trick, a piece of equipment came loose and struck his foot. A doctor in the audience came to his aid. Later, his foot was x-rayed at a hospital and put in a brace. Houdini insisted on continuing his tour. He went on to Schenectady, near Albany, and then to Montreal. Before leaving Montreal for Detroit, Houdini, who was still hobbled by his injured foot, was caught by surprise when an overly enthusiastic student struck him twice in the stomach to test his famous abs. On October 31, 1926, Houdini died in a hospital in Detroit. His cause of death was peritonitis following surgery for appendicitis. Neither his accident in Albany, nor the blows to the stomach he received in Montreal had done the magician any good. Houdini's erstwhile friend Sir Arthur Conan Doyle, the creator of Sherlock Holmes and a believer in spiritualism, fared better during his two visits to the Capital Region. In 1894,

Doyle spoke at the First Reformed Church in Schenectady during a cross-country lecture tour. On June 2, 1914, Doyle and his wife stopped briefly in Albany while en route to a vacation in Lake George. When they arrived in Albany at Union Station, they were traveling by private car attached to a fast mail train.

Edgar Allan Poe's visit to Saratoga Springs that McCabe mentions to Baxter is more mysterious and less well-documented. Suffice it to say that according to several sources, including secondhand accounts, Poe visited Saratoga and spent time at a tavern on the grounds of what is now Yadoo, the artists' community. It would have been appropriate if he had composed "The Raven" there. As for Albany, as McCabe tells her partner, there is also an unsubstantiated story told by an enemy that Poe came to the city in pursuit of a woman he was courting after his wife's death.

We do know that the Fox sisters, nineteenth-century celebrities in the Spiritualist movement, came to Albany while on tour. The Fox sisters, Maggie and Kate, became famous as young girls when they began to receive messages from those who had passed over (died). The messages were conveyed through a series of raps. Their older sister, Leah, stepped in to manage their successful careers as mediums. But after their personal lives went into decline, Maggie confessed that the rappings had been a hoax. She later recanted her confession, but the sisters had lost their credibility. The Spiritualist movement proved strong enough to survive this blow.

I should note here that the opinions about movements and institutions expressed by my characters are their own. This applies to Spiritualism. It also applies to religion and megachurches. And to the media—Hannah McCabe's strong reaction to the media is shaped both by her great respect for her own father's journalistic ethics and the unpleasant experience she had when she was nine years old and thrust into the media spotlight when she shot and killed a burglar. Her profession also comes into play. As a group, police officers tend to be as wary of the media as they are of politicians. A word about people—the police department in my series is fictional. Any corruption found in my fictional police department is not to be taken as a reflection of occurrences I am aware of in the real-life Albany PD. My detectives, uniformed police officers, and members of the forensic unit are not inspired by cops I know. The female mayor of Albany in my series was not inspired by the first real-life woman to hold that office. I was unaware that a woman would be elected mayor of Albany when I began to write the series. I chose not to change the sex of my mayor because my Albany in the near future is separate and apart from the politics of the real Albany.

My fictional Albany exists in a parallel universe. But many of the social issues that we are dealing with now in our world and will be dealing with in the future are common to both universes. For example, extreme weather conditions are causing problems for people, infrastructure, and the expensive surveillance system in which my fictional city of Albany has invested. However, it is possible to engage in ongoing surveillance of subjects with the use of cameras in public places. This is happening now in cities across the globe. This technology is a fact of modern life and will continue to be employed. Its use raises some fascinating issues about crime control.

Regarding technology, I should respond to a question that I have been asked several times since *The Red Queen Dies* was published: What does the acronym ORB stand for? ORB is an acronym for "Our Reach Beyond," a phrase used by the scientist who developed the communication system. In a lecture, he spoke of "extending our reach beyond time and space." ORB also refers to the web of the orb weaver spider, the inspiration for the system. Hence, ORB, WEB, and the people who post on the WEB are "threaders" not bloggers.

For the readers who missed *The Red Queen Dies,* the UFO mentioned in the first chapter of this book appeared in 2012 over the Mojave Desert. NORAD jets scrambled, but the UFO disappeared in a flash of light and has not been seen again. The people in my world are dealing with the long-term anxiety of the uncertainty caused by such an event. Teenage "space zombies" have dropped out. Adult survivalists have built mountain bunkers and armed themselves for the space armada they are sure will appear someday. Other people, like my detectives, just go on with their lives as best they can.